I0823299

EXQUISITE THINGS

ALSO BY ABDI NAZEMIAN

The Authentics
Like a Love Story
The Chandler Legacies
Only This Beautiful Moment
Desert Echoes

EXQUISITE THINGS

ABDI NAZEMIAN

HARPER
An Imprint of HarperCollinsPublishers

To every artist who awakens me, and every artist who awakens you.
And to all the lost souls who attempt to ban and burn art,
for recognizing its power and teaching us its value.

HarperCollins Children's Books, a division of HarperCollins Publishers,
195 Broadway, New York, NY 10007

HarperCollins Publishers, Macken House, 39/40 Mayor Street Upper,
Dublin 1, D01 C9W8, Ireland

Exquisite Things

harpercollins.com

ISBN 978-0-06-333968-2

Typography by Julia Feingold
25 26 27 28 29 LBC 5 4 3 2 1

First Edition

Behind every exquisite thing that existed, there was something tragic.

OSCAR WILDE,

The Picture of Dorian Gray

NEW YORK TIMES
ADVERTISEMENT SECTION

APRIL 1, 2025

BEAUTIFUL SCHUBERT,

Though it is spring again, the flowers no longer bloom. The lily has finally succumbed to the cold freeze of time. We will celebrate the flower exactly three weeks before May Day. You know the route. You may still despise me, but I know you still love our mother. She would want you to send her off. She would want us to be together. Forever yours,

WORDSWORTH

BRAM. LONDON. APRIL. 2025.

I walk through the lobby of Claridge's. Curious eyes take in my look. Baggy cotton pants. A denim blazer with graffiti on the back. Security cameras track me from ceiling corners. Perhaps I'll be found despite the veil I use to hide my face. I've led a life of risk. Will this be my final gamble? Coming back to London. Sleeping in the very suite where my father set my life on its unique course. Preparing to walk the same streets where I once knew happiness. Some risks must be taken. No matter how dangerous.

I step out of the hotel. Nobody snatches me from behind. No strong men throw me into the back of an unmarked vehicle. I exhale. London's architecture—like my physical appearance—appears unchanged. Same clutter of styles. Edwardian. Victorian. Art deco. Same rain and wind despite the rapidly changing climate. So strong that they almost take my colossal hotel umbrella with them. You have to look closely to see the transformations in the city. As you do with me. I look exactly as I did a century ago. Skin unwrinkled. Hair thick and black. Forever seventeen.

And yet—like London—I've been here an extraordinarily long time. As indestructible as this city, which I twice called home. First: as Shahriar. The name I was born with. It means "the king." The second time: as Bram. The name Lily gave me. It wasn't inspired by the man who wrote *Dracula*. That's mere coincidence. I may be immortal but I'm no vampire. I have no fangs. No lust for blood. Only for love. No occult powers other than the blessing or curse of eternal youth. Lily had named me after a weed. Herself after a flower. We are nature, after all. My father didn't care about my nature. He only wanted me to be a king.

And now I'm all queen in my sparkling veil. I know the danger of returning to the city I once called home. A city with cameras on every street. Lily's memorial is one of two reasons I would walk these pathways again. These junctions where my worst and best memories live.

The other reason is Oliver. I hope he's walking the streets of London right now. On his way to celebrate our mother. I have a brief fantasy of the wind carrying me up like *Mary Poppins* so I can search the city for the chestnut brown of Oliver's hair. The golden glow of his skin. The thick musculature of his body. The long graceful shape of his neck. Like a violin. I loved *Mary Poppins* when it came out in 1964. When I was either eighty-six years old or still a teenager. Depending on how you define age. Lily was like Mary Poppins. The magical muse who liberated the children she took care of. The woman who made life feel like flight.

I walk the thirty minutes from Mayfair to Covent Garden. That vibrant neighborhood where we once danced. Laughed. Felt seen in the darkness of the dance floor.

I walk past shops. Theaters. Pub awnings packed with beer drinkers avoiding the deluge. The rain goes from downpour to drizzle. The pub crawlers move out into sidewalks. Take over the streets with their boisterous cheers over the football game on every screen.

I know I'm getting close to the first stop of Lily's memorial when

I see them. Beautiful Azalea, Poppy, and Blossom. They walk reverently ahead of me toward what was once the Blitz Club. Their steps more careful than they used to be. Even the most vibrant of souls get old. Find themselves unable to sparkle as they once did. They've lost youthful energy and gained exquisite vulnerability.

I walk a few steps behind them. Find myself deeply moved by what they're wearing. Every stitch sewed by Lily. Sequins and crushed velvet and bright silk. The fabrics seem to glow as they turn onto the aptly named Great Queen Street. To our journey's starting point.

The street is flooded with two dozen fabulously dressed people who greet each other with long hugs. Tearful kisses. They've all gathered to celebrate Lily. The oldest ones are familiar to me. They were there in those glory days when I lived with Lily. Brixton. I can still travel back to it if I close my eyes. The only true home I've had in my eternal life.

I see Maud. My sister. My friend. She must be in her fifties now. No. Sixties. Time is hard for me to track. She looks so much younger. Holds the hand of a gorgeous woman who must be her wife. Simple gold rings on their deep brown skin. Beautiful.

The youngest ones are strangers to me. They must be Lily's children too. She was mother to so many. But mine first. I want them to know that. I can be quite petty. Selfish. Greedy.

Archie now looks as ancient and wise as an antique book. He stands atop the steps to what was once the Blitz. Announces to the group that the journey will begin in a few moments. With stops at all of Lily's old haunts on the way. Just as Lily mapped out long ago. When I was her son. Her firstborn. When she gave me a life.

Archie wears the ascot suit Lily made for him. It swims on his dwindling frame. His once muscular body has shrunk. Skeletal.

Fat lost in places. Gained in others. The side effects of the early HIV medications that saved his life. Lily always wanted to be the first of her chosen family to go. I'm glad she got her wish. And that Archie survived this long. His aged face is more beautiful than ever. It's a face with a story to tell. Those have always been the faces I've been interested in.

Oliver's face . . .

His eyes were my once-upon-a-time.

I can almost conjure his voice. Imagine the sound of his fingers on the keys of a grand piano. I wish I could travel back in time to the Boston of 1920. The first spring of a new decade of possibility.

Meeting him. Knowing him. Loving him. It's when I knew I had a chance at finally fulfilling my destiny. To love and be loved in a time and place where that love isn't a crime.

Archie lifts up his comically tall top hat as he addresses the crowd: "You know why Lily made me this hat? Because we would always lose each other when we went out dancing. When she gifted me this hat, she said, *Archie, you will never be lost again. At least to me.*"

I too felt found by Lily. Then I became lost again. The only way I can find myself is to get Oliver back. He holds my heart hostage. I shift my veiled eyes across the crowd of mourners. I sent Oliver a message via the newspaper. As we've been doing for over a century. He knows Lily is gone. Knows the memorial is today. Yet he's not here. Which must mean his hatred of me is greater than his love for Lily. The thought sends a chill through me.

Archie takes a deep breath. "And with this hat, you won't be lost either. At least not today. Just follow the hat. Shall we?"

Archie leads the way. The rest walk alongside and behind him.

They'll be spreading Lily's ashes into the Thames at the end of the day. It's what she wanted. Grief is in the air as they shuffle down the road. So is peace. The serenity that comes from commemorating a life well-lived.

I don't walk. Not yet. I know their route. I don't know where Oliver is. Is he running late? Perhaps he was too afraid of being seen by the others to show up on time. Though they're not who we fear being caught by. The people we're afraid of are the people we should all be afraid of. The kings of the world. Those willing to destroy in their quest for more wealth and power. My heart races as I scan the streets. I see no suspicious people or vehicles. Just the building that used to be our safe space. It's a strip club now.

A menacing-looking bouncer stands outside. He addresses me threateningly. "You coming or going?"

I reply coolly. "I'm waiting."

"Well, don't wait too long. You're blocking the entrance."

If only he knew how long I've waited. He wouldn't believe me. I wish I could tell him the strip club he now protects was once a space not for exploitation but for liberation. A home for trailblazers. The Blitz Club. Where Boy George was the coat check boy. Where everyone from Sade to Vivienne Westwood sought inspiration. Where I danced in Oliver's arms. Allowed myself to believe love can last. Some parts of London have changed. Some hidden parts of me have too. Now my heart knows true grief. Now this once-sacred spot is a seedy dump where women are exploited for the pleasure of men with enough money to do as they please.

And men tend to destroy when they can do as they please. Myself included. I've destroyed more than I care to admit. How could I not? With all these years behind me?

I've done it all. Traveled the seven seas. Seen the Seven Wonders.

Taken the polar plunge. Swum with a whale. Been to the Nile on a felucca. The only thing left for me to seek is the one thing I always wanted in the first place.

"Let's move it along now, kid." The bouncer shifts his muscular body closer to me. His threatening eyes are no match for mine.

I lift my veil up. My eyes appear brown at first glance. But stare at them long enough and they glow orange. Like a comforting sun. Or like a blazing fire. Depending on my mood. The bouncer recoils. "What was *that?*"

"I'll leave when I'm ready, thank you." I smile. Lower the veil back over my face. Take one last look at the building. Inhale the past.

A wealth of memories.

A series of lives.

I was born many times. Once when I took my first breath in 1878. Which of course I don't remember. I don't think it's fair that we don't remember being born. Surely one of the most important days in anyone's life.

Second birth: 1895. When my father lit the fire that would change my fate. In the hotel suite I woke up in this morning.

Third birth: 1920. When I fell in love. Truly. It took me a quarter of a century of adolescence to find something deeper than the typical teen lust. Or maybe all it took was meeting the right person. Oliver.

One final birth: 1980. When Lily baptized me as her child. Made me feel the power of true unconditional love and acceptance.

I head toward the next destination when the bouncer threatens to call the police. I can't risk arrest. I pray Oliver will be waiting for me at the lily pond. The memorial will last all day. Well into the night. There's time still.

And there's always hope when there's time left.

OLIVER. BOSTON. APRIL. 1920.

Sometimes, most times honestly, my own ability to pretend I'm something I'm not sickens me. I don't think of myself as a liar, and yet, I'm so skilled at it. Faking comes so naturally when I'm with Mother, Liam, my classmates, coaches and teachers. Perhaps I'm just weak. Or maybe, as my cousin Brendan says, I'm simply too concerned with pleasing others, Mother in particular. But what's wrong with wanting others to be happy?

I suppose it's the lying that's wrong. When Mother asks me to pick up some cuts at the butcher and he asks, "Oliver, you have a lass yet?" I find it too easy to offer him a conspiratorial wink and say, "Still searching for her, Mr. Barrett." It's horrible, isn't it? All I want is to live a life of honesty, to be as pure as a Chopin melody. Instead I'm like one of my signature wrestling moves, the one where I pull my opponent deep into a hold, almost like an embrace, before I turn him into my victim. That's who they think I am. A destroyer. If I'm a good wrestler, it's because the mat is where I take out my aggression at this cruel world that turns the purest of boys into the most deceitful of men.

But I must lie, mustn't I? To be honest and pure would be to destroy my beautiful mother's dreams. And she's worked so hard for us, hasn't she? Raising two boys all by herself and taking extra shifts at work after we lost my dad in the pandemic.

"No woman should raise two men without a man," she likes to say. In fact, she's downstairs saying it to the mailman now.

"But if any woman *can* do it, it's you, Mrs. Doherty," the mailman says in his jovial voice. That man has been delivering the mail to us for as far back as my memories go, and there hasn't been a day where he hasn't done it with a smile. Doesn't he have dark days like I do? Days when he doesn't want to leave the bed, when he longs to sink into his own gloom? Nights when he wants to ignore duty and indulge all his forbidden fantasies?

"You're too kind," Mother says sincerely.

"This one's postmarked from New Haven," the mailman says brightly. He knows, like I do, that nothing fills my mother's heart with pride like a letter from New Haven, an update from my brother Liam at Yale. "He's doing well, is he?"

"More than well," my mother says with a glow in her voice. "Full scholarship to Yale. He's made all the hard work worth it, and Oliver will too. He has his sights set on Harvard like his cousin Brendan. They have a wrestling team now, so perhaps there's a scholarship in his future. How could they say no when they see the way he overpowers the other boys on that mat?"

"Oh, I was at the last meet. Oliver absolutely pulverized the other boy," the mailman says gleefully, like destruction is sport, which of course it is.

"Yes, well . . . if it gets him a scholarship, it will all be worth it." Somewhere inside her, my mother knows wrestling means nothing to me but the chance to get into Harvard. She's the one who taught me piano, isn't she? Who guided my fingers from key to key, who would play the ends of my seventh chords when my hands weren't big enough, patiently waited for me to master a trill. Coached me to stop parking my foot on the pedal when it could finally reach it. "It muddies the sound," she used to say, as my father blurted out his own muddy sounds in the background. "You want your notes to be crystal clear." She knows me. Perhaps even the piece of me I hide. Or maybe not. If she did, she would have deduced *why* I'm using wrestling to get a scholarship to Harvard.

But she has no idea what Harvard means to me, what my cousin Brendan has shown me. A whole world of men like me, men who would shatter my mother's illusions of who her baby boy is.

"Oh my, our Liam is seeing a young woman," Mother says. "Her name is Mary. She's studying to be a secretary. He says she likes to bake."

"Just like you," the mailman says. "Every good boy falls in love with a woman just like his mother." I cringe when I hear that. If I do fall in love, and I'm not sure I ever will, then it certainly won't be with a man like my father, who drank too much, raged too loud, and lived impulsively. If anything, I want the opposite of him. A boy with clarity of vision. A boy without even a hint of cruelty in him.

Mother tells the mailman she's going to pack him some of her famous oatmeal cookies. "The secret's in the nuts," Mother says.

"Thanks, Mrs. Doherty. I'll see you tomorrow." Mother closes the door when the mailman leaves. I hear her deflate with a sigh. I know she pretends, too. Her happiness is a costume she wears for others. Underneath it is her quiet grief. It's been two years since we lost Father. My brother left us for Connecticut in September. Maybe I'm a born faker like she is. There could be some gene we don't know about. The imitation gene. If there is, my father didn't have it. He couldn't fake a thing. Not his hatred for me, certainly.

Sometimes, he would catch me singing a Bessie Smith song as I played its melodies on the piano, and he would slap me across the face with the back of his heavy hand for simply warbling a feminine tune. Imagine what he might have done if he knew that last week, I let Brendan and his friends put rouge on my cheeks.

"Oliver, are you awake?" my mother bellows from downstairs. "Would you like some eggs?"

It was thrilling, looking at myself in the mirror and seeing this rouged stranger. This soft boy who looks the way I feel. Not a pulverizer of men but a lover of them. I do imagine it sometimes, what he would do. Father, I mean. In my worst moments, I'm happy he's gone. If not happy, relieved. I feel sick admitting this, but I want a life of honesty, at the very least with myself. That's not too much to ask, is it?

"I'm not hungry," I yell. "I'm studying."

I hear her down in the living room. She lifts the fallboard of the piano and plays a few scales. Mother always likes to warm up her fingers with the scales that transport her. That sound like they come from some other place. Diminished scales. I can't help but push myself out of bed when I hear the eastern sounds. It's like she's calling to me to take a seat next to her, on that bench where we're always at our most connected.

"You remember how to play this scale?" she asks.

"Of course," I say. "The Phrygian. It sounds major, but it's minor. A deceptive scale." Like me.

I place my hands on the ivory. I like to play with my eyes closed. To know that I can create music from pure instinct. I play her a Phrygian scale. It's just a C major, of course, but you start on an E, which changes everything. Where you start the story, and where you end it, changes its whole meaning.

"It takes you somewhere, doesn't it? To some deserted Greek island perhaps, where everybody plays music and takes in the sun all day."

I can't help but smile, even as I correct her. "If memory serves, Phrygia was inland, and was in what would now be the Ottoman Empire."

"Those are the facts," Mother says. "This, my son, is a fantasy. Play me something. I want to be transported."

I open my eyes and begin to play one of her favorites, Mozart's "Rondo alla Turca," the "Turkish March." I offer her a smile as my fingers travel across the keys. She seems to relax into the music as she unties the straps of the apron she's wearing around her widening body. Ever since Father died, she eats what she craves, wears what feels comfortable, and seems much happier for it too. Father would chastise her if she ate too much or begged for a night off cooking. Never mind that they both worked all day. She had to cook all night as he kicked up his feet and drank. Those were his rules. Sometimes I wonder who she might have been had she never been a wife who had to sew other people's clothes to make ends meet and cook three men's meals every night. I finish the piece with a flourish, then play some improvised notes as I tell her, "I'm going out tonight, so you don't need to make me dinner."

"Where are you going?" she asks, unworried. She trusts me. She shouldn't.

"Brendan invited me to Harvard to study with him." A half-lie. I am going to Brendan's, but not to study. It's his friend Cyril's birthday, and they've planned a gathering in Brendan and Jack's room. "Studying with Brendan will really prepare me for Harvard. I'll understand exactly what they're assigning." I'm laying it on too thick now, so I stop.

"How kind of him. Please thank him on my behalf." She knows Brendan, but not as well as I've come to know him. Father tended to keep his own family at a distance, and Brendan is my cousin on his side. Mother runs a hand through my waves of brown hair. "You need a haircut. I could do it before you go."

"I like it long."

"It gets in your eyes."

"Well then, all I need to do is blow." I blow and my hair flies up. I can tell how silly I look. She laughs, and I laugh too, but mostly because I'm imagining Brendan's roommate, Jack Whitman, turning what I just said into some sharply delivered adage—*all I need to do is blow*—in his inimitably capricious way.

A wave of pain seems to stab me in the gut. I close my eyes. She must sense my change of mood because she asks, "What is it? Do you miss your father?"

"No, it's not that." I wish I could conceal the ache in my voice. Perhaps I'm not as good a liar as I think myself to be.

"Grief takes time, and it lingers under the surface," she says. "Reveals itself in unexpected moments. Is it because he used to cut your hair? Amateur barber, your father."

"Very amateur," I crack. I'm grateful for our laughter. It allows us to move on from her questioning. If there's one person I hate lying to, it's her. My beloved mother, who deserves an honest son.

The boys are already singing a slurred rendition of "Happy Birthday" to Cyril Wilcox when I enter Brendan and Jack's dorm room. Prohibition has been the law of the land for a few months now, but those rules don't apply at Harvard. The boys who come from money, the ones with fathers who can make problems disappear with a phone call to some politician or dean, can always take what they want, even if it's illegal, and in this room, no one wants anything legal.

"There he is!" Brendan exclaims when he sees me standing sheepishly at the door, holding a glass jar filled with Mother's famous oatmeal cookies. "And he's got cookies."

"Turn around, young man," Jack demands with a finger pointed at me. I turn awkwardly, unsure of why until Jack exclaims, "Yes indeed, he does have cookies." Jack raises one of his sharp eyebrows. Everything about Jack—his wit, his slender fingers, his imposing nose and devilish smile—feels sharp, like he was quickly sketched by an artist who forgot to blend and soften the lines. Sometimes, he calls himself "The Jackal," a nickname he wishes would stick, and an animal he bears a strange resemblance to. His joke is received with applause. I know it's meant in good fun, and I don't mind these boys admiring me even if I don't like any of them. Well, not that way at least. I like them very much in other ways. Their freedom, humor, and irreverence is intoxicating.

When I've thought of an appropriately witty response to Jack's comment on my backside, I turn to the group and smile. "Well now, I've just arrived and already I'm the *butt* of the joke." I'm learning to talk like them, to wrestle with words.

"Look at my baby cousin, giving as well as he receives," Brendan says as he puts a chunky arm around me. Brendan has the typical Doherty build. Thick all over, with hulking arms and legs, and a layer of baby fat on the cheeks that will likely never go away. But unlike us, he's also unnervingly tall, which gives his torso the feel of an old tree, and makes his thick limbs look like branches reaching out into the world. He takes the jar of cookies and holds it up. "Who wants the best cookies in Boston?" Brendan doesn't wait for an answer. "Birthday boy first." He tosses a cookie to Cyril, who catches it. Then moves on to the rest of the boys. One of them has rouge on his cheeks just like I once did. The room is littered with little hints of their hidden life. Women's makeup and jazz records. Pomade and a bouquet of green carnations.

When the cookie throwing is done, I ask Brendan, "Did I come too late? You've already sung happy birthday."

"We'll be singing throughout the evening. One happy birthday for each stop we make. Tonight, my cousin, you're getting a tour of all our spots."

"Well, perhaps not the tearooms and orchards," Jack says. "Baby boy is far too innocent for those haunts."

"I'm not a baby boy," I snarl defiantly.

"Is that so?" Jack says with a wink. "Care to prove it?"

"Ignore him," Brendan instructs. "He thinks everything is about sex."

"Except sex!" Jack squeals. "Which is about power."

"Thank you, Oscar Wilde." Brendan blows a kiss up to the ceiling, like Wilde himself is up there somewhere.

"If you're attempting to send some love to dear Oscar, he's not up in heaven. He's down in some gutter, looking at the stars." Jack's tone suddenly changes for a moment. He blows a kiss down to the ground, and with startling sincerity, he whispers, "Thanks, Wilde. You suffered for us. Rotted away in jail so that we could be here, drinking champagne, billing and cooing." Jack stands up and takes Brendan's hand. Twirls him around. "Dancing with each other." He leans in to kiss Brendan. "And also . . ."

But Brendan stops him. "Sorry, dear roommate, bank's closed."

"And what time does the bank open?" Jack asks.

"For you, dear roommate, never." Brendan pulls a pouty Jack

next to him. "You're my best friend. Let's not destroy it all for a night of sin."

"But why must it be a night of sin?" I ask.

"Because that's all Jack is capable of," Brendan says lovingly, like he doesn't really mind.

"Shameful but true," Jack admits. "I bore easy. Not to worry, dear roommate. I'll find myself some ripe fruit with less self-respect than you have later tonight." Jack approaches the Victrola and the sound of Sophie Tucker crooning "Some of These Days" fills the room. Brendan and Jack dance together like clowns, laughing, spinning, twirling. I see what they can't. That for all their jokes, there's real love in their gazes. Perhaps Brendan likes Jack's power. Jack is a son of influence and carries himself as such. His grandfather was a German immigrant and a chemist who started a small drug company. His father took over the company, renamed it Whitman & Whitman, and turned it into a pharmaceutical giant. As for what Jack sees in Brendan, that's obvious. Brendan is the only person willing to say no to him.

"These cookies are absolutely tremendous," one of the boys says with a full mouth. "Just tremendous."

"The secret's in the nuts," I say slyly.

"It always is," Jack snaps as he whirls Brendan's huge body around and cups his crotch. "The secret's *always* in the nuts." Jack transforms Mother's innocuous statement about oatmeal cookies into something raucous and bawdy. They speak in code, Brendan's friends, and I love that about them. It's like learning a new language. Or a new instrument. They're *in the life,* as they say, which means they know the hidden things, the things my mother doesn't see happening in her city, to her beloved son.

The birthday boy, Cyril, approaches me. "Brendan says you'll be coming to Harvard."

"Oh, I don't know," I say sheepishly. "I hope so. But I need a scholarship. I'm not like Jack over there. My father isn't a millionaire."

"Nor mine," Cyril says.

"How old are you today?" I ask.

"Twenty," he says. "You?"

"Seventeen. Eighteen this summer." I bite my lip anxiously, wishing I were older, ready for the rest of my life to begin. "So what can a twenty-year-old teach a seventeen-year-old?" I ask. "Is there some secret wisdom you've finally uncovered?"

"Yes, actually." His eyes brighten. Cyril isn't like Brendan or Jack. Those two feel like they've crossed the threshold into manhood. Cyril still looks and acts like a boy. Like he's still a sketch in a coloring book, waiting for someone to fill him in. "I've been thinking a lot about how twenty feels like the perfect age to stop thinking about nothing but the future. All my life, I've worked to get to Harvard. Now that I'm here, I'm constantly told to keep my head down and study so I don't get put on academic probation again."

"Why were you on probation?" I ask.

He shrugs. "Poor grades." Then he adds, "Sometimes, when the pressure feels too . . . overwhelming . . ."

I feel him struggling and say, "You don't need to talk about it if you don't—"

"It helps to talk," he says quickly. "Well, to a good listener like you."

I feel myself glow from the compliment. From the sense of belonging I feel in this room.

"I just get overwhelmed sometimes, that's all," he says. "And when I do, I break out into hives. It makes me look like a rotten cabbage, as Jack likes to say, and I get so scared that I'll break into hives again that I spin myself into a state of worry about it, even though worrying seems to be what causes it in the first place."

"I'm sorry," I say.

"But this is why I'm sharing the wisdom of my two decades with you," he continues. "Because I know now that we can't just worry about the future. If I can't live for *this moment,* then all I'll do is worry and fret until I die."

"That's morbid," I say. "You're not close to death."

"Aren't we all?" Cyril asks sadly. "After the Great War and the pandemic, it's hard not to think we must live every moment like it could be our last."

The words chill me. It wasn't just men like my father we lost these past few years. There have been boys too, taken by war, by the virus. The wails of grieving mothers who know all too well what a firm knock on their door means. Dreams and potential and lives, vanished. We tell ourselves, and each other, that it's all over now. But that's foolish, isn't it? Nothing is ever over. Everything continues. I saw Father's body buried and still I fear his wrath sometimes, don't I? He's not dead as long as the fear of him lives inside me.

"You're right," I whisper. "And very wise for a ripe twenty."

"Not you too," Cyril says with a shake of his head. "Jack loves calling me ripe fruit and chicken and brownie. Anything to get my goat."

I feel my face get hot. "I didn't mean it that way," I insist. "I just meant you're still very young. But not like a chicken. More like a wise old owl in a chicken's body."

We both laugh now. It feels nice. This is why I come here. For small moments of camaraderie. For brotherhood, which I never felt with my own brother, who takes after Father the way I take after Mother. Sometimes it feels like we were never a united family. There was the two of them, and the two of us.

"If I'm a wise old owl," Cyril says, "then listen to me and waste no more time. We're always being told that our happiness is in some distant future. What I'm saying is, be happy now."

Brendan approaches and pulls us both close. It really does feel like we're brothers here, or like what brothers should be. "I love this kid," Brendan slurs as he tousles my hair. He's a little drunker now. Spending too much time with Jack will have that effect. Jack loves to pour and pressure. "And I love this kid, too." Brendan firmly squeezes Cyril's cheeks.

"That sort of hurts," Cyril says.

"I'm sorry. I forget my own strength sometimes." Brendan laughs.

Jack stops the record mid-song. "Let's get to the Golden Rooster before you pansies start passing out," he yells. As soon as the decision is made, Jack pulls the green carnations out of the vase, and pins one to each boy's lapel.

I eye Brendan nervously. "I should go home. Mother will worry if I'm out too late."

"Stop living for her," he says. "Live for you."

"They won't let me into the Golden Rooster anyway. I look younger than the rest of you."

Brendan laughs off my trepidation. "You'll be with Jack. Nobody says no to Jack Whitman."

I feel my heart flutter in my chest. I've been to the dorm room. I've joined them for nighttime walks around campus. But I've never gone out into the city with them. Never to one of those establishments they've told me about where men from all over the city and beyond congregate. "I don't know . . ." I feel the eyes of the room on me. The record is off. There's no music. No conversation or laughter.

"Your mother thinks you're here at Harvard with me." Brendan puts a hand on each of my cheeks. "You worry too much."

"I just don't know if I'll— Well, will I—fit into that place?" I stammer out.

Jack taps an impatient heel on the wood floors. "Perhaps baby boy is right," he purrs condescendingly. "The Golden Rooster is positively rancid. It's no place for a clean-cut baby boy like him."

I throw an angry gaze at Jack. I don't like him baiting me like this, calling me baby boy twice in a row. But I don't change my mind because of Jack. I do it because Cyril's eyes catch mine, and his words of wisdom hit me anew. *Be happy now.* And so I reluctantly announce I'll be joining.

Brendan squeezes my shoulder, pleased with me. "If you want to use a bathroom, I'd do it here. You'll understand why when we get there."

"As for The Jackal . . ." Jack waves an arm in the air dramatically. "He loves to park himself in the bathroom of the Golden Rooster and wait for his next conquest."

"And that," Brendan says, "is why you should avoid it." I let Brendan pin a green carnation on me before we go. I'm officially one of them now. I hope I'm doing this for me, and not simply to please Brendan. I wish there were a way to tell why I do the things I do. A way to be certain of my own heart.

When we enter the Golden Rooster, it's the sounds that hit me first. Music. Laughter. The mashing of two young men's lips against each other. The pounding as they push each other against a wall passionately. The swish of men's eyes as they assess each other.

And then the most beautiful boy I've ever seen catches my eye. My age, I would guess. When I look at him, all the sounds seem to dissipate. The world goes quiet.

I don't know who he is, or where he comes from, but something tells me he doesn't belong here. Not the way the rest of us do, we children of Boston, we boys of Irish Catholic stock with our rosy cheeks, blue eyes, and doting mothers. Perhaps he's Italian. He has dark hair, slicked back with pomade, and a lithe body that wouldn't stand a chance on the wrestling mat. He has none of the nervous energy of these other boys, all drunkenness and performance. There's a stillness to him that mesmerizes me.

He raises a hand up. I'm curious who he's waving to. Perhaps he's meeting an equally mysterious friend. But when I look behind me, there's nobody there waving back. I turn to him. He points at me, then waves again.

"Me?" I mouth in disbelief, and he nods. So I wave back. He smiles. My heart leaps through my chest.

Just when I'm about to approach him, Brendan pulls me into a bear hug from behind. I keep my eyes glued to him as Brendan pulls me away. "Goodbye," I mouth silently to the mystery boy.

"Hello," mystery boy mouths back, his smile mischievous.

His peculiar eyes seem to glow like two fireflies in the darkness. "Who are you?" I mouth. "And how did you become so magical?"

SHAHRIAR. LONDON.
FEBRUARY TO APRIL. 1895.

I hate so much. The idiotic people who create the rules we must obey. This damp February morning. This wretched boarding school. These two carefree boys walking toward me as I rest on the stair tower of the imposing stock brick building. This is where we learn science's—and society's—secret codes. Most of all I hate the loathing inside me. It reminds me of the father I despise.

James—one of the wealthiest boys in our class—puts an arm around his tedious friend Theodore as they approach the stair tower. "Come on, just say yes."

"I wish I could, but speed skating."

"To hell with skating. It's opening night of Oscar Wilde's new play." Now I'm interested in what James has to say.

"Perhaps you should ask Alfie."

"Alfie has that cold that's going around. If I don't find a friend, my parents will invite my horrible uncle who smells like a sewer."

"I'm free to go!" I've never dared insert myself into the conversation between two classmates. They don't know I'm braver than any of them.

James is so tall he seems to be on stilts. His round blue eyes appear bewildered as they look down at me. The dark-skinned classmate he's never spoken to. Perhaps he believes I'm shy. That's not why I haven't spoken to him or his friends. It's because I've yet to hear one of them express an original thought.

"I invited Theodore, not you." A half note of cruelty in James's voice. His eyes are on Theodore's bright red cheeks. His plump pink lips. His golden hair. I've walked the city streets alone enough times to recognize illicit longing when I see it. James longs for Theodore. James is—in a vital way—like me. Perhaps I've been wrong about him. Perhaps convention is just his disguise. This excites me.

There is so much I love. Walking. Observing. Discovering. I realized years ago that no one was paying attention to us boys during our free hours. I began leaving the confines of school. A block or two at first. And then farther and farther. It's been seven years. I've seen clean streets and grimy ones. I love the rebels. Gamblers and prostitutes. Musicians and street poets. Men with illicit longing in their eyes. I've never been bold enough to speak to one of them. But I stop each time I see a nonconformist. Take a deep breath. Imagine myself inhaling a bit of them into my bones. Willing myself to transform into something else entirely.

"It's up to you. But I promise to be more fun than your fragrant cousin." A mischievous smile on my face. I want him to understand about me what I understand about him.

"Funny." He's not laughing. A shrug. "Valentine's Day. Be ready by six."

James seems to be searching his memory for my name. "Shahriar." I've been at the school since I was ten. Recently turned seventeen. But I've kept to myself. These other boys don't even register me. Perhaps it's because I come from a different country. Look and sound different in a sea of sameness. Too foreign to be understood.

"Tough name to remember. You have a nickname?"

"Perhaps you can invent one for me." I hold his gaze.

James laughs uncomfortably. Turns back to his friend. "We should get to class."

I feel triumphant as they leave. I've studied the city and its rebels. I know that Oscar Wilde is London's Rebel King. I've gained entry to his grand opening. On Valentine's Day of all days. The day of love. I sense something momentous coming. Life beginning anew.

It's a snowy evening as James and I head to the St. James in a carriage alongside his sharply dressed but dreary mother and father. His parents attend more out of obligation than passion. This is a business engagement to them. But it's much more to the throngs of people pushing to gain entry as we arrive at the theater. Wilde's devoted following is desperate. They *want* something they can't have. The evening is sold out. Need is what makes a person interesting. Those who have what they want care only about keeping it. There's nothing more boring than that. Need frightens me. Excites me.

"Follow me." James's father hands his tickets to one of the handsome ushers. We're escorted inside. Past some kind of commotion involving a man holding the strangest thing: a bouquet of vegetables. They look like congratulatory flowers from afar. But they're vegetables. Hard. Cold. Raw. Stalks and roots of asparagus. Eggplant. Carrots. Many of them visibly rotting. The man's eyes are mad. His hair a mess. He mumbles something unintelligible about Wilde corrupting his son. He's pulled away. His voice becomes one with the gusts of wind that underscore the stormy night.

Our seats are front and center. I learn that James's father is a solicitor who does work for the publishing house that has published Wilde to scandal and acclaim. He despises Wilde. Finds his work immoral. Yet he has no trouble profiting from depravity. Hypocrisy is a virus that has long infected the world.

The performance of *The Importance of Being Earnest* is magnificent. Underneath what appears to be a comedy is a seething rage for society. Disdain for the same things I disdain. And yet Wilde has somehow metamorphosed revulsion into humor. Pain into laughter. I wish I had that talent.

I feel James's long leg press against mine as Algernon says: "*The truth is rarely pure and never simple.*"

Does James mean to do this? Is it simply that his body is too long for these small seats? I find out by moving my leg even closer to his. An innocuous act. Too subtle to be noticed by anyone but him. He doesn't pull away. He pushes the full weight of his thigh against mine. There are layers of fabric between us. Yet it feels like our skin is touching. An undeniable heat. People lie. Temperature doesn't.

There are jokes only we seem to laugh at. Moments that appear lost on his parents during which we both lean in.

His fingers brush against mine when Lady Bracknell says: "*To lose one parent may be regarded as a misfortune.*" I imagine my mother. I have no idea what she looked like. All I know is she is my great misfortune. "*To lose both looks like carelessness.*" A charge within me. My brain stimulated by the words. My body by his touch. I take my thick scarf off my neck and place it on my lap. Hide the firm evidence of my lust.

James also lays his scarf on his lap when Jack says: "*It is a terrible thing for a man to find out suddenly that all his life he has been speaking nothing but the truth.*" I turn my gaze as James shifts in his seat. Our eyes communicate secrets.

The play ends. I leap to my feet. Roar in grateful applause. The ovation is furious. It doesn't even die down when Wilde himself takes the stage. Cigarette in his white-gloved hand. Sly smile on his childlike face. He exhales rings of smoke. Green carnation in the buttonhole of his black velvet collar. Green ring on his finger. He glows. Grins. I inhale. My attempt to draw his life force into me. Whatever I can steal.

"Bravo!" I shout. I clap. I feel exhilaratingly alive. "Bravo!"

James joins me. "Bravo!" We guide our hands toward each other so they touch with every swing. I think Oscar sees us. From up on that stage with his tanned skin. His selfish giant of a body. I think he sees what we're doing. Empowers us to go further.

"What if we walk back to school?" I suggest to James after the show. I don't want the night to end. Walking will slow it down.

"Walk?" His mother is aghast. "It's frigid."

"It's beautiful. The streets are blanketed in clouds." What I mean is: everything looks beautiful after you've seen a work of art that changes you.

James looks at the road. Seeing it through new eyes. His gaze finds mine. We seem to be sharing a joint memory of our legs pressing against each other. Fingers grazing. Hardness hiding under bundled scarves. "Won't we get lost?"

"I know the way." My body swells with pride. "I know every inch of the city."

"I'm not sure that's possible or advisable." His father's eyes are on a group of young men laughing too loud. Too girlish. Too *too*. Under a streetlamp that illuminates the green carnations in their lapels.

"Let's do it." James's eyes vibrate. "Let's walk!"

"Take my gloves." His mother peels off her leather gloves. But the father stops her. He won't have his son wearing ladies' gloves.

Neither of us speaks at first. We walk in silence as the sound of the crowds chattering outside the theater fades away. I lead James across Pall Mall. Past its gentleman's clubs and shops. Finally: "Thank you for inviting me."

James laughs. "You invited yourself."

I laugh too. Awkwardly. I haven't laughed often in my miserable life. I'm not sure I know how to do it right. "Then thank you for letting me invite myself." It was easier to connect to him without words. In the darkness of the theater. Using only our bodies.

James skips a step. I study his movements. Notice he avoids the cracks in the wet road. Snow turns to glistening slush from the carts. Horses. Carriages.

"I thought the play was superb." I move to avoid manure.

"Did you really? Or are you just saying it to be polite?"

"I despite *politesse*. Etiquette is a bore." I try to sound like one of the actors onstage. Adopt their rakishness.

He gazes at me curiously. His lips curl into a smile. "I loved it too. It was even better than *Lady Windermere's Fan*."

"I haven't seen or read it."

"I envy you getting to experience it for the first time." He jumps to avoid a large crack. "*A Woman of No Importance*?"

I shake my head no.

"You have read *The Picture of Dorian Gray,* haven't you?"

That's another no.

"It's the most exciting novel ever written. My father, of course, thinks it a menacing text. Those were his exact words. A *menacing text*."

"I've only read some of Wilde's poems." I feel a pang of shame for not being sufficiently in the know. I crave knowledge. I want to know everything. "I have catching up to do."

"Poems? I think I've read everything but his poems."

"I love poetry. It dispenses with everything but the necessary words."

He ponders. "But isn't it the unnecessary that makes life interesting?"

I laugh. "Perhaps."

"I'll lend you his novels and plays, if you like." His tone feels covert. Boys share school texts. This is different. This is menacing text.

"I would love that."

The word *love* hangs in the air. A provocation. He skips around the cracks a little faster. He's anxious. Also buzzing with life. I thought he was just another boring schoolboy. How wrong I was. "Want to know a secret?"

I smile. I love secrets.

"That abhorrent man with the bouquet of raw vegetables outside the theater. Did you see him?"

"Of course. It's not every day you see a man with crazed eyes and a bouquet of molding celery."

He's giddy with clandestineness. "That man's *son* is Wilde's *boy*." He pauses. "Wilde is a bugger." He allows the word *bugger* to waft like smoke. "A sodomite!"

"I know what a bugger is." I hesitate. "I don't love the word."

"The Marquess of Queensberry, what a silly title. What does it even mean? The man is frothing at the mouth over his son's infatuation with Oscar. I overheard my father and his friends discuss it. They called Wilde and Bosie and their ilk vile menaces to society."

I adopt an authoritative voice. "Menacing. Menaces. Mendiosus." I laugh. "Latin conjugation with Professor Hatcher."

"Who I suspect is also a bugger." He wields the word like a weapon.

"I think your father is jealous."

"Jealous?"

"Your father, his friends, our classmates, their lives are all so predictable. Exceedingly dull. And no one is having more fun on this planet in this moment than Oscar Wilde."

"Did you just insult my father and all my friends?"

"I—"

I'm prepared to stammer out an apology when he claps his hands together gleefully. "Where have you been hiding all this time?"

"In plain sight." I tap dance on the street. I'm not sure I knew what loving myself felt like before tonight.

"We must be friends. I can't tell the other boys the things I want to."

"Like?"

"Like how much pleasure it brings me to watch all our insipid parents cheer for Wilde and turn his plays into such ravishing successes, when all the while he's everything they claim to loathe in the world. Isn't it wonderful?"

"My father isn't cheering him on. He likely doesn't know who he is."

"Good for him."

"Nothing good about him." I hiss the next part out. "If you think your parents are awful, trust me, my father is worse."

"Is that so?" I'm used to competition from classmates. Everything at school is designed as competition. "My father eats with his mouth open."

"Mine whips me with a belt when I make a mistake."

"Oh." He bites his lip. "Mine spanked me as a child, but never a belt."

"My father has only visited me once since I arrived at school when I was ten."

His face falls in shock. "You've only seen him once in the last seven years?"

"No, no, I spend summers at home. Unfortunately." I look up at his face. He seems interested. I keep going. "I'm not a person to my father. I'm just . . . a project. He wants me to go to the best schools and study harder than anyone else so I can someday make him proud. Bring our family the glory he craves. All he cares about is money and power."

"He must have money and power if he sent you to school here."

I shake my head. "He wants more than he has. He *works* for the royal family. He wants me to *marry* into the royal family. To transform us into kings."

"And your mother?"

"She died when I was born." I step into a puddle. Kick off the mud. I know the true motivation behind my father's grand ambitions for me. He wants to transform me into a son who is worthy of his love. But that will never happen. Because I'll always be the son he blames for killing the one person he did love. "It's just me and my father. He thinks I'm going to move back home when I'm out of university. Work with him. Use what I've learned in England to help him ascend to even higher status."

"And what do you want to do?"

"I don't know yet, but . . ."

"But?"

"I'd love to write." It's the first time I've uttered these words.

Perhaps the first time I've had the thought. The improbable suddenly feels possible on this crisp February night. Admissible, at the very least.

"What would you want to write?"

"Poems, maybe." I allow for a short intermission in my words. "Menacing ones, of course."

He cackles. "You know what I'm fascinated by?" He skips over a crack. Almost falls. I hold him up. His long body in my arms. We remain frozen like that for a moment. We're in an alley now. A shortcut I know from my wanderings. No one else is in sight. "Book binding." His face below mine. My hands under his shoulders.

"Book binding?" That's not what I was expecting.

"I observed the physical creation of a book once and it was enthralling." He cranes his neck to make sure we're still alone. "Like you."

"Me?"

"Let's be buggers tonight." He waits. I say nothing. "What do you say?"

I grimace. "I don't like that word. Can't we be lovers instead?" I don't know why I say that. I don't love him. I desire him. He doesn't inspire that feeling the poems illuminate. When love's arrow strikes. One of Wilde's own poems comes to me: *We shall be notes in that great Symphony.*

James doesn't love me either. That is clear when he proclaims: "Men can't love men. But we can bugger each other." Before I can protest: "Would you let Oscar Wilde bugger you?"

"What? He's old enough to be my father." Wilde's poetry keeps coming to me: *One with our heart, the stealthy creeping years have lost their terror now. We shall not die. The Universe itself shall be our immortality!*

"My father, believe it or not, has some very handsome friends." James enjoys the sound of this shocking thought escaping his lips. "Does yours?"

"I suppose I would prefer to be with someone closer to my own age." I'm coming to these conclusions on the spot. Realizing what I want only when faced with what I don't. "What I want is . . . someone who might understand me. Truly and completely. And still, despite it all, love me."

"You'll need a woman for that. Men aren't meant to love. They're meant to do this." He puts a hand on my crotch. Rubs me until I'm stiff. The way he does it makes me think he's been taught how by someone else. Perhaps by one of the boys at school. "And . . . this." He presses his lips to mine. Shoves his tongue violently into my mouth.

Of course I crave him. But also more than him. Someone who makes butterflies fly inside me. A boy who makes me feel like a note in a great symphony. I push him gently away. "Let's not rush things."

"Who's exceedingly dull now?" He cackles.

"I'm sorry." I'm not sure what I'm apologizing for.

He quickly forgives me. He creates an elaborate fantasy of what our futures could be as I lead him back to school. "You'll write poems. Even better ones than Wilde. And I'll bind them. No, I'll publish them. I'll start a publishing house. We'll marry, of course."

For a moment, I think he's suggesting we would marry *each other*.

Then: "Our wives will be dear friends, and our children will be too. And when we need the company of a man, we'll visit each other surreptitiously. Doesn't that sound glorious?"

It doesn't. Not to me. All my father cares about are appearances, even if those appearances are lies. I don't want to pretend and deceive. But I can't confess this to James. There have been enough secrets for one day. It's clear to me that he's a bugger. I am not. I want something bigger than buggery. A love of the heart. A life of truth.

Whatever connection James feels with me seems to disappear once we return to the routine of school and sport. He goes back to his usual friends. Their pale faces and mundane thoughts. I finally find him alone in the library after eight days have passed. I catch his gaze. He quickly looks away. I wait for him to say hello. He doesn't. I sit next to him. "I thought we were going to be friends."

"That was before."

"Before what exactly?" I make no attempt to hide my annoyance. "Before you decided to go back to being a bore?"

He looks around to make sure no one is in proximity. "Haven't you heard? Wilde is taking the Marquess of Queensberry to court for calling him a sodomite."

"The deranged man with the vegetable bouquet!" I say this a little too loud.

"Keep your voice down. I don't know why Wilde couldn't just ignore the old man. Now the whole city's talking about it."

"Perhaps that's a good thing."

His eyes narrow. "A good thing?" He shakes his head. "There will be a trial. The whole world will be disgusted by him. By— By—"

I think he wants to say "by us." But I'm not sure. What I am sure of is that it won't just be Wilde on trial. It will be me too. My lust. My desire for love. My deviant thoughts. That will be what's debated in the court. Splashed across newspapers around the world.

"Perhaps there's something even more disgusting than being a sodomite." I wait for his curious eyes to find mine. "Being a coward." I stand up. Walk away from James.

He doesn't dare speak to me again. Not as news of the trial sweeps across the city. Boys in dorms do fey impressions of Wilde. They throw the word *bugger* around mercilessly. A dripping spittle of disgust on their lips each time they speak it. I hear James say it too. Mocking the very thing he is. Loathing himself as self-protection. Pathetic.

I go back to walking. Observing. Keeping my mouth closed. The streets are abuzz with talk of the looming trial. What was once gossiped about in private is now a public obsession. In the pages of the papers. I learn of the detectives Queensberry hired. Of Wilde's visits to male brothels. Tales of blackmail. Corruption. Cross-dressers.

They say: *Not since the Greeks.*

They say: *We must protect our children from the likes of him.*

The man all of London cheered for on Valentine's Day is despised by Easter.

SHAHRIAR. LONDON. MAY. 1895.

With the bloom of spring's flowers comes a surprise visit from my father. I know he didn't travel all this way for a friendly hello. Everything is a chess move to him. He arrives late and summons me to Claridge's. He's booked us a two-bedroom suite. Two bathrooms as well. He doesn't like sharing space with me. Why would he when he blames me for destroying his life simply by being born?

"I'm exhausted" is all he says to me on our first night.

"I understand" is my response. What I understand is that I exhaust him. It must be tiresome trying and failing to transform me into someone exceptional enough to warrant his love.

The suite is more luxurious than the boarding school dormitories I've grown accustomed to. There are sheets that feel like clouds. Curtains so thick they have the power to stop the sun. And yet I toss and turn all night. My mind spins with anxiety. Rage. Nervous to know why he's here. Angry that everything he does is in service of this unnecessary luxury.

Morning breaks. I watch the sunrise through the windows of the suite's living area. I remember something the king's cousin said to me and my father at some ridiculous party my father was over the moon we were invited to. *Everything looks better from above.* I hear the words in my head as I look out the twenty-eighth-story windows of our hotel suite. I want to be in the streets. In the gutters. One with people. Not above.

"Good morning." My father joins me by the window. No hug. No warmth.

"Good morning, Baba." I hope he'll say something kind. Perhaps about how much I've grown since he last saw me. Or a compliment on my latest accomplishments at school. But he offers no praise. Only silent judgment. I want to disappear. Hiding from each other is easy in our house back home. Lots of space. Always other people present. Human buffers. His friends or servants. The lovers he sneaks in. Their feminine scent and coy giggles. He thinks I don't see them sneak in at night and out in the morning. Or perhaps he wants me to notice. To learn. Emulate the way he disposes of women.

"Did you sleep well?"

"Fine." I turn to face him. He looks older. Wearier in the body. Even less muddy gray hair on his balding head than last year. His skin has a gloom to it. The sickly pallor of an empty life. I pray I won't age like him. I tell myself that the secret to eternal youth is loving and being loved. I must stop hating like he does. It's my greatest fear. Turning into him.

"This is not a social visit."

I say nothing. I know he prefers not to be interrupted. He's whipped me for speaking to him without being asked a question first.

"I have received a concerning correspondence from your headmaster."

A strained silence. I'm anxious to know more. I make the

mistake of speaking without being asked to. "I'm not sure what he might be concerned about. I'm top of my class—"

"I have been told that you are interested in being a . . . *writer.*" He says the word as if it were worse than being a bugger. The lowest of the low. "Even worse. A *poet.*"

I breathe a sigh of relief. I thought perhaps he somehow found out I kissed James. This feels small in comparison. "I did express an interest in poetry to my classics professor. But I—I have made no decisions on my future."

"Well, of course you haven't." He spits in my face as he speaks. Little liquid weapons. "Your future is not yours to decide. Which is why decisions have been made for you."

"What decisions?" I can't hide the tremble of fear in my voice.

"I sent you to London so you would master the language of power. You have evidently done that. You speak English like an Englishman and will be ready to do international business on behalf of your empire."

"I—I don't understand."

"London is no place for a boy like you. Not anymore. You think I don't read international newspapers. All those stories about men who . . . I won't even speak the word; it's beneath us. I can't have you influenced by degeneracy. Not when you're doing so well. Top of your class." *This* is when he acknowledges my accomplishments. As tactic, not praise. "I'm pulling you out of school. You're coming home with me."

My pulse races. I always knew he would bring me home someday. That day was meant to be years away. I was meant to stay through university before returning to Persia with my world-class education complete. I had resigned myself to returning after university.

To making my father proud by marrying well and making piles of money. But since seeing Wilde's play . . . I'd let myself dream of a different future. Studying writing. Finding love. Pursuing passion instead of fulfilling duty. I'm a fool.

Foolish enough to yell at him: "I'm staying here. This is my world."

"Your *world?*" His rage is a growing thing. A torrent. "I will decide what your world is. You have a duty to our family." He's my only family. My duty is to him alone. Mother died when I was born. My original sin. "You're a seventeen-year-old boy. When you're my age and your own son tells you what his *world* is, I hope you slap him across the face."

"Is that what you're going to do?" I dare him. "Wouldn't you rather take your belt off and—"

He uses the back of his hand. The sting of it feels worse than a belt. I won't give him the satisfaction of seeing my pain.

"Imagine, me, a nobody from Semnan, working for the king. And now you can join my team. You can bring English accounting practices to our country. You can be twice the man I am. Not some piece of filth in a city of vice!" His booming words sound like a jagged drumbeat. Each utterance a new shock.

"They might hear us in the other rooms." I'm embarrassed by him.

"Let them hear us! Let them know that if they don't do something about the crimes of men like that *writer,* the great families of the world like ours will stop sending their sons to be educated here. We want our sons to be real men, not, not—" Buggers. Sodomites. Those are the words he's too afraid to speak.

I gaze out at Hyde Park. Young men in three-piece suits walk—briefcases in hand—toward grim office buildings. Women in plush winter coats push prams. Walk their perfectly groomed dogs on tight leashes. Yank them to their sides if they stray too far.

"*Real men.*" I speak the words like a sigh. "Aren't we all real, whether we follow your rules or not?" It's not until the question escapes me that I realize it sounds more like a confession than a question. I await his response with fear.

"When I was your age, I would never have dreamed of talking back to my father."

"But I'm not you." Rage stirs within me too. Inherited anger. It bangs at my skin. Wants to be set free. Expressed. "I *never* want to be you."

"Watch yourself." A terrifyingly delivered warning.

I am watching myself. In the ornate mirror on the wall. I like what I see. He is *not* my only family. *I* am my own family. I feel a duty to myself. "You think my future belongs to you. That you can twist me into whatever shape you want me to take."

"You will respect me!"

"But I do respect you." My own words surprise me. "You created your own destiny. First in your family to go to university. A man who was born in dirt and ascended to the halls of power. All I ask is for you to understand that if your aim is for me to be a better version of you, then you must grant me the same luxury."

"I've granted you every luxury." He paces around the hotel suite. Throws a cashmere blanket onto the plush carpet. Runs his fingers on the gradient wallpaper. "Look at this place. I couldn't imagine a room like this when I was your age."

"I don't care about any of this." I gaze at the opulence with disgust. "I don't care about being at the right parties or marrying royalty or attending the very best schools."

"If it weren't for me sending you to the best schools, you wouldn't love poetry, so you have me to thank for that."

"I love it despite you, not because of you." My lips curl into a sneer. "I don't see poetry as a means to an end. I see it as the end, the goal. I want my life to be poetry."

"You won't understand until you're older." He catches his own reflection in the gilded mirror. Next to mine. Freezes for a moment. Perhaps he sees—for the first time—what I see. An embittered old man losing control of his only child. His turn at life is almost over. Mine is just beginning. "You haven't known the poverty I've known. I hope you never will."

"I only want one luxury from you. The luxury to choose my own destiny." I pause to make sure he hears the next part. "As you did."

I turn my gaze back to the window. The sun make its golden ascent over Hyde Park. Its rays illuminate the sharply dressed people beginning their daily rituals of obligation. Two young men in the park catch my attention. Foppish hair blowing in the winter wind like they just rolled out of bed. Wilted green carnations on their lapels. Shoulders held high as they swish like ladies of the evening. Backsides swinging like pendulums. They might be the most *alive* people I've ever seen. The bravest too. Unlike Wilde, they don't get to hide behind fame or wit. They're nobodies daring to be the kind of somebodies that scare the world into change. I'm overwhelmed by a surge of love for them. A swell of bravery in myself.

"There is no debate. The decision is made. We will visit the headmaster this afternoon and give him the news. Then you'll pack your bags, and we'll leave in the morning."

"Tomorrow morning?" Disbelief in my voice.

The mysterious somebodies disappear into the bareness of the winter branches. Take all their energy with them. Leave me weak. Depleted.

"Go get dressed. And look sharp. I don't care if this is the last you'll see of this country for the time being. You're still my son and you'll act the part." The way my dad lays claim on me—*my son*—chills me. But perhaps not as much as the fact that he is commanding me to play a part. I must perform the role of the perfect son once more. Forever, if he has his way. Make-believe might be fun onstage or in the pages of a novel. In life it's a curse.

"Everything looks better from above." My eyes are glued to the park below.

"That's what the king's cousin told me once."

"I know. I was there, don't you remember?" There's accusation in my voice. I hate him for not remembering my childhood. For rarely being there. For never filling my stories in for me. My first words. Favorite toys. Childhood likes and dislikes. All a void. "I was standing by your side. She said that when you're up high, you don't see any of the conflict and sadness of the world, only its beauty. She said that from above, one realizes each individual life is but a dot in the grand Impressionist painting of life, which even then I found a strange thing to say. That a single life was meaningless, when what is more important than each living thing?"

My father turns to me in shock. "You were just . . . How old were you when she said that? You must have been four or five. . . ."

"I was six."

"It's incredible you remember." There's a glimmer of respect in his voice. "You've always had a sharp mind. It cannot be wasted."

"I'm not planning on wasting it. Has it ever occurred to you that perhaps I have something to teach you, just as you've taught me?"

"No, it has not. When I was seventeen, I had a plan for my life. All you have is silly fantasies."

"My plan . . ." I take a breath. "Is to be free."

"Freedom has a price." Rage flashes across my father's face. There's violence in his eyes. He punches the wall. His frustration bubbles into a boil. Numbers are his domain. Not people. He always saw me as an equation. Plug in the right variables. Get the right answer. He got me instead. A wrong answer of a son.

The headmaster does not argue when my father announces he's pulling me out of school early and why. The headmaster shares my father's concern. He's equally disgusted by Wilde. By the details he's read of London's filthy homosexual underworld. He assures my father that the problems will disappear when Wilde is found guilty and put away. He calls it a cult of personality. As if our love for other men—which began long before the late nineteenth century—is due to one modern man. He speaks of Wilde as Dionysus. Putting others under some Bacchian spell. Not once in that meeting does the headmaster address me. It's my father paying the bills, after all. My education is simply a transaction. I its miserable product.

I pack my bags. Realize how little I own. Nothing belongs to me. Not even myself. Boys I've hardly spoken a word to say their goodbyes. There's a pang of sadness when I contemplate never seeing them again. Perhaps we've never been friends. But we shared spaces: Classrooms. Dormitory hallways. Cricket fields. Skating rinks. I go to James's room when my bag is packed. He's alone. Asleep. A book of Keats poems by his side.

I place a hand on the page that lulled him to sleep—"*Four seasons in the mind of a man: He has his lusty Spring*"—and the other hand on his hot cheek. "James."

His eyes flutter open. "What are you doing here?" Hazy panic in his voice. He pushes my hand off his cheek.

"I'm leaving." I keep my eyes on the poem: "*He has his Winter too of pale misfeature, Or else he would forego his mortal nature.*"

"Good." He rubs his eyes. Closes the Keats book. "I hope nobody saw you come in. I told you to—"

"James. Listen. I'm leaving. Forever. Tomorrow morning. My father is taking me back home. To Persia." I watch as he tries to decide if this news makes him happy. Sad. Perhaps both. "You were reading poetry."

"So, this is goodbye?" He flips the pages of the book anxiously. Words glide by.

"I'm afraid it is. I hope . . . that you find someone else you can speak honestly to someday. As we did."

His eyes soften. "If you're leaving, then what's the harm in one last night together. I'm due for dinner at my parents' tonight. Join us."

"My father—"

"Bring him. It's one night. One meal. What's the worst that could happen?"

My final night in London. We're seated at a long dining table in Mayfair. Eating an endless barrage of rich food: Soup. A roast. Stew. Sticky pudding. Cheeses. Tea. All served on ornate porcelain. The game was hunted by James's father only a few days earlier. He speaks of killing an animal and turning it into stew as a source of great pride. It sickens me to chew the meat.

James's parents offer my father a tour of their private gardens after tea and cheese has been consumed. They leave me and James mercifully alone.

"Come, I want to show you something." James leads me to his room. It looks untouched from when he was a much younger child. Perhaps since he's been living at school for years. Hand-painted underwater scenes on the walls. Fish. Octopi. Reefs. A world of magnificent colors. Where everyone and everything floats.

He closes the door behind us. "Look!" He pulls a manuscript from under his mattress. "I stole it from my father's office years ago."

I read some of the pages. Handwritten pages about Dorian Gray. "Is this . . ."

"It's Oscar Wilde's very first, unedited draft of *The Picture of Dorian Gray*. Well, not the entire draft, of course. I couldn't very well steal the whole book. And of course, by the time I took them, edits were made, subsequent drafts were created."

I leaf through the pages. Fifty or slightly more in total. I still haven't read the book. I've been too scared to ask for it. Wilde's name has become synonymous with sin. My eyes land on a passage that stuns me. I read it aloud. "*The aim of life is self-development. To realize one's nature perfectly—that is what each of us is here for. People are afraid of themselves, nowadays. They have forgotten the highest of all duties, the duty that one owes to one's self.*"

The words move me to act. I push James against a painted whale. Kiss him. He mutters a barely audible *oh*. Animal instinct takes over. He presses his body against mine. The hardness in his groin thrusts into me. A shocking hint of wetness in the fabric of his pants. I can hear my father's booming voice outside. I push James away. "I'm sorry. I shouldn't have kissed you. I should go."

"No." He pulls me back into his grip. "Why do you think I asked you here?"

"I thought perhaps . . ." I thought he would miss me. That we were friends. I was so foolish.

He smiles. "You're tempting, and as Wilde says, I can resist everything but temptation." He unzips his pants. Smiles. "Nothing you haven't seen in the showers before."

"I've never seen it like that."

"Show me yours." Lust pours out of him. I look nervously at the door as I put the pages on the small desk in a corner of the room. "Don't worry, my parents give garden tours to all their dinner guests. My mother takes a minimum of fifteen minutes to explain what each tree is, and what I have in mind won't take long."

"I-I'm too nervous. If we were in private—"

"There's nobody here. The servants are all in the kitchen cleaning and our tedious parents are discussing the wonders of urban botany. Now take your pants off. You know we want the same thing."

I don't want this rushed lust. I want a lifetime of love. Yet I pull my pants down. This is better than nothing, after all. Soon I'll be under my father's watch once more. I'll make the most of these hungry minutes before my lifetime of obligation begins.

"There we are." He pushes me against the wall. Begs me to touch him. Lick him. Pull his hair. He grabs a necktie from his closet. "Tie it around my wrists."

"What?" This, I wasn't expecting. "Really?"

"Please, make me feel powerless for just a moment. Power is so exhausting." He wraps the necktie around his wrists. He can't tie it tight enough without my help. I pull the ends for him. Give him what he wants. "Now I feel like a handcuffed criminal. Ready to commit the ultimate transgression." He lies on his bed. Spreads his legs apart. Begs me to press my weight against him. To place a hand on his neck until he's short of breath.

"Are you sure?"

"Quick, before they come back in."

I hesitate. I do it. Straddle him. Put one hand on his neck. Stroke him with the other.

That's how we're found. Me on top. Me in charge. Staring at his parents and my father. All aghast under the bedroom door's decorative moldings. James's hands are tied. He looks—as he wished—powerless. But he reclaims his power when he shifts his accusatory gaze to me. "He forced me! He tied my hands and pushed me onto the bed!"

"I—I didn't . . ." I look in his eyes desperately as I pull my pants back up.

"I should have known better than to befriend a foreigner. They're brutes." He's crying now. An expert performance. His tears are hot. His heart ice cold.

His mother rushes to his side. Unknots the necktie. "This was a gift from my mother." She glares at my father. "Please leave this instant. Go back to your vile country. Stop swamping ours with your savage ways."

"*Our* savage ways?" I hate to admit my father does sound savage. "I am not the one who creates legal defenses for the publishers of smut in court. That would be your husband's job."

"And I regret it every day. Never again. If I knew what Wilde was, I would never have accepted a publisher of his as a client."

"And yet you did." My father speaks with more controlled revulsion now. "You played a part in the corruption of this country and its youth. In the corruption of my son."

James's father fights back. "Your son is sick. He belongs in prison, and if you don't take him home as planned tomorrow, that's exactly where he'll be."

"I didn't . . . I swear I didn't . . . I didn't do anything wrong." I try to defend myself. Unconvincingly.

"Let's go." An order from my father.

I wait for James's father to notice the pages on the desk. To realize that it was his own son who stole them from his office. But all he can see is his own repugnance.

And so . . .

Before I follow my father out . . .

I steal those pages. What does James know about the duty one has to one's own self? He probably interprets those words as a call to selfishness and greed. Too much of a coward to stand by his own nature. I don't want to be like him. I want to be brave enough to be myself. To live a life of truth.

My father doesn't speak to me as we walk back to our hotel. Doesn't look at me until we're in the suite. It's a cold night. The staff lit a fire in the suite's fireplace for us while we were out. I sit in front of it. Close my eyes. Let the flames warm me. The first thing my father says as he kicks off his shoes is: "You disgust me. I have half a mind to leave you here to starve like those Irish beggars you see on the street, bringing their famine across the border with them."

"You're cruel." I say it plainly. My eyes on the flames. I was once told that staring at fire could blind you. I don't care. I need fire. I breathe it in. Welcome it.

"What did you say to me?"

"You heard me. Repetition is a bore. So are you." I pull out the pages I stole. Read aloud. "*Conscience and cowardice are really the same things. Conscience is the trade-name of the firm. That is all.*"

"What is that?"

"None of your business."

"Have you no shame?"

"Perhaps I don't anymore. Isn't that a wonderful thing? To have no shame. Tell me one good thing about shame. I dare you."

"It keeps people in their place!" He believes this. What a sad man.

"I've found my place. And it's not with you." I wish this were true. I haven't found my true home. Not yet.

"No? Then where is it? Among buggers?"

I read from the pages. I know Wilde's words hold answers. "*To define is to limit.*"

"You need limits! You want to be in the arms of another man?"

"YES." I cry this out. As if to the heavens. "And not James. He's incapable of love. I'll find someone else. Someone tender and honest. Someone who will give me the kind of life you never did. A life of love."

"YOU DISGUST ME!"

"You can repeat it and repeat it, and still, I won't care. I know I did nothing wrong."

"Nothing wrong? You tied a boy—"

"He asked to be tied. He wanted it."

"Stop talking. I can't hear this."

"Then leave!"

"Perhaps it's good you killed your mother in childbirth." His voice sizzles. He's been waiting so long to say these words. He's always blamed me for her death. He's just never been bold enough to say it. "At least you spared her this."

"You've never forgiven me for being born."

Finally.

The real fight.

The one we've been waiting seventeen years for.

"You killed her. She was the one good thing I had."

"Perhaps she died when I was born. But she would never have been pregnant if not for you. So you killed her too, didn't you? You set the stage, as you always do."

"And now you're killing me." It's as if he didn't hear a word I said. "You're a murderer."

"Then save yourself. Leave me to my own devices. I don't need you. I have these pages to read, and in them is more wisdom than you'll ever have."

My father snatches the pages out of my hands. "Dorian Gray?" A confirmation of his fears. "This is that deviant's handwriting. Wilde?"

"Indeed it is." I stand up to face him. I'm taller than him now. Grateful for that. He's exactly the kind of person I delight in looking down on. "And you know what? I'm just like him. A bugger. An invert. A homosexual. Pick your favorite word. It's who I am and none of your lessons, commands, or belts will ever change me. I delight in your disgust of me. It means I'm doing something right."

A long silence. The crackling wood of the fire. I wait insolently for what he might do next. Hit me. Push me. I think he has it in him to kill me. But what he does is perhaps even worse.

He flings those handwritten pages into the fireplace. "That's where filth belongs. That's where *you* belong."

"You belong in hell!"

"I already am in hell." He turns away from me. "I'm going downstairs for a drink. When I come up, you will either be here and ready to change your ways or you will be gone. Those are your only choices." He slams the door behind him.

"I wish I were never born!" I yell that to the closed door. But not existing is not what I truly want. Not at all. I whisper to myself. To God. My true desire. "I wish I were born in another time. I wish I could be alive in a time when my love isn't a crime. Please." Tears fall down my cheeks. Warmed by the flames. I long for those burning pages. Those words. Strokes of genius on paper. Once-in-a-generation words. Menacing text. Wisdom. Original thought. I won't let it burn. Can't bear to see art scorched like trash.

I throw my hands into the flames. My eyes glued to the fire. Desperate to save what I can. Words burn. *I am tired of myself tonight. I should like to be somebody else.* Pages warp. Black ink erupts into shades of rust and orange. *To cure the soul by means of the senses, and the senses by means of the soul.* Smoke fills the room. I choke as I pull three pages out. That's all I can save. Three of over fifty pages.

I pull my hands out of the fireplace. Realize my own sleeves are aflame. Drop the pages to the floor. Run into the bathtub fully clothed.

The water washes away my doubts. Makes me feel reborn. That's the only way I can describe it. Like a different person. With a new heart. A different soul. A renewed purpose.

I take off my wet clothes. Gaze at my curious reflection in the mirror. My eyes—when I stare at them long enough—glow orange. Like a cat. Like those burning pages. I don't know what it means. All I know is that I feel different in my body. I'm not my father's son anymore.

I walk right past my father as I leave. There's a tall glass of whiskey in front of him. He sits at the bar. Faces rows of bottles.

Wallowing in his own hate. I mouth a goodbye to him. In my left pocket is what little money I found in the hotel room safe. The combination lock was set to my mother's birthday. He probably doesn't think I know what day she was born. Doesn't think I'm worthy of knowing anything about the only person he truly loved. I take all the money. Feel no shame about it.

In my right pocket are those three pages I saved from the fire.

I walk out into the city. Toward one more sunrise. That's all I need. Just a little light to figure out the way forward.

OLIVER. BOSTON. APRIL. 1920.

Brendan pulls me to the back of the Golden Rooster. I wish I could stop him. Tell him that I want to find that mysterious boy with the spark in his eyes again. "Where are you taking me?" I ask my cousin.

"We're getting a private tour," Brendan says.

"A tour of what?" I ask. "I don't think I want a tour of the bathrooms, if it's okay with you."

Jack buzzes his way to me. "You really do need to loosen up," he says, chastising me. "I could help you with that, you know." His face breaks into a smile.

"I think you're plenty loose enough for the two of us," I snap back, and to my surprise, Brendan, Cyril, and the boys clap for me. I look up and see the mysterious boy has followed us to the back. He's clapping too, except his hands move toward each other slowly, like they're in thick water. They barely make a sound. He seems to want to remain unseen to all but me.

"Touché, baby boy." Jack claps for me too. "You know what touché means, don't you? It means touched. Now, if you ever wanted to touch me in a more *sensual*—"

"Jack, stop. Please. It doesn't have to be frivolity and innuendo all the time, does it?" I ask. I'm not sure who I'm speaking to in this moment. Myself perhaps. My eyes are closed. I'm swept up in a moment, in the now. "What I mean is . . . I don't want some night of fun in a bathroom. I don't want to love and leave. I want to love. Just to love."

My eyes open at the sound of Jack's laughter. "You have it all mixed up, baby boy."

"Please stop calling me that! I'm seventeen years old. I'm not—"

"You have it all mixed up, *big man*." He's holding court now. Preaching to his choir. "What happens here has nothing to do with *love*. We're having a lark, that's all. Some good fun before we begin our real lives."

"So this isn't our real life?" I ask.

"You're too literal," Jack snaps. "This is a brief period of fantasy so we get the sin out of our system before it's time for us to step up and be real men."

"Real men . . . ," I whisper woefully like I'm his faint, doubting echo. The boys we've come in with start to shift around us. Some of them—Brendan and Cyril included—move closer to me. The majority of them move closer to Jack. It's like they're picking sides. Are they here for some frivolous fun or for something more meaningful?

Only the mystery kid doesn't move. His eyes are on me. He doesn't blink once. I know because my eyes are fixed on him too. I want to know which side he's on. Mine or Jack's.

"Maybe I'm foolish for saying it, but I know I couldn't love a woman," I declare. "Well, not in that way. I love my mother, of course."

"Surprise, surprise. A fruit who loves his mommy." Jack's snideness is met with laughter.

I don't let the cackles deter me. "Laugh all you want, but I know I have so much love to give. And this place . . ." I wave my arm across the bar. "This might be the only place I'm safe to say so. I have love to give and what I want is to give it to . . . well, to . . ." I want to finish. To say I want to give it to another boy. But my mouth suddenly goes dry and my heart races. Mother told me before a piano recital to ignore everyone in the audience except for her. To play for an audience of one. That's what I do now. I speak only to the mystery boy. The warmth in his gaze inspires me. I feel clearer than I've ever felt before. My eyes are glued to him as I say, "I want a love that feels like a concerto. A concerto goes on and on, repeating motifs and building on itself. To me, that's what love should feel like. An epic lifetime of swinging back and forth from major to minor, always coming back to the same key in the end." My voice is full of confidence, but my heart shatters. Because I can't find this kind of love without breaking Mother's heart, can I?

Jack rolls his eyes. "As it turns out, I like swinging back and forth too. That's why I'm not wearing any underwear." More laughter. The room seems to have chosen Jack as the winner.

"I have an idea," Brendan says, offering us a détente. "Let's show Oliver the back room." Turning his gaze to me, he says softly, "I think you'll be fascinated by what's there."

"Brendan, if it's something to do with sex, I'd much rather—"

He shakes his head. "Trust me. There's more to the Rooster than dickylickers and deep-sea divers."

Brendan leads the way to a back room. I'm expecting to find some sort of dungeon, but to my surprise, what I find is a three-cylinder printing press. A thickly built young woman in a simple white shirt and gray slacks mans the imposing machine. It rolls out a stream of printed words and images about a labor union strike, and she cuts them into individual leaflets. She hands one to me first, then one to each of the boys. "We support your lot," she says. "We ask you to support ours. We demand better wages and work conditions, just as men have. And we won't give up, even if we never get the support of the men in charge of the labor unions."

"My mother works as a seamstress, and they don't even pay her during breaks," I say. "She works in the most cramped space you've ever seen."

The woman smiles. "So, you're not a golden boy like this lot," she cracks.

"Says the girl who just graduated from Radcliffe," Jack says.

"On a full scholarship," the woman clarifies.

Jack pulls an alarmingly large wad of cash out of his pocket and hands it to her. "For your cause, milady," he says.

The woman takes the cash. "Thanks, Jack." To my delight, she tousles his carefully combed hair.

"You're welcome," Jack says. "Now, can we talk about something more exciting than women's rights?"

"This is not what I was expecting to find back here," I say in awe.

"The Rooster is much more than a bar," the woman explains. "It's a center of community. Do you know why the owner put a printing press back here?"

Cyril raises his hand like he's in class. "Because whoever controls the written word controls the mind." He blushes. "My classics professor said that. It sounded more natural coming from him."

I gently insert myself into the conversation. "It makes me think that perhaps life was better before the written word. When no one could control others."

The woman kindly asks me, "You think early humans didn't exert control through other, more brutal means than writing?"

"I suppose you're right," I say sadly.

"Though I think *control* might be the wrong word for what we're doing," she says thoughtfully. "Some people use the written word to control the mind. Others use it to liberate thought, create empathy."

I want to be like this woman. A fighter for justice. A creator of a better world. Not through money like Jack and his family. Through action like her. "What about music?" I ask. "Can music be used the same way? To liberate thought and all that."

"Of course," she assures me. "Creativity is God's great gift to humanity, and like all gifts, it's also a challenge. Will you use the gift for ill or good?" I look around the back room. Flyers are littered about, as are stacks of paper, worn books, clippings from newspapers. She follows my gaze and quickly offers, "If you ever want to come back and read, just say the word. Eastman has set it up like a bit of a library. You can read Havelock Ellis or Freud, Wilde or Marx, all the thinkers the powerful are afraid of."

"I'd love to discuss Marx, but I'd much rather order another round of sodas and spike it with this." Jack pulls a small bottle of whiskey from the inside pocket of his jacket. "Who's coming?" Everyone follows Jack except me.

Left behind with the woman, I ask, "If I were to read one thing here, what would you recommend?"

"What are you looking for?" she asks. "Something to fill you with righteous rage. A poem to make you weep, perhaps. A scientific or psychological text about sex or gender."

I think for a moment. "No," I whisper. "I want . . . something to give me hope. That someday, I might be able to feel . . . I don't know . . . whole. With another man, I mean. You already knew that's what I wanted, didn't you?"

"Honey, my beautiful woman is back home waiting for me." She smiles as she hands me a copy of Plato's *Symposium*. "I think this will do the trick."

"Plato?" I ask.

"You've read it already?"

"Not yet," I say. "How will it make me feel better?"

"You'll have to read it to find out." She grabs her papers. "I'll leave you to it. It's time for me to go hand out some leaflets. You're all right in here?"

"I'm more than all right," I say. "I love it here. I could move in if you'd put a mattress on the floor. All I need is a piano."

"There's a piano in the main hall. They love it when someone plays for the crowd." She offers me her hand. "I'm Edna, by the way."

"Oliver." I take her hand and give it a squeeze. When she leaves me alone, I start to read the *Symposium*, curious about why she chose it for me. As I take in the words, I feel as if I'm ascending into some other time. Or perhaps just deeper into myself, into a part of me I'm just learning about. I can't help but shed happy tears at how beautiful it feels. I let the tears roll down my freckled cheeks, not bothering to wipe them.

Then I hear a slight creak. I look up and see him standing there. The mysterious dark-haired kid.

Embarrassed, I quickly wipe my face dry. "How long were you standing there?" I ask, annoyed.

"Long enough to want to join you," he says. "May I?"

"You stood there staring at me while I cried." I feel exposed and raw. "It's not right to watch a person like a spy."

"You looked so peaceful," he says. "I couldn't disturb you."

"I don't always cry like that," I say defiantly. "Only when a book moves me."

"And I don't always spy like that," he says. "Only when a person moves me." He smiles. "Am I forgiven?"

"I don't know," I say. "Can I trust you?"

"I'm not sure I can trust myself."

I laugh wryly at the truth of that. Every young man in this establishment can't trust themselves. We're all breaking someone's heart simply by being here.

"You shouldn't feel embarrassed by your tears," he murmurs. "A great piece of writing should make you cry. Or laugh. Or rage. I certainly cry reading Walt Whitman and Wordsworth. Every time. Have you read them?"

"I have," I say.

He begins to recite poetry to me. Wordsworth. I know the one. Mother loves it. "*Though nothing can bring back the hour. Of splendour in the grass, of glory in the flower.*"

"*We will grieve not,*" I continue from memory. "*Rather find strength in what remains behind.*"

He smiles. I do too. "*Now* am I forgiven?" he asks.

"If you promise never to spy on me again," I say.

"I promise," he assures me. I look up and focus on his eyes as they catch the light of the corner lamp. They're brown, but when I stare at them long enough, they seem to turn orange. Maybe it's the red lights from the main room still playing tricks on my vision.

"Were you looking for me?" I ask. "Is that why you came back here?"

"I didn't want to leave before saying hello," he says.

"Well then, hello." I quickly stammer out, "That wasn't, uh . . . meant to inspire you to leave."

"May I sit?" he asks. "I much prefer reading to . . . whatever is happening out there."

"What is happening out there?" I ask.

"Oh, just boys being boys. People chasing the thrill of immediacy when it will just leave them feeling lonelier. I know you agree. I liked the passion and intelligence with which you took on that buffoon out there."

"Jack Whitman?" I ask.

"His last name is Whitman? Like the great Walt. What a shame." He throws his face in his hands.

I laugh. "Jack could be worse. His parents are wildly wealthy. All things considered, he turned out better than one might expect." I'm not even sure why I'm defending Jack. I guess I do have a soft spot for the outspoken way in which he lives. I also loathe the way he treats me like an object. Treats us all like we're his playthings.

"Give him time to become fully corrupted," he says. "I know the type. Their kindness is predicated on their power. Once they feel the power slip, they'll cut even their closest friends to hold on to it."

"Gosh, I hope that's not the case." I hear the longing in my voice, and suddenly realize how invested I am in the well-being of all these friends. Brendan, Cyril, all of them.

"Trust me," he says. "Nothing is more dangerous than the wrath of the powerful who are feeling their supremacy slip."

"He's not a good friend of mine or anything, but he's my cousin's roommate. It would break my cousin's heart if Jack turned out to be as awful as you think he is."

"Is your cousin in love with him?" he asks.

"I—I don't know, honestly. We talk of fashion and music, we make jokes and mock each other mercilessly. But as you heard out there, talk of love . . . well, sometimes I think that in this world, our kind of love is the ultimate taboo."

His eyes light up when I say this, like he's sure that I'm a kindred spirit now. "And the sweetest one too. May I sit with you?"

"Yes," I say. "Thank you for asking."

"Thank you for giving me another chance." He sits next to me. Eyes the open book. "Good old Plato." He says the name like he's referring to an old friend.

"You've read it?"

"I've read everything." The sly smile on his face is intoxicating. "Well, everything I've gotten my hands on." He places his hand on the right side of the book. Mine rests on the left side. Our fingers almost touch as they wander across the words. Words like the *power of love* and *love is our best friend* and *children of the sun*. "What do you think of it? His theory of who we once were?"

"I love it," I say excitedly. "I don't know if it's true but imagine if it is. It would explain everything, wouldn't it?"

"And you . . ." He hesitates. "Are you a child of the sun?"

I glance over the passage our fingers rest on again. It says that in the beginning, we all had two sets of arms and legs and faces. There were three sexes then. The children of the sun were two men. The children of the earth were two women. And the children of the moon were a man and a woman. Being whole like this made us powerful, and that scared the gods. So Zeus split us in two, leaving us searching for our other half. "Yes," I whisper. "I am a child of the sun."

"And your other half?" he asks. "I take it you believe he's out there, since you believe this is all more than a romp."

"I have to be believe it," I declare. "If I don't, then I'll lose all hope. And if you have no hope, well . . . how do you move forward?"

"Hope is the only thing that's kept me going all these years." He sighs.

I laugh. "*All these years,*" I echo. "How old are you? Eighteen? Nineteen?"

"Seventeen, actually," he says, and for the first time, I notice him blinking. Finally, those feline eyes look calmer, less precise in their stare.

"Me too!" I squeal, excited to have found something in common with him, even if it's just a number.

"But I'm a very old seventeen," he says wearily.

"My mother sometimes says I'm seventeen going on forty, but that's because I work so hard. But in so many other ways, I feel like a kid, honestly," I confess. "I know nothing of love. Of intimacy. I hadn't read Plato until a few moments ago. I haven't read any of the material in this room. Havelock Ellis—"

"Overrated."

"Freud."

"Complicated."

"Wilde."

"Wild indeed." His eyes crackle like fireworks.

"Your eyes," I whisper. "Am I imagining it or are they . . ."

He closes his lids self-consciously. Turns away from me. I suppose, like so many of us, he's scared of being seen. "They're brown," he whispers, eyes still shut. "But when you look at them long enough, they turn orange. I've been told it's frightening."

"No, it's beautiful. Like a kaleidoscope." There's awe in my voice. "Or like a cat?"

"With nine lives." He finally turns back to me. Opens his eyes and looks at me with heartbreaking tenderness.

"I'd like to have infinite lives," I say. "I'd like to live everywhere, see the world."

"Traveling the world alone can be very lonely," he says. "You should start your adventures once you've found your other half."

From the main room comes the sound of Edna's voice. The music has stopped and she's giving a speech to some groans and some cheers. "Now, now, boys, I know you want to get back to getting sozzled and fondled, but this is important," she bellows authoritatively. "This country asked its ladies to step up when the boys went to war. There's no going back now that the boys are home." A few loud groans can be heard. "Apologies for bringing down the mood, but guess what? One copper walks in here and you could all be in jail. They're burning Negro churches in the South. Lynching human beings. Your rights are our rights are their rights. It's time to stand together as one human race." When she's done, "Tiger Rag" begins to play.

The speech changes the mood in the back room. What felt private suddenly feels public, like we're not alone anymore. "Shall we go back out there?" I ask. "My cousin is probably wondering where I am."

"Do we have to?" he asks. "I like it much better back here. With you."

I blush. "You're very forward."

"I just know what I want. More of your company." His eyes are locked on mine. "You're magic."

I bask in the glow of the compliment, which felt sincere, with none of the laced irony that is a trademark of boys like us. I enjoy the playful sarcasm and wit, but I think I like earnestness even more. It's important to be earnest sometimes.

I see him shift his hand a little closer to the spine of the book. I move mine toward his. Our fingers find each other at the center of the book, like we're uniting its two sides. He lifts my hand up to his face and rubs the back of my hand to his cheek as he reads from the book. "*And when one of us meets our other half, we are lost in an amazement of love and friendship and intimacy, and would not be out of the other's sight even for a moment.* Your turn."

"Oh, you want me to read?" I ask. He just nods, and I oblige. "*We pass our whole lives together, desiring that we should be melted into one.*"

He skips ahead a beat. "*And the reason is that human nature was originally one and we were a whole, and the desire and pursuit of the whole is called Love.*"

We gaze into each other's eyes for so long that his become a swirl of brown and orange and rust. They seem to have their own light inside them, an electrical charge that moves through him and into me, emblazoning me from within. I've never been kissed but I've seen the way it happens in pictures. Slowly. Passionately. With closed eyes. And yet, we don't close our eyes. We keep them open just like our mouths. I want to see him, and he seems to want to see me.

"I'm sure he's in there reading," Brendan yells as footsteps approach. I quickly pull away before the boys find us. They're each holding two cups of soda. They place the cups down and Jack fills them to the top with liquor. "And like I said, there he is. I take you to an establishment of questionable moral value, little cousin, and you treat it like a library."

"Perhaps he wasn't just reading," Jack says. "Our hopeless young romantic seems to have found a delicious new friend."

"Please, not now, Jack," I beg. I want to introduce my new friend, but then I realize I don't even know his name, and I feel so foolish. Just moments ago, we were ready to kiss each other. We were reading words of love like we were the characters in some romantic play. Now I'm reminded he's nothing but a stranger.

Sensing my sudden nervousness, he stands up and holds out his hand. "I'm Shams."

"Shams?" Jack asks. "What kind of name is that?"

"It's Persian," he explains. "It was the name of the poet Rumi's spiritual instructor, who some believe was also his lover."

"Rumi? Never heard of the guy," Jack cracks.

"Most ordinary chaps haven't," Shams coolly responds. He, unlike the rest of the world, seems unflustered by Jack.

"I'm far from ordinary, *chap*," Jack huffs haughtily. "But I'll forgive you because I love a full-lipped man, and yours look positively bee-stung. There really is an epidemic of thin lips going around Boston. People with thin lips and flat backsides should be barred from procreating, I say."

A few boys laugh. Shams and I don't. "You're not at Harvard, are you?" Cyril asks Shams. "I've never seen you before."

"Are you visiting Boston?" Brendan asks.

"Your accent is hard to place," Jack says. "Have you come from the United Kingdom? Are you attending university here?"

"He's just seventeen." I stand up. "And you can stop questioning him now. How would you like it if you were battered with questions like you were being interviewed for some newspaper?"

"Curiosity is a necessary quality in life," Jack counters. "Especially when you're faced with somebody named Shams. A sham is a lie. A thing that is not what it purports to be."

"The name is Shams, not Sham," Shams responds icily. "The *a* is flat, like your unfortunate behind." Jack claps, impressed. "And it's plural, because if I am a sham, then I'm more than one sham. I contain multitudes."

"Uncle Walt!" Jack exclaims proudly. He always calls him Uncle Walt because they share a last name, though he bears no relation to the great poet. "Now there's a poet I *have* heard of."

"And your name . . . Jack," Shams quietly whispers. "Perhaps it is a clue to your fate. You'll be cursed to a life of loneliness. Jacking off for eternity."

"On beautiful faces," Jack snaps, to applause.

"My goodness, enough now!" Brendan announces. "You two will kill me with these verbal daggers."

"He's right," Shams says. "You see, Jack. Curiosity might be necessary, but it also killed the cat." When he says this, his eyes glow orange in a way that startles us all.

"All right then, round one is over," Jack agrees. "Now I'd like to propose a toast."

I raise my glass up high. "I'll make the toast," I announce.

"You?" Jack asks. "You don't even drink. What kind of toast can you make?"

"Why don't you shut up so we can find out?" Shams asks, in a tone at once damning and ribald. I've never met anyone more expert at cutting Jack down to size. He's wonderful.

"All righty then." Jack backs down, impressed. Perhaps what Jack really wants, and needs, is someone strong enough to put him in his place.

My glass raised, I take a breath. "To all the romantics, who are far from hopeless. In fact, we're nothing but hope. And also, to Plato. To Plato for understanding us. Isn't life fantastic?"

"Something's come over your cousin," Cyril says to Brendan.

"I'm just happy, that's all," I say. "It feels a bit like a fog is lifting. Maybe it's just that I've finally come to terms with the grief of my father's passing. Or maybe it's meeting you lot. The . . . the camaraderie of being with you. I don't know. But it feels, for the first time, like I may not be all future." I look at Cyril as I say this, remembering what he told me about the lesson of his birthday. "It feels, finally, that I might be living in the present." I turn my gaze to Shams. There's understanding in his eyes. Without him saying a word, I know he empathizes with everything I'm saying. Perhaps he's a stranger to me, but our few moments together moved us, changed us, started something that I hope keeps going.

On our way back into the main hall, we see a beautiful woman swaying to the music alone. Jack gives her a wink and tells her, "You're absolutely stunning, doll. Did you pencil in those eyebrows yourself?"

"You think I'd let anyone else paint this face?" It's not until the woman speaks these words that I realize she's a man.

The boys must see the shock on my face because they all laugh and Jack says, "You're so delightfully innocent, Oliver."

"I—I thought you were—" I stammer. I don't want to say anything stupid. I want to be accepted here. I want to know all the unspoken rules. "Are those lilies in your hair?"

"Why don't you smell and find out?" the painted man asks slyly.

I feel my cheeks blush at the attention. "Well, they're beautiful. And you're beautiful. Like a film star, to be honest. I'm Oliver, by the way. And these are my friends—"

"Honey, I'll forget your names before I finish drinking this Hanky Panky. Come see me at the masquerade ball, children. I won't have lilies in my hair on the wrestling mat."

As she walks away toward the bar, I turn to the boys. "What masquerade ball?"

Jack pulls out an invitation from his jacket pocket. "Straight from the printing press in the back room. It's in two weeks."

I read the invitation, which promises a night of astonishing melodrama with a costume competition and a damsel wrestling match. "So these men, dressed as women, wrestle each other?" I ask, trying to make sense of it all.

"A wholesome evening of entertainment," Jack explains.

"I'm a wrestler," I whisper. "Are they really going to wrestle or is it just for show?"

"Why don't you enter the competition and find out?" Jack suggests. "I would pay good money to see you wrestle in a gown and heels."

With a raised eyebrow, I ask, "How much good money?"

"Enough to make it worth your while. And I'll even get you the costume."

As we shake on it, Edna finds us and approaches me. "Eastman said he'd love you to play some piano, if you're interested."

"Me?" I ask. "All the pieces I know are melancholy and old. I'm not sure this crowd wants—"

"Old, melancholy things are my favorite," Shams says. "I'd love to hear you play."

"So would I," Brendan says.

"Me too," Cyril adds.

"Me three," Jack declares. "Speaking of threes . . . has anyone ever tried a—"

"All right." I nod decisively, a small movement to help work through my fear. I let Edna guide me to the piano. She motions to an older man holding court on the other end of the room. Soon, the music stops, and Edna announces a special performance by a new member of our community. I like the way she says that. She sees me as something to be appreciated and welcomed, not used and disposed of.

I choose Schubert. Because he's my favorite. But also, because something in the melody feels deeply romantic to me, and I want Shams to feel I'm playing it for him. Perhaps we are strangers, I tell myself as I place my fingers on the keys, but don't all children of the sun and earth and moon start out as strangers before they eventually meet their other halves? I can't be sure he's my other half, but I want to find out. And seeing how he responds to "Fantasie in F Minor" might help me know. Because if his eyes don't moisten as the melody swells, I don't know if he can ever understand me fully. These aren't keys I'm playing. Not notes. This is my heart and soul, coming through my fingers, traveling into the world as music, as spirit.

He doesn't take his eyes off me as I play.

I don't take my eyes off him.

And then, as the piece crescendos and I let my fingers bang wildly, I see him flinch. Perhaps he thought it would stay soft the whole time. Thought I didn't have this kind of passion in me. I watch him take it all in. The gentleness with which I play can lead to a hardened passion before the melody takes over and I'm all softness again. I see a tear fall from his eye. And I know, if not that I have feelings for him, that I *could* have feelings for him. And that's certainly enough for today.

BRAM. LONDON. APRIL. 2025.

The rain has stopped. Replaced by the tears of Lily's chosen family. Downpours and drizzles in the eyes of young and old as Archie reads a plaque in the Victoria Embankment Gardens. "*This lily pond was presented in 1915 by Mr. Alfred Buxton.*"

"Who's Mr. Alfred Buxton?" That's one of the young queers. Beautiful Black boy. Hair tightly braided. Beard. Worn jeans. Baggy brown wool sweater. A soft knitted scarf in the colors of the Jamaican flag. I'm certain Lily must have made it. Her voice comes back to me: *Only national flag with no red, white, or blue. Jamaicans can't help but be unique.*

Archie takes his top hat off. Wipes the sweat from his wrinkled forehead. "I honestly don't know, Tobi. What matters is that this lily pond is where our beloved Lily chose her name." Archie's hair is gone. His scalp is bald. Spotted with discoloration.

I don't dare step forward and risk being seen, even though it's not them I'm afraid of being found by.

God, how I missed them all. Dancing with Archie. Learning from Azalea. Eating Poppy's home-cooked meals. She loved nothing more than emptying a tin of cayenne pepper into whatever she was making. We would all cry and laugh when we ate together. Jerk chicken. Pepper pot soup. Fried fish. We always wanted more.

"Poppy, it's your turn to lead the procession. Get up here."

The crowd parts so that Poppy can make her way up to the plaque. She lifts the bell bottoms of her red velvet jumpsuit to make sure they don't fall into a puddle. She's shrunk too. She leaps over one of the puddles carefully. "Move over, Archiekins." Poppy takes a dramatic pause before beginning to tell the story. "Lily and I wandered into these gardens on a rare sunny December day. It was 1973. Earlier that year, London had celebrated its very first Gay Pride march."

"It was 1972!" The beautiful Black boy named Tobi has his phone out. All the knowledge in the world in the palm of his hand. Except the things that can't be turned into data. The hidden emotional truths you can't ask a search engine about. How things *felt*.

Poppy doesn't bristle at being corrected or interrupted. "So it was. Back then, we didn't have no phones like yours to check a date on the spot. Nor to distract us from our *lives*. So when we would walk, we would observe. We would think."

I hide behind the trunk of an oak tree when I see Poppy's gaze travel toward me.

"You might think the first Gay Pride made for a joyful year, but as I remember it, this was not the case. It was a profound moment of despair for us. We hadn't found ourselves yet. Lily's heart had recently been broken by a little twat who—" Poppy stops herself. "You know what, he was a twat, but he died far too young and I won't speak ill of the fallen souls. What happened is this. Lily told me that she wanted her life to end. By this very pond, at this exact spot, in 1972."

In the crowd, a few audible sobs as the mourners contemplate never having known Lily.

"I asked her why, and she said that there was no future for her. She said that she felt no liberation when she attended that very first Gay Pride parade. None of the joy or freedom that her gay and lesbian friends felt. Because she wasn't like them. What she was, as we all know, was a woman. Like me, though she understood herself before I did. This was before the two of us saved up for our surgical trip to Casablanca. Thanks for nothing, NHS."

Lily understood so much before others did. This was one of her many superpowers. A profound understanding of the human condition.

"I begged her to stay strong. To keep going." Poppy wipes a single tear from her cheek. "I don't want to take any credit for what happened next, because I don't think she was even listening to me. She was staring at the pond as if in a trance. The sun seemed to be shining on her alone. Nature's spotlight. What I need you to understand is that she was being reborn in that moment. None of us are born only once."

How I know this to be true.

"When she came out of her trance, she turned to me and declared that from that day on, she would be known as Lily." Poppy nods. "And that is how our beloved Lily Summers came to be born."

The mourners bow their heads down to honor the personal history of this spot.

"On to our next destination, the National." Poppy turns to Archie. He raises his top hat into the sky. "Follow Archie's top hat. Funny, such a big top hat for such a big bottom!" Everyone laughs. No one louder than Archie himself.

I pick up a newspaper someone left on a park bench and cover my face with it as I follow them. Even in London, the *New York Times* can easily be found. That's why Oliver and I chose that paper. We had to make sure to choose a means of communication that would work no matter where we were. I took out the same ad every day for the last month, to ensure he would see it. He must have seen it. Where is he?

The mourners stop outside the National Theatre, where Lily first worked as a seamstress for the theater in 1980. It was for the National's production of *The Romans in Britain*. Oliver and I were at opening night. The play was magnificent. It juxtaposed the stories of Caesar's invasion of Celtic Britain with the country's relationship to Northern Ireland during the Troubles.

I feel a hand on my shoulder. Panic. Either Oliver is here, or I've been found and life as I know it is over. I turn around. I'm ready to bolt if I need to.

"Would you take a photo of us all together?" a tourist asks me as she holds out her iPhone.

I feel relief that I haven't been found. Disappointment that it wasn't Oliver. "Of course."

I take the phone and position myself with my back to Lily's memorial crew. I snap-snap-snap. Azalea speaks behind me. "Of course, no one remembers those gorgeous costumes Lily helped sew. No, what they remember is the moral panic the play caused because it dared to depict gay rape onstage. People threw things at the actors. Fireworks. Flour. Disgusting fools."

"Jesus." That's Tobi again. I get the sense he's learning Lily's history today. I wonder how long he knew her.

"Yes, exactly." Azalea laughs. "Jesus was indeed involved. A Christian activist sued the director for gross indecency. Mary

Whitehouse. An absolutely loathsome woman who knew nothing of Jesus's true teachings. Her hatred is the real gross indecency."

Gross indecency. The words remind me of Wilde. His life. His work. Those trials.

"Can you take a vertical one?"

"And some in portrait mode, please?"

I oblige the family. They're giving me a perfect way to be a part of the memorial without being a conspicuous observer.

Gross indecency. Wilde. The man who inspired me and destroyed me. And not just me. I'm not claiming his pages made others immortal. I do believe Oliver and I are the only ones. But Wilde slept with young men, then disposed of them. He insisted on suing for libel despite knowing the accusations against him were true. His trial created assumptions about gay men that last to this day. Sexual compulsion. Criminality. He doesn't deserve to be a symbol for our community. But perhaps Wilde isn't the problem. Never was. The problem is turning people into symbols in the first place. Defending their flaws because we think their mistakes belong to everyone in our community. Wilde wasn't perfect. That much I know.

Then again, neither am I.

I want to be loved as Wilde still is. For my beauty and my flaws. My light and my darkness. That's what I need from Oliver.

Oliver?

Is that him in the background of the photo I just took of the tourists?

I'm still in portrait mode. The background is out of focus. I go to the photo. Zoom in to the blurry chestnut-haired figure standing hesitantly by a lamppost. Half his face covered by the very newspaper I placed the ad in. It's *his* stance. He has a way of leaning forward. Always craning that gloriously long neck to see more of the world.

I return the phone. I feel dizzy with excitement as I search the crowds for him. Tourists everywhere. Splashes of street art in primary colors. A cluster of onlookers watch adolescent skateboarders athletically leap across ramps. The hungry line up at a Mexican food truck. Theatergoers flood into the National.

Where is he?

"Shall we go to our next stop?" Azalea is still in charge of the procession. She turns to Archie. "Follow the bottom's top hat!"

"I'm too old, too tired, and too talented to be bottom shamed." Archie cackles. "And by a nurse, no less."

"Same nurse who got you the meds you needed when the world turned its back on you." Azalea puts an arm around Archie. "Think that earns me the right to mock you mercilessly."

"I suppose so." Archie leans a head on her shoulder.

They head toward the Queen's Walk. I know the route. They'll head south to Brixton after the Queen's Walk. To our home. To Pearl's. Then back to the Thames for sunset. I don't follow them. I turn my head left. Then right. I search near and far.

I push through the crowds. Desperate to find him.

Memories flood my mind: London with Oliver.

And also: London before Oliver.

Those years before I met him. Those early days when I still wasn't certain those flames changed me forever.

"Oliver!"

I see a figure on the bridge. Staring out at the river. He's too far for me to be sure. I run. "OLIVER!"

The faster I run . . .

The closer I get . . .

The more certain I am it's him.

OLIVER. BOSTON. APRIL TO MAY. 1920.

While I'm at wrestling practice, Shams calls our new telephone, which we hardly ever use. Mother prefers letters. She begs my brother, Liam, to write from Yale instead of resorting to lazy phone calls. She believes written communication requires thought and intention. A phone call should be for emergencies. She only agreed to install the telephone after Father died. She knew Liam was right when he said that with a telephone, we might have been able to say goodbye to Father. "A friend called for you," she says as I come home from wrestling practice, my heart still racing from the exercise, my clothes sticking to me with sweat.

"Oh?" I ask, knowing it must be him.

"He left a phone number, but no name." She approaches me with a piece of paper. "I asked if he goes to school with you, and he said he doesn't. He said he met you through Brendan and that you had offered to give him piano lessons."

All true. I did meet Shams because Brendan took me to the Rooster. And after I played for the patrons of the bar, after he marveled at my musicianship and said he wished he could play like me, I said I could teach him. It wasn't meant as a serious offer, but perhaps that's how he took it. I snatch the paper from her hand and try to make a getaway.

"Oliver, honey, wait," Mother says with an ache in her voice.

I turn around. "I need to shower," I say.

"Why don't you shower in the locker room after practice?" she asks, without a clue as to why I might not want to be naked as an oafish team of boys mock each other's bodies and slap each other's bare buttocks and, when the mood strikes, find an opportunity to spit out what they would do if a pansy ever dared to so much as look at them. "Don't they have showers for you?" she continues when I don't answer the question. I want to start my life in college, at Harvard, where there are other boys like me congregating in Brendan's room. Not now, when I'm still in high school, surrounded by brutes who want nothing more than to pluck the daisies from the world before they've had a chance to bloom.

I have every intention of blooming, don't I?

"The showers are filthy." I grimace. "I much prefer washing up at home. You always keep everything so clean."

Mother approaches me and takes my hand in hers. Her eyes still sparkle with a hint of the girl she once was, but her hands betray the roughness of her life. The needle pricks she's suffered while sewing hems, the cuts from the old machine she's forced to use because her employers are too stingy to purchase the safer new models. I kiss her hand, pressing my lips against the deepest of her scars. I want to heal her.

"Son, I'd like to talk to you about something . . . sensitive," she says.

My heart sinks lower than my chest. It feels like it's in my groin somewhere, searching for a crevice that might allow it an escape from this body. Someone must have told her. Perhaps it was Shams on the phone. Did he tell her we were at a pansy club? Or was it Brendan? No, Brendan would never. Mother is his aunt. She would immediately call Father's sister and tell her. It could have been anyone, really. Jack's name suddenly hits me like a strong wind. If anyone would be cruel enough to break my mother's heart, it would be The Jackal.

I can imagine it in my head. Jack Whitman pulling up to our small home in some gargantuan limousine driven by a uniformed chauffeur. Knocking on our door. Telling my mother he's a concerned friend who has come to warn her that her son is going down a path of sin and damnation.

"Who . . . who told you?" I ask, the shake in my voice like those trills in Debussy's *L'isle joyeuse*.

"I already said," she explains, confused. "This friend you met called. He told me you were going to teach him piano."

I hold her gaze for what feels like an hour, but the second hand on our wall clock only ticks five times.

"Son . . ." She bites her lip. "You're a good boy. A dutiful boy. You've always made life easier for me. Keeping to your studies. Never causing trouble."

"I won't cause trouble," I promise.

"I know you won't." She sighs. "Sometimes I wish you would. Nothing serious, of course. But you're a young boy. You should be out having fun sometimes. All you do in your spare time is go to Brendan's room to learn from him."

"I'm confused," I confess. "What is the sensitive matter you wanted to discuss?" I hear the desperation in my voice. If she's going to confront me about spending time with homosexuals—about *being* one—I just want to get it over and done with.

"I don't want you working," she declares.

"That's—That's what you wanted to discuss?" I ask.

She nods. "I know you hate how hard I work for you. I see the way you look at my hands. But working for you to have a good life is what brings me joy. I want you focused on your studies and on that scholarship. You can teach people the piano later if you like. But hopefully you'll be doing something much more meaningful."

"What's more meaningful than music?" I ask.

Her eyes moisten. She offers me a pained smile. "Unfortunately, in this world, the most meaningful thing is money. I know that's why you offered to teach this boy. And I won't have you taking that on yourself. *I* make the money in this home. Is that clear?"

I nod in relief. I thought this was going to be *the* moment of truth. Turned out it was just *a* moment of truth. "It's clear, Mother. But I want you to know . . ." I pause, imagining the future I want for myself. A man by my side. Perhaps Shams even. He'll have to do for now to fill in the fantasy. A Harvard degree. A lucrative job in music. Are there lucrative jobs in music? Well, it's a dream, so let's say yes. Children. Can we have children? In my fantasy, we can. Not boys like me and Liam. Boys are so exhausting. We'll have two beautiful girls, and the firstborn will be named after Mother. Margaret. We'll call her Maggie.

"Yes?" she says. "What do you want me to know?"

I give her a strong hug. Her body feels at once powerful and frail. She's a bundle of contradictions, just like me. "I want you to know that when I do graduate and start working, it will be my turn to take care of you. I'll buy you a house on the Cape. You love the water."

"I do love the water. It heals the body and the soul. It inspires the imagination." She releases herself from my embrace and looks me in the eye. "But we have the Charles River right here, don't we?"

I nod.

"Besides, it will be your brother's turn to take care of me first."

I know what my mother doesn't know. That my brother is just like my father. If and when he makes money, he'll spend it on himself. Gambling and booze and girls. He'll never take care of her. Not the way I will. "Yes" is all I say. The last thing I want to do is break her heart.

Which I suppose is why I never call Shams back. I want to, of course. I desperately want to. But every time I pick up the telephone, the same thoughts stop me.

What good can come of this?

What if Mother finds out?

What if we get caught?

And who is he, anyway?

I know nothing of him. Well, almost nothing. I know he has kind eyes and a sharp mind, full lips and a romantic soul. I know enough to spend two weeks filling in the gaps of my knowledge with my own fantasies. I imagine he's the youngest student at Tufts University, a genius who was admitted to college at sixteen. I imagine he's a vaudeville performer, the son of a traveling circus star, royalty. In the absence of information, I create countless fictions.

Once two weeks have passed, I go back to Brendan and Jack's room. I tell Mother I'm going to study, and of course she believes me. But I know exactly where we're going tonight. The masquerade ball. It's been on my mind since I heard about it. I want to see those men in women's clothes wrestling each other.

Mother, of course, sends me with a jar of cookies. When I enter the dorm room, the whole group of boys is gathered in a circle, mumbling and laughing. "Hello," I say. "I've brought cookies."

"Cookie, that'll be your name!" Jack exclaims as he applies makeup to a boy whose face I can't see. "Cookie Nookie."

"Hilarious!' Brendan squeals. "Now what will my name be?"

"Hilda Homely," Jack suggests, and from behind, I see Brendan slap Jack's back.

"It's a compliment," Jack insists. "A handsome man makes a homely woman."

"What's going on here?" I ask.

Finally, the circle disperses and reveals Shams at its center. He's been transformed into Cookie Nookie by the rouge on his cheeks, the mascara on his eyelashes, and the lipstick on his mouth. Pointing to Shams, Jack announces proudly, "Ladies and perverts, I give you my latest creation, the belle of the masquerade ball, Cookie Nookie."

Shams looks at me warmly and waves. He mouths a "hi."

I wave back, then look around the room. Shams is not the only one in makeup. Brendan has some on too. So does Cyril. Jack, who seems to be in charge of the transformations, has left his own face untouched. "What do you think?" Jack asks.

"It's a start," I say.

"That would be because I've just begun," Jack snaps. "I have yet to reveal the costumes I borrowed from the theater. These gals will be absolutely gorgeous when the illusions are complete." Jack moves toward me. Puts a clammy hand on my cheek. His breath smells of gin and cigarettes. "You're next, I think."

"Absolutely not," I say.

"Let The Jackal paint that pretty face, baby boy." Jack pouts.

"Leave me alone, Jack." I move away from him, placing the jar of cookies on Brendan's desk.

"You're a bore," Jack says, matter-of-fact. "Boys, come look." Jack pulls a bag of costumes out from under his bed. He throws dresses and gowns around the room haphazardly. Ruffles and sequins. Scarves and hats. Gloves and heels. The boys cluster around him, fascinated by the illicit feel of these fabrics. Their bright colors. Their feminine softness.

"Tremendous," one of them coos.

Cyril drapes a dazzling velvet cape around himself. "It's incredible, isn't it? The power a frock can have to transform you into someone else entirely." Catching his reflection in the mirror, he adds bittersweetly, "Someone without a care in the world." He throws the cape off and grabs a corset.

In the opposite corner of the room, Shams finds me staring at them in quiet contemplation near Brendan's bed. "How have you been?" he asks.

"Oh, fine, busy." I glance at him quickly. The warmth of his gaze discomfits me. I glance away. "I'm sorry I didn't return your phone call."

"No apology needed," he insists. "I was only calling so you had a way to reach me. If you wanted to. But if you don't want to reach me, that's perfectly all right." His eyes gleam. "It will leave me devastated. Despondent. Hopeless. But it's all right."

"Stop, please," I beg. "I deal with enough guilt as it is. Always trying to be perfect for Mother."

"*Trying* to be perfect?" he asks. "You *are* perfect."

"Hardly." I giggle nervously. "I have so many flaws."

"For example?"

"I'm horribly afraid of . . . so many things." Before he can ask for an example, I give him one. "Like calling you back. I wanted to. But I was too scared. I'm not brave like you." Gazing at Jack, Brendan, and the boys, I add, "Like all of you."

He offers me his hand. There's red nail polish on it. "There's more than one kind of bravery," he says. "The way you express yourself. Your emotions. Your vulnerability. The way your heart speaks through the music you play. *That's* bravery too."

I hold his hand. Run a finger along the satiny crimson of his nails. "I almost called you so many times," I confess. "But each time, I put the phone down."

"Why is that?" he asks.

"I—" I think of all the easy excuses I could make. I was too busy with school, with wrestling. I wasn't feeling well. I had a big test. "I told you. I was scared." He seems to bring out the truth in me.

"Of?" he asks.

"Do I need to say it?" I ask.

"I find that when we speak our fears aloud, they lose a little bit of their power over us," he says.

"Really?" I wasn't raised to speak fears. I was guided into hiding them.

"Try it," he says firmly.

"Well, I—" I search for the words. "I suppose my biggest fear is hurting my mother. She's already lost her husband, and she's sacrificed her whole life for me. Works herself to the bone all day, and then comes home and cooks and cleans for me. My brother as well, I suppose. But he's in New Haven now. And besides, he never cared for her like I do. If she knew that I . . ." I drift off, unsure how to form the words.

"That you . . ."

"That I am . . ."

"The way you are . . ."

"It would destroy her," I declare with finality.

"May I make an observation?" he asks. "With a disclaimer that

I know very little of your situation and will be making some rather large assumptions."

"Sure." I turn my gaze to him now, waiting.

He smiles before he begins. "From what little I know, your mother is strong. You say your father is gone, and still, she holds her head high, working to raise her family alone."

"That's right."

"I would also wager she's kind and deeply intelligent, because she raised you." He bats his eyelashes quickly. They're thick and long even without mascara, but with the makeup, they're like wings taking flight each time he blinks. "You, Oliver, strike me as a person who was raised with love."

"I—" I nod. "My father was . . . I feel sick speaking ill of him when he's gone, but he was harsh. And selfish. But Mother . . . She . . . Yes, she always made me feel loved. *Makes* me feel loved. And I love her too. Too much to be a burden to her, ever."

"It shows." He moves a little closer to me. At the other corner of the room, the boys are gathered around Brendan, who squeezes himself into some kind of Elizabethan gown that looks worthy of Lady Macbeth. "I would hope a woman like your mother, a woman who loves her son and always did, would continue loving him no matter who *he* chooses to love."

"She won't understand it to be love," I argue.

"Perhaps in the beginning," he suggests. "But what I see is that your deepest fear is losing her love. The fear of losing love is . . . well, it's a fear I don't understand, I suppose."

I look at him with real sadness in my eyes. "Your parents—"

"Didn't love me."

"Brothers? Sisters?" I ask.

"Only child." He shrugs.

"But—But there must have been a kind aunt or grandparent who loved you . . . A best friend . . ."

"No, never." He shakes off the gloom. "Don't pity me, please. I've plenty of time to find love. Isn't that right?"

"Of course that's right," I assure him. "Of course it is. You're just a kid, really. In fact, we're the youngest two people in this room. When's your birthday? Mine is July seventh. Let's see which one of us is the youngest."

"Will you give me a birthday present if I tell you?" he asks.

"Of course I will," I declare. "What do you want?"

"Just this," he says. "To be in your company, speaking the truth to each other. I'm so tired of hiding."

"I feel exactly the same," I say, excited by the connection. "I'm always hiding, and it's so exhausting. Always wondering if someone will find me out. Afraid that some small slip of the tongue might give me away."

The boys who are masquerading are all dolled up now. Brendan is in Elizabethan dress and a frilly red wig. Cyril wears nothing but boots and a corset, his figure cinched into tight curves. "Howest doth we looketh?" Brendan asks, and everyone laughs and claps.

Shams turns to me with a smile. "You don't want to masquerade?" he asks.

"Oh . . . I . . . It does sound fun, but—"

"But you're scared?" he asks.

"That, yes." I stare at Jack, who places a floral hat atop a classmate's head. "Also, I don't want Jack touching my face."

Shams laughs, and I notice a red smudge on his front teeth. "There's lipstick on your teeth," I say.

"Which ones?" he asks.

"I can fix it," I offer. "Smile." He smiles big, and I rub my index finger over his two front teeth. When I'm done, he briefly closes his lips on my finger and pushes his tongue toward it. The wetness of his tongue on the tip of my finger sends warm shivers through my body, like I'm hot and cold all at the same time.

"What if I did your makeup?" he offers. "Then Jack wouldn't touch you."

I nod shyly. Shams crosses the room and snatches the makeup from Jack's desk. Jack is too busy dancing in the center of the room to mind. Shams returns to me and begins the process of transforming me from Oliver into whoever I'll become when he's done. Someone new, with no past, only future. Shams puts rouge on my cheeks. He draws a line around my lips before filling it in with a ruby-red lipstick. As he works on my eyes, framing them in smoky mystery, I whisper, "It's strange, isn't it? I've never been more honest with a person as I just was with you, and yet we're hiding behind these . . . disguises."

"*Man is least himself when he talks in his own person,*" he says, like he's reciting. "*Give him a mask, and he will tell you the truth.* Do you know who wrote that?"

I shake my head.

"Oscar Wilde." He speaks the name like he's summoning a ghost.

"Perhaps Oscar Wilde felt that way because he was forced to wear a mask," I propose. "Maybe if he had been luckier . . . to live in a time when men like him didn't have to . . . I don't know . . ."

"I know what you mean." Shams turns me toward the small, dirty mirror above Brendan's desk. In the foreground of the mirror is my unrecognizable self. In the background are the dancing boys, some dressed as girls. The reflection of us appears so joyful. Like we're frozen in this room, in this moment, far from all the fear and judgment outside. "He did what he felt he had to do, in his time. The wife. The children."

"I want children," I declare, shocked by my words. "I do. I want to love a child the way Mother loved me. But I don't . . . I don't want a wife. I don't want to deceive the people I vow to love. I feel cursed sometimes. Fated to have a family who will never know the real me."

"That may change," he suggests quietly. "Look at how society has changed in just this last decade. And what's family anyway? Perhaps this is a family." He throws his gaze toward the dancing boys. "A family we get to choose for ourselves. A brotherhood."

"I wouldn't want to exist in a brotherhood," I say. "I much prefer women to men. Can't we be a personhood? Not men and women, but simply people. Just the word *man* is so limiting."

"I think the maquillage has freed a piece of you," he says with a smile.

"Maybe." I look deep into his glowing eyes, under the spell of their browns and oranges. "I suppose I don't want to be limited to a world of men just because I am . . . what I am. Mother is the person I love most in the world. Even at the Rooster, the person I connected to the most was Edna, the sapphic Radcliffe girl."

"Not me?" he asks, only a hint of hurt in his voice.

"Of course, you." I squeeze his hand to make up for my thoughtless comment. "I suppose . . . I put you in a different category than Edna."

"And what category would that be?" he whispers in my ear.

"The category of people I'd like to kiss." I can't believe I just said that. We face each other and smile. There's lipstick on both our mouths and a gaggle of increasingly inebriated college boys around us. It doesn't feel like the right time to kiss, and so we let the moment pass. "My only point was that being a man feels so limiting."

He nods. "Man, according to the dictionary last I checked, means any human being, regardless of sex or age or color or creed. Simply a member of the human race. A person. Perhaps it's men who imposed limits on their own definition of themselves. Perhaps we were always meant to be whatever we wanted."

As I contemplate his words, Jack rushes toward us. "It's time to go, boys. Go pick out an ensemble worthy of the occasion."

Shams and I move toward Jack's bed, littered with unchosen costumes. We hold them up against each other as Jack mixes one more round of drinks. "Do you boys know why this drink is called an Aviation?" he asks as he mixes gin and maraschino liqueur with fresh lemon juice and crème de violette. "Because it will make you fly. And who doesn't dream of taking flight?"

Shams and I choose to throw matching Victorian dresses over our clothes. The dresses are large enough to fit over what we already have on. We find appropriate wigs and hats to complete the ensembles. I'm pretty sure I saw these costumes in the performance of *The Importance of Being Earnest* that Harvard put on last year, the one Brendan insisted I accompany him to. Mother came with us and loved the play. She laughed uproariously throughout, and no one clapped louder than her. I loved seeing her like that. Carefree in the dark. It struck me that evening that the true gift of theater is that as the performers play their parts, the audience gets to sit in the anonymity of darkness and *stop* performing for others. Just react from the purity of our own emotional responses.

"Aviations?" Jack asks, holding out two cups to me and Shams.

"No thanks, Jack," I say. "I'm a good Victorian girl."

"Of course you are, baby boy. And you, great sham of a person?"

"I don't need help taking flight tonight," Shams says. "I feel like I'm already in the clouds."

"You two are hopeless bores." Jack rolls his eyes dramatically as he empties both glasses into his stomach.

"Whoa there, Jackie boy." Brendan puts a protective arm around Jack. "You may want to slow down a tad. You wouldn't want to crash in midair."

Jack laughs uncontrollably. I've never seen him more sozzled. He speaks like he's onstage, playing the part of some European bon vivant. "Don't you tell me what to do, Lady Macbeth! The night is young, but our lives are short! LET'S LIVE."

Live we do. We stumble toward the masquerade ball, some because they're blotted, and some—myself, certainly—because we have no idea how to walk the cobblestoned streets in heels. If it weren't for Shams holding me up, I would certainly have tripped at least twice and added a layer of red blood to the rouge and lipstick on my face. With his help, I make it past the entrance door, which looks like any other door in Boston, dark mahogany with an arch above it. Nothing to suggest the world of revelation we've just entered.

"I need a drink," Jack declares, unaware that another drink is the last thing he needs. "Let's go order some ginger beers and I can mix up some Dark and Stormys to get the party started."

"Jack . . ." Brendan puts a hand on Jack's tense shoulder. "The party started hours ago in our room. I think we've had too much."

"And I say too much is not enough!" Jack sneers.

The other boys ignore Jack. They're too entranced by the sights all around them. Everything here feels exaggerated. The pearls too large, the feathers too abundant. It's a mockery of good taste and a reinvention of it all at the same time. It's wonderful.

"Did you hear me, world?" Louder, so his voice might reach the volume of the live band playing a syncopated ragtime, Jack yells, "TOO MUCH IS NOT ENOUGH."

"I don't think I can watch more of this," Shams whispers in my ear. "He's making an even bigger fool of himself than he usually does. Shall we take a walk?"

I don't need to answer. He already seems to know I'll follow him anywhere.

As we walk toward the band, where men in dresses dance with the joyous thrill of unexpected freedom, a mustached man in a tuxedo and a top hat beelines toward us, waving. He looks vaguely familiar, and I feel a sudden panic. It could be the mailman, or the butcher. My God, it could be one of my teachers, or my mother's employer, who I only met once. Did he have a mustache? I don't remember. He could have grown one if he didn't. My mind races with endless, equally terrifying possibilities of who this could be.

I hadn't thought of this before walking into this secret space, or when I went to the Golden Rooster for that matter. All this time, I've been worried that Mother might find out, without thinking of *how* she might find out. What if it's because I run into someone who knows her? Perhaps the reason the mailman is always so jovial is that he spends his nights dancing in dresses, filling himself up on freedom by night so he can be happy all day.

"Oliver!" the man says in a husky baritone that feels forced, like a performance. "Welcome to the grand rag."

I recognize something in the voice, but still, I can't quite place it. I feel sweat on my brow, and in my armpits. The Victorian dress I'm wearing over my clothes is thick and uncomfortable. I feel hot and trapped. I misjudged it all. "I—I don't feel well," I say to Shams. "I think . . ."

"You don't recognize me?" the voice says, no longer husky. It takes me a moment to realize it's a woman's voice. The top hat comes off. It's Edna in male drag. "It's me. Edna. The back room of the Rooster. Plato's *Symposium*. Even with all that makeup and the dress, I recognized you right away."

"I remember who you are." I wipe sweat from my forehead with the back of my hand. "I thought—I didn't . . . I was afraid you were someone my family knew. Someone who might tell my mother I was here."

Edna pulls me into a hug that immediately calms me. Support really can be medicine when administered correctly. And she knows just how to administer it. "I'm sorry I spooked you," she says when she releases me. "And I'm sorrier you have to live looking over your shoulder." She holds her hand out to Shams. "I don't think we've officially met. I'm Edna. But tonight, I'm going by Septimus Smith."

"A *Mrs. Dalloway* fan," Shams says.

"A well-read young man, I see." Edna seems impressed by him.

"I'm Shams," he says as they shake hands. "It's nice to meet you, Septimus."

The band's ragtime ends, and a man in Cleopatra drag takes the stage to announce the wrestling match will begin. Anyone who wants to enter the competition and challenge the reigning champion, Violette Ophelia, should line up by his side. As a smattering of queens—including the beautiful one we met at the Rooster—step into their spotlights, Shams tells me I should enter.

"Absolutely not," I protest. "Look at what I'm wearing. How do you expect me to pin anyone down in this?"

"It's just fabric. Let it rip." He smiles.

"Why don't you enter?" I ask.

"I'm no wrestler," he says. "But if that's what it takes to convince you, then let's go."

I think about it, then shake my head. "No. I can't. It's mortifying. Wrestling in women's clothing in front of a crowd. I couldn't." But then the man with the microphone announces that the grand prize is fifty dollars, which is more than double what Mother makes in a week. I could buy her something beautiful with that kind of money. "Come on," I say.

"Good luck!" Edna yells as I pull Shams onstage before it's too late.

Once we're onstage, I see that Brendan, Jack, Cyril, and all their Harvard friends are clustered at the very front of the crowd, and I have a moment of doubt. I can imagine Jack using this as ammunition to mock me mercilessly for years to come. Already, he's whistling at me. "Look at them pretty girls up there!" he yells out as he almost throws a cube of ice at me before Brendan stops him.

"You said you'd pay good money to see me wrestle in heels, Jack!" I yell out from the stage. "Double the pot?" I suggest.

"Nice try," he yells back. "Let's say ten for being a good sport, twenty if you win!"

I give Jack an elated thumbs-up as all of us onstage are paired up. We wrestle side by side. Winners stay onstage. Losers must walk offstage as the crowd playfully jeers at them. I win my first round. So does Shams. Two rounds later, we're down to four wrestlers. Me vs. a man in a satin gown that's now torn to shreds. Shams vs. the reigning champion. The emcee calls out, "On your marks! Get set! Wrestle!"

The band, who had been on a break, takes the stage behind us, underscoring our competition to a percussive beat. From the crowd come the sound of cheers. *Tear her down* and *pin that bitch* and Jack's inimitable voice yelling, "*RIP HER TO SHREDS.*"

My opponent is young and athletic, that much is certain, but he's no wrestler. He has strength to spare, but no strategy. He also loves the applause. The louder it gets, the more distracted he becomes. When he flashes a smile to our audience, I seize the opportunity his distraction provides. I lock his knees together until he tumbles down and pin him to the floor as the crowd goes wild. I look down and see my own dress has torn open, revealing the boy clothes I'm wearing underneath. It's not until the emcee declares me the winner that I turn to notice the reigning champion is no longer onstage. Shams is. He beat her while I was focused on my own opponent. We're the only two left.

The band begins a new tune, something appropriately triumphant. The speed of the song revs us up as we're given our cue to begin. We circle each other at first, smiling, our eyes locked. Something stirs within me. The feeling of connection consumes me. I want to feel his body against mine, and I take the opportunity by shoving myself into him violently and taking him down.

"Oh wow, I didn't know we were going to be vicious with each other," he says as he turns the tables on me, rolling himself atop me.

"I'm the best wrestler in my high school," I say with a smile. "Just give up now." I lock his head in my arms.

Once again, he has a surprise up his sleeve. He bites my arm. I'm so shocked I let go of him.

"I'm pretty sure that's against the rules," I say as we circle each other again.

"I'm pretty sure there are no rules here," he declares, and I know he's right. We could bite each other, kiss each other, tear each other's clothes off, and we would likely be met with cheers of approval.

"What if we declared it a tie and split the money?" I ask. We're just hopping in front of each other now, each one waiting for a moment of opportunity.

"I think we would disappoint our adoring audience," he says. "Besides, I don't care about the money. If I win, I'll just spend it all on you."

"On me?" I ask. "I don't need anything money can buy." I briefly ponder the truth in this. The things I want—love, freedom, a more accepting world—can't be bought.

"Then what will you do with the money?" he asks.

The answer comes to me like a tidal wave. "I'll get my mother a beautiful room overlooking the ocean for a holiday. On the Cape." I imagine her hair freely blowing in the salty wind. The sun warming her face. Mother deserves to glow. She would ask where I got the money. I would have to think of something, but that's a problem for later.

"You, Oliver, are too good for this world. You might be what I've been searching for all this time." His body language changes when he says this. He seems to deflate. The competitive tension is gone.

I take my opportunity and slam him down to the ground. I hold his body down hard. He doesn't struggle against me. Perhaps he's tired. Or perhaps he's letting me win. Either way, I'm declared the victor. The emcee helps me back up. Lifts my hand up into the air for me. I feel a rush of pride and adrenaline. Brendan is hooting for me. Cyril is jumping up and down. Jack is shouting to everyone near him that I'm his friend. Farther down the crowd, Edna watches with a delighted smile on her face. She tips her top hat to me. I wish Mother could see me now. I wish she could be proud of the person I am, not just the one I pretend to be. But perhaps that's asking too much. In this moment, I have more than I've ever had. More than I thought possible. I feel, for perhaps the first time, like a winner.

The elation of the masquerade ball lingers in my body, filling me with my own personal glow. Even Mother notices it. As she fries me some eggs one May morning, she asks if I'm in love. I grab my tall glass of fresh-squeezed orange juice and take a long, slow sip, using the cup to hide any reaction on my face.

"I'm sorry, I shouldn't have asked." She pushes the eggs around the pan. They sizzle, oil popping up like little fireworks that seem to mirror the crackling beat of my heart. "I remember being utterly mortified when my own mother asked me the same question when I was about your age."

"But you didn't meet Father until you were nineteen," I say, confused.

She plates the eggs and places them in front of me with a smile. "It wasn't your father she was asking about."

"Mother!" I exclaim. I laugh nervously, and she does too. It's been just the two of us for eight months now, and we've spoken about many things, but never anything like this.

"I did have a life before I met your father, you know. Perhaps not a very exciting one." She sighs. She pours herself a cup of coffee and grabs a breakfast roll. She dunks the roll in the coffee and eats it soggy and dripping. When Father was around, she rarely ate breakfast, too busy making sure his bacon was crispy enough to suit his peculiar taste for the burned and charred. Father liked things better when they had been destroyed. "And yet, no matter how dull our lives may be on the outside, we still have our dreams. Perhaps, and this is just your foolish old mother talking here . . . But perhaps the more mundane our lives, the more fantastical our fantasies."

"I don't think that's foolish, and I don't think you're foolish." I keep my eyes peeled on her as I eat, wondering who she was when she was my age. I've never, not once, asked her. How shameful of me. I've acted as if her life began when mine did. "Who was he, Mother? Were you really in love with someone before Father?" The question I almost asked, the one I didn't dare ask, is if she was in love with Father at all. There are so many reasons she may have married him despite not loving him. Duty. Fear. The pressure of parents. Social expectations. And of course, the most obvious one . . . she was pregnant with Liam and was forced to marry the man who would become her son's father.

"Oh, he's ancient history. We mustn't haunt the past. It deserves peace. You tell me about this girl who makes you feel like I once did in my youth." She utters these words like the beginning of shared intimacy. "This young woman who's making my son glow."

How is she to know her words have the opposite effect she intended? She can't possibly imagine it's not a girl I have feelings for, but a boy. Even this version of Mother, this cunning woman with a girlhood crush she's ready to reveal . . . Even she would be horrified by the truth of me.

"Son . . . Are you in love?" she asks tenderly.

I close my eyes. I can't answer. Besides, I don't know. Am I in love, when I don't know what love is? I know I think about nothing but him. I'm certain he's occupied a space in my mind and in my heart that will linger forever, no matter what the future holds. I'm aware I've barely been able to sleep since we met, and yet I never feel tired. In fact, I've never felt more awake, more certain that this is what life is meant to feel like. But I can't say any of this.

So I change the subject as fast as I can. "It's not a girl making me glow, it's a surprise for you." I wasn't planning on telling her this morning before school, on an average day, over an ordinary breakfast. I was hoping to take her out to a nice restaurant and tell her over baked pork chops and upside-down cake that I would pay for in crisp cash. But I need a way out of further inquiry into my romantic life.

"A surprise?" she asks, suitably surprised. "For me?"

"I won a contest!" I announce brightly. Shams and I came up with the idea on one of our walks. We take the longest walks around Boston together. Shams always arrives with a blue tin of Oreo cookies, and we promise to walk until the tin is empty. We nibble at the cookies slowly, desperate for our time together to go on forever so we can confide everything to each other. When we reach the Charles, we stop and stare at it. Let the river guide our conversation forward. I've told him all about Father's cruelty and my love of music. He's told me all about how harsh his own father was. How they don't even speak anymore.

"A contest?" Mother echoes. Her voice sounds hazy and far off, like the voices of Father's drunk friends when he would have them over for card games at night.

I don't answer her. I'm too busy fantasizing that on our next stroll, Shams and I will reach the Cape and discover we can walk on water. From there, we'll stride across the Atlantic, subsisting on ocean water and our tin of biscuit sandwiches. We'll walk through Ireland, where my ancestors are from. Through London and Paris, where I'll visit Chopin's grave in Père Lachaise and thank him for the nocturnes and sonatas that brought me closer to my mother and filled my heart with hope. I'll drag Shams to Vienna, of course, to breathe the same air as Schubert and Beethoven. And then I'll let Shams guide me to the part of the world his ancestors come from.

"Are you going to tell me what you won?" she asks impatiently. I pull myself back into the moment. These daydreams of Shams have been a problem lately. I can barely pay attention in class. We haven't even gone back to Brendan and Jack's room. We both decided we'd rather it just be us, just the two of us for now.

"Oh yes, sorry, I . . . It's a holiday weekend at an inn," I say. "In Provincetown. It includes meals and everything."

"A weekend on the Cape?" she asks. "How on earth did you win that? That must cost—"

"It was a trivia game at a local restaurant where I was studying. I stopped in because I wanted some water, and they said I could sit in a corner and study as long as the trivia wouldn't distract me." Shams and I landed on this lie when we walked by a trivia game in a local restaurant. I knew that if I told Mother I won cash, she would insist we invest it in my education. There was, after all, no guarantee of a Harvard scholarship in my future. The only solution was to tell Mother the prize was the excursion itself, and that it had to be used on a certain weekend. I couldn't give her any way to wriggle out of allowing herself a true getaway. "I couldn't help but enter the game. Half the questions were about classical music. They asked which composer's ridiculously long hands could span twelve piano keys—"

"Rachmaninoff!" she yells, like she's playing this game that never happened.

"And which composer had a wife who was a brilliant composer in her own right—"

"Schumann!" There's pride on her face as she answers. It's not just the knowledge she's proud of, it's the fact that she's the one who taught me about these great musicians and told me of their lives. Music has been our common language, the purest way we communicate with each other, free from the burden of words and freed by the key of pure emotion.

"So you see, I won and the prize is a weekend on the Cape for Decoration Day weekend and I'm taking you." I say it firmly, knowing what will come next. She will object because—

"Decoration Day is a sacred day. We can't possibly go. We need to place flowers on the graves of all the local boys we lost in the war." She shakes her head solemnly. Her eyes look unconvinced.

"Mother, for once in your life, do not do the dutiful thing," I plead. "Do the thing your heart *wants* to do. Be honest with yourself. Would you rather decorate graves for yet another year, or would you rather stare out at the ocean as you sip some tall, cold drink?"

"Those boys— They did their duty— They sacrificed their lives for us— For our freedom . . ." She's stammering through her guilt.

I want to tell her that yes, they did sacrifice their lives for our freedom, and yet still I'm not free. And neither is she. Her right to vote hasn't even been ratified yet, though we're both hopeful it will be by the next general election. But I know Mother. Politics are not the way to her heart. "I know they did," I say. "But Mother, think about it. If they sacrificed their lives for your freedom, wouldn't they be pleased to see you enjoying that freedom?" This, I think, might be the winning argument.

"That's a fair point," she whispers. "We can bring flowers back from the Cape, decorate the graves a few days later to show our gratitude."

"That's a fine idea, Mother," I say. My mother will always find a way to do her duty to others. I love her for that. "Then everything is arranged."

"I think there's someone else we need to thank too," she says. "We have just enough time before you have to go to school."

"Who?" I ask, genuinely curious.

She laughs giddily. "Rachmaninoff, of course. And Schumann. Come."

She leads me to the piano, and together we play Rachmaninoff's Piano Concerto No. 3 in D minor. Rachmaninoff was one of the first composers Mother taught me when I had the sufficient skill. She was thrilled to have a partner to play with because those massive hands of his made his pieces impossible for her to play alone with her dainty hands. Together, we muddle through his pieces, turning what were two-hand concertos into four-hand pieces. We've never played this piece with more joy. She feels lighter already. When I look down at her hands, their wrinkles and veins seem to disappear. The burden of her hard work evaporates, and I see what her hands must have looked like when she was just a young woman in love with a boy who was not my father, a boy who was, in my imagination, kind to her. A boy like the one I'm slowly realizing I might very well be falling in love with.

OLIVER. PROVINCETOWN. MAY. 1920.

Shams has a surprise of his own up his sleeve. On our first evening on the Cape, as we stare out at the ocean quietly, I hear footsteps and turn to see him there, on the deck of our inn, holding a cup of tea. Thankfully, Mother is so lost in the flow of the water that she takes no notice of him. We've seen other guests wander by and said no more than a quick hello. Mother, it turns out, doesn't want adventurous conversation with strangers. She just wants peace.

I open my eyes wide in shock, hoping to communicate an alarmed what-in-the-world-are-you-doing-here look to Shams. He just smiles coolly and addresses us like we're strangers. "Would it bother you terribly if I sat here? It's the best view and I don't want to miss the sunset."

"I—" I find myself unable to answer. My throat goes suddenly dry, like one of those mops Mother uses to clean after she's wrung it out.

Mother turns toward Shams, her eyes warm and serene. "Of course you can sit here," she says. "The sunset belongs to everyone."

"I couldn't agree more." Shams sits next to me on an Adirondack chair. Mother and I are on a bench. I'm in the middle, nervously turning my gaze from one to the other, wondering what will come of this moment. We sit quietly for what feels like a century to me. Then Shams says, "I've traveled quite a bit in my life, and one thing that's always given me hope is that no matter where you are on this earth, you're staring at the same sun, the same moon."

Mother turns to him curiously. Like me when I first met him, she must be wondering who this odd creature is, this boy who speaks like he's already lived a thousand lives. "What a beautiful observation," she says. "But I'm curious, why does it give you hope?"

Shams smiles. I can see he was anticipating this question. "Because it reminds me we are all connected, and that tells me that someday we might all live in peace with each other."

Mother leans toward him. "Yes," she whispers. "And may I add that on Decoration Day weekend, a wish for peace is well-timed." She looks out at the ocean longingly. "Nothing fills me with more pain than young lives lost to war. God should take the old and spare the young."

"Mother, don't speak like that," I plead. "God should take no one."

She laughs. "And leave us all here forever! No, thank you. When my earthly job is done, I look forward to ascending to heaven." Mother was never one of those mothers who imposed religion on the daily rituals of our lives. God was for Sunday mornings, and then we allowed Him to guide us through the week quietly. Realizing she may have been too morbid, she quickly lightens her tone. "Apologies. I suppose being here, by this glorious ocean, under this perfect sky, has made me feel closer to God than I've felt in a long time. It's a good feeling."

"Nature is God's truest house of worship," Shams says, shocking me too. He's never spoken of God either. I don't even know if he was raised with religion.

"I like that." Mother flashes a bright smile toward him. "What brings you here? Are you with your parents?" she asks.

"Oh, no," he says. "My parents are . . . far away."

She nods solemnly. She seems to intuit that far away is a euphemism for dead. "My name is Margaret Doherty, but my friends call me Maggie."

"May I call you Maggie?" Shams asks.

"Of course you can. And this is my son Oliver." She runs a hand through my hair. "His hair is getting unruly, but he's a beautiful son."

"Mother, please." I feel so embarrassed to be treated like a child in front of Shams. Our times together have been so grown-up. They've given me the illusion that I'm older than I am. A man, not a boy. But here with my doting mother, I worry that whatever spell I've cast that's made me appear interesting to him will wear off.

"Well, it's true." The gin and tonic in her hand is almost empty, but its effects on her are starting to show. Her voice is brighter than usual. "This son of mine, this boy who sits next to you . . . he won this weekend getaway for us in a trivia contest because he's so smart. And instead of taking his cousin Brendan or this mystery girl he's falling for, he took me, his mother."

"Mystery girl?" Shams raises an eyebrow. There's no jealousy in his tone. He knows *he's* the mystery girl.

"A mother knows these things." Mother leans her head on my shoulder. This small movement changes everything. Suddenly, it's her who feels like the child and me the parent. I hold her close. "He's been glowing lately. He disappears for long stretches. Always says he's studying, but a mother knows. . . ."

"She's a very lucky girl," Shams says, his eyes locked on me. "I'm sure wherever she is, she's thinking of him right now. Thinks of him constantly. And I'm sure that when she's lucky enough to meet you, Maggie, she'll be thrilled to know that his mother is as kind and charming as he is."

Mother doesn't lift her head from my shoulder, but she does throw a grateful glance his way. "If I'm charming this evening, it's the liquor and the breeze."

"That's not true, Mother. You are charming. And kind." I feel her shake her head into the fabric of my wool sweater. "And beautiful," I add. It suddenly dawns on me that I hope Mother finds love again. Or perhaps for the first time. Because Father didn't know how to love.

"All right now, that's enough of that," Mother declares, sitting upright once more. "What brings you here . . ."

"Shams." He holds his hand out and they shake. Because I'm between them, their hands grip each other above my heart. I close my eyes and freeze a mental image of this moment in my mind. "I'm here with a family, but not my own. I'm a tutor."

"A tutor?" she asks. "But you look like a child."

"I'm seventeen," he declares proudly. "Which is a strange age. Not a child. Not *not* a child."

"But how did you come to be a tutor at your age?" she asks.

"That's a long story and the sun is about to set but suffice it to say I was an advanced student who graduated from school early, and I've found tutoring to be a far more exciting learning opportunity than university. As a tutor, I get to travel with wealthy families to countries all over the world. I get to help young people learn, and as I've discovered, young people prefer learning from people closer to their own age than . . ."

"Than me!" Mother laughs.

"I didn't mean it that way," Shams says.

"Oh, I didn't take it that way," Mother assures him. Turning her focus back to the sky, she gasps. "Look at that."

The setting sun has turned the sky a devastatingly beautiful orange. Like the color of a calm fire, not the kind of flames that could ever burn or hurt you, simply the kind that will warm and heal you. I suppose all beautiful things are like that. They can be used to heal or to destroy. That is, perhaps, the magic behind their beauty.

Mother doesn't take her eyes off the sky. I can't help but look at Shams. I find his eyes already directed toward me. His eyes, they're the color of the sunset right now. Glowing. Warming me. This moment, the two of us sitting with my mother, becoming the three of us . . . It's the happiest moment I've known in my life. I feel, perhaps for the first time, that someday, she might accept him as more than a stranger on a deck. She'll accept him as part of our family.

When the sun sets, when Mother has drifted off into the deep sleep this day has gifted her, I creep out of our room and find Shams still staring out at the sky. It's darker now, but the stars shine in glorious patterns of constellations. "I can't believe you did this," I say.

"Are you angry with me?" he asks.

"Perhaps I should be." I smile to assure him I'm not. "Perhaps I would be if it hadn't gone so swimmingly. She adored you."

"And I adore her." He looks around. No one is on the deck. He grazes his finger against mine. Just that wisp of a touch creates constellations of light inside me. "I had to meet her, and this felt like the only way."

"Why did you have to meet her?" I ask.

"Because you love her," he says. "And the best way to know a person is to know the things they love. I know you love your cousin Brendan, and I've met him. I know you love music, and I've listened to nothing but your favorite composers since we met. But your mother, I do believe she may be your greatest love. How can I claim to know you, to love you, without knowing her?"

I feel my heart race around my body. "But I don't know any of the things you love."

"Yes you do," he declares. He taps my chest gently, the piece of it that houses my heart. "You know yourself."

And there, under the night sky, we kiss for what I hope is only the first time. I don't feel afraid in this moment. I feel empowered, like we're one with the nature all around us. Like we are nature. God's truest house of worship is our very bodies.

Shams is gone the next morning when we wake up. Mother asks the innkeeper after him at breakfast, and she's informed he checked out early. I think he wanted me to have this last day alone with Mother, and also, perhaps, he wanted to leave a perfect night alone. Mother and I explore the town during the day. We eat a whole lobster, laughing as we shuck its claws, its tail, its legs. Juice flies at us. She drinks two beers and lets me have a tiny sip. A waiter tells us that this part of the Cape has been an arts colony for two decades. Painters and playwrights and poets flock here, searching for inspiration in the dunes and shores. Mother asks if musicians come here too, and the answer is yes. She seems to love this place even more when she hears that.

On the street, a poet offers to write us a poem for twenty-five cents. "Why, that's the cost of three heads of lettuce," Mother observes. The poet brushes his beard away from his mouth with his dirty fingernails and asks if she believes a poem is worth more or less than three heads of lettuce. Mother laughs and says poetry is priceless. She pays him and he asks us a few questions about us before scribbling some words down on paper and placing them in an envelope that he seals with red wax. He tells us not to read it in front of him. His own words embarrass him. They're meant to be read and heard by others, never by himself.

We meet fishermen who tell us of the lasting damage of the Portland Gale on their trade even two decades later. We meet an actor who lives in Greenwich Village. He invites us to a show he's a part of that evening that he warns us is quite experimental. Mother wants to see the local church, and inside, we're told that the church was turned into a hospital during the flu crisis, and that all the town's residents wore antiseptic cloth on their faces for the duration of the pandemic. We're told this is a community that cares for its members, and Mother says, "Care is what makes community."

Every turn we take, people seem to talk to us. Perhaps this is just a friendlier place than the city. Or maybe it's us, so high-spirited here that people want to get to know us, this mother and son who wander the Cape together like giggly best friends.

As evening comes and we approach our hotel, I see a group of people laughing outside a theater, no doubt going to see the experimental play we were told about. I ask Mother if she'd like to go, but she says she's tired. "You should go," she suggests. "You're young and your feet don't hurt after a day of walking."

I'm about to say I'm tired too, but then I make eye contact with one of the people outside the theater and realize it's Edna. She stands with a group of young women who all appear to be recent college graduates like her. I wonder if these are her Radcliffe friends.

There's a look of urgency on her face, which could simply be because she's not sure whether to approach me when I'm with my mother.

"You know what?" I say to Mother. "I think I will see about getting a ticket. I can walk you to the inn first, though."

"I'm a capable woman, son. I can get myself across the street, but you're very sweet. And this time was very special to me. A memory I'll cherish forever."

"Me too, Mom." She flinches sadly. I realize I never call her Mom. Mother is formal. Mother is dutiful. This woman in front of me is Mom. "You sure you're okay?" I ask.

"I'm just too happy is all," she confesses. "I'm not used to being this happy, and I suppose it's made me realize that with happiness comes the fear that you might lose it. Or the certainty that you will lose it. Because no earthly happiness lasts forever. Soon, you'll be at Harvard."

"We don't know that."

"Well, some university. And then you'll start your own life, as you should. A wife. Your own children. Life might take you far from me. Another pandemic could come. A war could take you."

I hold her tight. She's never felt more human to me. It should go without saying that parents are humans, but it doesn't always feel that way. "Mother, I promise I'll never leave you. I'll go to school close to home. If life takes me far from Boston, you'll come with me. There will always be a room for you in our home."

"Wait until the woman you marry hears those words. It will scare her right off." She laughs off her fears and gives me a strong kiss on the cheek. "I'm sorry I burdened you with my thoughts," she says. "A mother is meant to be a container for her children's emotions, not the other way around. Go to the theater. Enjoy our last night here before real life puts its lobster claws in us tomorrow." She turns her hands into claws and mock stabs me with them. We laugh, but not as boisterously as we did earlier. The moment has passed, ephemeral like a sunset.

Mother takes her shoes off and holds them in her hand as she crosses the street. She looks back at me from the other side. Waves to me. I wave back as she disappears into the dark night.

I rush to Edna, who seems to be waiting for me. "What are you doing here?" I ask.

"What am *I* doing here?" she asks. "What are *you* doing here?"

"You're like the Cheshire cat," I say jokingly. "You seem to appear everywhere."

"Or perhaps *you're* like the Cheshire cat," she says with a sad laugh. "I suppose it depends whose perspective we're seeing things from."

I laugh at the truth of this. "What play are you seeing?"

"I'm not sure." She shrugs. "Some new young playwright now that Eugene O'Neill has become too big for us." A worried look crosses her face. She seems to search mine for similar concern. "Are you all right, Oliver?"

"Oh, Edna, I've never been better," I confess. "I brought Mother here with the money I won, and you'll never believe it, but Shams showed up. He pretended not to know us, but we had the loveliest time. And she *liked* him. She genuinely liked him. And more importantly, or perhaps not, I don't know . . . *I* like him. So much."

"That's wonderful," she says sadly, like she doesn't quite believe me. She feels different than before. There's a layer of defeat covering her like soot.

"And she was so wonderful today. We walked everywhere. We

met everyone. What a town. I wish every day could be like this." I hear the joy in my voice, and I love the way it sounds. Happiness suits me.

"You do know this has become a bit of a home for our kind of people?" she asks.

"The Cape?" I ask incredulously.

"No, just Provincetown," she says.

"Really? Why? How?" I ask.

"Asking why and how is always tricky," she says. "No question outside of mathematics ever has just one answer. It's an arts colony, and many of our people are artists, because we have repressed lives we need to find a way to communicate. Or perhaps it's simply because this is the very tip of the Cape, as far out as you can get. Land's end, as they say. Makes sense we'd want to get as far from what they call civilization as possible, doesn't it?"

"Yes." I look toward the water, but I can't see it from here. Not in the darkness. "That makes sense. We don't fit in anywhere else, so of course we would find a place at the very edge of the world, where earth meets water, and say, *This is us! This is where we belong!*" A few theatergoers look at me as they linger outside. "Oh gosh, sorry, I didn't mean to deliver that like I'm onstage. Perhaps it's because I feel like a stage star. Like my life is big all of a sudden. I belong, Edna. *We* belong. Isn't it grand?"

"You don't know, do you?" she asks.

"Know what?" I search her face for a clue. All I find is grave sadness. Inside the theater, lights flash and everyone enters. "You'll miss the show," I say.

"I don't care about that. I care about you. And all your Harvard friends." Some of her friends call out to her, and she tells them to go ahead without her. One of them, a beautiful woman with wild red hair, lingers longer than the others. This must be Edna's love.

"My Harvard friends?" I ask. "Why? Life is a ball for them."

"Oliver." She hesitates before saying, "Cyril Wilcox killed himself."

"No." That's the word that escapes my lips. No, this can't be true. No, Edna is mistaken. Brendan would have told me.

"I'm sorry to be the messenger," she says. "Were you close?"

"Close?" I echo. "No. But . . ." His birthday words come back to me. *Be happy now.* Why didn't he take his own advice? "How did he . . ." I can't even finish the words. They're too painful to speak.

"They say he inhaled gas and his mother found him. Can you imagine? A mother finding her son dead like that. . . ."

I feel my throat tighten. I can imagine it. I *have* imagined it. Throughout that whole dreadful pandemic, I prayed Liam and I would survive, more for Mother than for us. All for her.

"She says it's an accident, but of course we know." She sighs sadly.

"What do we know?" I ask.

"We know that our kind end their lives too often and too young." She looks in my eyes. "If you ever think of doing something like that, you call me, and I'll come talk you out of it."

"I—I would never—" I can't take the urgency of her in this moment. Minutes ago, I was the happiest I'd ever been. Time feels like a fickle friend, teaching me not to trust its illusions. There's no afterglow anymore. Just cold. "I have too much to live for," I say, as if trying to convince myself I don't have an unrelenting sadness hiding in the deepest parts of me. Did Cyril feel the same way? Always battling the gloom swirling through him like an incoming fog?

"I know you wouldn't," she says. "But if you ever feel alone—"

"Brendan!" I suddenly howl. "He must be so distraught. I haven't visited him in so long. I've been so wrapped up in . . . my own life . . . I've been so selfish. So thoughtless."

"You've done nothing wrong," she says. "You have every right to wrap yourself up in joy."

"Joy?" The word feels like a stranger to me now. Everything that made me happy just moments ago feels out of reach. Mother and Shams, shaking hands over my heart. The ocean breeze. The salt in the air and on Shams's lips when we kissed.

"Oliver, there's something else," she says gravely.

I can't bring myself to look at her. Cyril is gone. Death is final. How can there be more?

"It seems that after the suicide, some letters were opened by Cyril's brother from other Harvard boys. The letters were full of details. Not the sort of details Harvard wants to hear about its future titans." She takes a breath. I wait for more. "They've convened some kind of tribunal of sorts. They're questioning the boys one by one."

"But—Brendan? Is he . . . Is he being questioned?" I ask.

"I don't know. I assume he is."

"How did this all happen so fast?" I ask, almost to myself.

"That's how things happen," she says sadly. "Slow at first, and then all of a sudden. Cyril died a little over two weeks ago, and already—"

"*Two weeks?*" I croak. "But Brendan hasn't been in touch. Why would he keep this from me?" My heart sinks. The better question is why haven't I gone to see him? Because I'm selfish. I've been too focused on my own petty problems and illusory joys.

"He's probably trying to protect you," she says firmly. "From Harvard and their secret court."

"If it's so secret, how do you know about it?" I ask.

"They called my friend Harry to be questioned. He was seeing Cyril romantically. Did you know him? He runs Café Dreyfuss." I vaguely remember the boys speaking of that place. It was another meeting place for boys like us. "They seem hell-bent on putting an end not just to homosexual life at Harvard, but throughout Cambridge and Boston as well. And Harvard has the power to do as they please."

"But— Can't we stop them somehow? Can't we— Aren't there laws?" I plead.

"Of course there are laws." She puts a hand on my shoulder. "And they're not designed to protect us. That's why I fight so hard for the future. Because I must. *We* must."

"I can't . . . I-I'm not a fighter." A wrestler, yes. A fighter, no.

She lifts my chin up with her steady hand. "You may not think you are, but you'll see someday. We don't all fight the same way. My favorite professor at Radcliffe told me that. She fought by educating young girls like me."

I feel my emotions wrestling each other. Fear tries to pin sadness down. Rage drags anxiety across my body.

"Oliver, listen to me. If they call you in—"

"ME?! Why me?" I ask it in a reverent sob, like I'm asking God to spare me this pain. If I'm called in, Mother might be told. And what of my future at Harvard? All this time, I've studied and worked and mastered the piano and become my school's strongest wrestler so I could possibly be granted a scholarship to an institution that wants me dead. One of their students just lost his life, and their response is to investigate his friends. Why would I want to be there now? It's all tainted. My dreams, my world, my future.

"I don't know if they will. But if they do, make sure you're prepared. The other boys will surely be called first. They can tell you what to expect. Knowledge is power."

"No, it's not." I look at her firmly. "I didn't have any of this knowledge when I walked your way. And I felt so powerful. Like I was floating. I want to go back."

"You'll float again," she promises. "Time only marches forward. And so must we." She wraps her arms around me as I cry.

Mother notices the change in my mood when we check out of the inn. I tell her it's just the melancholy of a trip ending, and she believes me. She seems just as sad to be leaving this magical place. Land's end, where time seems to stop so we can actually enjoy it before it starts speeding forward again. On the ferry back, she says, "Perhaps the only bright spot of never having gone on a honeymoon is that I've never felt this particular sadness of ending a vacation before."

"You and Father never went on a honeymoon?" I ask.

"At first, we couldn't afford it," she says. "And then Liam was born." Once again, I wonder if Liam is the reason she married him. I can't help but think that's the truth. "Time passed, as it tends to do. You were born. There was never time for travel. Soon it was just forgotten. You can't take a honeymoon years after you're married, can you?" She's held back by social conventions once again. Boston is visible in the distance. The old rules and boundaries are back, more frightening than ever.

As we approach the house, I'm half expecting some sort of summons to appear from Harvard. What will it look like? Will Mother open it first and ask what this could possibly be about? How many more days of freedom do I have?

There is no summons, though. No letter. Just a void filled with my fear.

Before we enter, Mother takes me in her arms and holds me tight. "This was better than any honeymoon," she declares.

I want to tell her I love her. That I need her. But I'm afraid that if I speak, I'll break down. So I say nothing. I just hold her tight. My mother, as sturdy as the trunk of a tree that's survived the coldest of seasons. And me . . . I'm a leaf that wishes it could be blown away. To another place. Another time. Anywhere but here. Anything but this.

OLIVER. BOSTON. JUNE. 1920.

A horrible series of days go by, one blending into the next. In school and at home with Mother, I hide my fear, a master of deception. When I'm alone, I cry uncontrollably. I don't show up for a planned walk with Shams. I can't see him. Not now. What if someone knows we've kissed? What if they pull him into this? I can't have him being questioned and . . . he could be thrown in jail, all because of me. I'd rather break his heart than destroy his life. The person I need to talk to is Brendan. I need to know he's okay.

I go to Harvard. To Brendan and Jack's room, which feels more like a funeral hall than a space for revelry now. The records have been put away. There's no booze in sight. Brendan won't look at me when he opens the door. He hasn't shaved in weeks. He looks like he hasn't slept either. On his bed is a half-packed suitcase. "I'm sorry," he mutters.

"Brendan, you have nothing to apologize for," I say.

"You need to sit down." He moves the suitcase to the edge of the bed to make room for me.

But I don't sit. I can't. "Brendan, I *know*," I say urgently.

His bloodshot eyes finally land on me. "What do you know?"

"I know about Cyril," I say.

"Oh God." He turns away from me and lets out a sob.

I hold him from behind. "I'm so sorry. I know he was a part of your group. He was your friend."

"Please go," he pleads. "You shouldn't be here."

"I know about the secret court," I say. "I know they . . ." I look down at the suitcase and suddenly realize how stupid I've been. I didn't even think about why he's packing his things up. "They expelled you, didn't they?" I ask, feeling rage on my lips.

"It doesn't matter," he says. "Nothing matters anymore. Cyril is dead. Whatever life we thought we had is gone."

"You have to fight this," I beseech.

"Fight it?" he echoes. "How do you suggest I do that?"

"I—I don't know," I say. Then I naively suggest, "There must be a lawyer who could help."

He laughs bitterly. "One lawyer would be no match for Harvard's *team* of lawyers. Besides, I'm one of the lucky ones. The dean agreed to tell my parents I was expelled for plagiarism," he explains. "Which is a kindness they're not extending to all the boys."

"But you're no plagiarist," I snap back. "You're— You're honest. You're kind. You would never cheat or lie."

"Of course I would." He's holding back tears. His voice chokes. "I lie to my parents each time I talk to them. I'll lie to them when I get back home. I'll tell them that yes, I cheated. They can never know . . . what I am."

"What *we* are," I say. "You're not alone."

He suddenly grips my hands so tight it hurts. "Don't you go trying to save me. I dragged you into all this. It's my job to save you."

"This will be on your record forever," I argue. "Your future . . .

Your whole future will be trailed by this. Employers will think you can't be trusted."

"And if they knew the truth?" he snaps. "If they knew I was a great big piece of ripe fruit? Would they trust me then? Better a plagiarist than a faggot." His nostrils flare with rage, but I know it's not me he's angry with. It's them, the deans and the entire world of powerful men. The impenetrable density of their hate.

"Why is Jack not packing?" I ask, noticing Jack's clothes still hanging, his books on the desk.

"If you need to ask, then you don't understand institutions like Harvard," he says, and that's enough. Jack's filthy rich father wrote a check. Simple as that. "Besides, he quickly covered his bases when this nightmare began. Proposed to the daughter of a family friend named Agnes."

"Proposed?" I ask in disbelief. "Just like that? To an *Agnes?*"

"That's how things happen, cousin. Just like that." He sits on his bed and throws his stricken face into his hands. "I liked him. Everyone warned me not to be fooled into thinking he was a good guy. But I really did like him. His sense of humor. His confidence. If it weren't for him, I don't know if I ever would have . . ."

"Would have what?" I ask.

"Ever been with a boy," he confesses. "Ever explored that side of myself. Known who I am. Of course, now . . . Well, I'm not sure I can be grateful to him for that anymore. If only I had some boring roommate, I'd still be a student here. I'd be repressed and sad and I wouldn't know myself at all, but I'd get my degree."

"I despise him," I say. "He really is a jackal."

"Gods of the underworld," Brendan whispers.

"What?" I ask.

"That's what people in ancient Egypt thought jackals were.

Some kind of evil spirit. I should have known better. I should have kept him at a distance." He looks at me, his face knotted by his frenzied grief and anger. "Jack had a collection of men's physique magazines. You know the ones—"

"I don't," I confess.

"They're magazines about men's athletics. They're filled with articles on how to broaden your chest or build a strong back and . . . Well, photos too, of men wearing nearly nothing." He pauses. I'm waiting to understand why he's telling me this. "Jack would buy them all. I didn't have money to spend on frivolous things. I looked at them with him, sure. I enjoyed them." He lets out a heavy breath. "He told them they were *my* magazines. He said the only reason he was even involved in any of our queer underworld is because of me. He made me out to be some kind of ringleader when it was always him egging everyone on."

"But— But that's evil," I say. "And it's a bald-faced lie."

Suddenly, I hear his voice. Jack. The Jackal. The god of the underworld who has destroyed my cousin's life. "Lies must be told in service of the greater good," he says icily.

"Ignore him," Brendan says to me.

"No worries, I'll come back later," Jack says. "I just needed a jacket for The Jackal." He picks up two options. One made of brown wool, the other a navy-blue cashmere. "What do you think? Agnes and I are going to the symphony with our parents."

"Look at you. Cyril's dead and you're not even grieving," I spit out.

"We all grieve in our ways," he declares, unbothered. "So, brown or navy for Tchaikovsky?"

"Tchaikovsky would despise you," I seethe.

"Have you summoned his spirit?" he asks with a smile. He's

enjoying this. He wants me to attack him. Treats this . . . Treats life like a game.

"Leave it be," Brendan begs. "There's nothing we can do." Brendan sits on Jack's bed.

"We can tell him how much we hate him!" I yell as I sit next to my cousin.

Jack approaches me calmly. He stays standing so he towers over us both. "You can hate me now. You can question my decisions. But I have plans. I'm going to run my family's pharmaceutical company someday. And when I do, I'll cure every illness out there. I'll make humans indestructible. Immortal. Tchaikovsky would have loved me if I had been around back then to cure the cholera that killed him."

"But you weren't, and you didn't," I protest.

He's unfazed by my rancor. "Someday, your life, or the life of someone you love, will be saved thanks to me. And when that happens, I want you to remember this moment. I want you to ask yourself, was it worth sacrificing your cousin's Harvard degree to save the lives of millions?"

"Is that what you tell yourself to sleep at night?" I ask.

"I sleep just fine at night," Jack says. "Just ask my roommate. He's the one who's had to get me out of bed in the mornings."

"He's the one you betrayed!" I yell, standing up.

Jack sits next to Brendan now, taking my place. "Yes, I did. And I'm sorry I had to do it. But I had more to lose." He looks at Brendan. "Yes, I said the magazines were yours. The parties too. I said all of it, and I freely admit it. But I did this for the good of humanity." He puts a hand on Brendan's knee and squeezes it. "And as I've already told you, I'll help you until you get on your feet."

"I don't want your money or your pity," Brendan snaps.

"All righty then," Jack says with a carefree shrug. "Just for the record, it's Ernie and Harry you should be upset with, not me."

"Who's Ernie?" I ask.

He eyes me with suspicion. "You never really were one of us, Oliver. You never even met Ernie and Harry, for God's sake. They're the ones who wrote the letters to Cyril that were intercepted. If it weren't for them, there would be no investigation and we'd all be in here, drinking whiskey and raising a glass to our friend Cyril before pouring our grief into some bloke in the bathroom of the Rooster. Which is already shut down, by the way."

"Forever?" I ask.

Jack laughs. "Harvard practically owns this whole city," he explains. "You really think they're going to allow these establishments to stay open now? The Rooster is gone. Café Dreyfuss is gone. No one affiliated with our lot is getting hired for a job anywhere near Boston."

"No one but you," I say.

"True." He smiles. "But I did nothing wrong. Blame Cyril for being so selfish."

"He wasn't selfish," I croak. "He was sad. Desperate. Hurting."

"Fine, then blame Ernie and Harry."

"You're truly horrible," I say to Jack. "I can't think of anyone else who would come to the conclusion of blaming the victims of the situation. Not the deans. Not the president of the university."

"President Lowell?" he asks. "That prick is probably doing this to distract everyone from the fact that his sister is a lesbian. All anyone has to do is read her poetry to know. He thinks he's some hero for letting the Irish and the Germans attend Harvard, but he's just a scared fool. Still, he's not to blame. Ernie and Harry were stupid, and I hate stupid people."

"Stop, please," Brendan begs. "I can't hear any more of this."

But Jack doesn't stop. "They didn't learn from history. What was it that sent Oscar Wilde to jail, after all? *His letters.* I'm all for fun and games, but for God's sake, do not put the unspeakable in writing." Jack delivers this like a sermon. Like he's the wise sage and we're the idiots who haven't learned how to successfully hide a secret self.

"But if no one ever writes it . . ." I'm trying to piece the thought together. "Then it will never be real."

"Of course it will be. Real to us." Jack stares at his two clothing options again. "I think I'll go with the navy." He flings the other jacket onto the closet floor. These fancy fabrics mean nothing to him. "Perhaps life will bring us together again. If it does, I do hope we can all be friends. Life is too short for enemies. And remember, go have your fun, but don't put any of it in writing. You'll live to regret it." With that, he winks and heads to the symphony. He probably doesn't understand the first thing about music. Mother and I should be hearing Tchaikovsky. Brendan too. And Shams.

Why does it always seem like the worst people get the best of this world? Then I think that perhaps they become the worst people *because* they're so spoiled by the world.

"Oliver." Brendan says my name urgently and I turn to him. Jack's shifty presence lingers in the room. "I want to assure you of something."

"What?" I ask.

"I—" He takes a deep breath. Almost inaudibly, he mumbles, "They asked why you visited so often. They knew your name and where you go to school."

"Oh God," I mumble. It's exactly what I feared most. I'll be incriminated. I'll break Mother's heart. Ruin her life.

He looks at me with desperation in his eyes. "I told them you visited me because you're my ambitious little cousin and your dream is to be a Harvard boy. I assured them you knew nothing about the rest of it."

"Brendan . . . I'm so sorry they've done this to you. If I could, I would . . ."

"You can't do anything. Just stay away from me until all this settles down. If this ruins you too, I'll never forgive myself."

I can't help but cry. He still fights back his tears. We were both raised the same way. Taught that men don't shed tears. But I'm not a man by their standards anyway, so I let myself sob out the sadness.

"I made all the boys swear they wouldn't say a word about you," he promises. "You're safe. But Oliver . . . ?" He finishes without asking his question.

"What is it?" I sit next to him, staring out at Jack's clothes, all that hanging luxury when my cousin has been thrown out like some disposable rag.

"If I were you, I would stop. Find a nice girl before it's too late. Pretending is better than being dead like Cyril." Now he sobs too. Whatever he was holding back comes flowing out in a wave. "I never said goodbye or told him how smart I always thought he was. I'll never know who he might have been. I didn't know. If I knew he would do such a thing, I wouldn't have let him out of my sight."

"You can't blame yourself," I say. But I'm replaying the one conversation I had with Cyril. Wondering if perhaps I also missed the signs. Blaming myself.

He looks at me with his big eyes. "Oliver, you're not . . . I just . . . Sometimes I notice you seem sadder than usual. If you ever feel so alone—"

"I'm not Cyril," I say.

"I know." He cocks his head toward me. "But if you ever need me, I'll always be a phone call away."

"Me too. I'll never stop being your friend."

"You might have to," he says. "I'm so sorry, cousin. I really am so—"

"Stop," I whisper. "I'm the sorry one. I'm just so sorry this happened to you." I don't know what else to say, so I say no more.

At church on Sunday, I cry when the choir sings "Abide with Me" as Mother harmonizes, her voice more radiant than any of theirs. If she had the time, she could be the choir leader. She could guide these voices into something approaching transcendence. "*Come, friend of sinners,*" she sings. "*Abide with me.*" I close my eyes and pray that I can abide with her. I've never felt closer to God. Never further either. I wonder how that can be.

When we return from church, I go to my room and see something. Shams has managed to slip a note into the crack of my window: *I know what's happened at Harvard. If you're ignoring me to protect me, please don't. I want to support you. Please walk with me.* He leaves a time and place to meet. I don't go. He calls every night. I know it's him because when Mother answers, he hangs up. He's waiting for me to pick up, but I never do. She thinks it's a prank and bemoans ever getting a telephone.

Finally, one night, he speaks to her. She puts her hand over the receiver and addresses me as I read a history book for school. "Oliver, you won't believe who it is. The young man we met at the inn. The tutor!" Into the receiver, she asks, "How did you get our number?" After a moment, she says, "Well, that was nice of the innkeeper to give it to you." Moments later, "Of course you can pay us a visit. Let me give you the address. How's dinner tomorrow night? We rarely have company. I'll cook something special." When she hangs up, her eyes look dreamy. I know she's thinking back to our magical time by the ocean. I wish I could tell her those days are behind us. Our land's end days have ended.

SHAMS. BOSTON. JUNE. 1920.

Oliver's mother cooked for me. Meat loaf. Green beans. Sweet potatoes. I wonder if my mother would have cooked for me had she lived. Would she have lovingly seasoned vegetables like these are? Would she have lit a fire to set the mood like Oliver's did? Would she have softened my father into a man who might have loved me?

"Mother must really like you," Oliver comments as we finish. "She rarely lights a fire because we both hate cleaning the fireplace."

"And I very much like *you*," I say to his mother. "You too," I joke to Oliver. How I wish I could declare my love for him right here. Right now. In front of the person who matters most to him. I stand and try to pick up the dirty plates.

"No, no, you're a guest," she insists. "You relax. I clean."

"Mother, you've worked hard enough today," Oliver says as he stacks our plates. "Sit and talk to Shams."

"Just leave everything in the sink." His mother shrugs. "What can I say? I enjoy scrubbing dishes."

Oliver carries the plates and trays to the kitchen. I continue chatting with his mother. We didn't discuss anything personal at dinner. We focused on books and politics. Now we reminisce about that beautiful deck by the ocean.

"The ocean is a symphony," his mother says.

Did my mother love the ocean?

Did she think of ocean waves as a symphony?

We're still discussing music when Oliver comes back. I beg him to play something for us.

He throws me a sharp gaze. "I'm tired. It's been a long night."

His mother intervenes. "I'll play with you. We can't say no to our guest's request for some live music."

They look so beautiful. Mother and son. Side by side at the piano.

Oliver bites his lip. "I'm nervous."

His mother glances my way. "We rarely have an audience. At least not an appreciative one."

Oliver laughs. I love his laughter. "Father found classical music ponderous and Liam just ignored us most of the time."

I can't imagine anyone finding them ponderous as they play a Chopin nocturne. Oliver knows the piece so well that he keeps his eyes closed as he plays. His mother keeps her own eyes on her son. She beams with pride as they create magic together. I've been tutoring other people's children for decades now. Never have I seen a parent and child this connected. It makes me long to be a part of their family.

The nineteenth-century melodies they summon at that piano bring my own nineteenth-century memories flooding back to me. Surviving without my father. Leaving school forever. Needing money on the streets of Victorian-era London. Stealing from the rich to feed myself. They were easy dupes. Bespectacled men. Overly painted ladies. I spoke their language and knew their world. I had no qualms about it. I would imagine they were my father when I robbed them. It gave me a frisson of revenge.

The Chopin piece reaches its melancholy conclusion. I burst into grateful applause. Oliver's mother takes her son's hand and guides him into taking a dramatic bow together. They're a perfect pair. So connected.

I've been running for so many years. City to city. Country to country. Never have I found a pair like these two. And a tutor sees families in their private moments. I've taught languages and literature to so many kids. Always tried to teach with more love and compassion than I had ever been given. Told every child I had the privilege of working with that the goal of learning is not achievement but knowledge. Grew attached to so many of them. Always had to leave them. I came to realize that three to five years was the average time it would take people to notice I wasn't changing the way they were. I left before the questions came. I didn't want to be studied. Didn't want to be some freak. I would change my name with each departure. Start anew. I perfected so many languages that I could successfully pretend to be Phillipe or Benicio. Mohammad or Luca or Günter. I once called myself Dorian. Just for fun.

"Bravo!" I yell as they enjoy their well-earned ovation. "Bravo!" The word brings me back to the St. James. The premiere of *The Importance of Being Earnest*. Wilde. Why are these memories so present today? Why does the past suddenly feel so close?

His mother blushes. "Well now, it's time for me to clean up." She stands and straightens the creases in her dress. "Oliver, why don't you give him a tour while I do the dishes? It's not a very big house, but perhaps Oliver can make it seem big with memories."

He leads me up. I wish we could never stop ascending. Take me to the heavens, Oliver. Take me to the sky. Let's live on a cloud.

The staircase walls are littered with framed photos of Oliver and his family through the years. He always had those dreamy eyes. I ponder the photos as we pass them. His generically handsome brother's plastic smile. His father's harsh eyes. The way his mother holds on to Oliver in every photo. She can't let go of him. He's her life raft. In their family and in the world. Each family photo makes me try to visualize my own father again. I don't have a single photograph of him. Do I remember him as he was? Or have my tormented recollections morphed him into something else entirely?

"Mother loves to have our photo taken." Oliver keeps his gaze on me as I keep mine on the photographs. "She says she'll need the photos to keep her company when we're all gone." He sighs. "Of course, only I'm left. . . ."

I do know this about my father: He began losing his hair at the age of nineteen. What little he had left was a dark muddy gray. Nothing of the sort happened to me. That was my first hint that I was both immortal and ageless. I wasn't sure in those first years after he burned the pages. I knew I felt different. Reborn. Powerful enough to make it on my own. To never see my father again. Never ask for his help. I didn't find out Father died because I stayed in touch with anyone from home. I obtained the information when I robbed some Persian visitors. I didn't reveal I was his child. Merely asked about him as if he were a distant acquaintance. They told me my father was taken by some plague or another. I don't wish that on anyone. Yet it didn't inspire any forgiveness for him. Perhaps one of the reasons I'm forgiving of the flaws of a person like Oscar Wilde is that he did more good than bad. My father did more bad than good. And that's that.

"Stop staring at my baby pictures!" Oliver tries to pull me up the final steps.

I look at a photo of him as a baby. Then at beautiful

seventeen-year-old Oliver. I sigh. I lower my voice to a whisper. "You were always magic."

"Shh." He looks over his shoulder with worry. Hoping his beloved mother didn't hear me.

He pulls me up the second story. I love that each floor of a home is called a story. As if every level is an opportunity to spin a new tale. Perhaps a better one. Each story building atop the one below. Oh, Oliver. Take me high up above this. To a place in time where no one would judge our love. To a land of fairy tales and enchantment. A land where a prince can find his prince.

Oliver pulls me anxiously into his bedroom. Closes the door. I take it all in. The mattress his body lies on. The sheets that have the privilege of touching his skin. The pillow his beautiful cheeks rest atop. His scent is all over the room. I never want to leave. I could be happy spending the rest of my life here. In this one room. With him.

He turns to me. Speaks in an urgent whisper. "What are you doing? Calling us incessantly? Inviting yourself over for dinner? Are you crazy?"

I try to change the mood with humor. "My sanity is certainly in question. Love will do that to a person."

He doesn't laugh. "Is this a joke to you?"

I take his hands in mine gently. "Not at all. I'm sorry, I—I just needed to see you."

"I've been avoiding you to protect you."

"I don't want to be protected. I want to be—"

He pushes my hands away. "Don't you dare say loved."

"I have to dare." I smile wistfully. "And you do too. If we don't, they've won."

"We'll win someday. Maybe not in our lifetime, but—"

"Listen to yourself!" The harshness of my tone jolts me. "You've already written off your whole lifetime. Accepted loneliness as your destiny."

"What choice do I have?" His eyes well up. The fog of his sadness isolates him from me. "Do you want me to end up dead like Cyril? Or expelled like Brendan?"

"Those aren't your only choices."

"Yes they are!" He spits his words out bitterly. "You expect me to break Mother's heart." He looks down. As if he can see his mother one level below. She's in one story. We're in another. Oliver knows the two stories can never be a part of the same life. Not here and now.

I plead with him. "I expect you not to give up. To fight for yourself. For us."

Oliver sighs sadly. "I always told you I was afraid. That it was the worst of my qualities. Now you understand."

I try to soften my tone. I don't want my passion to scare him away. "Let me be brave for you."

"I don't *want* that. Don't you understand that the only reason I wasn't dragged into this is that Brendan protected me? And by extension, *you*."

"I know all that. But I can't stop loving you." He turns away from me when he hears the word *love* again.

I put my arms around his torso from behind. Turn him toward me. I can't resist one more kiss here. Where we're safe. Our breath feels heavy. I want to inhale him into my soul. So we can be one. Forever. A mockingbird chirps outside. Oblivious to how fraught this moment is. I thank God for the birdsong. For the optimistic melodies that nature can't help but play.

His mother yells from below. "Boys!"

He pushes me away. Yells down to her. "Yes, Mother?"

"I'm going out for some S.O.S. pads to clean the pots and pans with. I'll be right back. Oliver, offer our friend some tea."

"I will, Mother!"

We stare at each other in nervous silence. Footsteps. The click of the front door. She's gone. We're alone.

I've never felt more excited. It's all I want. To be alone with him.

But all I see when I look in his eyes is anguish.

I pull him gently toward me again. He resists. "Do you want me to leave?"

He shakes his head sadly. "Of course not. But you must leave. You must be gone when she gets here. I can't see you again."

"Give me a reason that isn't based in fear."

"Fear protects us." He looks out his window. Lovingly watches his mother cross the street. He keeps his eyes on her until she turns the corner. "You want to know what I'm most afraid of?"

"I want to know everything about you."

He turns to face me. "I'm afraid of how easy it is to talk to you."

"Then talk to me. I'm here."

"I'm afraid of how *myself* I feel when we're together."

I put a hand on his cheek. Hold it there. "Then be yourself. What other choice do you have in the end?"

He lowers his voice to a hush. "I'm afraid of how much I want to kiss you."

I smile. "Then kiss me."

And so he does. He brings his lips to mine. Passionately at first. And then softly. We kiss like we have all the time in the world. He finally removes his lips from mine. He smiles as he leans back against his blue wall. Runs his hand along its chipped paint. "We all painted my room together. Me, Mother, Father, Liam. Mother chose the color. She said it reminded her of the ocean."

A memory: me and James alone in his room. It was almost two decades ago but I can still see the underwater world painted onto his walls. Still remember the humiliation of being caught with him. I did see James once again after that horrible night. But I didn't speak to him. James has lived a long and prosperous life. Marriage. Children. He never went into bookbinding. He became a lawyer like his father. Lived someone else's dream life instead of his own.

Oliver must be haunted by his own remembrances because he suddenly looks away from me. The fear returns to his gaze. "I can't break her heart. I'm sorry."

"Maybe our love won't break her heart. Maybe, in time, it might even fill her with joy. To know her son is loved."

"By a man?" His sharp eyes tell me there's no counterargument to this.

Still, I have to try. "Your mother loves you. Nothing will change that. I've looked into her eyes and into her soul. She may struggle at first, but she's a good woman."

"Even good women have their limits." He's speaking to the walls he painted with her. Staring at the color she chose. "And how will I support her if I stay in the life? How will I get into a good school, get the kind of job that will let me care for her as she has for me?"

"You're still young. There's time to figure all that out. I certainly never imagined I'd be a working tutor at seventeen."

His lips tighten bitterly. "I'm not young anymore. Not since Cyril died and Brendan was expelled."

"You could make music. You're talented. Your mother would be proud if you—"

"Music isn't a job!" He scoffs loudly. He looks at me in confusion. I'm not making any sense to him. "And if you're so adamant I chase my passions, then what about yours? Is tutoring moneyed children your lifelong dream?"

"No. Once upon a time, I dreamed of being a writer. A poet, perhaps."

"And?"

"Writing is too dangerous." I remember how James's father once described Wilde's words: *menacing text*. "Every time I tried to write a poem or any sort of story, it turned into *my* story. And my story can't be told."

"Exactly! Because what we want . . . who we are . . . it's unspeakable." He throws his arms up into the air in exasperation. "You think we can be together when writing about our life would be a crime?!"

"I don't need to be a writer anymore. I don't need the world's approval. I don't even need anyone to know. All I need . . . all I desire . . . is right here in this room." I take a reverent breath. "My dream is to have the privilege of loving you."

That seems to stop him cold.

"I've scared you." I hold my hand out for him to shake. "Perhaps I've said enough. If you can't love me back, then let's part before things—"

"But I do love you back!" He scratches his head in frustration. I'm afraid he might rip his beautiful hair out. "That's the problem. I want this and I'm scared of it all at the same time."

"What if we could be together forever?" I ask the question without thinking it through.

"No one can be together forever. That's just fantasy. Just like *we* are a fantasy. And maybe that's okay. Maybe we're not all meant to love and be loved. Being a good son is enough for me. Taking care of Mother and giving her grandchildren she can help raise and—"

"Does your brother share your concerns?"

"I am not my brother. My brother chose to leave. My brother is already engaged to some girl he hasn't even brought by the house. He hasn't introduced her to Mother. It makes me feel sick when I think of how thoughtless that is."

"And yet your mother has met me." I smile impishly. "So if ever *we* become engaged—"

"That's a fantasy for another world. A better one."

"And who creates this world we live in?" I take a hold of his shoulders. I feel dizzy as I gaze into his eyes. "We do. We make the world. Men and women. People. We make the rules."

"You see, this is why you have to leave. You put these ideas in my head . . ." He closes his eyes.

"The ideas were already there in your head before me. I first began to fall for you before we officially met. Do you know why?"

"Why?" He opens his eyes. Dares me to give him a good answer.

"You were with your cousin and his friends. They were doing what boys do, turning the sincere into the frivolous, having fun. And you were brave enough to say that you wanted more than a little fun. That you wanted—"

"Love." He smiles. Remembering that moment. Those more innocent times.

"You didn't let Jack's quips stop you from expressing your truest self. You said you had love to give. You said you wanted your life to feel like music and poetry, like an endless concerto. You were brave. And clear. You were—you are . . . magnificent."

He blinks rapidly. "How do you remember all that?"

"Because I've always wanted the same thing. You made me feel seen. Understood. Not alone. I wasn't sure I would love you then, but I'm sure now. I love you. I want to give you a life that feels like the endless concerto of your dreams."

"I want the same thing." He shakes his head. "But it's impossible. Wrong place. Wrong time. If we just lived in some better future—"

"Is that what you want?"

"Of course it is. But we don't. This has to be goodbye."

He pulls me close. Kisses me. Our tongues throb with desperation. With need. I'm breathless as I pull away. I want more of him. All of him. I kiss him again. It feels like we're enveloped by steam.

I pull away and take in the glory of his face. "That felt more like hello than goodbye."

"I love you. So much. But please go before Mother comes home."

"You hadn't said you love me before today."

"Well, I do." He fixes his gaze on me. "Now will you leave?"

"If that's what you want. I guess this is goodbye, then?" I turn around, slowly, giving him time to change his mind.

The birds keep singing outside. He calls out to me. "Wait!"

I turn to face him. "What is it?"

"What do you imagine they're saying?" His eyes wander to the window. "The birds."

"You beg me to leave, and when I do, you ask me what the birds are saying." I can't help but smile. I love that he can't seem to let me go. To let *us* go. "I think they're telling you to kiss me one last time."

"Funny, I was thinking the same thing." He practically lunges on me. Pins me onto the bed with feverish anxiety.

"Whoa there. This is love, not wrestling." I remember James again. The way he asked me to tie him up. The aggression he craved from me. I want that sometimes too. But not right now.

I kiss Oliver's long neck tenderly. Little kisses as I travel back to his lips.

He sighs. "That feels nice."

I keep kissing him. I try to put James out of my mind. To be in the moment. The last time I saw James was a few years after that fateful night when my life changed. I was asleep on the street outside one of the brothels where Wilde liked to find his young boys. I watched as James walked toward the brothel alone. His hat worn low to cover the top of his face. His scarf wrapped over his mouth. He had grown even taller. Thicker. Hairier. He sported a bushy beard that didn't suit his face at all. He had changed. I had not. He didn't see me. I could feel the shame in his every step as he entered the brothel. Off to bugger some lad before going home to the woman he would marry someday. That was when I realized I had to leave London. James wasn't the only person I knew there. There were others. Students. Professors. Deans. I couldn't risk being found out. I began my life of escape.

Oliver takes my face in his hands. "What are you thinking about?"

I shrug. "Nothing."

"I wish I understood you the way I understand the piano. But maybe that's the whole point of love, that it's not an instrument that can be mastered. It's meant to leave you guessing, isn't it?" He smiles. "You leave me guessing." He tries to take my shirt off.

I pull it back down. I want a lifetime of love from him. Not a frenzied night. "Your mother will be back very soon. This might not be a good idea."

The tables seem to have turned now. I'm pressing the brakes. He's the one pleading to speed ahead. "But this really is goodbye. If we don't do it now—"

"Stop pretending you know the future." I walk to the door and open it. "You're the one who wished we lived in a better place and time. Anything could happen."

I walk out of his bedroom and down the stairs. Descend the staircase. My eyes on all those images of Oliver's past. The boys he's been. He follows behind me. Argues as he chases me. "But anything can't happen! That's the whole point. The only time we have is the time we live in. And right now, Cyril is dead, Brendan is expelled, Mother is overworked."

I could keep arguing. But my mouth feels too dry to speak. Our conversation and our kisses have left me parched. I desperately need water. I go to the kitchen and pour myself a glass.

He hovers at the kitchen door. "Being ourselves is a crime!" His sharp gaze challenges me to contradict him.

I'm so nervous that I spill the water on myself. "Oh, come on." I'm soaked. I remember the fire is still raging in the living room.

I head there. Sit in front of the fireplace to dry my shirt. Oliver sits next to me. Leans his head on my shoulder lovingly. He whispers sadly into the flames. "Mother will be home soon."

I look into his eyes. Illuminated by the glow. "Tell me one last time. Do you love me, sincerely and eternally?"

"I do." He bites his lip. "I can't be with you, but I'll always carry you in my heart."

"And if you could be with me in some other world—"

"Stop with the fantasies. Of course I want that. Of course I do. I would do anything if I were a magician."

He kisses me on the lips gently. I pull him close feverishly.

"I don't want to stop." He scrunches his face up into a mask of torment. "I don't know what to do, Shams. Tell me what to do."

"Shh." I can feel the crumpled remaining pages of Wilde's manuscript in my pocket. They seem to be vibrating. Telling me to pull them out. The pages have remained with me since that day in 1895 when I saved them from burning. Parting with them would be like parting with a piece of myself. I often wondered about their power. Could they do to others what was done to me? I never burned them, though. Because I never found someone I wanted to join me in this journey. Not until Oliver. Immortality has been like a curse without him. But to be immortal together with the one you love . . . eternal love . . . isn't that what we all dream of? "Let's not rush the best thing either of us will ever find." I take a breath. "Oliver, there's something I need to tell you."

He stares at the pages in my hand. Tries to make out the handwriting. "Are those pages from your journal?"

I shake my head. "This isn't easy to explain."

"Is it a love letter you wrote and never sent?" I try to find the words to begin telling him what I am. What these pages can do for him. For us. But he keeps talking and I love the sound of his voice too much to stop him. "It's a poem you wrote for me! Do you know something? A street poet in Provincetown wrote a poem for me and Mother. We haven't opened it yet. We're saving it for a time when we need poetry, I think. That's something Mother and I have in common, I suppose. Always living for the future, putting others first and our own little pleasures last."

"Oliver, please. Listen to me. We don't have much time. These pages—"

"BOYS!" The front door creaks open. Slams shut. She's home. I missed my chance to tell him.

We need more time.

We deserve more time.

From the foyer, his mother loudly explains what took so long. "Would you believe there was an accident involving a truck full of peaches? Peaches everywhere. I had to take a detour."

I frantically turn to Oliver again. I can hear his mother's footsteps. There's no time. I ask him urgently: "Oliver, tell me the truth. Would you want to be with me in a different, better time and place?"

"Yes, yes, a million times yes." He scoots a little farther away from me. Anticipating his mother's entry.

I can't lose him. His mother approaches. She's seconds away from the living room. This could be the last time I see Oliver. I want to tell him my name isn't Shams. That I'm immortal. Eternally young.

But there's no time.

We need more time.

And this must be a sign. That he and I are in front of a fire in this very moment. The fates are sending me a message. *Make him immortal,* they're telling me. *We provided the fire. Now do your part.*

And so I do what I think I must. I throw one of the pages into the fire. I watch as Wilde's words burn: *"The basis of optimism is sheer terror."*

Sheer terror. That's what I feel as the page burns. "Say it again, Oliver. Tell me you wish you were born in another time, a time when your love isn't a crime. Please. Say it."

His eyes are moist as he says, "I wish we could be alive in a time when our love isn't a crime."

I sigh. He did it. He made his wish as the page burns. I'm not even certain it will work. But if it does . . .

His mother enters. Oliver turns to her. A nervous smile on his face. "Hello, Mother."

His mother squints. "Son, how long have you been staring at that fire? Your eyes look positively aflame."

Oliver looks at me. That's when I know it worked. He's like me now. "I feel different, Shams."

Optimism. That's what I feel as I lose myself in his fiery gaze. Our eyes are the same now. Our fates forever tied. I have to tell him that I made his wish come true. Granted him the fantasy life he dreamed of. We have no limits any longer. We're not stuck in this horrible time and place. But there's time to explain all that. An eternity of time and an eternity of love.

BRAM. LONDON. 2025.

"Oliver?" I approach him slowly. He doesn't turn to face me. I haven't seen him in forty-three years. That was the average human being's life expectancy when I was born. It feels like a blip in time to me right now. The years without him seem to disappear now that he's here with me again. "Oliver. Please. Look at me. Talk to me."

Finally he says: "I hate this." His eyes are on the river. The water that by dusk will contain Lily's ashes.

"I know. Lily's gone. Our mother."

That's when he turns to me. I examine his unchanged face. Search for signs of warmth behind the smoldering rage. He doesn't bother wearing a veil. He lets his eyes burn for all to see.

"*Your* mother. I loved Lily. You know that. But I *had* a mother. You took me from her."

"Oliver, we discussed all this over a century ago. . . . You could have—"

"Could have what?" His eyes are scorching. I forgot what it's like to be looked at with those feline eyes in these decades without him.

He repeats a variation on the same words he spoke to me by the Charles River. It was the first sunrise after I had transformed him. He knew something had changed inside him. I knew I had to tell him the truth. I thought he would thank me for making his wish come true. That's how naive I once was. How stupid.

What he said then was: *Now I must tell Mother that not only am I a homosexual, but I'm also immortal?! This is the state where they burned women at the stake. You think the same people who put our friends at Harvard through a secret trial will be kind to the woman who birthed a freak like me?!*

What he said then was: *I promised myself I would never love someone like my father. And you're just like him. Selfish. Mercurial. You take what you want without a care for others.*

What he said then was: *I hate you. I'll hate you forever.*

His words came out like a waterfall back then. Now they're more a gush of resentment as his aching voice plays the same sad theme. "I never wanted this. Mother is gone. Brendan is gone. And now . . ." A lump in his throat. His voice cracks. "Now Lily's gone. Everybody I've ever loved is gone."

"I'm here." I pull him close. He sobs into my chest. Hot tears that warm my heart. "Look." I pull a vintage Oreos tin from my satchel bag.

"You think I'll forgive you because of some hundred-year-old cookies?"

I laugh. "The tin is vintage. I found it online. The cookies are fresh." I open the tin to reveal rows of Oreos. "We walk until we finish them all, remember?"

"I hate you."

"I love you." I repeat those three words until his tears subside and his body relaxes. I know I made him this way without his consent. I hate myself for it. I tried to justify what I did for years. I would remind myself that I had no idea if it would even work until I burned that page. I couldn't be sure the magic would work twice.

But I *wanted* to make him immortal like me. Of course I did.

My desire is my guilt.

He accused me then of being like his father.

I worry I'm like my own father. Greedy. Insatiable. Cruel. The thought sickens me.

"Why did you do this to me?"

"Because I love you." I know that's no reason. Love is everything. Love is also not enough. I lift my veil so he can see the sincerity in my eyes. "And because I thought . . . You said that if we could live in another world, a better time—"

He pushes me away from him. "Over a century and your argument hasn't changed one bit."

"It's not an argument. I know what I did was wrong. But at the time I thought . . . that you would thank me."

"*Thank* you? For cursing me?"

"For making your wish come true."

"You and your silly fantasies. That's what I thought it was when you asked me if I would choose to live in a different world with you. A fantasy. It's like if you asked someone if they want some superpower. Like the power of invisibility. Of course they'll say yes, yes, a million times yes, because they don't think it's a *real option*. They haven't pondered what it truly means. Just like you didn't think of the implications of what you did to me."

"I know that." I don't dare say more. I know myself well enough. I'll say the wrong thing.

"You didn't have anyone you loved when this happened to you." There's a new cruelty in his voice as he says this.

"What?"

"You didn't have to *leave* anyone. Your mother was dead. You despised your father. You had no other family. No friends. You didn't stop to think of what it meant for me. Never seeing my mother again. My brother."

I step closer to him. "You *hated* your brother!"

He backs away from me. "Everyone hates their sibling at some point. You robbed me of the chance to resolve our issues. My nieces are both dead and I never met them. I don't know their children. I have nothing. You took it all."

"You're right. I was never loved." I pause. "Maybe I envied you. The love you had with your mother. It was so pure. Maybe I did what I did because I wanted pure love so badly."

"So you admit you were selfish?"

Of course I was selfish. Still am. Greedy for love. For a life of meaning. I know how much it hurt him to leave those he loved behind. Brendan—believe it or not—was readmitted to Harvard two years later. Became a dean at the university. Lived and died single. He never exposed what Harvard did. No one did. The secret court wasn't discovered until 2002. There were two more Harvard suicides after Cyril. Eugene Cummings checked himself into the university's infirmary after being questioned by the secret court. Took an overdose of medicine. Keith Smerage died by suicide in 1930 by inhaling gas. Just as Cyril once did. I think of Keith often. He made it to New York City. Appeared to have a good life. Yet the ghosts of his past won in the end. Edna remained a lifelong activist. She lived long enough to see the Daughters of Bilitis, the Mattachine Society, Stonewall. Long enough to see homosexuality removed from the American Psychiatric Association's list of mental illnesses. But she passed before Harvey Milk was murdered. Before AIDS. I hope she died feeling hopeful about our collective future. Passed into the next world feeling the sheer terror of optimism.

"Say something!" His lips curl defiantly. "You summon me back to London, and you can barely say a word to me?"

"I'm sorry." I bite my lip. Keep my head down. Looking at him when he's angry at me is too painful. "I've tried to grow. To truly see myself. Which means accepting the unforgivable thing I did to you." I take a deep breath of cold air. It feels like the distant fog enters my body. Becomes one with my thoughts. "And yet, I beg your forgiveness. You forgave me once."

"And I was proven wrong."

"Were you? We were happy, weren't we? Living with Lily and Maud. Dancing. Music. Brixton. The Blitz. Pearl's. It was our time."

"Until it wasn't." He closes his eyes. I wipe the tears from his cheeks. His skin still as youthful as ever.

"Until it wasn't." A melancholy echo. I know all too well what I put him through. The escape. The loss. The grief. The fear.

"Do you forgive yourself?" He's never asked me this before.

"I do." I can see he's surprised by the answer. "It took time. It took Lily teaching me how. I know what I did was horrible. I also know I did it because I want what we all want. Eternal love."

"No one wants eternal love in a literal sense. Some in our own community don't desire romance or sex at all. This need of yours to put romantic love above all else . . . It's delusional. I did love you. Perhaps I still do. But that doesn't mean I would choose you over my mother and my friends and family. Over being a *human*. What you gave me isn't eternal love. It's eternal . . . loneliness."

"I know that now." I let out a sob. "I'm so sorry, Oliver. If I could go back . . ."

"Do you still have the last page?"

I put my hand on my heart. Inside the chest pocket of my

jacket is the only remaining page of Wilde's original manuscript in my possession. I pull it out. Hand it to him. He seems to contemplate throwing it into the Thames. Drowning any possibility of cursing another poor soul. But he puts it in his own pocket. "It's safer with me."

"I agree. You're certainly less impulsive than I am." I shake my head sadly. "I've spent over a century thinking about what I did. How it happened. Why I did it. How much I regret it. How to forgive myself for it. But—"

"But?"

A pain in my chest. My weary heart aches. "Is it too much to ask to make today about Lily? They're probably leaving Queen's Walk right now. Headed to Brixton. Our home. We can trail them together."

He hesitates. His love for Lily pours through him as he speaks these words reverently: "Today is for Lily."

I open the tin again. "We walk until the cookies are gone?"

He takes a cookie reluctantly. I do too.

I say: "You look good."

He laughs. "I look the same. As do you."

"No, I meant . . . You look happy."

He shrugs. "I'm ashamed to say this, but I've found a medication that works for me. Those melancholy spells are gone."

"Oliver, there's no shame in mental illness."

He laughs again. "I'm not ashamed of my depression. I'm ashamed because the medicine is manufactured and distributed by Whitman and Whitman."

My heart sinks at the mention of that company. Jack Whitman. The Jackal. His evil sneer comes back to me. I feel the need to escape again. To move as fast as we can. I take Oliver's hand. Lead him across the bridge. Down the steps. Just as we walked that first morning after I burned the page and made him immortal.

On that walk . . .

One hundred and five years ago . . .

I confessed.

He raged.

Begged me to reverse it.

I had no idea how.

Still don't.

His biggest fear was how he would ever explain it to his mother. He never did tell her.

My biggest fear was never seeing him again. Not being able to find him. He wanted to know where I was too. He still loved me. Despite his hatred of me.

We devised a system to let the other know where we were. Classified ads. Paid ads when the classified section got shut down. I would refer to him as a classical musician. He would address me as a great poet. He told me he never wanted to see me again. I said the entire reason I did what I did was to be with him in a better time and place. That's when he said, and I remember every word . . .

If you ever find that time and place, I'll come to you. I promise.

I thought I found that time and place with Lily. Here in London.

And I was right.

Until I was wrong.

BRAM. LONDON. DECEMBER. 1979.

Poetry has saved me time and time again. The verses themselves have been a big part of my salvation. The human ability to transform the mess of life into beauty has never ceased to amaze me. But poetry *physically* saves me in this moment. Specifically: Audre Lorde's collection *From a Land Where Other People Live*. I thank the heavens that this particular book is visible in my pocket. I feel grateful my attempts to shield its pages from the December rain are unsuccessful. Lily may never have taken notice of me without the Lorde as our point of connection. And she did. She does. She has. She's here.

She's like a guardian angel as she lies to save me. "My name is Lily Summers and that's my son." A subtle accent in her cadence. Rhythmic hints of a Jamaican childhood that mirror the syncopated beat of my heart. No woman has ever called me her son.

The two police officers who threaten to arrest me for loitering don't exactly look convinced. "Your *son?*" Venom on the cop's tongue. He's a snake. Just one more member of law enforcement who breaks laws to bash queers like me. Their slithering hatred of us was always there. But it's become worse since that wretched Iron

Lady took power. Margaret Thatcher hates everyone and everything I hold dear. Queerness. Hair that moves. Bodies that sway. Clothes with style. Human decency. And most especially: working people.

I've been a working person since I was seventeen years old. And I've been seventeen for eighty-four years. That's a lot of toil. I suppose my early years of thieving might not be classified as work by some. But they required planning. Strategy. Expertise. Long hours. The drudgery of labor.

"Your son?" I sound just as confused as the officers.

I don't know why she bothers trying to save me. Until she points to the book in my pocket. "Of course you are. Isn't that the book you borrowed from me? Audre Lorde."

"Who?" The second officer clearly doesn't want an answer.

She answers anyway. "Audre Lorde. A genius. A radical. A lesbian. A feminist. A warrior for Black people." The way she says the last part tells me she too is a warrior.

"So she's a criminal like your . . . *son* here." Officer number one's evil eyes look like they're boiling. The spite in his tone speaks volumes. It says he doesn't think a person like her can have a son.

I defend myself feebly. "I'm not a criminal. I just fell asleep."

"You can't sleep on the street." Officer number two slaps his baton into his hand threateningly.

"Well, he can't help it. My boy is a narcoleptic." Lily comes up with this falsehood quickly. Speaks it with confident assurance. Something tells me this is a woman who has gotten herself out of plenty a jam with police.

"A what now?"

"It's a medical condition. He can't control when, where, or how he sleeps. Would you like the phone number for our family doctor?" She remains relaxed. Nonchalant. Her eyes dare them to call her on the bluff.

The baton-hitting cop approaches her threateningly. "You're telling me that you, with your black skin and your man's voice—"

"I am a woman. My name is Lily Summers and my address is—"

"You're telling me you are the mother of this brown boy who looks nothing like you."

She has an answer for this too. "You haven't heard of narcolepsy *or* adoption, I see." I'm in awe of how fast her mind works.

The cops get an alert on their police radios. Just in time to save us. They're off to terrorize some other deviant.

Lily holds her hand out to me and lifts me up. I accept it gratefully. "Why did you do that?"

She pulls some lipstick from her purse. Reapplies the cherry red of her mouth. "Do I have lipstick on my teeth?" She smiles. It's luminous. I shake my head. "You ever slept in jail?"

"No. Never."

"Once they lock you up, they try to keep you there."

I ponder what would happen if I ever ended up in prison. What would they do once they realized I wasn't aging? Nothing good, I'm sure. "I—I don't know how to thank you."

She eyes me curiously. "What's a kid who reads Audre Lorde doing sleeping in a rat-infested alley?" Most of the city's grimy and rat-infested these days. Not Mayfair of course. Not Sloane Square. Not wherever the hell the Iron Lady lives. I'm certain she's cozy and warm as she devises legislation to make our kind extinct.

"I—I don't know. But thanks for saving me. I'll be back on my feet soon. I work as a tutor, I just . . . I just came back to London and—"

"*Back* to London? You look like a child. Where are your parents?" She seems genuinely concerned. No one has been *genuinely* concerned about me since Oliver.

"Don't you remember?" I smile. "You're my mother."

She laughs. "That was all I could think of in the moment. I could not let a boy who reads radical poetry end up in prison for needing a place to sleep. I loathe bobbies."

"I do too."

She shakes her head. "They don't patrol the streets to protect us. They do it to scare us. They can throw us in the nick for existing. They can kill us and get away with it. And we all know that when someone *does* kill us, they look the other way." She seems to be thinking of something, or someone, specific. "You're queer, right?"

I nod. "Gay. Queer. Both. Yes."

"Listen, kid, you'll come over for a shower and a bite to eat, but that's it. I have a full day ahead and I need a nap."

"What do you do?" I walk by her side. Her high heels click along the pavement with purpose. She smells like a night of dancing. Like sweat. Glitter. Escape.

"I make clothes." She says it with delight. I can tell she fought for her life. "Custom orders. Alterations too. Where are you from?"

"I suppose I'm from Iran."

"Oh." She looks at me differently now. "I'm so sorry. Did you have to escape because of the revolution?" I don't say yes or no. "Your parents? Did they . . . Are they . . . I heard a lot of people—"

"Yes, my parents are dead." It's not a lie. They are dead. Just not in the recent revolution. I let her make her own assumptions.

"My God, I am so sorry." She puts an arm around me as we walk. "How did you make your way to London?"

"I—I know some people here." Again: not a lie.

"Then why are you not with them?" I evade her gaze. She nods. Fills in my history for herself. "Ah. Your people don't know you're gay?" I don't answer. "This world isn't easy for us, kid." She shakes her head. "Look at us, two of the colonized living in the city of the colonizers."

The British didn't technically colonize Iran. They manipulated and meddled in insidiously covert ways to quench their thirst for oil. Still horrible. Perhaps not to the same degree. I don't correct her. Not when she sees us as allies against the same enemy. "Where are you from?"

"Kingston. Jamaica." She practically sings the words. Fills those three syllables with both joy and sadness. The faint accent feels more pronounced when she speaks of her homeland. "I haven't been back since I left. Always meant to. Never had enough money. And then it got . . ." She doesn't look at me. It's like she's speaking to someone else. Doesn't finish the sentence either. "Well, there's no reason to go back no more. Not since my mother passed."

"She didn't move to London with you?"

Lily shakes her head. "She sent me to live with my Uncle Alton in Brixton when I was twelve. Said I'd get a better education here. Said I'd be safer too. She was right on one count."

"So the last time you saw your mother . . . you were *twelve?*"

"When did I say that?" She laughs. "I said I never went back. She visited us when she could. Always hated it here. Rubbish on the streets. Judgment in people's eyes. Gray skies." She switches to a much heavier accent. A warm imitation of her mother. "*It always be raining in London cuz dis place fills God wid sorrow.*"

I smile. "She sounds wonderful."

"She was."

"I'm sorry she's gone."

"No pity!" She waves a manicured hand into the air. The nails are hot pink. *"I got no time for boo-hoo backstories."* She smiles. "My mother used to say that." She switches back to her mom's voice again. Clearly enjoys being her. *"Clock always be ticking, pickney. Who got time fi sadness? God give yuh one life. Live it."*

If anyone has time for sadness, it's me. "Is your Uncle Alton still in London?"

I see the pain in her eyes. I wonder what happened. Perhaps her Uncle Alton rejected her. Cast her aside. "Tell you what, kid. You don't ask about my past and I won't ask about yours." Perhaps her Uncle Alton is dead.

"Is that a promise?"

She looks at me with a smile. "It's a promise."

She holds her hand out. I shake it. We seal the promise this way. The past will never be discussed. This one promise already makes me feel so much safer. I won't need to lie if I don't have to discuss my past. I can start anew.

She leads me onto Oxford Street and then down a side alley toward Covent Garden. Three men sleep. Liquor bottles by their side. We barely glance at them. It's not such an odd sight anymore. The rulers create poverty. Then force the poor into dark alleys. Overcrowded prisons. They can't stand to see the human toll of their freedom.

We stop at a red light. Next to us: two teenage girls dressed like they're coming home from a debaucherously champagne-soaked all-nighter at some members-only club. "It's up to sixteen girls." The one slurring right now wears a tight pink sequin miniskirt. "And he's still out there."

"Well, he's not here in London, is he?" This one is in short shorts and a tight-fitting designer blazer.

"He's not far. He could take the train in. Is this light ever going to change?"

Behind us, a man screams something about nuclear power stations destroying us all as he turns a corner.

The light finally changes. We cross the street next to the girls. There's a haunted tone to Pink Sequins's voice as she worries about this serial murderer on the loose. I know that feeling. The suspicion that danger is one wrong turn away. "My mum said he's only killing prossies."

"Must make her feel better, thinking it's just prostitutes."

Pink Sequins rolls her eyes. "Nothing to be terrified of if it's *them* and not us."

Lily turns to the left at the next intersection. The girls turn right. It's just us on a quiet street. Lily looks at me with steel in her eyes. "At least the press gives a fuck about those Yorkshire girls. When we disappear, nobody pays it no mind."

"We?"

"Queers. Queens. Freaks. Fag folk. Trans folk. Black folk. Brown folk. Shall I go on?" She offers me a bittersweet smile. "Us."

"Us." I've felt so alone for so long. So far from Oliver. Loveless. "At least there is an *us,* though." The last time Oliver left me a classified message was a month ago. He addressed me as T. S. Eliot. Identified himself as Vivaldi. The message simply said that the weather was warm in Buenos Aires. That told me he's in Argentina. That's all he's granted me since we parted in Boston almost six decades ago. His location. Nothing more.

She stops when she reaches a run-down building on Floral Street. Two punks drink from the same container on the stoop of the building. One of them has a shaved head. Wears nothing but a leather vest. Even in this freezing cold. The other has an orange Mohawk. He's wrapped in a ragged blanket. I think I see bedbugs crawling on the wool. "Good morning, boys. Nice to see you're sticking to a healthful diet."

"And you?" Shaved Head glances my way. "Looks like you'll be eating chicken for breakfast."

"Bite your booze-soaked tongue, baldie. I'm helping the kid out, and you turn it into something dirty. You're no better than the Tories who think queers shouldn't be allowed to teach children in schools."

"Oi, I'm no Tory." Shaved Head takes an insolent slug from his bottle.

"So you say." Lily unlocks the front door. Gazes down at him. "Bet you would've been burning records at Disco Demolition Night."

"DISCO SUCKS!" That's the last thing I hear out of the punk's mouth.

Lily looks down at the punks with real empathy. "So does booze. Look what it's done to you two." I can't help but agree with her. I've lived long enough to know I never want to experience another hangover.

Lily slams the door shut behind us. There's no lift. She makes her way up the stairs. I follow. "I would've introduced you if they were worth knowing. Pissed punks. At least Thatcher and her buddies look the part. But the punks. They think they're so cool. Deep down, they're just conservatives in secondhand clothes. They think their rage is more valid than ours, their art more meaningful. Disco is manufactured to them just like my tits are." She unlocks the door. "It's a mess, kid. You've been warned."

"Wow." I almost shed a tear when I first lay eyes on her flat.

"Come on, it's not that bad." She closes the door behind me.

"It's . . . fabulous." I turn my gaze from one end of the flat to another. Living room. Dining nook. Kitchen. All connected by open arches. Fabric *everywhere*. Patterns of embroidered satins thrown onto a fuzzy brown couch. Monochrome polyesters on a hard wooden chair. Plaids. Wools. Explosions of color. Crushes of velvet. Bunches of chiffon. Like pastel clouds. A sewing machine on the dining table. The scent of home-cooked food. A small television with a machine I don't recognize under it. A record player. Crates and crates of vinyl.

"Wow, you have so much music. This must have cost a fortune." I look at her curiously. "Are you rich?"

"Never ask a lady how old she is or how much money she has." She laughs. "I'm thirty-three and just getting by. None of the records belong to me. I make clothes for all my DJ friends, and store their records for them as payment."

"I'd like to be the kind of person who says *all my DJ friends* as casually as you do." I gaze at her with reverence. "You're fabulous."

Next to the record player is what can only be described as a shrine of sorts to Donna Summer. I approach. Photos. Magazine covers. Records. All carefully placed next to each other. Three candles underneath them. Dried wax dripping down their edges like withered tears.

"We all have our saints." She kisses her knuckles. Places her hand gently on Donna's face. "I was raised with God and now I worship a goddess."

"I love her too."

"So you don't think . . ." She imitates the punk now. Raises a fist up. ". . . disco sucks?"

I snort. "No, of course not."

I know why she's sore about this. Disco is her music. Black. Queer. A reflection of her world. Over fifty thousand twats blew up disco records just a few months ago in Chicago. Disco Demolition Night. It was during a baseball game. America's pastime is burning us down. London's no different. Perhaps nowhere is. The powerful always want to destroy the powerless when their dominance is at risk.

"Good, because I'm going to put a record on and get to work while you shower." She reaches into a hallway closet. Hands me the striped towel she pulls out. "Here." She eyes my filthy clothes. "Do you have something to wear that doesn't smell like a rubbish bin?" I shake my head. "I've got some for you. I tried my hand at menswear a few years ago and the results were terrible, but they should fit."

"Thanks."

"Go wash up. You smell like a sewer and I've got deadlines."

She picks out Donna Summer's *Once Upon a Time . . .* record. Donna looks like a goddess on the cover. Hair like ocean waves. Lips parted suggestively. Eyes soft. Skin dewy. Lily holds the record up next to her face. "Do I look like her?"

"You do. A little."

"Why? Because my skin is black and my hair is big?"

I feel my heart sink. I've upset her. "I— No— Just—"

She cackles. "Relax, kid. I'm teasing."

She puts the needle on the record. Approaches the sewing

machine. I enter the bathroom. Close the door behind me. The opening strings of the title song lead to her crystalline voice. *Once upon a time there was a girl, who lived in a land of dreams unreal.* I imagine Lily is that girl Donna is singing about. It pleases me to think of her story being told by her goddess. I turn the shower on. *Family in name alone, no place left to hide.* I think perhaps the song is about me now. Family in name alone. Exhausted by hiding. Escaping. Creating new identities.

The shower feels heavenly. The warm jets relax me. Lily has a seemingly endless collection of bath products. Lemon shampoo. Lavender soap. Some kind of shampoo with nine herbs in it. Rainwater-soft rinse. Antiaging this and that. Even baby shampoo.

That's what I choose. Shampoo for a baby. I feel like a kid again. Like someone else is taking care of me.

The song changes as I linger in the shower. The next song is far more dramatic than the first. It's about the city closing in on Donna. *Help me. I want to get out.* I think to myself that I never want to leave this place. I wonder what Oliver thinks of disco music.

Do they play it in Buenos Aires?

Does it remind him a little of his beloved classical music with its instrumental breaks and recurring motifs?

Does he go out dancing?

Does he have a dance partner?

My mind has worked this way for fifty-nine years now. Always wondering after Oliver. What was he doing when Martin Luther King Jr. was assassinated? When Kennedy was shot? When Marilyn took her final breath? When Judy died? During the Stonewall uprising? What does he make of jet engines and the atomic bomb? Of birth control pills, Barbie dolls, heart transplants?

When I first heard that a successful heart transplant was performed . . .

I dreamed that they could take my heart and transplant it into his body.

Make us one forever.

Did he have the same thought?

Does he think of me like I think of him?

Has he loved another?

Does he feel like I do? Desperate to love. To be cared for. To find his place in the world. To belong. To be of his time. Not out of time.

I make the water as hot as it can possibly get without burning me. Let the heat bring me back to life in some new form. I don't know why I first came back to London. It wasn't to see any of my old schoolmates. They would all be over a hundred years old at this point. Either they're all dead or they'd think they were suffering from dementia if they recognized me. Perhaps it's the haunting memories that brought me back. Some need to track my past. To reconsider it. See it in some new light. I needed to see the streets where James and I walked. The hotel where my father burned me into youthful immortality.

A knock on the bathroom door. "You all right in there?"

I turn the water off and yell out. "Yes, sorry, I didn't mean to use so much water!" I wrap myself in a towel and open the door a crack.

"There are clothes for you outside the door. Breakfast is ready. And please moisturize your skin. You're cracked all over. You'll look my age soon if you don't take care of yourself, kid."

I dry my body. Rub myself silly with lotion that claims to have egg yolk in it. Grab the clothes she left out for me. A pair of boxer shorts. Baggy cotton pants with two strings near the waist. A white T-shirt. A light denim blazer with bright graffiti on the back. *The National Front Is an Affront.*

"Hi." I find her at the sewing machine. Doing something that looks like magic to me.

Lavender fabric glides through her fingers like a gleaming river. She doesn't look up at me as she speaks. Too focused on her work. "Eat your breakfast. Porridge and banana fritters. Rich in fiber and potassium. It'll give you energy for the day ahead." She laughs to herself. "You sound just like your mother, Lily."

"Thanks." I sit. Taste. The porridge is so hot it burns the roof of my mouth. I don't show or even feel displeasure. I'm too happy. She seems to have spiced the porridge with turmeric. The flavor reminds me of being a child in Persia. That smell always traveled from the kitchens of my homeland. "What are you making?"

"A dress for some rich girl's sixteenth birthday party, which will be held on some polo ground somewhere in the countryside, where the attendees would be horrified to find out whose hands made the birthday girl's dress." She continues sewing as she speaks. "Just what I dreamed of when I graduated fashion school."

"They can't be so horrified if they hire you." I'm trying to raise her spirits.

She throws me a quick side-eye. Doesn't stop sewing. "They don't hire me, silly. You think the earls and dukes of the world are going to do business with me?"

"I'm sorry—I thought . . ." I put some food in my mouth to stop myself from putting my foot in it again.

"There's a posh girl I went to school with who takes the orders. Cordelia Biddlecombe, but her friends call her Biddie." She threads the sewing machine.

"What do you call her?"

"I call her Lady Cordelia." She giggles. "Her family owns this place. Rent comes out of my pay."

"So she doesn't pay you?"

"She does. A tiny fraction of her price to do the work."

"Oh." I put a banana fritter into my mouth. Enjoy the fried sweetness.

"Beats working in a garment factory. I get to play my music. Use the leftover fabric to create beauty."

"Still doesn't seem fair."

"Life isn't fair. Sooner you realize that the better off you'll be. But . . ." She stops sewing. Looks at me with a funny sort of pride in her eyes. She pulls the collar of my blazer up. Brushes my shaggy hair off my face with her long fingernails. "You know what, my menswear isn't as bad as I remember."

"Bad? I've never felt sharper."

She shrugs. "Maybe I just hate men." A beat. "No, no, I don't hate men. Sadly, I love them. But why do they have to be such bloody twats so much of the time?"

"Did you want me to answer that, on behalf of all men?"

She laughs. "You're not even a man yet. You're a boy."

She's right. I'm still just a boy. Still full of the same angst. Same longing. Perhaps it wasn't just my body that was frozen in time by those burning pages. Perhaps it was my mind too. My soul. My spirit. "You said life isn't fair, *but* . . . What's the *but?*"

She takes a moment to gather her thoughts. In the background,

Donna sings. *Queen for a day. Queen for a night. Dressed head to toe. So you'd never know it's me.* Lily takes my hand in hers. "But it's still *life,* and isn't life the greatest gift God can give us?"

"I—" I don't know how to answer that.

"Yes, it's unfair that I'm the best damn designer in London and I have to make these dumb party dresses for the daughters of Tories, but it's not all I do. I make dresses for the real queens of England. I help them transform into the creatures they always dreamed themselves to be." She squints. "Boy, do you know your eyes glow like neon?"

"Oh." I feel self-conscious. "Only sometimes. It's strange. Some people think it's frightening. I'm sorry."

"Don't apologize for being unique." She looks at my empty bowl. "You done?"

I nod. She picks up the bowl.

"I can clean it." I'm not just being polite. I'm trying to find a reason to stay longer. "I can clean all of this. Help you organize. I'm good at that, and this place is a . . ."

"I know what it is." She laughs. "I know it looks like a tornado passed through here just last night."

"I could use a job. I could be your assistant."

"Boy, I can't afford no assistant." She cackles. "Besides, you should be in school."

"I finished school early." Not really a lie. I am done with school.

"University, then."

"I'm a tutor. I swear I am. Before you found me on the street, I tutored kids. Wealthy kids just like the ones you make dresses for. Maybe your posh friend could find me kids to tutor. I'll give her a cut. I'll give you a cut too."

"Honey, you're getting way ahead of yourself. I'm a busy bitch, and I've done my good deed for the day. This is goodbye . . ."

I know she's waiting for my name. I feel suddenly sick. I've assumed over thirty names since going by Shams. I've pretended to be so many people. I don't want to pretend with her. To my surprise, I tell the truth. "My name . . . Well, the name I was born with . . . It's Shahriar . . . But I hate that name. I don't want to be . . . I'm *not* his son anymore."

She places a hand on each of my cheeks. Her fingers are strong and soft at the same time. "You don't need to be anyone you don't want to be. You think the name I was born with was Lily? No, I named myself after my favorite flower while staring at a lily pond."

"And your last name? You named yourself after Donna Summer?"

She laughs as Donna's silky voice continues to fill the room. Singing about finding a sweet romance. "No, no, no. I really am a Summers. Of the Kingston Summers, darling. That's just a lovely coincidence. Of course, her name is one singular summer. And mine is plural. I'm all the sunshine." She sings to the tune of Chaka Khan. *"I'm every summer. It's all in me."*

"Will you give me a name?" I'm tired of birthing new versions of me. All I want—finally—is for someone to create me not from duty or from ambition. But from love.

"Honey, that's a big responsibility. I don't know enough about you. What do you love?"

"Poetry." I close my eyes. "Poetry and words, and nature and spring, and love. I *love* love. And this horrible city that makes God cry. I love it, too, for all its flaws, because the streets here seem to rise above their memories. I came to London when I was younger, and it was horrible." I open my eyes. "But now here I am with you, in a new London."

"It's still the same city. Horrible. Wonderful."

I pull a piece of fabric from the hard chair. "What about Polyester?"

"As your name? Have you lost your mind?"

"It can be Polly for short."

"Are you a woman?"

"No."

"Do you plan on pursuing drag?"

The question brings me back to the masquerade ball. All those decades ago. It still feels like yesterday sometimes. And like three dozen lifetimes ago at other times. "No. I did do drag once. I don't think it was my calling."

"All right then. You're not Polly."

"What did you have in mind?"

"I have nothing in mind, you wild thing. Now go. I have to work." She makes her way back to the sewing machine.

"How about this? Once you get to know me a little better, you can name me. It'll be fun. Like a game." I try to catch her gaze. She ignores me. "All right, I'll go. But thank you for saving me from the police, and for the clothes and the shower and the food and—"

She looks up at me in exasperation. "Honey, come to the Blitz next Tuesday. I'm there every week with my friend Archie. Now go."

"Yes, ma'am." My smile feels like it takes over my face. I leave satisfied that this isn't the end of us.

The two drunk punks are still out on the stoop when I leave. One of them whistles at me in my new outfit. I'm pretty certain it's an insult. But I take it as a compliment. I twirl around to show off the flow of those baggy pants. I feel free.

On Tuesday, I make my way to the Blitz Club on Great Queen Street. Still in the clothes Lily made. I stand in line outside. The dramatically dressed people ahead of me are all desperate to be let in. They tap their sharp heels. Smoke cigarettes as they lean against the dilapidated wall. Partially exposed brick. Torn posters. A sign reads: *Keep gates in locked position when premises are open.* I feel nervous as I inch closer to the entrance. I've now heard the creature at the door turn multiple people away with stinging judgment.

To a man in slacks and a cashmere sweater: *Would you let yourself in?*

To a pair of girls in Audrey Hepburn–inspired black dresses: *Try harder next time, luvs.*

To an androgynous figure in a fuzzy leopard overcoat and thigh-high boots: *You wore that last time, Bertie.*

To a rugby-built boy: *This is the Blitz, not your local pub.*

The man at the door wears a suede cape. Huge geometric collar. No shirt. Short shorts. Knee-high suede boots. He flings his cape back every time he lets someone in. He eyes me up and down when my turn comes. Turns me around. Hums curiously. "So how do you know Lily?"

"Oh, uh, she's . . . a new friend."

"I'm surprised she let someone wear her abandoned menswear collection. You must be special to her." He leans closer to me. Gazes curiously at my eyes. "Your orange contact lenses are fabulous. Where did you get them?"

"Oh, I— Well, they're not—"

"Oh, fine. Don't reveal your secrets. I wouldn't either. Have fun." He waves his cape to let me in. I can't believe my luck as I take in the extravaganza. I feel a sense of wonder again. For the first time since leaving Oliver.

I enter to the sound of Petula Clark singing "Don't Sleep in the Subway." I approach the cloakroom near the DJ booth. An androgynous stunner asks if I want to check my jacket.

"Be careful. George is famous for stealing from coats." I turn to see who's speaking. Another androgynous beauty. Hair like a punk Veronica Lake.

"Blow me, Marilyn." That's the coat check creature. His voice is velvety.

"You wish, George." They both laugh. Their ribbing of each other seems grounded in affection.

There's a gleam in my eye as I hand my jacket to George. "It's all right, I've stolen from my share of coat pockets in my day." Stealing is stealing. No matter the century.

"A fellow thief." George flashes me a charismatic smile. "Rest assured someday I'll be famous for more than theft."

That's when I hear Lily's voice behind me. "That's right. Someday George will be famous for stealing Jamaican music." Lily kisses George's cheek to let him know she's joking.

Lily gives me a nod. I feel my face open up into a smile. "I came!"

"So you did." She eyes me up and down. "Boy, have you changed your clothes or washed up since I last saw you?"

Lily is interrupted by a man before I can answer. "There you are!" He's Tom of Finland handsome. Like something out of a physique pictorial. Chiseled face. Body like a Michelangelo statue. "I need to introduce you to someone."

Lily rolls her eyes. "Archie, if this is another doomed attempt at matchmaking—"

"Career matchmaking." Archie pulls Lily close. "A film producer. You could do costumes for his next film."

"What's the movie?"

Archie laughs. "Darling, I didn't get that far. But he's gorgeous and I'd gladly offer myself up to him if he promises to hire you."

"Archie!" Lily wags a finger at him.

Archie cackles. "What? I'd do it anyway. May as well get something for it."

"First, introductions." Lily puts her arm around me. "This is the boy I told you about." It pleases me to know she's told her friend about me.

Archie introduces himself. Tells me that Lily was thrilled that her menswear pieces were finally being put to use.

I turn to Archie. "How come you never wore them?"

Archie laughs. "She refuses to design for me. She hates my body."

Lily slaps his shoulder playfully. "I just think you work too hard to conform to some masculine ideal, at the expense of your own joy."

"*You* bring me joy, darling friend."

"I can't go out to dinner with you anymore." She turns to me now. "This man thinks raw celery and boiled chicken is a meal."

Archie defends himself. "I have to watch my calories—"

"You already don't drink. Half the calories in the British diet come from the pubs. I'm telling you, the human psyche needs *flavor.*"

Archie laughs. "The boys like me ripped, I like the boys to like me, and trust me, I enjoy boys of *every* flavor."

"That'll be enough of that now." Lily puts a protective arm around me. "We have a young innocent in our midst."

"As if I wasn't thinking far worse at his age." Archie rolls his eyes. "All my teenage thoughts were of boys. I never dreamed I would live in a world where I could be with one. Besides, I've had this body since I was a teenager. I blame the boarding school crew team for my unhealthy obsession with looking healthy." I gaze at Archie curiously. He must come from wealth and privilege. I wonder if his posh parents know where he is. Is he still a son to them? "Now let's go see if we can't get you a better job."

Lily follows Archie to the back of the club. I gaze over at George and Marilyn. They giggle about something or other. George looks at me. "Go have some fun, kid. What are you standing with us for?"

"Oh, I don't know."

"Don't worry, Rusty won't play Petula Clark forever." Marilyn laughs.

George talks as he checks a man's ruffled coat. "The beauty of Rusty is he'll play Bowie, Kraftwerk, Roxy Music, but then he'll throw in something so unexpected, so square, that you can't help but reassess it."

I stroll over to the small dance floor. Throngs of assembled freaks sing along with Petula. *Don't sleep in the subway, darling.* I join the sing-along. *Don't stand in the pouring rain,* we sing. We raise our arms up. We belt the words. We're proud of sleeping in subways. In squats. Wherever we might find a place to rest before another night of dancing. All these queers. Claiming a piece of the city as our own. We'll sleep where we want. Be whoever we want. Look however we want. It's a powerful feeling. Dancing and singing alongside people who have suffered the same rejections.

The song ends. A new one begins. Roxy Music. "The Thrill of It All." Lily and Archie dance in a corner. Archie spins her. I can see the details of Lily's dress in the light. Multicolored patchwork.

Dazzling. The dress is so long that you can barely see her heels. The sleeves even longer. Her lips are a rust color. Her lashes glitter in the light. Like she's layered them in diamond dust. Archie wears nothing but a leather vest and tight denim shorts. A hint of jock-strap. A burst of friendship as they laugh.

I wish Oliver were here. Every smile here is beautiful. But none are his. The song feels like it's about us. *Everywhere I look. I see your face.* Perhaps every song is about us. Every word ever written about us. *Though you've gone. Still I recall. The thrill of it all.*

Lily drags Archie to my side. "So what do you think of the Blitz, kid?" She fixes my hair as she asks the question.

"It's incredible. Like what utopia might look like."

She laughs. "I don't know about that, kid. Needs more melanin. Lots of colorful clothes. Not enough colorful faces."

Archie nods in agreement. "Also strange that it's named after that wretched bombed-out period when people supposedly came together as one."

Lily quickly jumps in. "Which of course they didn't."

"I said *supposedly*. I know true unity is a myth."

Lily sighs. "A beautiful myth, perhaps even a necessary one."

Would Oliver agree? Does he believe humans can ever come together as one?

From his booth, the DJ announces a band is about to play. "They played their first gig over a month ago right here at the Blitz. Give it up for Spandau Ballet!"

Five costumed men take the stage. They wear jumpsuits. Skirts. Plaid. Ruffles. They begin to play jangly music that feels both dark and light at the same time. The lead singer wears an Elizabethan dress. It brings me back to that night when we all attended the masquerade ball decades ago. Who was it who wore an Elizabethan dress that Jack stole from the theater closet? Was it Brendan or Cyril? Some details come back so clearly. Others fade. The lead singer's transportive croon seems to exist in a realm beyond time. His voice feels like the past. His lyrics speak directly to the present. *Oh, look at the strange boy. He finds it hard existing. To cut a long story short, I lost my mind.*

Archie applauds loudly when the band's set ends. "The music is fantastic, but why must they be called Spandau Ballet? It's so depressing."

I ask Archie what the band name means.

Lily's the one who explains. "Supposedly, they got the name from something scribbled on a bathroom stall in Berlin. From what I understand, a Spandau Ballet was a term coined to describe Nazi prisoners jerking about while being hanged at Spandau prison."

"Well, they *were* Nazis. But I still don't love having to think of men being hanged. It's gruesome. No one should be tortured." There's pain in Archie's voice as he says this. A raw vulnerability barely hiding beneath his brawny surface.

"The club is called the Blitz. The band is named after Nazis. I guess this country is still reeling from the ghosts of the world war." Lily sighs. "Of course, this country also takes all the credit for ending the war. As if we Jamaicans didn't provide safe haven for countless Europeans. And the biggest military contingent from the Caribbean."

"I'm sorry I got us onto politics." Archie turns to me. "This place should be a refuge from all that."

Lily takes my hand in hers. "Let's go for curry. I'm starving and I don't want to see these queens get sloppy." It's then that I notice that—unlike the majority of the blitzed crowd—neither Lily nor Archie had anything but water to drink.

We go for curry. Followed by ice cream. Archie pays for dinner. Lily for dessert. It feels like we're a traditional family. Mother. Father. Son. Out for a family meal. We couldn't look more mismatched as any kind of wholesome ideal. Lily with her black skin and riotous fashion. Archie with his bulging muscles and barely there gay uniform.

Me: This strange brown thing that's been here as long as some of the city's historic buildings. This ancient thing that still looks and feels seventeen.

The ice cream disappears. Archie says it's time for him to get to his date for the evening.

"Do you know this one's name?" Lily teases him. Gently. Lovingly.

Archie climbs atop a newspaper rack. Orates like he's onstage. "What's in a name?" My eyes focus on the headline of the paper in the vending machine. *Three Boys Dead. Hunt for Arsonist Continues.* Archie's joy stands in contrast to the bleak news. "That which we call a rosebud by any other name would taste just as sweet."

"You are filthy!" Lily says this with love too.

"Filthy and fabulous." Archie leaps off the stand. Kisses Lily gently on the lips. Pats my head awkwardly.

Lily asks where I'll be sleeping that night when he's gone. I say nothing. She puts her arms around me like I'm the stray cat that I am. "You'll sleep on the couch." She raises a finger. A warning. "But just for one night. After that, you're out."

Back at her place, she fixes the couch up for me. Uses long swaths of soft fabric for sheets. Wraps a pillow in yellow silk. "I'll have you know this is not just any couch. It once belonged to Francis Bacon."

"Did it really?" I touch the couch softly. Like it's in a museum.

"Well, that's what the queen who sold it to Lady Cordelia said, and it's what we've chosen to believe. And if we believe it, then it's true." Her eyes turn to me curiously. "What about Francis?"

"Oh, I think he's a fantastic artist. Don't you?"

"I meant as your name. I've always thought it was a beautiful name. Very soft. Poetic. Like Saint Francis of Assisi, who stood up for the poor."

"I don't know. . . . It feels too much to live up to. I'm not noble or glorious or anything like that. I'm just a wild thing that somehow survives—"

"Bramble!" She blurts the word out decisively. A burst of inspiration.

"What?"

"Well, why not?" She pulls a fluffy blanket from a closet. Throws it onto the couch. She's completed the task of creating a bed for me. "A bramble is wild and prickly, with sharp thorns that could either hurt you or stun you with their beauty."

"That does sound like me." I look at her. "And I like that it feels related to your name. Lily is a flower. Bramble is a vine. We're both plants of summer."

"Hmm." She nods. I wonder if she likes this connection between our names. Or perhaps regrets it. "I'll say good night now. In the morning, you'll need to start telling me what your plans are for making money and finding a place of your own. There's gay squats up and down Brixton now. You can start there. I don't want you sleeping on the street."

"Yes, Mommy." I say the word sarcastically.

"I'm being serious. Gay boys like you are disappearing off the streets. No one knows why. No one cares why."

"You do."

She nods. "Yes, I do." She approaches me menacingly. "And next time you call me Mommie, you will add the word *Dearest*, you hear. Mommie Dearest."

"Um . . . Okay . . ." I feel like I've let her down somehow.

She cackles. Tousles my hair. "It's from the book, kid. *Mommie Dearest.* Written by Joan Crawford's daughter. Oh, it's both a nightmare and a dream of a book. You'll read it before bed." She goes to her bookshelf, which is haphazardly stacked. Everything from James Baldwin to Oscar Wilde, Maya Angelou to—of course—Audre Lorde. The genius who first brought us together. She pulls *Mommie Dearest* out. Throws it to me. I catch it. Notice she's underlined passages. Written notes in the margins like a student.

"Follow me." She leads me to the bathroom, where she hands me an extra toothbrush. Points to the tube of toothpaste. "Now I know I'm a mess, but I do have my pet peeves. You will push the toothpaste from the bottom of the tube. You will put the toilet seat back down at all times, and you will not piss on it. I do not like to sit on piss, is that understood?"

"Yes, Mommie Dearest."

"Now let's get ready for bed, Bram." She calls me Bram naturally. The nickname sticks. "Mommie's tired and has a full day of work tomorrow." She takes the bathroom first. I start the book as she showers. She sings as she engages in her elaborate nighttime ritual of creams. Toners. Powders. A song I don't know. *I've got no time to live this lie. No time to play your silly games.* The smell of lilac and lavender wafts out of the bathroom. Fills the space with femininity.

I skim through the book. The first sentence is just one word. Capitalized. DEAD. A dramatic way to start. I skip the sections that cover things I already know about Joan Crawford. I go straight to the shocking allegations of child abuse. Think back to my father. The chillingly casual way he used violence to control me. I close my eyes. Remember it so clearly.

I will decide what your world is, he said before he struck me with the back of his hand. As if his words didn't sting enough.

I realize something in this moment. Perhaps the reason I failed at romantic love with Oliver is because I was never properly taught how to love. Lily switches to singing a new song. This one I know. Donna Summer's "Could It Be Magic." I have a chance to be loved by her the way I should have been as a kid. I'll be a new person if that happens. A secure person. The kind of person Oliver deserves. Capable of loving and being loved.

"Your turn, boy." Lily emerges from the steaming bathroom. Robe wrapped around her. Towel over her head. Her face looks dewy. Her whole being emanates a floral paradise.

I head to the bathroom quietly. It's too soon to tell her of my dreams for us. I'll call her Mommie Dearest as a joke for now. But soon it won't be a joke. She'll feel what I feel. Come to the same conclusion I have. That she is the mother I need. And I—please let this be true—the child she wants.

BRAM. LONDON. JANUARY TO MARCH. 1980.

We live in temporary and inconsistent cohabitation for a few months. Lily tells me often that she can't very well have me sleep on her couch forever. She asks me to leave. So I do. Then she sees me at the Blitz. Or wandering Covent Garden. And she takes me in again. She hates to see me dirty. She makes me new clothes. Washes my grubby ones for me. I find some kids to tutor in time. I try to give the majority of what I make to her. She refuses to take a cent. Says I'm just a kid. So I hide the money for her in envelopes all over her apartment on the nights I'm lucky enough to sleep there. I hide one under her pillow. One in her jar of oats. One in an Audre Lorde book. I think that's a nice touch.

I refuse to take the money she tries to return. I say she can just spend it on me if it makes her feel better. That's what she does. Buys me new shoes. A beautiful leather journal. She forces me to write in it every day. Says getting your thoughts out of your body is crucial to staying grounded. She invests in a new pillow for me to sleep on when she notices me massaging my neck too often. We watch every movie she owns on VHS countless times. She takes me to the store to select new ones. Each videotape will be a new shared memory. A new set of inside jokes and scenes we'll re-create together.

Her friends often join us for movie screenings. Lily is the only one with a television and a VHS machine. Archie lives in a squat in Brixton. Azalea and Poppy live together a little farther up Lambeth. We love to imitate the voices of the movie stars. We speak in screwball voices. Or like we're in a film noir. We sing and dance like we're in a musical.

We watch *Mahogany* so many times that I learn it by heart. It's Lily's favorite. Poppy's too. Poppy loves Diana Ross the way Lily loves Donna. When Lily tries to kick me out of her apartment, I use the same quote from the movie to change her mind. "Success is nothing without someone you love to share it with."

"But I hate you. You're a nuisance!"

And yet she lets me stay.

And stay.

And stay.

Cordelia Biddlecombe pays us a visit on the afternoon of Valentine's Day. It's the first time she's been to the apartment since I started staying there. Lily is at the sewing machine working on lilac bridesmaids dresses. Asks me to open the door. What I find is a bony blond woman in dazzling Paco Rabanne. Gold. Pleated. Expensive. "Who are you? Where's Lily?"

"I'm here, Lady Cordelia!" Lily doesn't stop working.

Cordelia lets herself in. It is her apartment after all. "Lily, I do wish you'd call me Biddie. We are friends, aren't we?" Cordelia stares at the couch with her thin eyes. Turns to me. "Are you living here?" Turns to Lily. "Is he *living* here? Who is he?"

Lily stops sewing. Rises to face Cordelia. "His name is Bram. He is not living here."

"It appears he is from the looks of it." Cordelia places her hand on the corner of a wall. "The paint is chipped."

Lily takes Cordelia's hands in hers. "You seem worried about something. Is everything all right?"

"I'm not worried." Cordelia's voice trembles.

"The dresses will be ready in time, if that's what you're—"

"I told you I wasn't worried." Cordelia pulls her hands away. Anxiously flattens her hair. "It would be nice to have a couch to sit on, but the couch is occupied by your friend who is *not* my tenant."

"Biddie, you look beautiful today." Lily smiles. I can tell she used Cordelia's nickname to change the mood.

Cordelia smiles. Finally relaxes. "I have a date with a duke. He's taking me to see *Beatlemania* in the West End. Listen . . ." Cordelia looks at me. Back at Lily. "Is it all right if we speak alone?"

Lily cocks her head toward the bedroom. I scram. Close the door. Lily puts on a record. Nina Simone sings about a wild wind. I hold my ear to the door. I can't hear every word. But I can hear enough. Lady Cordelia's father is selling the apartment. Covent Garden has become so seedy. He wants no part of it. It's out of Cordelia's hands. She'll keep employing Lily, of course. They can discuss new terms when Biddie is in more comfortable clothes. It really is out of her bony hands.

Lily calls a meeting to decide what to do. Azalea and Poppy arrive first. Then Archie. I clean the kitchen as they talk. I insist she lets me clean. She wants their advice on where to live. Archie suggests she join his squat.

Lily quickly shuts that down. "I'm not living with a bunch of men."

Azalea says that she and Poppy already live in a cramped one bedroom. Lily is welcome to their couch. But they have no room for her fabrics or a sewing machine.

Archie tries again to convince her to join the squat. "Everyone in the house is a queen. I promise you'll love them."

"I would like to be back in Brixton." Lily's voice is contemplative. "But I can't be living in no squat. Not at my age. And besides, there's two of us now."

"Oh, you mean . . ." Everyone's eyes turn to me. I don't dare look at them. I scrub the sink clean.

"I was thinking that Bram should live with me permanently."

Poppy smiles. "He's very lucky to have you."

"I feel lucky to have him." I can't help but smile when I hear her say this.

Archie puts an arm around Lily. "You're a born caretaker, Lily Summers. No other sponsor could've kept me sober this long."

"Five years." She says this with pride. "Not bad for someone who came into his first meeting looking like death was around the corner."

"I have an idea." Poppy stands up as she speaks. Joins me in the kitchen. "Boy, stop cleaning. I haven't even cooked yet. Clean up when I'm done making you the best meal of your life."

"What's the idea?"

Poppy takes some chicken out of the fridge. Places it under hot water in the sink. "Some of the queers in Brixton have started a housing co-op. The Lambeth Council is, believe it or not, working with them."

Archie pipes in. "I hate it. They're going to destroy the magic of Brixton. All the squats will soon disappear."

Poppy shrugs. "Everything changes. But this could be right for Lily. They're mostly single-family units, but there are some family homes. They want people with ties to the community. That's you, Lily. The whole neighborhood wants you back." Poppy throws the chicken into a pan. Begins to season it.

"I do miss Brixton." Lily stands up. Grabs the pepper from Poppy's hand before she can add too much spice. "You trying to kill us with the pepper, girl." Lily turns to me. "What do you think, kid?"

"I think . . ." I smile so big that I can feel my face expanding. "I think that a house is nothing without someone you love to share it with."

We move in on the first day of March. Thick flakes fall from the sky. London feels like a snow globe. Perfect and fragile. Ideal weather for carrying boxes into our bright new home. Archie, Poppy, and Azalea help unpack along with one more of Lily's friends, an Indian drag queen named Blossom. Lily makes extravagant costumes for Blossom's legendary shows. But today she's dressed in everyday clothes. The kind you wear only at home. Only in front of people you trust enough to see you in baggy sweatpants. We organize the books together. Decide which blanket should go where. Re-create the Donna Summer shrine. Blast the new *Bad Girls* album to make more mundane tasks—putting the plentiful beauty products away and making the beds—seem fun and glamorous. Donna sings, *love will always find you*. Like she really means it. Lily makes plans for the house. We'll get a phone line. Make it a helpline for queer people. We've been gifted a home. We'll need to give back. I tell her I'll sit by that phone as long as she needs me to. I'll help. I'll give. I'll do anything for her. For these walls that will keep us warm and dry. It took me over a hundred years to find a place that feels—finally—like home.

I feel an ache for the old place as the days pass. We were always together because the flat was so cramped. Lily would be working in the same living area I slept in. Always bumping into each other in the bathroom. The new house is bigger. Lily disappears into her workroom for hours. Door closed. Singing as she creates. I'm afraid to disturb her process. We have our own bathrooms. I miss brushing our teeth next to each other. Miss finding her long black hair in the shower. This new place feels like home. It also feels empty with just the two of us. Could use more life in it. Barely anyone even calls the queer helpline we've set up. Not that anyone would know about it. We put a sign on our front window: *Queer Helpline. You're Not Alone. Call between 5 and 7. Weekdays Only.* We distribute some leaflets around town. I spend lonely hours alone by the phone. Waiting for it to ring. All I get is cranks. Groups of boys huddled by the receiver together. They call me a sod. Then laugh. Call me a tosser. Laugh some more.

One slurring boy takes it further than the rest. Doesn't hang up after he and his friends get their laughs. "You a pillow biter, then?"

I decide to play along. To try to get the last laugh this time. "There's other things I'd rather bite. Like your head off."

"Which head?" Hysterical laughter from his end of the line. He must have at least four friends listening in. "Did the good old MP bugger you too? Tell us the truth. Me nan's from his district. She don't deserve to be represented by a sodomite."

"She doesn't deserve a piece of shit grandson either. Such is life, my friend." His friends clap in approval of my comeback. I know their kind of boys. They love nothing more than a fight.

He spits out one more *bugger* before hanging up.

I get my first genuine caller a week into March. Not an asshole trying to look cool for his friends. An actual human being in need of help.

"Hello." Azalea gave us a few hours of advice on how to talk to callers. She is a nurse after all. A professional giver of care. She told us to ask gentle questions. Open questions. To listen actively. Never judge. Clarify by summarizing what they said. Ask if they're thinking of harming themselves. Call for professional help if we suspect a caller is at risk of suicide. "Hello, is anyone there?"

Deep sighs on the other end. Not the heavy breathing of a prank caller. The desperate exhalations of a person in need.

"Hello, this is the queer helpline. May I help you?"

Finally: "Yeah. Yeah, I'm here." Her voice is weary.

"My name is Bram. What's yours?" No response. Azalea told us to open up. To make them feel they're not alone. "I'm gay. Hasn't been too easy for me. How about you?"

"I'm not gay. I'm a girl."

"There are gay girls out there. Plenty of them."

"Black butch girls like me?" Her tone dares me to contradict her. "Haven't met one yet. I don't fit in anywhere. Don't have no one. Don't even go to school no more. They put me in an educationally subnormal school. I could teach the teachers. Every other kid in that school was Black. What does *subnormal* even mean?"

"Apparently, it means Black."

She chortles. "No, really though."

"I don't know exactly what it means, but it sounds a lot more fun than being normal."

That gets a real, honest-to-goodness laugh. I feel my chest rise with pride. For giving her a tiny moment of joy. I remember something Lily said to me. I think maybe it might help her too. "Don't apologize for being unique."

"I didn't. Apologize."

"No, you're right. You didn't." I'm afraid I'm losing her. "Do you have a place to sleep?"

No answer.

"Are you considering harming yourself or . . ." I can't even say the words. Azalea told us to ask about suicide. But she didn't say when to ask. Have I rushed things? Is that what I do? I did it with Oliver. Jumped right into loving him. Did it with Lily too. Latched on to her and haven't let go.

"No. I swear." Her voice chokes up a little. "Not even after my mum died. I want to be here. I just want here to be somewhere different, yeah?"

"Yeah." I try to erase any judgment from my voice. Speak from pure empathy. "I'm sorry about your mother. How did she . . ." Stupid question. I don't finish asking it. Why would she want to relive something so awful?

"Officially, cancer. Unofficially, murder." She huffs angrily. "Every doctor who saw her told her she just needed to change her diet. Said she was having stomachaches because she ate rich foods and didn't get enough sleep. By the time someone took her seriously, it had spread all over her body."

"I'm so sorry."

"Yeah." I think she's crying. "You didn't kill her though, yeah?"

"Yeah." I think this is the right time to ask: "What's your name?"

A long pause. "Maud. No last name. Don't want that man's name."

"I'm sorry. I don't use my father's last name either." All the pain of being his son comes rushing back to me.

"I'm sorry too."

"You live with him?"

"Not any longer. Only reason I didn't leave sooner is for her. Mum wasn't strong like I am. She let other people walk all over her. I'll never be like that."

I want to reach through the receiver. Give her a hug. Tell her I understand. At least I think I do. "Are you in London? You could come by the house. Brixton is full of all kinds of lesbians. The Rebel Dykes are just down the street. You'll see."

"Not sure I'm a rebel dyke." She chortles again. A half laugh that charms me. "They sound cool though."

"You don't have to be anything or anyone. Except yourself. Will you remember the address? It's on Chaucer Street." I give her the address. "*Flee from the crowd, and dwell with truthfulness.*"

"Sorry?"

"No, I'm sorry. That was from a Chaucer poem."

"I don't do poetry. I'm educationally subnormal, remember?" She giggles. She sounds like the kid she probably is. "But if I were in a proper classroom, I'd say it sounds like what Chaucer was saying there is *fuck what other people think and be yourself.*"

"Exactly." I can hear Lily dancing on the second story. Her steps like a drumbeat. I can faintly hear the song she plays. Louisa Marks. "6 Sixth Street." *Tell me, tell me, tell me, baby, tell me why?* "Maud, are you all right tonight?"

"Yeah, I'm good."

"You're not alone?" Azalea told us these were three very important words. But she told us to say it as a statement of fact. I just posed it as a question. I'm afraid I messed up. I say it again. With complete sincerity. With utter belief that these three words will always be true: "We're not alone."

"Yeah, thanks. I'll come by. Maybe."

"You can also call again. Between the hours of five and seven every weekday evening."

"I know. I'm holding your leaflet right now."

"Maud, you're—"

She hangs up before I can tell her she's not alone again.

It's on the tenth of March that the idea hits me. Two things happen that morning.

The first: Lily plays Donna's *A Love Trilogy* album while we make soft-boiled eggs with slices of toast for breakfast. "Could It Be Magic" fills the house. Lily's favorite song of all time. I feel Oliver's presence in the room.

Spirits move me, whirling like a cyclone in my mind.

I feel that in my core. He's been the cyclone in my mind for over fifty years now. Then she sings the chorus.

Could this be a magic at last?

The question feels like a dare. Like Donna Summer herself is asking me if I'm ready to finally have the magical life I've always dreamed of.

Another thing happens. Poppy barges into the house just as we're finishing up breakfast. Asks if Lily has heard the news. Poppy says that the BBC is going to re-air *A Change of Sex*. More than that. They'll be airing two new chapters about Julia's gender transition.

The news isn't enough to stop Lily from sewing. "That's great, or maybe it's not."

"It's one of us on the telly. No one's afraid of the people they see on the telly."

Lily shrugs. "I see Thatcher on the telly, and I'm terrified of the woman."

Poppy cackles at that.

Lily does a chilling Iron Lady impression. "*People are really rather afraid that this country might be swamped by people with a different culture.*"

"She really said that, didn't she?" Poppy shakes her head in disgust. "Okay, Thatcher is evil, but at least now we have a party that's truly on our side."

"Are they?"

"They say so, at least. I think maybe things are changing, finally."

"Finally maybe."

And then Poppy says the words that send chills through me: "I think this is our time, Lily."

I don't hear what Lily says next. My mind turns into a haze when Poppy says that this is our time.

Isn't that what I promised Oliver I'd wait for? *Our time*. An age when we could love freely and openly. Without fear or shame. Isn't this that time? I have a real home. A beloved mother. I can dress how I want in the streets. I can dance alongside other freaks and queers at night. This is it. A moment like this may never come again.

I knock on Lily's workroom door late that night. She tells me to come in. I find her frustrated. Unable to get the dress she's working on just right. She's a perfectionist. Even when she's making dresses for people she hates. This one is for some society ball.

"Can I ask you something?" I hear the shake in my voice.

She takes her hands off the sewing machine. Waves me over. I pull a chair next to her. "What's going on, kid?"

"There's someone I once . . . well, I know we said we'd never discuss our pasts again, but I think that's because our pasts are painful, right?" She waits for me to say more. "But there's one part of my past that's beautiful."

"You've been in love?"

I nod. "He doesn't live here though. But I was thinking . . ." I bite my lower lip. I can never turn back once I ask. "Well . . . Now that we have this big place, maybe he could visit for a holiday. Meet you. Maybe I could see him again and know if what we once had is still real."

"Where does he live?"

I can't bring myself to say he's in Buenos Aires. It seems too absurd. She'll wonder how and why he ended up there if she meets him. There will be too many questions. I tell myself it's not a lie to speak of the Oliver I knew. Not the one who leaves me cryptic classified ads. "Boston. I was visiting the city with a family I was a tutor for, and we met there. It didn't last long, but it meant more to me than any relationship I've had." A beat. "Until you."

"Boston's not very close, but if he makes the trip, he's welcome here for a holiday." She smiles. "What took you so long to tell me about him?"

"I don't know." Of course I know. I'm afraid I'll say something that might reveal the truth. "What about you, Lily? Have you ever been in love?"

She nods. "Only once, sweetie." She shakes her head. "But it wasn't a good love. There's good love, the kind that lets you shine in its glow. And there's destructive love that makes you less of who you are. That pushes you into a place of fear. I did love him, but he was destructive."

"Did he—" I don't want to ask the question.

"He never laid a hand on me." She knew precisely what I was

going to ask. "He was more destructive to himself than anyone else. And I suppose he brought me down with him. Lots of drinking. Eventually, the drugs killed him. Which saved me, I suppose. Nothing like burying the man you watched overdose to shock you into sobriety."

"I'm so sorry."

She pushes my chin up. "No boo-hoo backstories, remember?"

"Yeah, but still . . ."

I realize something about Lily. She sees all that's wrong with the world. Doesn't ignore it. But she refuses to let the awfulness define her. I think it's her knowledge of the brutality around us that makes her work so hard to provide light.

I don't leave a classified ad for Oliver right away. I decide to wait two more weeks. The first day of spring feels like a symbolic day to summon him. That's what this feels like. A summoning of the past into what is now my present. I race out the door to place an ad in the newspaper.

"Where you going, Bram?" Lily calls to me from the living room. She's sitting on the floor. Cutting fabric rolls into manageable pieces. "Come here."

I enter sheepishly. "I—" I've already gotten her permission to invite Oliver for a "holiday." But telling her about our covert way of communicating with each other through newspapers would invite too many questions.

"Happy New Year." She looks up from her fabrics. A warm smile on her face.

"What's that?"

"It's your new year, isn't it? Nowruz. First day of spring."

"That's right. It is." It's been so long since I've been around any of my own people. So long since I've celebrated Nowruz properly. The last time must have been before my father sent me off to London for boarding school. Lifetimes ago.

"Nowruz means new day, right?" She knows she's right. She's done her research. "Thought this could be a new day for us too. You didn't have plans, did you?"

"I— No, not really. Where are we going? Out for kabobs?"

"Nothing says new day like kabob." She laughs. "You'll see."

What I see soon enough is this: Lily leading me to the South Bank. Down to the Thames. Lily tells me she'd like to be cremated and scattered into the river someday.

"I don't like thinking about you dying."

"Then don't." She takes my hand. "Think about me floating for eternity. I love water. I'll be happy here."

"Is it because it reminds you of Jamaica?"

"You think this filthy river reminds me of Jamaica?" She puts a hand in the dirty water. "You never had a mother, did you?"

I shake my head.

"I was thinking. What if I baptize you here? With the water from this city we call home."

"Baptize me?" I don't think of Lily as particularly religious.

"Maybe it's a silly idea. I just thought it would mean something. Like a wedding symbolizes a union. This can too. My commitment to you. To be a mother to you."

"And mine. To be a son to you." I smile. "It's not a silly idea. It's a beautiful one."

She nods. Takes my hands in hers. "In the name of Donna Summer, Grace Jones, and Oscar Wilde, I now baptize you as my son."

I don't know why she chose Oscar Wilde of all people. Perhaps, like Donna and Grace, she thinks of him as some kind of patron saint.

She bends down. Cups some water into her right hand. Sprinkles it onto my face with her left. The filthy water feels like it cleanses me. I do feel reborn as she declares me: "Bram Summers of the Brixton Summers."

"I love you, Lily."

She holds me tight. "I love you too."

Have I told her I've loved her before? I'm not sure. One doesn't track those three words with a new mother as one does with a new lover. And yet they're just as meaningful. There are so many ways to love.

I separate from Lily by the Waterloo Tube station. We hug tightly outside a restaurant with an obscenely large portrait of Queen Elizabeth in its window. The crown of jewels atop her head glimmers behind the glass. Next to her face are brightly colored words. *Breakfast. Dinner. Teas. Sweets.* A young girl in tattered clothes stops outside. Stares at the queen's image. Is she inspired by the queen's opulence? Or perhaps shamed? Likely both.

I take the Tube to the newspaper office to place the ad. I've never felt so sure it's the right day. I have something concrete to offer Oliver now. A home. A mother. A life. I imagine him somewhere in Buenos Aires. Looking just as he looked when I left him. Same soft face. Locks of brown hair. Blue eyes glowing orange as he reads my message. Addressed to Tchaikovsky from Walt Whitman. He heads straight to a travel agency. Asks for options on how to get to London. He doesn't think through the decision. Doesn't need to. He's forgiven me. He's ready for our life together to finally begin.

I see a tattoo parlor in Soho on my way home. Displays of elaborate designs. Dragons. Chinese characters. Arabic scripture.

Astrological symbols. I go inside. I don't know why exactly. I suppose it feels right. To mark myself for him. I can't very well tattoo his name on my chest though. Not when he's likely changed it dozens of times like me. I tell the tattoo artist I want a simple oval shape on my heart.

"Like an egg?" He raises an eyebrow.

"Like a capital O."

An O. For him. And for life. Which is a circle, after all. Always bringing us back. Familiar emotions. Frustrations that feel like old friends. A love that won't let go of our hearts.

NEW YORK TIMES CLASSIFIED ADS

MARCH 20, 1980

MY DEAR TCHAIKOVSKY,

It is the first spring of a new decade and the world is in bloom at last. I have finally found the time and place we have been waiting for. If you are still open to fulfilling your promise, meet me at the *Young Lovers* statue in Festival Gardens in exactly one month, on the 20th day of April, 1980, at noon sharp and we can discuss the details. I hope you understand that I would never summon you were I not certain this is our time.

YOUR DEVOTED WALT WHITMAN

OLIVER. LONDON. APRIL. 1980.

The young lovers, like the boy who transformed me, are frozen in time. The bronze they're sculpted from makes them appear ageless, genderless. Love, in its purest form, must be beyond age, time, gender, mustn't it? I wish I had the answers. Seventy-seven years on this planet and I understand less than I used to about life's biggest questions. Perhaps knowledge isn't accrued over time. Sometimes I wonder if we're smartest when we're born. When we're nothing but instinct. The young lovers, clutching each other tightly, don't look like they knew much, other than how to love.

Is that all there is to learn in the end? Life's one, only, and hardest lesson.

Bright yellow daffodils grow from the ground around the young lovers. A hint of spring sunshine gives them a technicolor sheen. The sun also lights Shams, or whatever he calls himself now, like a movie star. His brown skin glows with youth.

Are we young? Or old? I don't know how to answer that question.

Do I love him? Hate him? No answer for that one either.

If I still loved him unconditionally and passionately, wouldn't I run into his arms like he wants me to as he glances back at the

St. Paul's cathedral clock? Then again, I'm here, aren't I? I came, didn't I? I couldn't stay away.

The minute hand of the cathedral clock ticks forward: 12:01. I pull the straps of my backpack tighter. Make sure my synthesizer keyboard is safely on my back. It's lighter than the accordion I relied on for decades. Playing music in Berlin U-Bahn stations. On the Miami Beach boardwalk. In the medina of Marrakech. Survival through music. Living off whatever money people threw into my hat. Francs and liras and dirhams. Exchanging currencies each time I escaped a farm, a city, a country. Exchanging my identity too. Being everyone and therefore no one. Feeling empty. Sometimes, not getting out of bed for days, weeks, months if I had enough food to survive. Then again, I always survive.

12:02. He taps his feet anxiously on the pavement. Leans over when no one's looking and picks a single daffodil. Holds it close to his heart and whispers something to himself. A silent prayer, no doubt. That I'll show up. That we'll live happily ever after like he thought we would when he made me immortal.

There is another version of this moment. A fantasy as grand as a Tchaikovsky concerto. In this fiction, I do run into his open embrace. We clutch each other like the bronze young lovers. Declare our eternal love for each other. Live our endless days inseparably, dancing and laughing and kissing. That version would be the end of something. This is only the beginning.

12:03. His hair is different. Long on one side. Chopped short on the other. What's left of it is dyed mauve. His tight, torn jeans reveal the smooth skin of his knees. He wears a blazer with large words on the back. *The National Front Is an Affront*. He's the same person I knew sixty years ago. He's also completely different.

The cathedral clock keeps moving forward, one minute at a time. He glances at it. Looks around at every face, wondering if it's me. I keep myself safely hidden behind a tree. The cherry blossoms are in bloom. Mother always loved them more than any other flower. She would take me to the Esplanade to see them every spring. We would stare out at the Charles River as we bathed in the mesmerizing explosion of pink. The last time she took me was just before that fateful spring day when I met Shams. On that day she said to me, *What makes the cherry blossoms so special is how ephemeral they are. They last such a short time.*

I'm ashamed to say that I felt a pang of hurt in that moment. In my mind, I was wondering whether Mother appreciated Father and Liam more than me because they too lasted a short time in her life. Father died so young. Liam chose Yale instead of a closer university. My plan was to stay by her side forever.

I wouldn't be a cherry blossom. I would be the perennial flower that would never go away. Until I had to. I left her and never spoke to her again. No matter how desperately I wanted to call and hear her voice.

"OLIVER!" Shams yells out my name. He sounds like Marlon Brando yelling out for Stella in *A Streetcar Named Desire*. "Oliver, are you out there? Oliver!" I was in Vienna when that movie came out. Saw it in a theater full of enthralled Austrians. I stayed in Vienna as long as I could, among people who cared for classical music as I do.

"OLIVER!" he roars.

"Oliver?" he asks.

"Oliver," he finally sighs.

The clock strikes one. We've both been standing in the same

spot for an hour. Finally, he gives up. Walks away. Throws the daffodil he had picked for me into a puddle of muddy water. I rush to the puddle when he's out of sight. Fish the bright flower out. Hold it in my palm as I clandestinely follow him.

The city streets are packed. It's Sunday and the clouds are moving south. So are we. He doesn't look back as he crosses Blackfriars Bridge. The water of the Thames looks murky. Like there are secrets buried at the bottom of the river. I hate secrets. A secret destroys its guardian, always. Pulls him away from those he loves. Secrets isolate.

I didn't plan on following him like this. I thought seeing him again would give me the certainty I needed. To be with him or not to be with him, that is the question. Now here I am, doing neither. Living in the indecision.

But I do have a plan. I'll observe him in his new habitat. Try to understand why he feels this is our time. I'll deduce how I feel about this city independent of him. I've been free of him for sixty years. Free and lonely. Free and yet chained to him by the fate only we share. What's a little more time to figure out how I feel when all we have is time?

The winter of discontent I read about in the papers is officially over, but the smell of garbage still fills the city. Trash is everywhere. Heaps of it. A couple of rats scurry in and out of a trash bag. I watch as a fat rat shares its bounty with a feebler rat. I almost stop following Shams to watch the rats a little longer. I had no idea rats had empathy for other rats. All these years, and still I have moments of revelation. Perhaps there's more empathy in the world than I thought.

The smells change as Shams approaches the Brixton Tube

station and turns onto Railton Road. The warm smell of food fills the air. Spices from faraway islands, brought to London because of economic necessity.

A handsome adolescent approaches me. Wavy brown hair. Bright blue eyes. The Oxford shirt he wears is about three sizes too big, his jeans a size or two too small. "You lost?" he asks.

"I— No, sorry—" Shams turns another corner. I need to keep him in my sights.

"Here, this'll help." The guy hands me a copy of *Gay News*. "We're working on a new paper. We're calling it Gay Noise. Get it? *Gay News. Gay Noise.*"

"I get it, yeah." I see a bookshop on the corner Shams turned on. I walk toward it.

The paper boy follows me. "Not implying it's me starting it. I'm the errand boy. The guys in my squat are the heroes. We're one of the last squats standing. You're American, aren't you? I'm good with accents. I'm from Sheffield. Up north."

I ignore my overeager new friend as I search for Shams. He's gone. Disappeared on Chaucer Road. It's almost too poetic. Shams and his love for poetry. He infected me with it. I must've read hundreds of thousands of poems by now. Neruda and Rumi and Emily Dickinson. And yes, Chaucer. He who said, *So short our lives, so hard the lessons.* Well, he was half right in my case. If a short life is full of hard lessons, what is the longest life full of?

"If you're new to the city, you can peek through the London section of this. Lots of great spots. If you're sticking around Brixton, just avoid the George at all costs."

"The George?" I ask.

"Racist pub. They banned gays a few years ago. One of my friends was beat up in there earlier this year."

"I'm sorry," I say.

"That's why I dream of travel. There must be somewhere on this planet where we can be truly free without fear, right?" He pulls a copy of the *Spartacus Gay Guide* from his bag, and hands it to me. On the cover is a photo of four macho white men in front of an eighteenth-birthday cake. A birthday I'll never reach. Eternally stuck at seventeen. "Sometimes, I flip through the pages and dream of going to some gay beach in Spain, or to a disco in New York. But look who I'm talking to. You been to New York?"

I flip through the pages of the gay travel guide and feel shocked to find not just guides to gay bars and gay-friendly hotels in cities all over the world but also a "*Paedophile Vacations Holiday Help Portfolio,*" for "*boy-lovers.*" It makes me feel sick. Thinking that this book lumps me in with men booking their travels based on a country's age of consent. I thrust the book back into his hands too aggressively. "I'm sorry, I'm meeting a friend," I say. "I'll need to say goodbye now."

"Right." It's not until I let him down that I see his loneliness. That's why he wouldn't let me go. The poor guy is desperate for love, company, belonging. I wonder why he's living in a squat. What kind of home did he escape from? He shuffles away.

I enter the bookshop, wondering if Shams is inside. It would be just like him to drown his sorrows in the poetry section of some charming local bookshop.

"Can I help you?" I look up and see a young butch standing in front of me. She has dark skin and a short Afro. She wears a long-knit sweater that travels down below her knees. The pattern is captivating. Colors blend into each other, like she's wearing an Impressionist painting.

"Oh yes, I . . . Do you have a poetry section?" I ask.

She nods. "We do, but it'll be Black poets only. This is a Black bookshop, yeah?" She looks at me hard, like she's trying to see if this scares me. "You did know that, right?"

I didn't know that. But how wonderful that a Black bookshop exists. A gay newspaper. A Black bookshop. All unimaginable when Shams and I met. Perhaps someday I'll be accepted too, as this strange immortal creature I am now.

I stupidly recite a poem aloud to her. *"I know you've heard the boogie-woogie rumble of a dream deferred."*

She laughs with the warmth of someone who is letting down their guard. Whereas the squatter emitted desperation, she glows with contentment. "All right then, the white boy from America knows his Langston Hughes. But do you know Phillis Wheatley, Gwendolyn Brooks, Claude McKay?"

"Yes, yes, no," I say as I follow her to the poetry section.

She recites a poem as she pulls a book out for me. *"If we must die, O let us nobly die. So that our precious blood may not be shed in vain. Then even the monsters we defy shall be constrained to honor us."* She lets the powerful words linger a moment. "He wrote it in response to the Red Summer." Seeing the blankness on my face, she explains, "Whites in America attacked Blacks in riots all over the country. In dozens of cities. Killed hundreds."

"When was this?" I ask.

"1919." She catches the alarm in my eyes. "Long time ago, yeah?"

"Yeah." It was the year before I met Shams. It was the year Liam left us for Yale. There were people being attacked all over America because of their skin color and I had no idea. I read the papers, didn't I? Were these atrocities unreported? Or did I skip over it because it didn't immediately concern me? I think of Edna, of her fight for people's rights. I've fought for nothing. Not even for love. I feel suddenly sick.

She seems to notice the ache inside me and puts a hand on my shoulder. "I'm Maud," she says.

"I'm . . . Oliver?" I say it hesitantly. It's been so long since I've used my real name. But now, with Mother gone, Liam gone, Brendan gone, Edna gone, who's left to suspect it's really me?

"You sound unsure about that." She laughs.

"No, no, I'm sure. I'm Oliver. I've tried to be other people, but that's who I am." I feel my chest rise with pride.

She nods. "We all try to be someone else before we learn to be ourselves. Well, at least all us queers."

"I'll take the book." She walks me to the counter and rings me up. I hand her the pounds I got at the airport currency exchange when I landed with a fake passport. I've gotten very good at obtaining false documents. "How long's this shop been here? It's so cool."

She puts the book in a bag and hands it to me. "A few years, I think. I just started here a few months ago. There was another bookshop here before. Unity. First Black bookshop in Brixton."

"It closed?"

She lowers her gaze. "Blew up because of a racist firebomb in the letterbox."

"Oh." I don't want to leave without saying something more. "It wasn't the firebomb that was racist, was it? It was the asshole who put it there."

She nods. "Indeed." She offers me a smile as she looks up at me again. She flinches in shock. "Your eyes," she exclaims with a gasp.

"I know, sorry. It's a genetic thing. My mother was convinced our family is part feline." This is the lie I've told people who ask for decades. *A family trait. Part feline.* I've repeated those words so many times that they've lost all meaning.

"I think I might be living with someone you're related to, then," she declares.

"Sorry?"

"My brother Bram has the exact same thing. His eyes glow when you look at them too long."

"Your brother?" I echo. And then, in a hush, "Bram?"

She nods. "We live just down the street on Chaucer. I've only been there two weeks, but it's home. When you know, you know. You know?" She sees another customer come in. "See you around."

She approaches the new customer, who says, "Hello, Sister, could I leave some flyers in the shop for an upcoming rally?"

Maud takes the flyers. "Of course, Brother. These sus laws have got to go."

I wander down Chaucer Street, searching for the house he lives in. Bram. Leave it to him to choose a name that stands out. That makes him sound like the almost-vampire he is. He always was dramatic. I peek into every window until finally I find him. On the second floor of a run-down house. He's crying. No, bawling. He holds his head in his hands. I did this to him.

He weeps until a woman enters. Holds him. I imagine she's asking him what's wrong. He buries his head in her bosom. Cries into her sweater. She consoles him. Runs a gentle hand through his strange new hair. I wonder if she knows why he's so upset. He couldn't possibly have told her about me, could he? Unless, perhaps, he made her immortal too. With his last page from the manuscript.

When the tears have dried, the woman rushes out and comes back with a bag of old clothes and fabrics. She and Bram—it'll take some getting used to calling him by this name—throw on new clothes. Wrap fabrics around each other. Bram puts on a baggy suit. A cowboy hat. A leather vest.

Someone else enters. A man in his thirties. He's unbearably handsome. He wears a tight white T-shirt and short denim shorts. They laugh now. Uproariously. Happily.

Soon, Maud comes in too. She jumps on the bed and offers them a thumbs-up or thumbs-down as they all change clothes. How I wish I could hear what they're saying. Maud referred to Bram as her brother. Are they some kind of family? Then again, she also referred to the customer after me as Brother. Perhaps it's just how she sees people. As part of her extended family. When you really think about it, we are all family, aren't we? All descendants of the same mysterious path to existence. I despise how my loneliness has turned my thoughts toward philosophical spirals.

I want to stop spiraling. To stop somewhere. To have a life. One life. Not one hundred lives.

They all head downstairs from the bedroom to the kitchen, where Bram and Maud set an eight-person table in the living area. More people arrive. Three women. One man. One of the women arrives cradling three large casseroles. They eat together. I scurry toward the house. Hide just under the open window near them, next to a sign advertising some sort of queer helpline. I quickly memorize the number. I'm close enough now to hear some of what they say, even if I don't always know who's saying it.

"The party is Tuesday night. It's Sunday and you lot are already planning your outfits." That's Maud. I recognize her voice.

"Bite your tongue, child. I didn't start planning our outfits today. I started on Wednesday morning."

"Steve won't let you in if you don't look the part." That's Bram. His voice sounds . . . lighter. "Can't wear the same thing twice. Can't look boring."

"Sounds like exclusionary bullshit to me." Maud again.

"It's not." Bram again. "It's fun. Lily takes other people's trash and transforms it into a *look*. That's magic."

Maud says, "She spends more time creating your looks than you do wearing them. Seems like a waste of time."

"But creativity is God's greatest gift to humanity. It's never a waste of time." This must be the woman named Lily.

Bram adds, "Besides, Steve keeps the people who don't dress the part out to keep us safe. To create a space where freaks like us can feel at home."

"I feel at home right here," Maud says.

"But one home isn't enough, is it?" This is one of the women. I'm not sure which one. "When my family moved here, they were so scared of racist violence that they wouldn't let me leave our council flat. I went to school and came home. Which made my home feel like a prison. I needed a home away from home, and a home away from my home away from home."

"It's true," Bram says. His voice gets closer. He's standing by the window. Looking out. Completely unaware that I'm crouched and breathless underneath the windowsill. A spy in his house of love. "But some people don't even have one home. They're cursed to wander the world alone."

I roll my eyes up. I can see him leaning forward. If he were to look down, he would see me. Perhaps he'd be thrilled. Welcome me in. Perhaps he would hate me for eavesdropping. But he doesn't look down. Instead, he closes the window. Shuts me out. But that's all right. I know exactly where to continue my exploration of his new life. I'll observe him until I've made a decision.

I play my synthesizer at run-down Tube stations with fancy names. Park Royal. Marylebone. Marble Arch. When the police chase me out of the Queensway station, I run fast enough to evade them, the coins I've gathered jangling in my pocket.

On Monday evening, I enter a red telephone box. There's trash inside. I kick it to the corner of the booth. I get the sense someone slept here last night. Better than sleeping in the rain. I push a button marked *A*. Place some coins in.

I dial the queer helpline. His voice comes from the other side. The voice I've tried to escape for decades. The voice I've longed to hear for decades.

"Hello, this is the queer helpline. My name is Bram. How may I help you?"

I freeze, realizing he may recognize my voice, even after all these years. I hide any trace of the Oliver he knew behind a heavy Irish accent. I spent years in Belfast, thinking perhaps I'd feel at home there, in the land of my ancestors. "Hello" is all I say at first.

"I'm gay and I'm here to help if you are too," he announces calmly.

"Gay as in homosexual?" I ask, confident he can't identify me with the accent. "Or as in happy?"

"A little of both," he says. Then, "No, sorry, I'm a hundred percent homosexual. Perhaps fifty percent happy."

"Better than most."

"You're probably right." He sighs. "I should feel lucky. I do feel lucky."

"It's sad, isn't it?" I ask. "That the vast majority of the world is so deeply unhappy."

His voice rises a little. "It's not sad. It's enraging. We made it this way. Humans. We have all the tools for happiness. We could take care of each other. Provide for each other. Instead, we destroy each other. For what?"

"Greed," I say. "To have more than others."

"Yes, greed," he echoes. "I've been guilty of greed."

"Is that why you're volunteering for the helpline?" I ask. "To ease the guilt?"

He takes a moment. "I'm supposed to be asking the questions," he says quietly.

I hear a click. Place another coin in. Outside, an impatient woman taps her foot on the pavement. Rushes me with her urgent blue eyes.

"I wasn't greedy for money," he explains, filling the silence. "Just for love. I did something impulsive and terrible because I thought it would bring me the love I craved. The kind that lasts forever."

I gulp down hard. I feel I've taken this far enough, or perhaps too far. And yet, I need to hear this. I must know if he understands what he did. How he might explain it to a stranger. Which is what I am to him from the other end of the line. "So you never found it, then? Love that lasts forever."

"No," he mumbles. "And perhaps, yes. Not romantic love. I only experienced that once, and I'm afraid I bungled it forever. But . . ."

"But?" I ask as he collects his thoughts.

Finally, he speaks, reverently. "Well . . . I once believed romantic love was our only chance at exaltation. Now I think . . . No, I know—that love takes different forms, and they're all equally transcendent. Romantic, yes. But platonic too. Familial. Parental. Communal. Artistic. And of course, the most important love of all . . ."

"Which would be . . ."

"Loving ourselves, I suppose."

"So, you love yourself?" I ask.

"I think so." He seems surprised by his answer. Like he's still figuring out if he's worthy of love.

"You think, or are you sure?" I murmur.

"It's hard to love yourself," he declares with ease. "But I think so."

"So you forgive yourself, then?" I ask.

"Forgive myself?"

"For your greed."

"Oh." Complete silence. He's not breathing. Finally, "I think I do. Do you love yourself?"

The woman outside knocks on the glass of the telephone box. I shrug sheepishly, letting her know I won't be leaving anytime soon.

"You did call the helpline," he says. "If you're feeling unloved, I'm here to help. You're. Not. Alone." He speaks those last three words carefully. Giving each word emphasis.

"I've felt alone for a very long time." I feel a lump in my throat. I wish I were saying this to him directly. As myself.

"I'm sorry." There's sincerity in his voice. "Are you in London? There's an incredible gay community here."

"Yes," I say. "But this isn't home. There's no one here who could replace my mother."

"She's in Ireland?" he asks. Now I'm certain he doesn't recognize my voice. If he did, he would know it was Mother I'm speaking of. "Did she kick you out of the house when she found out? Too many kids are on the streets because their families won't accept them. It's disgusting."

"No, she was wonderful." I close my eyes. Imagine Mother in the kitchen. By the Charles. In Provincetown. At the piano. Her hands, wrinkled from working for me. Her eyes, always full of love for me. Her smile, always ready to warm me. She lived for me and I deserted her. "She was warm. She was my best friend." I laugh. "I sound like such a queen, don't I? A mother for a best friend."

"Nothing wrong with being a queen," he snaps. "Unless you use the throne to colonize and oppress."

I laugh. Gently at first. And then uproariously. I feel, once again, that I could talk to him forever. Like we used to on our walks. Just us and a tin of Oreo cookies. It scares me. That even here, in a new time, in a new country, I can still talk to him so naturally.

"I'm Bram," he says. "What's your name?"

"I— It's—Liam." It's the first name I could think of. I feel so stupid. Giving him my brother's name.

"Liam?" he asks, his voice haunting the past.

I suddenly panic. I can't do this anymore. I'm afraid I'll slip up. And I've heard enough, haven't I? He's happy. He's loved. He forgives himself. Knows what he did was wrong. Isn't that all I need to know?

"I—I have to go, I'm sorry." I'm so anxious that I hear the accent disappear.

"Wait!" he says.

But I hang up. Catch my breath in the telephone box as the woman outside pounds on the glass.

I leave the box. She enters. She presses the *B* button and fetches the coins from my remaining time. Now I'm the one pounding on the door. "Hey, that's my change," I yell.

"Not anymore, kid." She puts my money into the box and makes a call.

I walk away. I use what money I've made to scour vintage clothing shops for clothes that might gain me admission to this club. I remember reading about the army surplus store where the Beatles found the costumes for the cover of *Sgt. Pepper's Lonely Hearts Club Band*. Laurence Corner Army Surplus, near the Warren Street station.

I sing a song from that album at the Warren Street Tube station for good luck. *Will you still need me, will you still feed me, when I'm sixty-four?* An elderly couple in ratty coats dances as I play. Their dance is precisely choreographed. I imagine it's their wedding dance. Perhaps they return to those steps when they need to be reminded of what young love felt like.

They tip me generously. Enough that when I enter Laurence Corner, I go straight to one of the more expensive items on display, a centuries-old red British Army jacket. I throw it on. It's too snug and has holes in it. It's perfect. I buy it. I ask if they have a pair of scissors. I use them to cut the holes into hearts. I turn a symbol of war into a symbol of love.

I search the streets for the one thing I'll need most. I finally find it on a mannequin in a shop called R. Soles. A Venetian masquerade mask. White, red, and gold. I enter and ask how much it is.

"The mask isn't for sale," the shopgirl says. "Sorry."

"I need it," I plead. "How much to make you change your mind?"

She glances behind her, no doubt checking for a manager. "A fiver should do."

I count the coins I have left. Fifty-pence coins, ten-pence coins. I can see she regrets our deal. She expected a crisp bill, not this pile of tips received for playing in Tube stations. "That's five," I say.

She looks behind her again. Then she pulls the masquerade mask off the display mannequin and hands it to me. "It's papier-mâché. Be careful with it. You going to a ball?"

"Sort of," I say. Then, "Thanks."

I sleep on the Tube. Lay my head on the bag that contains my few belongings in it. My synthesizer. My new poetry book. My just-purchased clothes. On Tuesday evening, I buy a pass to a gymnasium. I need a shower and a place to change. The muscle men in the locker room eye me suspiciously as I put on the red military coat with heart-shaped holes in it.

I don't put the mask on until I reach the lineup outside the Blitz. I stand waiting for what feels like an eternity. Eventually, I see them arrive. Bram and the woman he lives with, along with the handsome man who was with them in their home. Bram is dressed like some kind of post-punk priest in a white ecclesiastical robe that he pairs with platform boots and a leather biker cap. He looks ridiculous. Then again, so do I. But perhaps not ridiculous enough. The closer I get to the front of the line, the more rejections I hear. One person after another is denied entry. I make a spontaneous decision. I tear off my old pants and throw them in my bag. They're beige. Boring. The jacket is long enough to cover my underwear. And bare legs are anything but dull.

The guy at the door, who's dressed in some modern version of Tudor royal, eyes me up and down. "Just you?" he asks.

"Just me," I say.

"Funny to think the British Army once wore bright red," he

says. "Suppose they didn't need camouflage before weapons could shoot their targets down with horrifying precision."

"Yes, I suppose so," I say.

"No camouflage needed at the Blitz neither. You can be your real self here. The one you keep hidden under that mask." He waves me inside.

My real self. Who is he anyway? I wonder as I enter the smoky club.

Music fills the space. Something metallic. Germanic. The voice isn't a voice, exactly. It's humanity as filtered by modern technology. *We're functioning automatic. And we are dancing mechanic. We are the robots.* Among the most fascinating things of traveling across borders of time and place is the changing of sounds. From country to country. From era to era. Pianos replaced by synths. Microphones swapped out for talk boxes that make the singer sound like an alien being. Acoustic turned electric. Cultural traditions blending together to create something fresh.

I search the tiny space for Bram. It's really more hallway than club. Long and cramped and strangely old-fashioned for a place that feels like the future. Portraits of Churchill everywhere. A poster of Marilyn Monroe, who wasn't born and hadn't died when Bram and I last saw each other. Ornately gilded mirrors that reveal reflections of the brazenly dressed crowd laughing, dancing, smoking. It's hard to see over all the hats. So many hats. Tall vertical hats that reach up to the ceiling. A tower of flowers on a beautiful woman's head. A metallic spiral sculpture attached to a man's skull cap. A golden eagle seemingly flying out of someone's hair.

I push my way through the smoke. In a booth, the DJ uses a

drum machine to add carefully placed percussion to the music he spins. The robot song gives way to something far more romantic. Something Italian and sweeping. The dancers sway slowly. They look more like waves than dancers. No one seems to be dancing *with* anyone.

I take my backpack off and pull out a pair of sunglasses. I throw them on. Between these and the mask, my face is completely invisible.

I hand my bag to the coat check boy stationed near the DJ booth. "I would remove any valuables if I were you," a teasing voice says. It's Bram. He's walking our way in his post-punk priest getup. Now I notice the slashes of makeup on his face. Smoke around his eyes. A hint of scarlet on his cheeks, just like how we used to rouge our faces back in the Harvard dorms. "George is a famous thief," he says, unaware it's me he's speaking to behind the mask and sunglasses.

The coat check boy unzips my bag. He pulls out my synthesizer and exclaims, "Yamaha PS-3! Oh, I would most certainly steal it. You're a musician, then?"

I freeze. I need another vocal disguise. I put on a Southern American accent. Turn myself into a Tennessee Williams character. "I play a little," I drawl.

"You in a band yet?" George asks.

"No." I keep my eyes on Bram. I can feel them glowing orange behind the black lenses of my sunglasses. Bram has no idea it's me. "I'm all alone."

"A solo artist, good for you. Oh, and look at this," George says, pulling out my recently purchased poetry book. "Claude McKay. I love his poem 'December, 1919.'"

I see Bram flinch a little when he hears the year 1919 spoken aloud. Is he traveling back to that first version of us in his mind?

George flips through the book until he finds the poem. He sings the words aloud, like he's trying to find a melody in the words. "*'Tis ten years since you died, mother. Just ten dark years of pain. And oh, I only wish that I could weep just once again.*" George closes the book. Takes a deep breath. "That's enough of that now. I can't bear to think of my mother dying. Best woman in the world."

I gulp down hard, thinking of Mother. The obituary said she died peacefully in her sleep, but how would they know? Perhaps she was asleep, but it may have been a fitful slumber, full of nightmares and questions from the past. Was she still wondering about me until her last breath? Or had the grandchildren Liam gave her filled her heart full enough to forget me?

"First time at the Blitz?" Bram asks me as I take my backpack from George.

I panic. Will he recognize my voice? Am I ready to reveal myself to him? Or do I want to run away into the safety of solitude again? "Yes," I say with a twang. "You're a regular?"

"Nothing regular about me." Bram smiles devilishly. "Perhaps that's why I like it so much here. There is no normal here. Most subcultures thrive on uniformity. Punks, beatniks, surfers, zootsuiters, hippies. They all dressed just like each other. It's not like that here. There's no uniform. Look around."

I gaze out at the crowd. He's right. There's no uniformity here. Everyone is unique. One man dressed like a futuristic robot kisses another man wearing a three-piece suit right out of a 1940s film noir. The only commonality is individuality.

Bram's eyes light up as he speaks about this place. "The thing many queer people who long to be *normal* forget is that the whole fun of being queer lies in running counter to culture," he says with awe. "We deserve rights, not *boredom*."

"So everyone here is queer?" I ask.

He shrugs. "If by queer, you mean that they live in defiance to whatever society decides is the norm, then yes. And isn't it wonderful?"

"What's wonderful?" I ask.

"That we have to fight for what we want. It's so much more fun to earn something, isn't it? In order to merely exist, our love for each other, our belief in our own identity, must be so much bigger and deeper than theirs. And they know this. They know that queer love is the truest love, because it's the one that's been fought for. I think that scares them. They know we're stronger. They know our skin's thicker."

"I suppose I've never thought about it that way." I miss the way he makes me think about the world. His perspective and his impenetrable hopefulness, even when his heart is broken. I can't take my eyes off him. He looks so alive. He doesn't wear sunglasses or a mask like I do. He lets the fiery glow of his eyes shine for all to see. In this space, they don't look strange at all. "How long have you lived here?" I ask.

"London?" he asks.

"No, Earth."

He laughs. "Earth, seventeen years. London, a year and a half." He pauses, considering what to say next. "I lived in London for a short spell when I was . . . younger. But it wasn't *this* London then. Or perhaps I wasn't *this* me then."

I nod. "People change," I say.

"Thank God for that," he says. "Are you visiting? You sound

American. Southern? Let me guess. Alabama? Louisiana? North—"

"I—I came for a visit, but I'm . . . considering staying, I think."

"How could you leave after seeing this place?" he asks. "This is freedom." With a note of sadness in his voice, he adds, "I never thought I could find a place where I could truly be happy. But here I am."

"You don't sound happy, though," I observe.

"Oh. Yes. That's just because my heart was recently bruised."

"Not broken?" I ask.

"Not yet. I thought perhaps I could have it all. But what I'm realizing is that what I have might be enough." He looks toward the dance floor, where the man and woman he walked in with are laughing in a huddle with a group of mesmerizing creatures of the night. The woman waves to him. "That's my mother Lily and her best friend, Archie," he announces proudly.

"I'm sorry about your bruised heart," I say. "I hope it heals."

"I hope it doesn't," he replies quickly. "Love, even unrequited, makes me feel alive. If my heart healed, it would mean I didn't love him anymore."

"Him?" I ask.

He smiles. We're both haunting the past now. I can feel us traveling from the Blitz back to 1920. We're at the Golden Rooster again. Wrestling each other. Holding each other. We're walking side by side, sweet cookies in our bellies. "I'm sorry," he says. "I must be boring you. Other people's love stories aren't interesting to anyone else."

"Tell that to Romeo and Juliet," I say. "To Antony and Cleopatra. To Tristan and Isolde."

"Those aren't love stories," he says. "Those are tragedies."

I nod, realizing he's right. "Perhaps the only love stories anyone's interested in are the ones that end tragically." I think of the movie *Love Story*. It captivated the world with its doomed tale. The lead character's name was Oliver. The love of his life died. Mine never will. I feel a sudden swell of warmth for Bram. Maybe the two of us really can have eternal love.

"I've had enough tragedy for one lifetime, thank you very much," Bram says. "I'll hold on to hope as long as I'm alive."

"Really?" I ask. "As long as you're alive?"

I must put too much emphasis on the question because he gazes at me curiously. "Yes," he says. "I should go. I'm Bram, by the way. You never told me your name, did you?"

"Didn't I?" I reply. Then, "Bram is a beautiful name."

He smiles bashfully. "I was named by a beautiful person. Everyone here is beautiful. Living boldly and freely . . . that's true beauty."

"Yes," I say.

"If you were coming on to me, I'm sorry, but the bank is closed," he says, using an expression that reminds me of Boston. *Bank's closed* is what Brendan would say when The Jackal would hit on him. "Mending a bruised heart, as you know." He pulls his shirt down, revealing a tattooed *O* on his chest.

"O?" I ask.

"For the boy I'll love forever. Oliver." He rubs his heart gently. "He's always on my heart."

I feel sick inside. I want to walk away from him, but I just can't. He's had the first letter of my name tattooed on his body. He's done everything I haven't been able to do in all this time. Found his place in the world. Accepted himself. Remained resolute in his feelings for me, in his belief in us. All I've done with my time is isolate and mope. Leaving him was a mistake. I know that now. The truth is, I need him to be happy.

I feel like the DJ's drum machine is in my body now. My heartbeat is percussive. It races around my body. Bram. His name is Bram, not Shams. He's a different person. A happier one. More himself. There's a glow to him. Maybe it's the red lights of the club. Or maybe it's that he's found his place in the world. I feel like I could love this version of him. Be happy with him. Figure things out. Be accepted for the immortals we are by this beautiful band of freaks.

"Isn't that the mask from the shopwindow of R. Soles?" a young androgyne asks. "Can I try it on?" The dazzling creature reaches for my mask.

My sunglasses fall to the floor first.

Then the androgyne pulls my mask off.

Reveals my face.

I feel the fire in my anxious eyes.

The song changes. Bowie. *In the event that this fantastic voyage should turn to erosion and we never get old.*

I feel exposed and raw. The lights seem to land on me like a spotlight.

"Oliver?" Bram asks. His eyes are inscrutable. Happy and sad at the same time. "It's you? I thought . . . Was it you on the phone? You called the helpline? I thought maybe . . . but then I thought . . . Oliver wouldn't do that. He doesn't have deception in him."

Bowie knows. Never getting old is the real erosion. Even Bowie, symbol of youth, innovation, boldness, is aging. He'll probably settle down someday like everyone else. Get himself a wife and a kid and make music that sounds like an echo of the music he used to make. When he was young.

"Oliver, say something!"

I feel exposed and humiliated. I feel like the liar I am. Guilt floods my body. Sends me rushing out the door. Into a downpour.

NEW YORK TIMES
CLASSIFIED ADS

JANUARY 18, 1962

HELLO HOMER,

I find myself in Berlin, on the west side of a wall that divides a city and a people. Everything here feels cold and sharp. More a gray blade than a city. It suits me. I feel divided from myself too. At home among a people devastated by war and guilt. Don't come find me. The wall that divides us is there for a reason. East and west, perhaps, were never meant to meet.

LUDWIG VAN BEETHOVEN

BRAM. LONDON. APRIL. 1980.

There's still a line outside the club. Despite it being so late. Despite the rain destroying the outfits these poor people spent a week creating. Feathers are flattened by the torrent. Wind blows even the most carefully matted hairstyles.

"OLIVER, STOP!"

He runs away. He has no pants on. His wrestler's legs are faster than mine. A man in a sleeping bag on the street whistles at him as he collects rainwater in a bowl for his mutt. "Nice gams, soldier."

"OLIVER! PLEASE, DON'T RUN AWAY AGAIN!"

He doesn't stop. He races past the Royal Opera House. Covered in scaffolding. It's being refurbished. Expanded. There's always money for opera houses. Never for the people on the streets.

"OLIVER, HAVE PITY. I'M WEARING PLATFORM BOOTS!"

I think that might make him laugh. Remind him we can be light with each other. He sprints even faster. Past the Savoy Theatre. Currently playing something called *Not Now, Darling*. A ridiculous title. A perfect one too. *Not now, Oliver,* I want to scream as he crosses the Strand. Rushes toward Waterloo Bridge.

Finally: He stops. Catches his breath.

It's the dirty old river that stops him. Water means something to him. Land's end. A new beginning.

I don't get too close. Can't risk scaring him off. I remind myself to speak gently. Ask open questions. Give him time. "Oliver. Look at me. Please." I try to use my helpline voice. It's no use. I don't sound gentle. My voice is too urgent. It bursts with need.

He keeps his eyes on the Thames. On the lights of a city that suddenly feels so far away. We're not in London anymore. It's Boston again. The past is present. Sixty years erased with one gust of wind.

"How long have you been in London?" I step a little closer to him.

"Long enough." He reaches into his bag and pulls out a pair of beige pants.

"How did you know where I'd be tonight? You must have planned it. The mask. The sunglasses so I wouldn't see your eyes."

He doesn't speak. Takes his sopping shoes off. Pulls his pants up. Buttons them. Puts his shoes back on.

"Were you ever going to reveal yourself?" I take his hands in mine. "Please. Tell me. Were you going to run away without even talking to me?"

"I don't know." He finally looks at me. Those eyes. I've missed their warmth. The way they always look like they're melting. Moist and alive. Years of accumulated sadness in their afterglow. The most beautiful things in the world always look like they're about to break. I speak a Wilde quote that comes to me aloud. "*Behind every exquisite thing that existed, there was something tragic.*"

He shakes his head in disbelief. "Why are you quoting Wilde right now?"

"Because you're exquisite and tragic." I feel my heart tremble. "Tell me. What was your plan? Were you just going to spy on me and leave?"

"I really don't know what I was going to do. I was just—unsure."

"Of me?" I bite my lip.

"Of you, yes." He nods. "Of us, too."

"So you thought you'd play some kind of trick on me."

"It wasn't a trick. It was—" The downpour stops suddenly. I wish his doubts could disappear as fast as a London rainstorm. "I needed to know you again. Who you are now. To see your life. To see this city. I couldn't just pick up where we left off without more information."

"Funny, I have all the information I need. It's here in my heart." I place a hand on my chest. "The heart I had tattooed in your honor. But you know that already."

"Yes. And I know you're happier than you've ever been. And that you have a home. A family of sorts."

"Not of sorts." I hear the annoyance in my voice. I soften my tone. "We are a family. Lily is my mother." I realize I never told him about Lily or our home in the club. "Wait. How do you know about them?"

He shrugs. "I followed you from the *Young Lovers* statue." He reaches into his bag. Pulls out a crushed daffodil. Places it gently in my hair.

"You *followed* me?" I want to hold him. Want him to kiss me. I also want to rage at him. For lying to me. For making this harder than it had to be. I ponder the lengths of his deception. Putting on fake accents to observe my new life. Making me suffer. But then . . . I caused him more pain than he could ever cause me.

"I'm sorry." He means the apology. I know that. He may be unsure of us. But he's still Oliver. Still the same kind soul who wouldn't want to hurt anyone. "You did spy on me once, so we're even, I suppose."

"When?"

He looks up at me sharply. "When I was reading Plato and crying."

I suppose I did spy on him. For a few minutes. Not for days. But I don't fight. Not when I need to win him back. "Do you know why I chose the *Young Lovers* statue for our reunion?"

He shrugs. "They're young lovers. We're young—" He stops himself from saying the word. We're not lovers anymore.

"That was part of it, of course. But the real reason is because the sculptor, Georg Ehrlich, had to escape Austria for Britain. His wife joined him later. She brought much of his art with her. Saved it from the Nazis. They made a life here together, in a country that wasn't their own."

He stares at me curiously. Confused. It's like I'm speaking an alien tongue he can't decipher. His hieroglyphic old love. Speaking in incomprehensible fantasies. "Do you seriously think a Jewish couple fleeing persecution is *romantic*? You're more twisted than you ever were."

"No, I—I never said it was—romantic. But it is—" I stumble over my words. I need to explain myself to him. "It's a testament to the power of two people to survive. Together. Because their love was their strength."

"You don't know that. Maybe their faith was their strength. Or his art. You always think you know things you couldn't possibly know."

"Like what you wanted sixty years ago. . . ."

"Yes." He doesn't say any more.

"Still, they made a beautiful life despite the greatest odds. We can too."

"Can we?"

"I thought of you every day. Wanted to share every mundane detail of my life with you. And the big things. I always needed to know where you were. What you thought. Vietnam. The moon landing. World War II."

"I thought of signing up to serve." Melancholy swirls around him. His eyes emit little fireflies of sorrow. "Figured I'd make quite the Allied soldier. Nazis can't kill me, can they? Then I thought of all the medical exams the military performs. The questions they might ask when a submachine gun fails to kill me. I realized I can't even serve my country. If it was even my country then. By World War II, I had long deserted America."

"Let me be your country." I pull him into a hug. "A country with no rules. No laws. No border lines."

"But you're not a country. You'll always be the person who made me this way."

I take a deep breath. Exhale. "*Whenever a man does a thoroughly stupid thing, it is always from the noblest motives.*"

He scrunches his face in annoyance. "Stop quoting Wilde. Just because he said something doesn't make it true."

"So you know your Wilde as well as I do."

He nods. "You think I haven't scoured his writing for some sign of why this happened to us?"

I smile. "I've done the same." Then: "Don't you see that I'm the only person you can confess all this to? The only person you can be yourself with?"

"I don't know if I want to be myself is the problem." He tucks his chin. His graceful neck slumps. "Don't know if I even know who I am."

"Then let me remind you. I know who you are. I'm sure of us, still." My heartbeat skips. "Are you still unsure?" I want an immediate answer. I don't get one. "That's a very long and concerning pause."

"You ruined my life." He doesn't say it with anger. More with acceptance.

"I know that now." I swallow hard. "I didn't know then—I couldn't know . . . How deeply you loved your mother. It wasn't until I met Lily that I knew how fiercely one could love their family. Now I understand. Your mother—"

"Please let's talk about anything but Mother." His voice chokes up. "All these years . . . all this time . . . and she's still my biggest regret."

"You have nothing to regret. It's all my fault."

"But I do." He sighs. "For years after leaving, I would write her letters with no return address. Just telling her I was fine and that she ought not to worry. I debated creating an elaborate lie. Telling her I was studying music in Europe. That I had married a woman. Had children of my own. But lies lead to more lies. Evasion is a stronger tactic."

"I've learned the same lesson."

He takes in a long breath. "The last letter I sent her was a decade before she died. I told her I loved her. I told her not to waste another thought on me. But I begged her to keep me in her prayers."

"I'm sure she did."

His eyes look to me desperately. "How can you be so sure? What if she cursed me in the end? Hated me?"

"She didn't. She couldn't. You're impossible to hate."

He rolls his eyes.

"It's true. Your mother knew it and I do too. And the way I see it, you have two options. The first is to run away from me, which you've already tried. Has it made you happy?"

"No." He shakes his head sadly.

"Then try the second option. Be with me. Let me make it up to you. Let me prove to you that we can be happy."

He laughs. "Here? In this city with trash piling up on the streets, where queer bars are raided by the police, where punks and vagrants call me a bugger and a screamer when I'm sleeping on the Tube. Where boys like us are beat up at the George. This is where you want us to find happiness? In a country where the prime minister is at war with working people, immigrants, and . . . people like us."

"You're right. There's injustice here. Poverty. Greed. People still hate us. Maybe they always will. I don't care about all that right now. I care about you. What do you want, Oliver? In your heart."

"I—I don't know."

"You do know, but you're not brave enough to take it." I shock myself with my own anger. I've craved his forgiveness for so long. Accepted my wrongs. Now I see I also resent him. For holding on to a sixty-year grudge. For allowing his beautiful tenderness to morph into defeatist weakness. "You've spent sixty years blaming me for your fate, haven't you?"

"Yes, yes, I have, and—"

"And have you ever wondered what your fate might have been had you not met me? Cyril would still have killed himself. Harvard would still have put all those boys on trial. What would you have done?"

"I—I can't answer that. No one can."

"I can. Because I know you. You wouldn't have dared break your mother's heart. You would have taken a wife you didn't love."

"You don't know that. You can't—"

"Doomed her to loneliness. To always wondering why her beautiful husband shudders at her touch. You would have been a distant father."

"Stop it!"

"Never able to truly reveal yourself to your own children. A life of secrecy. You would be in a seventy-seven-year-old body by now. Watching rebels change the world."

"Why are you being so cruel?"

"Wondering why you couldn't have played a part in your own people's liberation. Well, this is your chance."

"For what exactly? Is being together some form of liberation now?" He cracks his knuckles nervously.

"Isn't that exactly what it is? To love when you're told that love is a crime. What else is that but liberation?"

"Greed." He shakes his head. "Fantasy."

He shifts his gaze to a man and a woman kissing against the bridge. The ease of their passion stabs me like a blade. Queers have to learn where we can kiss and where we can't. We don't get to be carefree. Part of me likes that we have to fight for our love. Another part of me is enraged by it. I want to kiss Oliver defiantly and lovingly.

"You could've told me what you are." He holds my gaze. He's been waiting a long time to say this. "I might have understood. Perhaps I would have loved you. You never gave me the chance."

"Loved me?" I'm full with the desire to defend myself. "You told me we couldn't be together. You were ready to end us."

"So you cursed me—"

"Because I thought it was what you wanted. Because I thought it was destiny. And yes, because I was greedy and selfish and stupid. I admitted as much to *Liam* on the phone, didn't I? But you're not Liam. You're Oliver. I don't have to be a gentle voice on the other end of a helpline with you. I can be myself. I must be myself. And I am sorry. And I was greedy. But please hear me when I say I don't want *fantasy* from us." I put a hand on his cheek affectionately. My fingers tremble on his warm skin. "I want the opposite of fantasy. I want a *life* with you. Real life. With fights and laughs. Ups and downs. Sickness and health and all that."

"There's no sickness for us though, is there?"

"Listen to me. Please. Don't shut me out. I want—I want to make mistakes. I've made mistakes. Grave ones. And I want to make more. I want to do stupid things because I'm too passionate to make a sound decision. I want to want things. To need things. To need you. I want to be full of regrets. But to be the kind of person who tells people I have no regrets and actually makes them believe it. Don't you see that a life without regrets is boring? I don't want to be bored. I want to be *us*. Alive and unpredictable and exciting."

He actually smiles. I might be getting through to him.

"I'm not begging you to stay here because the world is perfect. Yes, yes, yes, the world is as fraught and enraging as it ever was. I'm pleading because *my little world* is perfect. And I want to share it with you." I get down on one knee. Like I'm proposing. I want to give the moment the weight it deserves. "I live in a home with enough room for you. I know a community who will welcome you. Where there are more than enough spaces for us. You saw the Blitz.

All those freaks. Living freely. And it's not the only place. There are bars and shebeens and shops just for us. We don't need the whole city. Just a block here. A bar there. A shop or two that welcome our kind. And each other."

He tries to pull me up. "Get up. You're making a scene."

I resist. Stay on my knee. "Let people look at us. I don't care. I'm done hiding myself. Done hiding my love for you."

He looks around. Glimpses disapproving strangers staring at us. "Bram, please."

"I love you, Oliver. So much that I did the stupidest thing of my life. I don't know what else to say to make you understand. I love you and I'm sorry and I love you and I'm sorry and I'll say the words again and again until I drive you mad."

"Oh, you've already driven me mad." He says those words evenly. Without anger. Something is shifting in him. I feel it. He's traveling back to the Oliver I once knew. The one who didn't run away from risk. Who didn't push me away.

"You're scared. You're angry. And you have every right to be. I know you're still holding on to the past. But all I want to know is if you love me too. Do you?"

He turns his face to the river. It glimmers from the city lights. Then he looks back at me. "I wouldn't have come back if I didn't."

I smile. "Then come with me. You're soaked. You look like you haven't had a proper meal in weeks."

I start to walk. He pulls me back. "What will we tell people? They'll ask how we met. Why we both have eyes that glow."

"I've already told Lily about you. I said we met when I was tutoring in Boston. The eyes . . . We'll say that's why we met. We saw each other in a bar—"

"No, not a bar. A library. We were both reaching for the same book."

"Wilde!"

"*The Picture of Dorian Gray.*" He smiles now. He's enjoying himself. We're building a story that will belong to us. A lie we'll share with each other. So then, not a lie. A bond of trust.

"We reached for the book. I snatched it away from you."

"Of course you did." He laughs. He switches to a thick British accent. You *arsehole*." Back to his own voice. "Wait, that shop. R. Soles. It's meant to sound like *arseholes*, isn't it?"

"Brits have a cheeky sense of humor. You might like it here."

"I might."

I take his hand. Lead him across the bridge toward the South Bank. We'll walk to Brixton. The rain has stopped. The wind is placid. The ever-changing London weather is telling us the storm has passed. "What happened after I snatched the book away from you?"

He smiles. "I wrestled you to the ground and took it from you."

"You wrestled me to the ground in a library?" I laugh.

"Okay, fine. No wrestling. I politely asked if I could read the book first?"

"And I said perhaps we could read it together. We sat side by side at a long wooden table and read. You read faster than me, so I would tell you when I was ready for the page to be flipped."

"We read it aloud to each other."

"In a library?"

"Yes, in an empty nook of the library."

"When we finished, we looked into each other's eyes."

"And that's when we realized we're both part feline."

"Part feline, I love that." I pull him closer. "Nine lives."

"I've lived more than nine lives already."

"No, you've only lived one. So have I. It's all one journey. And it's led us here."

No one is home when we arrive. I give Oliver a quick tour. Then lead him up to my room. I want to shower with him. To scrub him clean. But I don't dare move too fast. We're still a fragile pair. A push or a pull in the wrong direction could break us again. I offer him some of my clothes when he's dry. He runs his hand through the rich fabrics in my closet. "These are all so beautiful."

"Lily makes it all. She's a genius. She'd be the next Coco Chanel if there were any justice in the world." There's pride in my voice when I speak of her. My mother who baptized me.

"I met Maud." He quickly puts on a T-shirt and a pair of baggy wool pants with a drawstring waistband. I love the way his body elongates as he stretches himself to get the clothes on. "At the bookshop where she works. I didn't know she was your . . . sister?"

"I told you we're a family."

"She said she's only lived here a few weeks. Already family?"

I meet his skeptical gaze. "How long should it take a mother or father to love their child? More than a few weeks? I'm sure your mother loved you the minute you were born."

He sits on my bed. "Please don't bring up Mother again. It's too painful."

"I'm sorry." I sit on the floor. I want to be beneath him. To worship him. I rest my head on his lap. He caresses my face. "I didn't mean to hurt you. I want to be all future and no past, but that's not how it works, is it?"

"It's all present anyway." He places a palm on my cheek. It feels warm. He runs his other hand through my hair. "Your haircut is ridiculous."

"That's exactly what I was going for." We laugh. Our breaths synchronize until they sound like one inhale and one exhale. His stomach rumbles into my ear. I raise my head from his lap. "You're starving. Come."

I lead him to the kitchen. Open the fridge. There are some leftovers of Poppy's beef stew in the fridge. I empty what's left onto a pot on the stove. Throw some leftover rice in. "Poppy's the best cook. You'll see."

"Who's Poppy?"

The sound of a door closing. Lily and Archie are home. Lily's voice fills the room. "Poppy is one of my best friends. And who are you?"

"This is Oliver." I pull Oliver close to Lily.

She doesn't look amused. "We were worried. You disappeared. I asked everyone where you went. No one knew. No goodbye. Archie even walked away from a swarthy man without getting his number."

"Every word she says is true." Archie fills a glass with tap water. Drinks it fast. "He was quite gorgeous. Greek accent. Thighs as thick as the pillars of the Parthenon."

"I'm sorry you were worried, but Lily, this is *Oliver*. From *Boston*."

Lily's eyes open wide. "Well, why didn't you say so, child?" Lily's entire body language changes quickly. She wraps Oliver in her arms. Presents him to Archie. "Archiekins, this is *Oliver*. From *Boston*."

Archie squints in confusion. "Is that meant to mean something?"

Lily kicks Archie in the shin. "I told you Bram had a friend in Boston."

"Oh." Archie stands a little straighter. "You're the *friend*. I thought perhaps you were merely a figment of Bram's imagination."

Lily grabs a wooden spoon and stirs the stew. "Bram, you need to stir the food so it heats evenly."

"Yes, Mommie Dearest."

Oliver laughs at that.

Lily turns to Oliver again. "You're a little late. We were expecting you days ago."

Oliver nods. "Yes."

Archie stands up. Puts a hand on Oliver's shoulder. "Better late than never. You're here now." Archie backs away in shock. "Your eyes. They glow just like Bram's."

This is our time to try out our story. See if anyone believes it. I start the lie. "It's part of how we met, actually. We were in a library."

Oliver steps in. "We both reached for the same book."

We tell our elaborate fake tale. Lily and Archie don't question it. They seem charmed. Two teenage boys meeting in a library while reaching for Oscar Wilde. What could be more romantic? Of course it's a lie. But Wilde himself said secrecy is the one thing that can make modern life mysterious or marvelous. *The commonest thing is delightful if one only hides it.* And I do feel delighted as I watch my beloved mother and her best friend welcoming my love into our life.

Oliver leans toward Lily. "Bram gave me a tour. I love the Donna Summer shrine."

Lily's eyes light up. "You like her?"

"I don't think *like* is sufficient to describe how I feel about a woman who revolutionized music. There's music before 'I Feel Love' and music after 'I Feel Love.'"

"Exactly!" Lily turns to Archie. "Haven't I said the exact same thing?"

"You have." Archie looks at Oliver. "She has."

Oliver keeps going: "What they did with the electronics in that song . . . The delay on the bass line. The way they manipulated the Moog to sound percussive. It's the first drum machine click track ever released, as far as I know. It's all so precise and yet so free. It's like the musical equivalent of a moving train. It just *travels,* you know."

Lily smiles. "I do know, even though I'm not sure I understand music like you do."

I don't dare interrupt them. But I do think of how much I love the song. And also how much I love riding the Tube. Its speed. The rattling motion that makes me feel like I'm going somewhere. That's all I want. To keep moving forward and farther forward. Headfirst. Always accelerating. Who wouldn't love a song that gives them that sensation?

Lily asks: "Do you know why the song was written in the first place?"

Oliver shakes his head. "I don't."

Lily smiles. She's excited by the conversation. "Donna was working with Giorgio Moroder on an album that was a tour of music through the decades. They decided if they were going to chart the history of music, they also needed a song to represent the future."

"Wow." Oliver closes his eyes. Moves his body. He seems to be playing the song in his imagination. "And they were right, weren't they? They created the sound of the future. But then, what makes the song so powerful is the way she delivers the melody in her head voice. So angelic. So human. So incongruous with the electronic world of the song."

"She's a church girl at heart. She knows how to channel God when she sings."

"My mother always said music is our way of communicating with God."

"Said?"

Oliver bites his lip. "Oh. Uh . . . She passed." I can tell Oliver regrets bringing her up. He says he doesn't want to talk about his mother. And yet she's still the person most on his mind.

Lily reaches for Oliver's hand. Squeezes it. "I'm sorry." They clutch each other. Their hands are over my heart. I've never felt happier. Lily adds: "Perhaps all creativity is our way of letting God communicate *through* us."

I can tell Oliver loves Lily already.

Lily smiles. "And Donna really was in love when she wrote and recorded it. You can fake a lot of things. But not love."

Oliver's gaze catches mine when Lily says this.

Archie leans on the kitchen counter. "Music can be a revolution."

Lily nods. "Music *should* be a revolution."

"When I saw Queen in Hyde Park—"

"Archie, this story again!" Lily throws Archie a playful gaze.

"Well, the boys haven't heard it, have they?" Archie turns his gaze to me and Oliver: *the boys*. "The crowds were massive, but somehow Freddie had every one of them in the palm of his hand. I felt pride watching him. As he strutted across that stage in his tight-fitting white leotard, cock bulging—"

"Archiekins, no need to be so graphic!"

"Well, it was." Archie laughs. "It felt to me, in that moment, that life is limitless. All the rules and boundaries of society felt so weak in the face of a power like Freddie Mercury. When the main set ended, we all cheered for an encore that never came. Two hundred thousand people, cheering and shouting and begging. What we didn't know at the time is that the bobbies had forced the band into the back of a police van and threatened them with arrest."

I didn't know this story. I hear myself respond in shock. "Wait. Seriously?"

Archie nods. "They said it was because the concert was becoming unruly. But let's be real. They were afraid that one more song from that magical creature might have tipped the scales of power forever in our favor. That's the power of one song, one person, one moment. Remember that, won't you?"

Before any of us can respond, Maud gets home. "I'm proper famished." Maud opens the refrigerator without even glancing at Oliver. "Aw, come on. Where's the beef stew? I had my heart set on it."

"Here." Oliver pushes his plate toward her. Offers her his fork.

She takes out her own fork and stands next to him. "Wait, it's you. From the bookshop. White boy who knows his Langston Hughes."

"And now my Claude McKay, thanks to you."

Maud sits next to Oliver. They eat side by side. She's no doubt had a long night at some shebeen or another. The Blitz isn't for her. The Brixton shebeens are where she finds her necessary doses of freedom and abandon. "Wait, so what are you doing here?" She speaks with a mouth full of stew.

"He is Oliver. Bram's friend from Boston." Lily pronounces

friend with just the right amount of emphasis. Maud immediately understands he's more. "He'll be staying with us for a little while."

I smile. My heart feels full. My mind has one question. How long can this *little while* last? Forever, I hope.

Nothing less than forever will do.

OLIVER. LONDON. 2025.

Nothing could prepare me for the feeling of emerging out of the Brixton Tube station with Bram by my side. We're greeted by bikes for rent, a bus advertising *The Phantom of the Opera,* Sainsbury's, old red telephone boxes that no one uses anymore. Street vendors selling souvenirs. And of course, CCTV cameras. I can feel them spying on me. Almost a million cameras in this one city alone. Watching me. Watching Bram. Keeping digital eyes on these crowds of busy people rushing to their destinations. One camera for every ten people in London, apparently. Every Londoner is captured seventy times a day. I anxiously try to do the math in my head. If I only stay in London for a few hours, that's still at least a dozen opportunities for me to be caught.

"Bram. I'm scared. Someone who has access to all this CCTV footage must be friends with—"

"Wow!" Bram says, pointing to the striking mural of Brixton boy David Bowie. "Let's read the messages."

I take in a deep, calming breath as Bram and I take in all the messages written from those Bowie moved through sound and vision.

I miss you, David.

Thank you, Bowie.

Shine bright, Starman.

We walk to Railton Road. I don't know which punches me in the gut harder, the things that have changed or the things that haven't. There's a gated community where a school used to be. The squats aren't squats anymore. They're refurbished homes. They probably go for a million pounds. Gentrification is everywhere. *To Let* and *For Sale* signs pepper the buildings. Everything has its price. Thatcher's legacy.

The record shops are all gone, lost to new technology, rising rents, and the grim reality that this isn't the community it once was. Reggaeheads used to hang out outside the record shops, gathering materials for their sound systems, shebeens, and blues dances. There are no rebel dykes anywhere. No women's centers. No Race Today Collective. No anarchist news service. The energy of the place is more comfort than anarchy. There are odes to the past everywhere. The Black Cultural Archives. A poster of Olive Morris outside the Brixton Advice Centre. Olive, a once vibrant activist who changed the world, is now a memory. An image in a window. What once was present is now archival.

"The best of our life is ancient history," I say.

"The best part of everyone's lives turns into ancient history," Bram counters. "That's not unique to us."

"I suppose." I look around. There's graffiti everywhere. Also advertisements. The words of the ads say things like *Fire Broadband Is Here* and *Hot Coffee*. The words of the street art declare *Free Sudan* and *Black Power*. The contrast is stark.

"Come on," Bram says. "Let's get to Chaucer."

"Doesn't it make you sad?" I ask. "Why are there bougie coffee shops and Pilates studios where there used to be shebeens, Brixton Faeries, and Rebel Dykes?"

"Maybe because people want them?" Bram looks around. "Everything changes."

"Except us," I say, my voice sad and ominous. I can't shake off my fear. "Bram, is this a good idea? What if we're caught?"

Bram closes his eyes. "If we let them keep us away from Lily's send-off, then they've won. We have to be here." He opens his eyes again. They look uncertain as he says, "Besides, maybe they're not looking for us anymore."

He doesn't convince me, but I let him lead the way. Even after all this time, it feels good when he guides me into the unknown. I notice that time is everywhere. It's on the post office box with its collection times. It's on the Ethiopian and Jamaican and Greek restaurants with their opening and closing times. It's on the parking signs. Time haunts me. The way it lurches forward.

And yet, remnants haunt the neighborhood like ghosts. It's the smells that hit me hardest. The familiar scent of jerk chicken being cooked, fish being fried, turmeric and curry powder. Food, I suddenly think, is our most direct link to the past. Everything else changes. Sounds and sights evolve quickly. But not food. Sure, some trendy chef might deconstruct classic dishes with molecular flair, but it will never stick. As long as there are humans, I bet there will still be dumplings and rum cake. I think of Mother's recipes. Her meat loaf and green beans. What I would give to taste them again. To be transported back to her love.

We stop just shy of what was once our house. Bram lowers his veil. I put on a large pair of sunglasses. A floppy hat that falls over my face.

Maud speaks to the group. Her voice is deeper than it used to be. Her hair, once a short Afro, is now in beautiful braids. She holds a woman's hand. They both wear wedding rings. "Miraculously, the Brixton Housing Co-op still exists," she says. "One of the few survivors from our time. So much is gone."

"But we're still here," Azalea calls out.

"That's right." Maud nods. "The first time I came to the house, I was a lost person. I called the helpline first. A lot of you know the story by now. I spoke to Bram before I met Lily."

There's a hush when Bram's name is spoken aloud. People whisper to each other.

"I'm sure wherever he is, Bram is thinking of Lily. Oliver too." Maud pulls her wife closer. The supportive look on her wife's face fills me with agony. Maud did it. She found love that lasts. A true partner. Happiness, I hope.

"We shouldn't be here," I say to Bram. "If they see us—"

"They would be thrilled to see us," he says. "Didn't you see Maud's face when she spoke of us? She doesn't hold a grudge."

"If they see us, Lily's memorial will become all about us. The ageless wonders. We can't do that to her. Today is about her, remember?"

"Right." He takes my hand, just as Maud took her wife's hand. I know comparison is the enemy of peace. Lily said that once. Still, I can't accept how much easier their touch felt. Maud and her wife touch each other in a way that feels natural, automatic. Ours is forced.

"Lily left the home after Bram and Oliver left. Too many

ghosts, she said. Lily didn't like living among ghosts. You know how she was. Always changing. Curious. Maybe those boys did the right thing, she told me. Children are meant to fly away. She told me to fly away and I did. But never too far. She walked me down the aisle, didn't she?" Maud kisses her wife's cheek. "She didn't move far, of course. Found a house just a few roads down. Kept taking in children. Kept telling them to fly away when they were ready. And eventually, she took in her last child. Her own Uncle Alton. That man spent four decades in prison for a bogus charge before he was finally exonerated. All those years Lily missed with him."

"And we're still dealing with racist cops," Azalea calls out, bringing back the energy of the old uprisings.

Poppy chimes in. "They're exonerating the old cases but arresting new boys. It's youth they want to take from us. They'll let us be free when we're too old and tired to take what's ours."

Now Archie steps forward. "Look at Turing's Law. Passed only eight years ago. Not until 2017 did our government think to overturn the convictions of gay men arrested for doing nothing but being brave."

"We're still fighting the same fights," Maud says. "Black Lives Matter. Police brutality."

"Anti-trans bullshit," a young Black boy calls out as he scratches his beard.

"Who's that?" I ask Bram.

"His name's Tobi. I've never met him. Probably one of Lily's last children."

"He's so young. He looks like he's our age." Bram shoots me a curious look. "You know what I mean," I say.

Tobi keeps going. "The prime minister wants to remove legal

protections for trans people in the Equality Act. Families are leaving the country because their children are being bullied. She-who-must-not-be-named has devoted her magical powers to attacking us. Hate crimes against us are at a record high." Tobi's voice thumps with righteous rage. The fury of youth. "I'm just so filled with . . . with . . ." I think he's going to say anger, rage, frustration, but what he says is, "Hopelessness. Lily's gone and hope is too." Tobi buries his head in his hands and breaks down crying.

Maud rushes to Tobi's side and puts an arm around him. "Hey, it's an emotional day. Let it out."

Tobi cries on Maud's shoulder. "I'm sorry. I know this is meant to be a celebration of life."

"In all its beauty and brutality," Maud says. "Celebrating life means acknowledging all of it. Not just the pretty parts."

"I know Lily didn't want no boo-hoo backstories," Tobi blubbers.

Maud lifts Tobi's chin up. "Hey, this isn't a boo-hoo backstory. This is grief. For the mother we lost and for the joy they want to take from us. This is *your* story. *Your* time. You're how old now?"

"Seventeen."

"Seventeen." Maud exhales the word luxuriously, elongating the last syllable. "Your life is ahead of you."

Tobi wipes the tears off his face. His jaw hardens into defiance again. "She gave everything she could to this country and look at it now. Moving backward instead of forward. I'm scared of what's ahead."

"I know you are. I am too. But the arc of the moral universe bends toward justice."

"Too slowly," Tobi says.

Archie awkwardly inserts himself into the moment. "It's true there are challenges still. But these times are the best we've ever had. Poverty is in free fall. More humans have access to food and education and clean water than ever. Children used to die of scarlet fever. Our community used to die of AIDS."

"Still do, last I checked," Tobi says.

"Because of ignorance and greed," Archie replies.

Tobi grunts in frustration. "But ignorance and greed are the problem. Don't matter how many lifesaving medicines we discover. How much water we clean. Is it too much to ask for a world without ignorance and greed?"

Archie puts his thin arm around Tobi's powerful young shoulders. "Tobi, what you're asking for is a world without humans."

Tobi laughs at that. Looks at the others sheepishly. "Sorry, friends. We should keep moving."

"Forward we go," Maud says with a wink to Tobi. She leads them to 103 Railton Road, where Pearl's shebeen once welcomed us. Pearl's is where Maud truly found herself. Only in community can we find ourselves and that was hers. It's gone now. Just one more nondescript forgotten building. The trash bin outside has the numbers 103 written on it in white. If only the tourists and teenagers walking by knew the magic this place once held. But then, each generation makes their own magic, in their own ways.

Tobi turns toward us. Bram quickly pulls me behind a truck. "We should go," he says. "We know where they'll end up. We can see Lily off there."

"Then what?" I ask.

"Then I don't know," he says. He pulls me down Shakespeare Road. Takes his veil off. I put my sunglasses in my pocket. Throw my hat in my bag.

Poets Corner, they call it. Of course, it's where we made a home. In a neighborhood where the streets are named after Chaucer, Shakespeare, and Milton, but where the people were Black and brown and queer and defiant. There's a poem on Shakespeare Road commemorating the Brixton Uprising.

"You always know, though," I say. "You always have a plan."

He leads me into Brockwell Park. Green everywhere. A glorious spring. Seasons, like us, never get old. They arrive every three months fresh and new.

"I don't have a plan anymore. I want to be with you. I know that. But I'm done chasing you. Done trying to convince you that we're enough."

"But we're not enough. We would have been enough if only we could age. I could have loved you until the day I died."

"I would have died first," he says. "I would have made sure of it. I could never handle seeing you pass."

I shake my head. He's ever the morbid romantic. "This way is doomed though. Never aging. We'd get bored with each other because we'd never change."

"I was never bored of you. Not in Boston. Not in Brixton."

I lean against an ancient oak tree. Gaze out at a large open meadow. Families play together. Parents coo over their babies. A very young mother sings Lana Del Rey's "Video Games" to her newborn like a lullaby. Perfect pitch. F sharp minor. Adagio. *It's you, it's you, it's all for you.* She turns a song about romantic love into one about parental love. I feel every ounce of her love for her child.

It's Mother's love, which Lily taught me how to feel in a new way. It's Lily's love. It's every parent's love.

Grandparents walk their grandkids. Couples hold hands. The cycle of life is everywhere, like the seasons. Change. It's essential to happiness.

"I didn't last two years in Brixton," I say. "You didn't have me long enough to get sick of me. Maybe if you hadn't been so stupid. If only you had left well enough—"

A heavy hand on my shoulder.

My heart sinks.

I was about to blame Bram for what happened to us that last night in London, but I don't need to.

Because we've been found.

Whatever freedom we thought we had ends here.

But when I turn around, it's not some goon I see. It's Tobi. His eyes are misty and confused as he asks, "It's you two, innit?"

"Sorry?" Bram asks.

I clutch Bram's hand tight, afraid of being found out. In the calmest voice I can muster, I say, "We should get going. We have an appointment, remember?"

We try to walk away but Tobi follows us. "It's you. I know it's you. I've heard all about you. Look at your eyes. You look just like how Lily described. Except . . . you should be ancient by now. It makes no sense. *You* defy the laws of time."

I look at Bram. We could run away from London like we did decades ago. But then, it's not our family we were running from, and Tobi is family. I feel Lily's presence around me. I close my eyes and feel her like she taught me to feel Mother. Lily tells me to let Tobi in. When I open my eyes, I say to Bram, "We're brothers, aren't we?"

Tobi takes his knitted scarf off and ties it around his waist. "That's what Lily told me. That you were my oldest brothers."

I smile. Of course Lily said that. Of course she considered us her children long after we deserted her. "Walk with us," I say to Tobi. "It's a long story."

OLIVER. LONDON. JULY. 1980.

I'm a session man now. I've graduated from playing in Tube stops and on street corners to accompanying artists as they record the albums that will make them famous. The Blitz is not only where I find liberation through music. It's also where I find work. Word gets around that there's a young kid who knows how to play the synthesizer like he's an avant-garde Rachmaninoff. Lily urges me to dream bigger. To be more than an invisible name. But she doesn't understand that I *can't* be famous. Fame means being seen. It invites questions. Besides, I like the background. Staying in the shadows suits me fine. And I love the music I'm playing. Love the way the world sounds right now. I'm exhilarated by the way music, culture, fashion, and life itself is being reinvented in real time.

I feel inspired as I leave a session with George's band. He never did steal my synthesizer, but he's stolen my heart with his melodies and lyrics. He has something to say on behalf of us all. I don't know if the world is ready for him, but it'll be a real shame if it's not.

I turn the key to our house. Lily just had an extra bolt installed. Too many cops arresting Blacks and queers for nothing but their suspicions. Too many young gay kids disappearing without a trace. I open the door and hear—

"SURPRISE!" A chorus of sound. Baritones and sopranos and tenors and contraltos. They're all there. My new family. Bram, Lily, Maud, Archie, Poppy, Azalea, Blossom. Friends from the Blitz and friends from Brixton. The lonely kid who tried to talk to me when I first arrived is here. He's not lonely any longer. Neither am I. He has a name to me now. Charlie from the squat up the street.

"I— How did you know?" I blush as I look around. Balloons everywhere. A large banner that reads *Happy Birthday, Oliver.* A full spread of Poppy's greatest culinary hits. Brightly colored fabrics rain down from the ceiling. All for me. "It's amazing, but—I didn't tell anyone when my birthday is."

"You told me when we first met." Bram approaches me with a gift in his hand.

"I did?" I race back in time, but it's been too long. My mind is a clutter of memories. Flickers of loneliness in Buenos Aires, despair in Tokyo, solitary strolls through the streets of Madrid, seclusion in Berlin.

"You certainly did. I remember it all. Every moment we've shared. You not only told me your birthday, but you told me what you wanted for your birthday. Of course, I had to leave Boston so I never got to celebrate a birthday with you."

"I haven't celebrated my birthday in a long time," I murmur, my eyes fixed on Bram.

He seems to know what I'm thinking. *Does it even count as a birthday when we don't age?*

"You deserve to be celebrated," Bram says.

"What did I say I wanted? For my birthday? All those—I mean . . . Back in Boston."

"My memory isn't perfect, but I think you said all you wanted was to be in my company, speaking the truth to each other. You said you were so tired of hiding."

It all comes back to me now. Brendan and Jack's dorm room. Boston. 1920. The camaraderie. The merriment. The carefree youth that fooled me into thinking it could last forever.

"Hmm," I say. "Now that I'm in your company, I want more."

"Ask and you shall receive," Bram promises. "What else do you want, birthday boy?"

"A puppy!" I declare. "Or a kitten. I've always wanted a pet, but Mother said they were—"

"Too expensive!" Lily blurts out.

"Exactly," I say. I take the gift Bram is holding. "This is for me?" I ask.

"Open it."

"Let's do gifts later," Lily announces. "It's bad luck to open gifts before you eat the birthday cake."

"That is a completely made-up superstition," Blossom says with a laugh.

"Every superstition is made up by someone," Lily replies. No one argues with that. Lily pulls me to her side. "Tonight, you must share him, Bram. Everybody here wants to give the birthday boy some loving."

We all take turns choosing music from the record collection. Lily has even more crates than usual. She must have asked every DJ she knows if she could borrow a piece of their collections for the party. We cycle from genre to genre. The sound of *right now*. How I love it. How I wish Mother and Brendan could hear the evolution of music. We play it all as we eat, laugh, dance. The Cure. Kate Bush. Blondie. Bob Marley & The Wailers. Gal Costa. Spandau Ballet. Gregory Isaacs. Chico Buarque. Roxy Music.

Dalida. Michael Jackson. Johnny Osbourne. Queen. Gainsbourg. Our beloved Bowie. Françoise Hardy. Manu Dibango. Prince. My goodness, Prince. My imagination couldn't have dreamed him up back in Boston. He blurs the boundaries of gender, color, time. He's everything all at once. Old and new. Male and female. He wants to be the world's lover. In a country devoted to its monarchy, he's our Prince. True royalty doesn't live in a castle. Doesn't colonize. It gifts the world new ways of existing. Music has never felt more vital. Neither have I.

After Poppy's spread of food has been devoured, Lily turns the lights and the music off. She reemerges moments later from the kitchen with a rum cake on a blue porcelain platter. Eighteen candles light her face below. On her left, Bram. On her right, Maud. My new family. Everyone sings. Archie adds an off-key "*and many more*" at the end of the song.

"Make a wish!" Lily yells out happily.

"Make it a good one!" Blossom adds.

"No, make it a naughty one," Archie advises. "You're only eighteen once."

I close my eyes and blow. I wish for life always to *feel* like this. Warm. Connected. Full of love and laughter. Not to be young forever, but to *feel* young forever. That's what Dorian Gray *should* have wished for.

When I open my eyes, there's still a single flickering candle left. I feel a flash of the old fear coming back to me. Does this mean my wish won't be granted? I pull as much air as I can into my lungs, and exhale as hard as I can. The final flame goes out. The lights come back on. Poppy cuts the cake into thick slivers. Places them on paper plates and hands them out.

"So, how does it feel?" Lily asks, her arm around me.

"How does what feel?" I ask.

"Being another year older at an age when another year isn't something to be afraid of."

Archie approaches Lily. "You, my dear beautiful flower, are a mere thirty-four years old. You should hardly be afraid of another year."

Lily pats her cheeks. "Everything is starting to sag. There are lines around my eyes. It's all downhill from here."

"Your vanity is your most charming flaw," Archie says, taking her hand in his.

She pulls it away and slaps him in jest. "It's my *only* flaw!" Everyone laughs. Lily turns to me again. I have a piece of cake in my hand now. A belly full of sweetness. "Ignore my vanity, child. But heed my advice and appreciate your youth. With every year that passes, time speeds up on you. The days, weeks, months, and years go by faster and faster."

"It's true," Azalea says. "Scientists are researching why. They think it's because the young brain takes in information faster. Learns more. Which makes time *appear* longer. More meaningful."

"But surely time is time," Poppy says. "A minute is the same minute whether it passes for an aging woman like me or a young soul like Maud."

"All time is not equal," Lily says with certainty. She takes a piece of cake but doesn't touch it yet. "Think of the most beautiful moments of your life. Archie, think of the moment you broke free from your family. Azalea, think of when we saved up enough money to fly to Casablanca and become the women we knew we were. Oliver, think of that moment in the library, when you first laid eyes on Bram. Surely, these are the minutes we all replay in our minds millions of times. Which makes that single life-changing minute more valuable than a million dull minutes."

Azalea nods. "What you're saying is that all that matters is our perception of unknowable things like time, space, love, pride. These things *feel* unstable because *we* are unstable creatures."

"Unstable and vain," Lily cracks. Everyone laughs. "The sad truth behind my charming vanity . . ." Lily throws her gaze toward Archie. ". . . is that I don't *feel* old. My body is aging faster than my soul. Maybe every soul is eternally young."

"Absolutely not," Archie blurts out. "I assure you that my parents do not have eternally young souls. Perhaps you do because you're curious; you're open to new sounds and ideas and experiences. But people like my parents have decidedly old souls."

"That makes them sound very wise," Maud observes.

"Then let me rephrase." Archie thinks for a moment, then, "My parents have eternally decayed souls."

"My point is this," Lily says. "Souls don't age. They can't. Perhaps all of us have souls that are fixed at one age. Mine is eternally young. And Archie's parents are eternally decayed."

"I think I might be eternally middle-aged," Azalea blurts out, and everyone laughs.

"I think I'm in an eternal midlife crisis," Poppy cracks.

"Eternal life would be nice," Charlie says. He's still so young. He has no idea what wishing for immortality can lead to.

"No, it would not," Lily says firmly. "Who wants to be some decrepit one-hundred-year-old anyway?"

"Eternal youth, then," Poppy suggests.

Lily shrugs. "Doesn't sound so great either. The only thing worth living for is discovery, isn't it? Of the world . . . Of our selves . . . Once we know everything, once we've seen everything, what's left?"

"This is why I hope to always be a little unsure of myself," Bram declares, his eyes on me. I realize that Bram and I have not stopped looking at each other since this conversation about time and age began. "Because if I'm not, then life is over. The interesting part of it, at least. And I never want life to end. Not when it's this beautiful."

"Can Oliver open the gifts now?" Maud asks. "All this talk of getting old is freaking me out."

"Gifts!" Bram squeals happily.

I tear open wrapping paper and fling it across the room. After six decades of solitude, it feels so extravagant to accept so many presents. A pair of Levi's from Archie. A Claude McKay novel from Maud. It's called *Banana Bottom,* which inspires a round of hilariously dirty jokes about what a bottom might do with a banana. A Walkman from Azalea. Unbelievable that you can carry music with you now, in your pocket. You can score your own life like it's a film. Azalea and Lily must have coordinated their gifts, because Lily gives me cassette tapes as well as records. All classical. Tchaikovsky. Chopin. Rachmaninoff. Schubert. All my favorites. I've embraced the new without discarding the old.

"I wanted to make sure we played your favorite music once in a while," Lily says.

"Thank you. I'm so . . . touched." I give Lily a meaningful hug. She's not Mother. She never can be. But she is *a* mother. And like Mother, she understands what music means to me. Not revolution, but salvation.

"Which one should I play?" Lily asks.

I unwrap Tchaikovsky's *Romeo and Juliet.* It wasn't long ago that I was masked. Telling Bram that the only love stories anyone's interested in are the ones that end tragically. He told me he's had enough tragedy for one lifetime. I have too. I choose hope now. I choose life. Perhaps that's why I choose this record. Because being this happy allows me to enjoy tragedy as entertainment. As something that won't catch up with me again.

Lily carefully positions the record on the turntable. The modern sounds that have filled our home give way to the haunting fantasy overture written by a man who I know with all my heart was never allowed to love as he wanted to.

"Mine now," Bram says, handing me his gift again.

I unwrap it carefully. There's a leather journal inside. Lined paper, empty but for an inscription on the first page. *Let's never hide from each other again. If there's ever anything too difficult to say to each other, let us write it in this journal instead. I love you. I will forever.*

I look into Bram's eyes. It feels like we're finally picking up where we left off sixty years ago. I give him a kiss. I find a pen on an end table and jot seven words on the next page. *No more hiding. I love you too.*

BRAM. LONDON. AUGUST. 1980.

The crash of the front door wakes us up. Then Lily yelling. "Children, downstairs now. Come meet your sister."

I nuzzle my head into Oliver's chest. Take a whiff of his pure scent in the morning. "What time is it?"

Maud barges in. Opens our blinds. She wears gingham pajamas sewn for her by Lily. Unfazed by the sight of us in bed. Bare chests pressed against the other. My now-long and straightened hair on his pillow. Our bare feet popping out from under the covers. Our bedroom. One queen bed. Two queens. "Sister? She's brought another one of us in already. She'll soon be the queer Mother Teresa."

Oliver and I both laugh as we kick off the sheets. Reveal our naked bodies. It's nothing Maud hasn't seen before. The three of us share a bathroom after all. She still takes the opportunity to tease us. That's what siblings are for. "Why must teenage boys smell so foul?"

I tickle Maud playfully. "Why must teenage lesbians sleep in gingham?"

She laughs. "Hey, I chose this fabric."

"Oh. I know." I turn to Oliver. He grabs his ripped pair of jeans off the floor. "Oliver, back me up here."

Oliver looks at her as he pulls his jeans up. God, I love watching him get dressed. And undressed. The shapes his body makes as he bends and pulls. The sun perfectly illuminates his angelic face in the morning. Before any anxieties or memories have crept into his eyes. Peaceful. "It is a hideous fabric, Maud. But you pull it off because you're so beautiful. Besides, who cares what you wear to bed when you sleep alone?"

"Ouch. That began as quite the compliment. Ended as quite the insult." Maud wrestles Oliver back onto the bed and pins him down.

"Beware who you tackle. Oliver was a wrestler, once upon a time." I find my pants strewn on the floor too.

"Sweet gentle Oliver, a *wrestler?*" Maud eyes him with surprise. "What other secrets are you hiding?"

That question—asked at the wrong time—could fluster either of us. Send us into a panic. But not here and now. This is our right time. Oliver smiles. "Only that despite teasing my sister, I think she's absolutely wonderful."

Maud musses up his hair. "You little shit. You know I do better with being teased than being complimented."

"Then let us help you practice accepting praise." Oliver pulls her close. "Someday you'll meet a woman as beautiful and smart as you, and she won't be able to hide her adoration."

Maud cackles. "Please! I'm odd-looking and educationally subnormal."

Now I throw myself in bed too. Maud in the middle. Three siblings staring up at the cracks in the ceiling that keeps them safe and dry. "You're striking, and you're brilliant. You spend your days in that bookshop reading every book in there."

Maud shrugs. "Well, I try at least. Because after all, *genius lasts longer than beauty. That accounts for the fact that we all take such pains to overeducate ourselves."*

Oliver and I both look at each other. Eyes wide. He asks the question for us. "I thought you'd never read Wilde."

Maud's eyes gleam. "I made an exception and read the words of a white man. How could I not read that book after your story about how it brought the two of you together? I read every pithy little word imagining the two of you reading it out loud to each other in some American library."

"CHILDREN. RISE AND SHINE. NOW!"

We all bolt up. Oliver and I each grab a shirt that was thrown on the floor last night. Evidence of our lust after another night at the Blitz. Dancing to Rusty's eclectic choices. Oliver behind the percussion machine for part of the night. Me holding him from behind. Oliver adding synth sounds to the songs. Watching from the DJ booth as the crowd swayed blissfully.

"YOUR SISTER IS WAITING TO MEET YOU."

"You reckon she's a lesbian?" A sigh of hope in Maud's voice.

"Maybe she'll end up shacking up in your bedroom." I'm in Oliver's shirt from last night. He's in mine. We swap clothes like this. We share everything. Most importantly: a life. "Wouldn't that be something? Me and Oliver in one room, you and the new girl in your room."

"Margaret Thatcher's nightmare!" Oliver zips up his pants. Heads down first. We both follow.

We arrive downstairs to find Lily next to Archie. A muddy tabby cat in her hands. "There they are. Children, meet your new sister. She don't have a name yet, but she's as sweet as can be."

I turn to Maud with a raised eyebrow. "A little pussy. Just your type."

"Fuck off." She swats me playfully.

Oliver's eyes gaze at the cat adoringly. "I love her."

"I thought pets were too expensive." I approach Lily and pet the sweet animal. It purrs at my touch.

Lily turns to Archie. "Things are about to change around here." Lily hands me the cat. She digs her claws into me. It hurts a little. Also makes me feel loved. Like she doesn't want to let go. I know what it feels like not to want to let go of someone.

Lily digs through a crate of records. In search of something. She finds it. Dennis Brown. She carefully removes the vinyl from its sleeve. Puts the record on the turntable. "Sing it with me, children." We all know the song by now. It's on heavy rotation in the streets of Brixton.

"Money in my pocket but I just can't get no love."

"Louder!" Lily starts to dance. The island girl seems to come alive in her. She's no longer a middle-aged mother. She's full of youth. Exuberance.

"Money in my pocket but I just can't get no love."

Lily takes Maud's hand. Spins her around. Archie sways his hips. Oliver throws his hands in the air. I'm the last to join the dance. I savor the sight of them first. The freedom of the moment.

The song ends. Lily collapses onto the couch. "Children, guess who will be working as part of the costume department for the National's new show?"

I raise the unnamed cat into the air. "Our new sister?"

"You little shit." Lily laughs. "We have Archiekins to thank."

"I did nothing but make an introduction to a bloke I buggered—"

Lily lifts a scolding finger. "Archie! Children!"

Archie shrugs. "Apologies. To a lovely gentleman I made very pure love to. He happens to work in *the theatah*. Lily did the rest." Archie turns to Lily. "It's your talent that got you hired. Not me. If I had half your talent, I would have finished fashion school with you and pitched myself for the job. Alas, my only talent is choosing the right friends."

"You wanted me to be *more* than a friend when we first met, if memory serves." Lily cackles. She's loose. Giddy from the promise of a new future.

I turn to Maud. We both can't believe what we just heard. A little secret from the past. Maud is the one who digs. "Come again. Did you just say that you and Archie once *dated*?"

Archie brushes the question aside with a wave of his wrist. "Maud dear, you should know by now I don't *date*. But yes, I did have my eyes on Lily when we first met. And she was wise enough to reject me."

Lily smiles knowingly. "You children think you know all there is to know about me? But I've lived more lives than this little cat." She stands back up. Too energized to stay seated. Takes the cat back into her arms. "I can't wait to call Lady Cordelia and tell her I won't be sewing for her any longer." Lily smiles. "Mind you, I'm not the costume designer. Just a seamstress. But it's a step, isn't it? And I like steps. Change. It's the key to staying young."

"That's exactly why I cycle through men so quickly." Archie raises a sly eyebrow. Dares Lily to scold him again.

"Maybe we should call the cat Lady Cordelia?" Oliver's suggestion.

"Over my dead body." Lily shakes her head.

"Blitz." My suggestion. I feel my face open up into a smile. The memory of Lily naming me comes back to me. My rebirth.

Lily shakes her head. "That name's already taken. This cat's an original."

"The Iron Kitty." Archie's contribution.

"Poor thing has nothing in common with Thatcher." Lily pulls the cat closer. "Well, maybe the claws."

"Okay, I've got it. I think we should call her Changeling." We all turn to Oliver. Sensing he has more to say. "Because, well . . . as you said, you love change. And she represents change. In a sense. And in another sense, we're a happy home of changelings, aren't we?"

Maud leans in. "What's a changeling exactly?"

Oliver explains. "They're children placed in human homes by demons. They're strange. They don't fit in. They scare the ordinary humans with their otherness. But the thing about changelings is that they're always alone in a human home. No one's ever considered what might happen in a home full of changelings. A world of nothing but otherness." Oliver pauses. Looks at me with what I think is gratitude. "A happy world."

Lily pulls him close. "Changeling." The cat purrs. "I think she likes the name. It suits her. Look at her eyes." Lily turns to me and Oliver. "Now there are three members of the family who are part feline."

She places Changeling down. Lets her slowly explore her new home. The cat paws at the furniture. The framed photos of us haphazardly placed around the living area. The record player. Lily joins Changeling by the turntable. She puts a new record on. The just-released new album from Siouxsie and the Banshees.

I think of all the times I've seen Siouxsie at the Blitz. Now she's changing the way the word sounds. Looks. Feels. The new record is called *Kaleidoscope*. A word that sounds a lot like my life. So many ways for it to reflected. So many patterns that there's no pattern at all. But all that matters is what it looks like now. Bright.

The first song comes on. "Happy House." When Lily plays DJ, she always picks the right song. We start to dance again. We sing along at the top of our lungs. *We're happy here in the happy house.* Oliver rushes to our room and emerges with his synthesizer. He adds some live instrumentation. He hits the keys with his eyes fixed on me. I dance with mine fixed on him.

Changeling seems to dance too. She wants to join the party.

Oliver smiles. "She likes music!" He picks her up. Places her in his lap as he creates sonic magic. Changeling's eyes glow. She's happy here. In the happy house.

OLIVER. LONDON. SEPTEMBER. 1980.

After three days of thunderstorms and five days of drizzle, the sun peeks through our bedroom window on a Sunday morning. Changeling purrs in delight. She sleeps in our bed every night. I love nothing more than waking up and realizing she's curled up between us. Neither of us has to work today. Bram never tutors on Sundays. I have no sessions booked.

I pull Bram out of bed and into the sunlight. We scour the city for Oreo cookies, but they don't seem to exist in the United Kingdom. We rush through the aisles of Tesco and land on Spooks biscuits. They're made from colored dough, and each one has a ridiculous monster name. Red Devil. Yellow Peril. Green Gremlin. We eat the biscuits as we walk the streets of a new city. Stroll through Brixton, up to the river. We gaze at the National, where Lily now works. We make the city ours. Even in Mayfair, where the rules of the old world still apply, we hold hands. We ignore the glares of clenched women and vicious men. When a teenage boy pretends to sneeze so he can croak out the word *screamers* for the amusement of his friends, we walk on.

Bram stops outside Claridge's. An unnerved look in his eyes, like he's seen a ghost. "That's where it happened," he says.

"What?" I ask stupidly.

"Where my father burned the book. Well, some of it at least. Where I became . . . like this." His hand tenses in mine. For perhaps the first time since I've known him, he seems genuinely terrified. Like he's his father's son again, existing in a time before I was born. A time before Mother had met Father, when she might have chosen some other path. Perhaps a happier one.

"Let's go in," I say.

Bram shudders. The hairs on his arm stand up.

"You're scared," I say. "But you shouldn't be. This is our time, remember?"

I have to be the brave one today. I lead him inside the majestic building. Into the decadent art deco lobby. Everything inside screams money. The grit of *our* London doesn't exist in this shiny land of marble and gold, of checkered clothes and glass chandeliers.

"It's changed," he says. "There used to be a carriage drive."

"There used to be carriages," I say. And then, "Everything changes."

"Except us," he says wistfully.

"We have definitely changed," I say. "We used to eat Oreos. Now we eat Spooks."

He laughs. "A monumental transformation."

"We used to be apart. Now we're together. How's that for monumental?"

The fear exits his gaze. He steels himself with a long inhale. "Let's have afternoon tea."

The hostess looks us up and down when we ask for a table. She's not the only one. Every gentleman and lady seated in the art deco foyer seem to be hissing at us with their eyes. Some leer at us directly. Others stare at our reflection covertly in the many mirrors that line the walls, reflecting opulence back at itself. The cost of the flowers in this one room alone could probably feed a whole neighborhood.

I see us through their eyes. Bram's platform boots. His long hair, now with streaks of hot pink. The jacket he loves to wear. *The National Front Is an Affront*. Me with my new waves of gelled hair. My tight Levi's. My T-shirt with a decal of Donna Summer's face on the front. I like us so much better than I like them.

"Are you guests of the hotel?" the hostess asks.

"No, but we can pay in cash," I say.

I'm about to pull my wallet out to prove it when Bram stops me. "I'm guessing you would've seated us already if we were wearing Armani suits."

"That sounds like an accusation," the hostess says coolly.

"It's not," Bram responds. "You don't make the rules. You simply follow them. I stayed in a suite here with my father once. If he were still alive, he'd be just like those men inside. Sneering at the filthy faggots invading their pristine little world."

"I-I'm sorry," the hostess says.

"Because my father is dead, or because I'm a filthy faggot?"

"I don't know . . . Both." She puts a hand on Bram's shoulder. "I'll put you at a corner table where you won't be bothered by the . . . clientele."

The afternoon tea doesn't disappoint in its grandeur. Seasonal fruits. A special blend of tea unique to the hotel. Once the other patrons have tired of gawking at us, we're free to gawk at them. We make up a story about each of them.

The lady sitting alone reading *Madame Bovary* has recently had her heart broken by the young man she's been sleeping with behind her husband's back.

The young, blandly beautiful couple feeding each other finger sandwiches like babies are royalty from some Scandinavian country.

The angry-looking man barking at his waiter because his eggs were undercooked has three children, none of whom speak to him.

When we've finished eating, my eyes travel to the grand piano in the center of the room. "Do I dare?" I ask Bram, my eyes on the instrument.

"You absolutely do dare."

I stand up and walk toward it as if possessed. I don't ask for permission to play. I simply sit on the bench like it belongs to me. Put my fingers on the keys and take a deep breath.

I can feel Mother by my side. I warm up with a Phrygian scale just for her. The diminished, eastern sound that always transported her into a world of fantasy. I smile, imagining she's playing the scale an octave higher next to me. I feel such gratitude to her for gifting me her love of music. As long as I have music, she's still close, isn't she?

I debate playing Bowie. Donna. Queen. Something rebellious and incongruous with this luxurious room. But I choose Schubert's "Fantasie in F Minor" instead. I played it for Bram once before, when he was Shams, when we were strangers to each other.

I look up. The stuck-up guests are learning to love me now. They're reconsidering the wild child they thought they could dismiss. Forced to remember what they once knew when they were young, that we are all capable of creating beauty.

My eyes land on Bram as I play the devastatingly romantic melody that feels as vibrant today as it must have when it was written in 1828. Great music has no age. The joy in Bram's eyes stirs me. Makes me feel as vibrant as I once was, long ago.

The first time I played this piece for him, I wondered if he might be my other half.

Now I know he is, and that knowledge allows me to play the piece with a new depth of understanding. I didn't know what love is then. I do now. We're children of the sun who found each other.

I close my eyes as I reach the end of the piece. The piece is meant for four hands, but I play a two-hand version that works.

The notes I can't play ring in my head, Mother's hands playing them next to me.

The melody brings her back.

Music is time travel.

I'm in charge of the destination.

For the first time in my life, I feel powerful. My destiny is of my own making. It feels wonderful.

BRAM. LONDON. DECEMBER. 1980.

It is the last day of the last month of the first year of a new decade.

Oliver is gone when Changeling wakes me up by crawling atop my face. She meows until I acknowledge her. She misses Oliver when he's gone. I do too. She prefers Oliver to me. I do too.

"I know, sweetie, I'm not him. But he has a session today. He'll be back."

On his side of the bed is the journal I got him for his birthday. Now filled with our thoughts and fears. We keep it carefully hidden under a loose floorboard, for our words would give our secret away.

I flip the pages until I see his new note: *I didn't think it possible, but I think this was the best year of my life. Thank you.*

I write my own: *Next year will be better, I promise.*

I place the journal back under the floorboard. He'll see my message soon enough. I feel a sudden wave of superstitious panic. Am I tempting fate by promising an even better year?

But the anxiety doesn't last. I'm too happy. Too certain that the best is yet to come.

OLIVER. LONDON. DECEMBER. 1980.

I wander the streets with Bram and Maud on the last afternoon of the year. We're giddy with excitement. A new beginning starts tomorrow. We're unafraid. Excited for what each new sunrise will bring. Charlie sees us as he approaches the squat he lives in. "You all going to the wrestling meet?"

"The what?" I ask.

Charlie blushes. "I know it's macho bullshit. But it's not all we do. We have a knitting circle too. And a sewing bee. And of course we all work on *Gay Noise*. Do you have our latest issue?" Charlie pulls out the paper and hands it to me.

"Oliver's a wrestler," Bram says as I stare at the front page of the paper. The headline reads

**WHEN IS A KILLER NOT A MURDERER?
ANSWER: WHEN HE'S IN THE SPECIAL
AIR SERVICE OR THE BRITISH ARMY.**

The piece makes a connection between the brutal killings in Northern Ireland by British forces and the treatment of gay people by police. A cartoon on the next page shows police officers preparing for duty. The caption reads

Right, lads—before we start on the pickets,
some practice on a few minority groups.

"You're a wrestler?" Charlie asks. "You have to come in. You can join the meet!"

"No, I *was* a wrestler," I say. "Those days are over."

"Come on, please!" Maud begs.

"Absolutely not." I turn my attention back to the newspaper. An ad for a new gay bookshop: *"Haven't You Hard? Gay's the Word. London's Gay Community Bookshop."*

"What if I join too?" Bram asks.

"I've already seen you wrestle," I say. I flip to the last page. The classifieds. An ad that reads *"BOOKS ARE WEAPONS!"* from *"Edinburgh's comprehensive left / radical bookshop. Browsers welcome."*

"What if I join?" Maud asks. "Bet you can't take me on, little brother."

I raise an eyebrow. "Who are you calling little?"

She smiles. "You, baby boy."

The way she calls me *baby boy* reminds me of Jack. The Jackal. How I wish I didn't have to read his name in international newspapers. He's taken over his father's empire, as planned. Whitman & Whitman has become the world's biggest pharmaceutical company, and eighty-year-old Jack one of America's richest men. Thinking of him awakens my competitive spirit. "Let's go!"

In the basement of the squat, men wrestle. Some play up their masculinity in tight-fitting singlets that hug their hairy, muscular bodies. Others rebel against gender norms by wrestling in dresses and heels.

Charlie signs us up for the meet. They pit me and Maud against each other. We hop onto the dirty old mattress in the center of the basement floor. Men surround us, cheering loudly as we circle around each other. An aggressive song plays. Peter Straker's "Real Natural Man."

Maud pulls me into a tight hold. She pushes me down onto the mat. Pins me to the floor. Our audience hoots and hollers for her as Straker yelps about being a real natural man in a voice so high that it's clear he's not interested in being some masculine stereotype.

I wrap my legs around Maud and overpower her. I flip her over. Now I'm on top. She laughs happily. "You really are a wrestler."

"Told you," I say.

"Don't get too comfortable," she warns. She locks my head in a grip. Uses her knee to destabilize me. Boom. She's on top again.

Bram cheers her on. "Come on, Maud!"

I turn to Bram, feigning dismay. "You're rooting *against* me?"

He laughs. "It's fun to see you pinned down," he says impishly.

Maud slams me down onto the mattress. Clouds of dust rise up and make us both cough so hard that we can't help but laugh. I struggle against her, but it's no use. She's got me. And I want her to win too. That's the beauty of being surrounded by people you love. You want them to win, even if it means you lose.

BRAM. LONDON. JANUARY. 1981.

"Ten. Nine. Eight. Seven. Six. Five. Four. Three. Two. HAPPY NEW YEAR."

We all hug. Lily holds me close. Says she loves me. Maud pulls me and Oliver into a group hug. Archie, Azalea, Poppy, and Blossom gather us into a circle. The first song we dance to this year is Johnny Osbourne. "Truths and Rights." The whole shebeen sings along. Loudly.

"Children, run, come, the truths and rights. That's what I'm about. You know the truths and rights. Teach it to the children."

There's something so beautiful about this moment. So wholesome. No one is drunk. Pearl stopped serving alcohol since the police raids started getting worse. Thatcher and her *moral values*. Mary Whitehouse and her *moral values*. Lily's first show might have led to threats and protests. Thankfully it also led to another show. A new career in theater. Archie and Lily prefer Pearl's without alcohol. No pushy people asking why they aren't drinking. No need to explain their sobriety to drunks.

We sing out: *"When you think it's peace and safety, Lord. It could be, could be sudden destruction."*

The song ends. More reggae plays. We order sodas at the make-shift bar that once served Red Stripe and Tennent's.

We share our favorite memories of 1980.

I say: "Oliver coming to London."

Oliver says: "Changeling moving into the house."

Lily says: "This moment. Right now."

Maud says: "But it's already 1981!"

Lily says: "Well then, perhaps I like 1981 even more than 1980. A new year. A new start."

We dance in the cramped and smoky space until Pearl kicks us out. We walk home singing Johnny Osbourne as a police siren interrupts us from a nearby street. They all ignore it. I try to as well. But I'm suddenly filled with another wave of superstitious panic. The siren feels like a bad omen, a warning that sudden destruction could puncture our peace and safety at any moment.

OLIVER. LONDON. VALENTINE'S DAY. 1981.

Valentine's Day. A day that celebrates the saint who dared perform weddings for Christians who were forbidden from marrying each other. A day that should therefore belong not to all lovers, but to forbidden lovers. *Our* day. My day to show Bram how much I love him. He's chased and celebrated me. Today, I want to celebrate him.

"Good morning, my love," I mutter, still groggy. Changeling meows happily. Paws gently at my cheek. "Yes, good morning to you too, but I was talking to—"

I reach for Bram. He's not there. I check the time. It's almost eleven. I've slept in. I suppose secretly planning a surprise trip for two in between sessions has exhausted me. I've spent months saving enough money from sessions to book what I think and hope will be a surprise worthy of our forbidden love. I haven't told him a thing about the trip. Simply asked him to clear his calendar from this afternoon until tomorrow night. He almost looked disappointed, like he wanted to be the one to plan our first proper Valentine's Day together.

Sixty-one years we've circled each other. Now, finally, we get to celebrate our love. Our flight leaves in four hours.

I stumble past Lily's workroom. I imagine she's in there, working the day away. I expect to find Bram in the living area, reading quietly so he won't wake me up. Maud should be at the bookshop. But when I enter the kitchen, it's full. Of people and also of tension. Lily, Maud, Azalea, Poppy, Blossom, and Archie are clustered inside. Bram is missing. Nobody looks happy.

"Ah, Sleeping Beauty has arisen," Lily says when she sees me. She pulls me close. Her hair is in curlers. Her face isn't on yet. It's rare to see Lily without a single stroke of blush, eyeliner, or lipstick. I love the untouched warmth of her face. She is the sun we orbit around. I wonder if all families are like this. One member the sun. Another the moon. Me . . . which planet would I be?

"It's ENRAGING," Maud yells at all of us, and at none of us, and at the walls and the ground. Maud would be Mercury maybe. Hot and mercurial. A bubble of rage boiling just beneath the surface. "I feel sick to my stomach."

Lily lets go of me and shines her light on Maud now. "We all do, child. But we can't do anything reckless—"

"Reckless?" Maud spits her words out, barely breathing. "Our kind don't need to do nothing reckless to get arrested or worse. They can stop us for *suspecting* us. And they *always* suspect us."

"What's going on?" I ask, afraid of the answer. I wanted to start the day with kisses and declarations of love. Dreamed of sweeping Bram off his feet and into a new city. I wanted to orchestrate the day like a conductor. Packing our bags would be the overture. Dancing to an accordion player on the Seine would be the crescendo.

No one answers my question. Lily shakes her head, indicating I shouldn't interrupt. I should let Maud burn like Mercury.

"And you know what pisses me off the most?" Maud asks.

Lily clutches Maud's hand both tightly and gently. It's a rare gift

Lily has, the ability to be both firm and tender in the same breath. "That human life is not valued equally."

"But you already knew that, didn't you?" Poppy asks.

Maud lets out a sad grunt. Almost a laugh. "Sure. Yes. Of course I knew that. What pisses me off the most is that they're taking *my* humanity from me."

"Don't let them do that," Lily urges. "Then they've won."

"But they *have* won." Maud's words sizzle. "Look around. They've colonized the world. Put us in prison because they feel like it. Built their empires with our slave labor. Test their medicines on us, and then make sure we don't have access to them when they're approved. I'm so angry that I can't even grieve those poor people in Dublin. Forty-eight young souls dead and instead of mourning them like I want to, I'm just so angry. Thirteen dead and nothing said."

"What happened?" I ask. Then stupidly, I add, "Is everything okay? Where's Bram?"

Maud's nostrils flare. "Everything is certainly not okay, Oliver. And it's not about Bram. I'm sure wherever he is, he's just fine. There was a fire in Dublin. Just like there was a fire in New Cross. Remember?"

"Yes, of course I—Maud, of course I remember the New Cross fire." I feel a surge of unexpected guilt enter my body, like a dark and ominous string section. The world goes from major to minor. My romantic visions for the day feel suddenly inaccessible, replaced by nightmares of that fire almost a month ago, in our city, that ended thirteen young Black lives. It's all Maud's talked about since. That fire seemed to light something in her. A dormant spark that blazes wildly now. She's not the only one. The neighborhood has changed since the fire. The same song blaring from every home. Johnny Osbourne.

Thirteen dead and nothing said. Oh, what this world is coming to?

Maud flings her words at me. Filling me in on what I missed by sleeping in. "Thatcher and the queen have written letters of condolence to the victims of the Stardust fire. And they're *Irish*, for fuck's sake. Mother England hates the Irish, but apparently, they hate us more. Where are *our* condolences? Where's *our* investigation?"

Azalea shakes her head. "They don't want no investigation. If they find out it was some racist firebomb, which we all know it probably was—"

Maud looks at me with fire in her eyes. "It wasn't the firebomb that was racist, was it?"

I smile. She remembers the day we met as vividly as I do. The summoning of this memory allows me to breathe again. Of course Maud isn't angry with me. I didn't light the fire. I don't put Black kids in jail. I release my guilt and offer Maud a smile. "No, it was the asshole who put it there," I say.

Maud gifts me a tiny nod of acknowledgment.

"Which is exactly why they won't investigate," Lily says. "Thatcher loves the National Front. They're doing her dirty work for her."

"What do we do?" Maud asks. Then she quietly whispers the lyrics to Johnny's song. *"Oh, what we gonna do?"*

"We will do what we've always done," Archie says. "We'll keep living. Not merely existing, as Wilde accused the masses of. But *living*. It's our life they want after all, is it not? We won't let the National Front or Thatcher or the queen stop us from experiencing joy. This is our time."

I flinch when Archie speaks those words. *This is our time*. Four words I believed in with all my heart. Four words that suddenly feel perilous and confusing. *Our.* Who is included in when we speak of what is *ours?* And *time.* What is time anyway? A single year on Neptune amounts to one hundred and sixty-five years on Earth.

Perhaps Bram and I would be Neptune in the galaxy that is our new family. We're out of sync with the way the rest of them experience time.

Maud clears her throat. "Easy for you to say, *Archiekins.*" She pronounces his nickname with disdain. "If *you* burned in a fire, someone would investigate. Your mother is probably friends with half the nitwit inbred members of the royal family—"

"Maud, that's enough of that," Lily says curtly. "Archie is not the enemy, and you have no idea what he's been through because of his mother."

"I know that," Maud says with resigned weariness. "I'm sorry, Archie."

"No need to apologize, my dear," Archie says calmly. "We're all others here. All refugees from the same empire."

"Really? How are you a refugee exactly?" Maud asks Archie. "With your handsome white face and your posh accent. Your parents probably live not far from here."

"Unfortunately, they do," Archie says sadly. "But there may as well be an ocean between us. Perhaps more than an ocean. A solar system."

Venus. That's who I want to be. Not the planet. The goddess of love. This was meant to be my day to let my love shine. To not let Bram make all the decisions for us.

"Archie, don't be a fool now," Lily chastises without cruelty. "You know that comparison is the enemy of peace, and we need peace in here when there's war raging outside."

I know Lily is right. I also know that I was just doing the very same thing Archie did. Comparing what's happening now in Brixton to what happened in Boston in 1920. It's a version of the same thing, isn't it? The powerful trying to keep the powerless in their place. One big swirling galaxy of injustice?

Lily continues, "Your experience, my beloved Archie, isn't comparable to Maud's or mine or to any Black person forced to make a life in countries that still see them as slaves and subjects."

"Thank you!" Maud says. "Finally, you're making sense!"

"Child, I always make sense," Lily says. "Sometimes it's your listening skills that need work."

"I'm sorry if that's how it came out," Archie says to Maud.

"I suppose you can't help it," Maud says sharply.

"Maud." Lily speaks Maud's name with the authority of a parent about to lay down the law. "Treat Archie with respect. You have no idea—"

"If I have no idea, then tell me!" Maud pleads.

Lily simply says, "There are things grown-ups don't tell children to protect them from the horror of it."

"Like what?" I ask, curious to know more.

Maud gives me a nod of solidarity. "Yeah, like what?" With Maud's eyes on me, it's not Archie's secret past I'm thinking of. It's my own. All the things I hide from these people I love, from my new family. My immortality and eternal youth. But perhaps more importantly, the heartbreak I suffered because of Harvard, the boys I cared for who died, the family I had to abandon . . . Mother. I close my eyes, silently begging God and Mother for forgiveness.

Just then, the slam of a door. Bram's sunny voice. "Happy Valentine's Day, everyone! Oliver, are you upstairs?"

"In the kitchen!" I yell back.

He recites a poem as he approaches, unaware of the big bang

that awaits him. Our world is being re-created anew this morning. I can feel the change like an explosion of particles. *"For this was on Saint Valentine's Day,"* Bram bellows like some Shakespearian actor. *"When every bird cometh there to choose his mate."* He enters holding a dozen red roses and a framed page of poetry. He seems too elated to notice the glum looks on our faces. "Oh, hello, everyone." He raises the poem up. "It's Chaucer. I thought it would be a nice gift because we live on Chaucer Street. And his poem is said to be the first time Valentine's Day was associated with love. They say he wrote it for King Richard II and his bride—"

Maud rolls her eyes. "The royals strike again. They're also to blame for the commercialization of love. What didn't they fuck up with their greed?"

Bram deflates. He finally takes us all in. Realizes we're not floating atop the same cloud he's floating on. We're under a different cloud. A black and stormy one. "Did I say something wrong?"

"No, it's not you," Maud says. "I'm sorry I snapped. The poem is beautiful. The roses are gorgeous. You and Oliver make me sick with how adorable you are. Living with you two is like eating too much candy. Makes you smile and make your stomach turn all at once."

Everyone laughs, no one louder than me and Bram. That's the Maud we love. The one who teases us mercilessly and lovingly.

Bram hands me the flowers and the poem. "They're for you. I had to do something for you this morning since we're taking a mysterious trip later."

"You're leaving?" Maud asks. "Today? After what's happened?"

Bram looks to me, still unaware of all that's transpired. Maud also looks to me, her eyes like steel. "I—I had planned something special for—for me and Bram."

"We all had other plans today," Maud says. "And we're all changing them." She turns to the grown-ups. "Right?"

"I don't know," Lily says. "We need to think. To be careful. Strategic."

"What we need is to be *prompt*," Maud argues. "We can't wait for the moment to pass. We need to flood the streets while our hearts our pounding." She looks around. "Or is my heart the only one that feels like a hammer right now?"

"I'm with Maud," Poppy says. "This is no time to sit back."

"Me too," Azalea says. "And there's safety in numbers. The more of us out there, the harder it will be to stop us."

Archie approaches Maud apprehensively. "I would love to join you in whatever you're planning," he says. "But if you'd rather I not be there because . . . because . . ."

"Because you're white and your mummy attends polo matches with Duchess Cuntlesby?"

"Maud!" Lily tries to sound stern, but she's also laughing.

"My dear Maud," Archie says with a smile. "Duchess Cuntlesby insists on always being referred to by her full name, which is Her Disgrace, *the* Duchess *of* Cuntlesby. Words matter, you see."

Maud manages a smile. "So do you, Archiekins. Of course we want you there. White faces. Brown faces." Maud looks to Bram and Blossom. I see Bram bite his lip, debating what to do. "We need the numbers. And maybe they'll be less likely to arrest us with some white faces in the mix."

My fingers twitch when Maud mentions getting arrested. Considering what this would mean for the first time. Sure, I've run from cops here and there for minor offenses. Busking. Sleeping outside. But what's happening now feels different. More dangerous. What Maud sees as protest, they see as inciting violence. Fear possesses me so fully that I can barely stand upright. Bram puts an arm around me.

"Maud, Oliver planned a surprise for me," Bram repeats quietly, sensing my weakness is about the trip. And it is. But it's about more now. It's about the terror of what's coming.

"What's the surprise?" Maud asks aggressively.

I feel myself shrink into Bram's body. His strength. I don't know how I ever wrestled. I feel so powerless. "It's not about that," I croak out.

Bram holds me close. "He can't reveal the surprise, right? Then I won't be surprised."

"Maud, I-I'm sorry," I stammer. "But I'm scared. For us. But mostly, for you. I don't want you making a target out of yourself. I—I want you here. With us. Safe."

"Guess I shouldn't be surprised," Maud says sadly. "Just go."

"Maud, let me discuss it with Oliver," Bram says firmly. "Just give us some time."

I turn to Lily desperately. "Lily, you must see my point."

Lily nods. "Go on your trip, Oliver. You already asked me for permission. Come back tomorrow. It will be a new day."

"But that's exactly what I'm worried about," I argue. "I don't want a new day. I want yesterday back. When we were all happy. Nothing has happened. Yet."

Maud throws her hands up into the air. "And that is exactly the problem. *Nothing* said. Ever. It's time we said it."

"Lily, she's your responsibility," I implore. "Tell her it's not safe for her to be out protesting. They'll arrest her. Everything will change."

Lily sighs. Closes her eyes. When she opens them again, she's a different Lily. The warmth of her sunshine has been replaced by a cold edge. She speaks with controlled precision, unwilling to let herself break. "Children, I suppose it's time I told you a piece of my boo-hoo backstory." A brief pause, a caesura in the concerto that is Lily Summers. "I moved to London when I was twelve to live with my Uncle Alton." I can see she's haunting the past, as Mother used to say. She speaks to us, but her spirit time travels. "Uncle Alton was . . ." She laughs. "He was a tornado. He drank too much. Danced too hard. Loved too many. Worked just as hard as he played. For me. So he could buy me the sewing machine I begged for. If he ever managed to sleep with a posh girl, he'd steal her scarves and bring them home so I could make something out of them. Never told me to go into the streets like the other—"

She stops herself. She's journeyed back to a time we've never talked about. A time before she had introduced the world to the Lily we know and love.

"He loved music. The music that reminded him of home. And the music that let him dream of America. Ray Charles. Chuck Berry. Little Richard. But he never judged me if I cried in my room listening to Joan Baez. I would lie in bed at night, repeating her song 'Girl of Constant Sorrow,' until he came home from whatever trouble he was causing and tucked me in bed with a prayer. The other kids said I wasn't Black enough, which was code for not being man enough. Uncle Alton never cared. He took care of me. Just like he promised my parents he would."

Another silence. Longer. Not a caesura. A fermata. A full stop as Lily prepares for the next movement.

"When I go to my Alcoholics Anonymous meeting on Sundays, I'm really going to visit him in prison."

"Wait, what?" Maud asks softly. "Lily . . . I'm . . ."

"I do go to meetings on other days. But on Sundays, I give him back the love and the gifts and the devotion he gave me."

"But . . . why was he arrested?" Bram asks.

"Why?" she asks. "For *nothing.* Three of them were arrested fleeing a house party. The police said the party was illegal. It was. But what were they supposed to do when pubs wouldn't serve them? They said Uncle Alton was selling drugs. He wasn't. They piled one accusation after another on him. He couldn't afford no fancy barrister. The first time I visited him after he was put away for life—"

"For *life?*" Maud echoes.

I look around at the grown-ups. Azalea, Poppy, Blossom, Archie. They all look unsurprised. They know all this already.

Maud paces across the sliver of free floor space in the kitchen. "How can you just accept that he's in some cell— How can you— How can you live without talking about him all the time—"

Lily puts her hands on Maud's shoulders, stopping her from nervously wandering the area. "I don't tell you about it because . . ."

She doesn't finish so I say it for her. "Because it's too painful," I whisper. I'm thinking of Mother now. Of how warm and wonderful she was. Of how rarely I bring her up to my new friends and family. "Because anything you might say would diminish the magnitude of what he means to you."

Lily's gaze freezes on me. I know she's wondering who I'm talking about. "Exactly," she says. Her eyes burn with contemplation. Like speaking about this aloud has helped her see it differently. "I do want to protect you children from the horrors of the world. But maybe, well, maybe I also want to protect myself from living in that sadness and anger. If we live in sadness and anger, they've won."

Maud looks up at her. "So you're saying we shouldn't go out into the streets? Shouldn't fight?"

"No, child, not at all. Protest isn't giving in to sadness and anger. It's rising up as a community. It's connection and hope. It's exactly what we must do. But maybe . . . The truth is I don't like thinking of myself as a victim. That's why I don't talk about the things that hurt me most. Why I don't like boo-hoo backstories."

Hearing Lily open up like this, allowing her powerful facade to melt into vulnerability, shifts the energy in the room. It fills me with a longing for the person who loved me into being. The woman I'll never see again, no matter how long I'll live. Time only marches forward. I wish it could also bring me back. Just one more sonata played by her side. Just one more taste of her cookies.

Lily hoists herself up onto the kitchen counter. Crosses her legs. "I want to tell you what he said to me that first time I visited him." Lily rubs her lips against each other, then she speaks in a different voice. Her uncle's voice. "If dem arrest me fi stealing fabric from posh girls fi you. Well, mi would hold mi head up high. Serve mi time proud. But dem yah charges is lies. I'm . . . living a lie now. Look at me. You know wah dat means? Means you haff tah live true enough fi both of us, child."

"Live true enough for both of us," Maud repeats, almost to herself. Then she sighs out, "Fuck me."

Lily wipes a tear from her cheek. She's not done. "I don't like wallowing. And I didn't want to tell you kids about Alton because I want you to carry hope with you always. Not sadness. Not regret. Not the realization that this world is full of people like him, sentenced for crimes they didn't commit." Lily turns to Maud. "I'm telling you this now because you need to understand that what happened to him can happen to you. If I'm protective of you, it's because I'm scared of losing someone else to a jail cell. But I won't stop you from rising up either. In fact, I'll join you. Because that's living true, isn't it?"

I don't dare say what I'm thinking. Which is that living true shouldn't mean taking such unnecessary risks. I know Maud will end up just like Uncle Alton if she goes out there. She's a butch Black lesbian. She's everything they fear. I want to protect her, and I also know that expressing that will feel like the opposite of love. It will come across like I want to control her. Put her in another kind of prison.

Lily pulls some lipstick out of a kitchen drawer.

Azalea sees an opportunity for a mood change and takes it. "Girl, why do you keep lipstick next to your forks?"

Lily raises a shoulder coyly. "A lady must have lipstick handy everywhere." With that, she puts the first piece of her face on. Turns to me and Bram with glossy red lips. "You two go upstairs and get yourself ready for a beautiful Valentine's Day." She hands me a vase. "Be sure to put those in water right away. Wouldn't want them to die."

As Bram and I head upstairs, that horrible word lingers in my mind. Die. Death. It will happen to them. Inevitably. Maud, Lily, Archie, Azalea, all of them. These people I now love. Just as I loved Mother and Brendan, and they're gone.

I feel, for the first time since following Bram into his new life, a sincere and painful pang of regret. I shouldn't have allowed myself to welcome all this love. It will only end, like all the most beautiful concertos, in the melancholy silence that longs to recapture the beauty that's passed forever.

BRAM. LONDON. VALENTINE'S DAY. 1981.

We shower together. He holds me from behind. Soaps my body up. I get the sense he doesn't want to look at me. That he's hiding. I felt so vital when I walked into the house. Roses in one hand. Poetry in the other. Love in my heart. Connected to him. To life. Now he feels distant from me. Even as his skin pushes against mine.

He squeezes some shampoo out of a tube and rubs it into my hair.

"That smells like soup. I swear, Lily and her antiaging potions."

He doesn't laugh. He's in no mood for jokes.

"We shouldn't go." I speak the words quietly. Wonder if he heard me over the sound of the shower jets.

"Shouldn't go protest?" He speaks directly into my ear. "Or shouldn't go on the trip I spent months planning for us?"

"Oliver, don't be like this." I immediately regret saying it. He's only being himself. Scared. Averse to risk.

"Be like what exactly?"

"Nothing. I'm sorry, that came out wrong."

"I want to know. Like what? Tell me? What am I *being like*? Like . . . oh, maybe like a person who actually has an opinion of his own? Doesn't just follow you around like a lapdog?"

"Oliver, what's going on in that beautiful head of yours?" I attempt lightness. But my question only magnifies the vast expanse of energy between us. I don't understand him anymore. Perhaps I never did.

"It doesn't matter." He lets go of me. I don't move. I'm the one hiding now. I keep my gaze on the chipped tiles of the shower. A herringbone mosaic pattern I let myself get lost in. The countless shapes the same pattern can make. Depending on how it's perceived.

"Have you thought about what would happen if we end up in prison?" Oliver grabs my shoulders and spins me around. "What would the guards say when they realize we don't age? What will this government that's so willing to sacrifice their own do with us, do you think?"

"I—I don't know." It's not a thought that's crossed my mind. I suppose it should have. They raid queer bars. They lure men into toilets, then arrest them for cottaging.

"Well, I know." He turns the shower faucet until the water is freezing cold. He needs it to cool the heat inside him. "They'll try to kill us out of fear. Then they'll realize we're indestructible. Which is what they long to be. Then they'll use us."

"Use us? How?"

"I don't know. As soldiers. Or spies or assassins. As—as—as something that will give them more power. If I were evil enough to mastermind such a thing, then I would be a president or a prime minister or in charge of some sort of empire!"

"So it's not Maud you're concerned about? It's you—"

"Oh, don't accuse me of being selfish. Not you, the most selfish person I know." He exits the shower. There's still foam on his lower back.

"That was harsh." I whisper the words. I'm not sure he hears them.

Oliver grabs a damp towel hanging from the door. It's black

with bright pink palm trees on it. He dries himself ferociously. Like his skin is covered with insects. "And how dare you accuse me of not caring for Maud? Or for you. We're happy. Finally, we're happy. Why would we risk all that right now? For what?"

"I don't know. For a more just world." I hear myself say the words. I'm not sure I believe them. The world has always been unjust. Always will be. Destruction and injustice will survive as long as human beings do.

"Good luck with that."

"Look, I know what you're saying. I get it."

"No, you really don't." He looks at me with scorn. It's Valentine's Day. This is the last thing I imagined happening today. "You say you *get it* because you want the conversation to be over. Because you can't stand being wrong, but you really don't get anything at all."

"I— You're right. I don't get it. I feel like you're in one conversation, and I'm in another. All I'm saying is that we waited a long time for the life we have now. Perhaps we need to do what we can so Maud and Lily and everyone else has their chance before their time is up."

"Great. Fine. Message received. But today? On the day I spent months planning for us?"

"Nobody planned this, Oliver."

"I PLANNED IT!" His eyes blaze with fury. He screams so loud that I'm sure they can hear him down below. It's not just a lover's spat anymore. It's a public fight. We've made it everyone's business.

"I—I know you did. I'm sorry. I get it. I wasn't thinking. Or I was, but not of you."

"Because you never think of me." He hangs the towel back up. Stands naked in front of me.

"All I think about is you." I turn the shower off. Stand in the steam. Let it evaporate around me.

"As the object of *your* obsession."

"Not obsession. Love."

"*Your* love." He lowers his voice. He can't risk too much being heard. "*Your* decision to make me this way. *Your* life here in London. *Your* mother. *Your* sister. *Your* home. It's always you leading us—"

"I thought—I always—I thought you liked that about me."

"I did." He huffs. "Maybe I do. Most times. But this was *my* day. I asked you to hold the day for me. I wanted to be the leader *for once*. I was going to take you to Paris. I—"

"Paris, really?" I open the shower door. Join him outside. Try to pull him close.

He pushes me away. "You're wet and I'm angry."

"Will you forgive me? If I come to Paris with you?"

He shakes his head. Looks at me with even more rage than before. "It doesn't matter anymore. It's over now. The surprise is ruined. I don't want a Valentine who spends the day with me out of guilt."

I grab the same towel he dried himself with. Wrap it around me. "I have never spent time with you because of guilt, Oliver." I catch my reflection in the mirror. As youthful as ever. Unblemished skin. White teeth. Eternal glow. "If I do feel guilty, it's because of them downstairs. We can go to Paris anytime. Because we have all the time in the world. They don't."

"Sure, yeah, you're right." He nods. "Let's go to Paris another time. Anytime, in fact. Which we both know means it will never happen. I certainly won't be getting my money back."

"Is this about money now?"

"It's about . . ." He hovers under the door frame. "It's about everything!"

He doesn't get dressed. He throws himself in bed. Raises the covers over his face.

I sit by his side. "Oliver, come on. This isn't like you."

He speaks from under the sheets. "You have no idea how *like me* it is. I'm so good at hiding, and I hate it. We're still hiding. Not because we're gay anymore. Because we're immortal. But it feels the same. Lonely and horrible."

"Then let's tell them." I try to think through the repercussions. "Let's go downstairs and tell the truth. They're our family."

"Which is exactly why we can't tell them. What good could possibly come from their knowing what we are? A distance will grow between us and them. It will all come crashing down. And all I want . . . is for our happy home to never crumble."

"Maybe nothing will crash down. Let's talk this through."

"I don't want to talk."

"Then come downstairs with me. Let's be with Maud. She needs us."

"You go."

"She needs you too."

"I won't be a part of her destruction. Someone has to tell her how risky it is for her to go out there."

"Then go convince her. But don't shut us out."

He gets out of bed. I feel hopeful he's coming out of his dark fog. He takes the journal I gave him out of its hiding spot in the floorboard. Grabs a pen.

He writes me a message: *Please leave me alone.*

Somehow, I can't argue with him in writing. I scrawl a message out under his: *Okay. I'm sorry I ruined your Valentine's Day. I love you.*

He puts the journal back into its hiding spot. Returns to his cocoon. "At least it was memorable." He pulls the sheets over his face again. I close my eyes and think of the last memorable Valentine's Day I had. 1895. James at the St. James. The premiere of Wilde's play was on this very holiday. The event that set my life as I know it into motion. I feel a sudden chill. It feels like a new version of my life is being set into motion once more.

I head downstairs. I pray that whatever has changed between me and Oliver will shift back with a sunset or a sunrise. A passing storm. Nature's way of releasing pressure. That's all our fight was. Pressure relief. I hope. Everyone but Lily and Maud are gone when I get to the living area. They make posters together.

Lily's reads, *No Police Cov—*

Maud's reads, *Blood ah go run if—*

I sit next to Maud. Grab a poster board. "Is it cool if I make one?"

Maud nods. "Of course." She continues adding to her poster. Draws a capital *N* in block letters. "That sounded like quite a row up there."

"Yeah, sorry."

"Everything okay?" That's Lily. Concern in her voice.

"I think so." I shrug. "I don't know."

Lily places a hand on mine. "Was Oliver always prone to melancholy spells?"

I want to deny ever noticing Oliver's moods. I feel as if his sadness is all my fault. Guilt washes over me. I can't lie to Lily so I say nothing.

The certainty in Lily's eyes tells me that I've told her everything. Without uttering a single word. "Should I go up there?"

I try to put myself in his shoes. He asked me to leave him alone. But Lily might get through to him in a way I can't. "I don't think it would hurt."

Lily stands up. Gives us both a pat on the head. Then she heads upstairs. I hear her knock on Oliver's door. Sweetly speak his name.

I grab a red marker. Contemplate what to write. But first, there's something I need to say. "Maud, please don't be cross with Oliver."

"Cross? I'm really not." It's not her rage that slaps me in the face when she looks at me. It's the hurt. "But quite the choice of words after the New Cross fire."

"He'd just been planning the trip for months. It meant a lot to him."

"More than *thirteen Black lives?*" Maud reacts to her own words. "Sorry."

"You have every right to be upset."

Maud shrugs. "Thing is, I'm not upset. I'm . . . frothing with rage. I don't know how to live like this. Always looking over our shoulders." She breathes slowly. Attempts calm. "And I suppose—it's made me see how different things are for all of us. Oliver can go ahead with his plans today because the world didn't just end for him."

I put the marker down. I haven't written a word yet. I take her hands in mine instead. "The world has not ended for you. You still have us."

"For now."

"You have Pearl's."

"They've already stopped her from selling liquor. How long until they throw her in jail like Lily's Uncle Alton for running an underground bar for Black queers like me?"

I feel caught by two opposing forces. Oliver's gloom still swirls around me like a cloud. And now Maud's anger approaches like a tornado. All I want is to help them both. I have no idea how.

"What should my poster say?" That's all I can think of to ask in the moment.

Maud raises an eyebrow. "Whatever you want it to say. You're the poetry lover. Write us a poem, yeah?"

I smile. I want to make her laugh. To change the mood. To recite the worst poem ever written. "Justice for all. Thatcher will fall. You saw what happened at Stonewall. Now prepare for your curtain call." She laughs. I've succeeded. "Now let's have a ball?"

"You're such a little know-it-all." She swats me with a marker.

"I'm not going away with Oliver. I want to join you." I start writing words on my poster. I start with the word *Never.*

"Don't do it if you'll resent me." Maud looks at me meaningfully. "I mean it. I don't want you annoyed with me because you missed your goopy romantic trip."

"I won't." I add the word *Going* to my poster as Lily keeps knocking on Oliver's door. He's not letting her in. "I promise I'll find you just as annoying whether I go or not."

Maud laughs. "All right then, what's your poster going to say? Never going what?"

I write in the last word. *Never Going Underground.* I stare at the words, satisfied. Oliver is right that we're hiding a piece of us. But that doesn't mean we need to hide the rest. I won't let fear drive me into the darkness they prefer us in.

I spend Valentine's Day in the streets. Chanting. Singing. Raging. Connecting. I see a plane in the air. I wonder if it's the one I was supposed to be on with Oliver. I feel terrible that he's spending the day alone. We march down Railton Road. Chants of *Thirteen Dead and Nothing Said.* The protest gains steam as we forge on. The crowd grows louder as more police show up. Someone blares the Johnny Osbourne song from a loudspeaker. We all sing along. The whole crowd erupts into cheers when the song ends. I wish Oliver could see how celebratory it is. Catch the look of elation on Maud's face as she morphs rage into action. I wish he knew he shouldn't be so afraid.

The protest circles the neighborhood. We end on Railton Road where we began. Thirsty from screaming and walking. Everyone needs a drink. Lily suggests we go to Pearl's. Maud has a more rebellious idea: "The George." Maud says the words spitefully.

We all know we're not welcome at the George. We've never dared go inside. Maud doesn't wait for anyone to express a concern. She marches toward the public house that houses the pub.

We find a sea of white men's faces inside. Staring at us scornfully. Daring us to move farther.

Maud takes a seat at the bar. "I'll have a Red Stripe."

Lily quickly joins Maud. "What my daughter means is that she'll have a Coca-Cola. *Please.*"

The woman behind the bar narrows her eyes at our lot. Her lips are pursed. Her hair is yanked. Her body is hunched and shriveled. "I have to serve you Black folk. But the queers will have to leave." Her thin eyes land on me. Then on Archie. His far-too-tight jeans. His leather cap. His white tank top with the rainbow flag that now represents our community. "Can't call the Race Relations Board if I refuse to serve degenerates, can you?"

Lily leans forward. Practically spits in the woman's mouth as she speaks. "Well, my dear, I am Black AND queer, as is my daughter Maud, so what will you do with us?"

"You the one who kept reporting Pearl to the police?" Maud can't conceal the venom in her voice as she asks the question.

The bartender pours Maud a soda and places it in front of her.

"How old are you, child? Don't talk about things you know nothing about. These were *our* neighborhoods before you lot moved in."

"We lot moved in to rebuild your country after the war." Azalea stays calm as she speaks. "I've probably nursed some of your friends back to health."

"Job well done then." The woman claps her bony hands together condescendingly. "We don't need you no more. War's been over for a good long time. You can go home."

"*This* is home." Lily pulls a large bill from her purse. "Sodas for everyone. Marching against bigots like you is exhausting."

Maud glances at Lily with pride on her face. We take over the counter. A few of the men hiss at us.

One says: *Go home.*

Another: *Perverts.*

The drunk old men spread their legs like they own the world. I stare hard at the lines of cruelty on their faces. It's not time that has ravaged their faces. It's hate. People who hold love in their hearts age with warmth. One man so drunk he can barely walk stumbles toward us. Spits at the ground beneath us.

We ignore them. Maud raises her glass when our sodas arrive. "To family." Her eyes land on me. "Especially to my brother Bram for choosing to be here today. For not deserting me when we needed support."

"And to Oliver." I give Maud a pleading look. "Who loves you just as much as I do. Who stayed away because he's afraid for you."

Maud nods. Accepts this. "To Oliver too, of course." She says the next part loudly, so everyone can hear. "And to *Mother England.* Our country. Our home. We forgive her trespasses against us. Cheers."

OLIVER. LONDON. VALENTINE'S DAY. 1981.

It's dark when I hear the front door close. They sound happy. More than happy. Elated. If Lily wasn't sober and didn't forbid us from drinking, I would say they were drunk. They sing that protest song. "13 Dead (Nothing Said)." All these years of loving music. Studying music. Playing music. Decoding its theories. Thinking about how it reveals our souls to us. And yet this is the first time I've pondered music as a call to arms. As a conduit to the kind of heartbreak and wrath that frightens me. Because it demands a response. They may be giddy from the rush of it now, but what of tomorrow? Of the day after? What song will they be singing when Thatcher and her Black Rats have had time to devise their plan to fight back?

A knock on the door. Lily's voice. "Oliver, may I come in now?" Changeling purrs.

I told her I needed a little time when she knocked earlier. But what's a little time anyway?

"Oliver, please. I care about you. We all do." Changeling's eyes urge me to let Lily in. Shames me for shutting her out earlier.

I roll myself out of bed and open the door for her. "Hey," I whisper.

She places a hand on my hot cheek. "May I come in?" she asks.

I nod and walk back to the bed. We sit on the edge of the mattress together. It feels like a boat. I'm afraid I might sink into a dark ocean at any moment, and take Lily down with me. I feel like I'm the worst thing that's ever happened to her. To Bram. To Maud and Mother and Archie and Brendan and everyone who's ever had the misfortune to cross my path.

"Bram loves you so—"

"I don't want to talk about him!" I snap. I immediately feel spoiled and ungrateful for raising my voice.

"I love all my children equally," she says. "I hope you know that." Lily seems to understand what I'm feeling without my saying it. Maybe all mothers do. Is that what being a parent is?

"He was your firstborn," I say.

"So what?"

"You're right. My brother Liam was my mother's firstborn." I can see her surprise at the mention of my previous life. She doesn't dare interrupt me when I'm finally letting her in. "And she loved me more than Liam. I know she did."

Lily crosses her legs. Takes my hands in hers. "Perhaps it felt that way to you." She pauses. "Perhaps it felt the same way to your brother. A good mother makes every child feel like her favorite."

I shake my head sadly. "She was the best mother. And I never—I didn't—I'm sorry, I can't . . ."

"Oliver, you can tell me everything or nothing." She guides my head onto her shoulder. "But if your brain is busy convincing itself that you let your mother down somehow, you need to stop. You're a beautiful soul. Any mother would have been proud to have you as her child."

Tears roll down my cheeks. I didn't feel them come. They gave me no warning. "I didn't say goodbye to her."

"What would you have said?" Lily asks. "If you could have said goodbye."

My voice cracks. "I would have thanked her. For . . . for everything. And I would have begged her forgiveness. For . . . for everything."

"Oh, sweet child." Lily strokes my hair. "She forgives you."

"How?" I croak. "She's gone. She's dead."

"Love doesn't die," she whispers with certainty. "Neither does forgiveness. And your mother . . . I think she's here with us. Perhaps not in body, but her soul is watching over you. You just have to learn how to feel her presence in a different way."

I raise my head and look at Lily. It's like Mother is with me. They're so different. And yet . . . they share something. A purity. Looking into Lily's eyes . . . I can feel Mother's forgiveness. Her love. I let it envelop me. "I love you," I whisper, to Lily, and to Mother, and maybe even to myself.

"I love you too," Lily says. She opens her arms up and I allow myself to deflate into her warm embrace. "And if you ever feel sad, I'm here. But Oliver . . . If I'm not enough . . . If you think you need to talk to someone—"

"A head shrinker?" I ask dismissively.

She sighs. "I know they don't have the best track record for our community, trust me, *I know*. But there are some good ones out there."

"I'd rather talk to you," I say. "Please don't make me—"

"Hey, I'm not making you do anything. It's a discussion. We're a team. All of us. We all love you." She takes a deep breath. "Bram loves you. He's downstairs. Afraid to come in. Afraid you're mad at him."

"Bram makes everything about him," I say.

"Then teach him not to. We can only grow through honesty delivered with love."

I nod. I take Changeling in my arms when Lily stands up. "Tell him to come upstairs. It's his room too." Changeling licks the dry tears on my cheeks.

Bram steps into the bedroom quietly. "We missed you," he declares.

"Maud isn't angry with me?" I ask.

Bram peels his clothes off until he's in nothing but his underwear. He jumps into bed. Straddles me. "Of course not. She even raised a glass to you at the George."

"The George?!" I sit up, alarmed that they would step into what we all know is enemy territory.

He laughs. Carefree. Drunk on nothing but his own righteousness. "It was fine. It was fantastic. If you were there, I would've kissed you in front of every vile man who called us perverts."

"Then I'm glad I wasn't."

He bends down and kisses me hard on the mouth.

"Bram, stop. I'm not in the mood."

He throws himself off me. Lies next to me. "*Je t'aime,*" he whispers.

"Don't remind me," I say.

"That I love you?" His eyes are on the cracked ceiling. "Or of Paris . . ."

"Both." I stare up at the ceiling too. "I saved for months. Booked our flights. Got us a little hotel on the Seine. Felt it was time to walk along a new river."

"That sounds beautiful," he says. "Let's do it another time. We can walk the Seine while eating a box of—"

"Macarons?" We look at each other. "That was already a part of the plan. Macarons and the Eiffel Tower. I even memorized a French poem to read to you on the Pont Neuf."

"We don't need to be in France for you to read me French poetry," he says. Then, "Which poem?"

"*Romance.*" I pronounce it *en français*. "Rimbaud."

"*When you are seventeen, you aren't really serious.*" Of course, he knows it by heart already. Probably in multiple languages.

I echo his words in the poem's original French. "*On n'est pas sérieux, quand on a dix-sept ans.*"

He smiles, impressed. Perhaps even moved. A love poem written just for him, my unserious seventeen-year-old taking all he can from life, too lost in eternal youth to see the premonition of what's to come.

"He's one of my favorite poets," Bram says. "So sad he was taken so young."

"Is it?" I ask.

"Of course it is. He was, what, forty when he died?" he asks.

"Thirty-seven," I say.

"Even worse." He sighs. "Nothing is sadder to me than artists who die before they've expressed all they had to say."

I shrug. "I spent years wandering foreign cities thinking of sadder things."

"Hey," he whispers as he holds me close. "I'm here for your happiness and for your sadness. I'm here for all of you. Just . . . don't push me away. Please."

"I won't," I say, but I hear the uncertainty in my own voice. "I'm not . . . leaving you. That's not what this is."

He seems to exhale gratefully when I say this. "Then what's going on?"

"I suppose I wanted a redo of Paris. I wanted the city of love to be something new for me. Not a place that houses lonely memories. I hated Paris when I lived there. I was all alone. It's a terrible city to be alone in. Lovers everywhere. I let myself believe life had cursed me. That *you* had cursed me."

We rarely talk about the lives we led apart from each other. What is there to say, really, other than that they were lost and lonely years for us both? Sometimes debauched. Often merely dull. A well of experience that amounts to nothing but more longing.

He raises a curious eyebrow, wondering what I'll say next.

"But then I came here," I continue. "And we started this new life. And I felt . . . happy."

"Past tense?" he asks.

I try to find the right words. What I come up with is, "I guess—I don't know how to explain it, but I feel . . . haunted."

"Haunted?" he repeats.

"By a premonition," I say. "Don't tell me I'm being silly. I feel something shifting."

"In us? In you? In the world?"

I nod. "Yes. All of it. And it's not . . . I know I can be melancholy . . . Lily sees it, I know it, I'm sure you've seen it too. But this is different. This feels . . . like a warning inside me."

He puts his head on my belly. I haven't even gone downstairs to eat. I can only imagine what the rumbling of my stomach must sound like to him. Perhaps like the avalanche of change I know is coming.

"All you're saying is that things are changing," he says. "I feel it too. It's a new day. A new time. That's just reality. Things must change, but maybe for the better."

"You're not listening," I say. "What I'm saying is that I'm scared.

What I'm saying is I'm not ready for things to change. I liked us the way we were."

"Then let's be the way we were." Bram raises a fist up like Rosie the Riveter. "We can do it!"

I almost laugh.

"Be sad, be angry, be scared," he says. "But we're still us. Lily is still Lily. Maud is still Maud. Don't mourn the life you love before it's been taken from you."

Those words wake something up in me. "I'm starving," I say.

"Then let's go warm up some food for you."

Bram pulls me out of bed with a smile. We both throw clothes on.

Changeling follows us as we descend the stairs toward the sound of Donna Summer and Barbra Streisand singing together. Bram takes my hand in his. "You know, perhaps it's for the best we didn't go. You know what Oscar Wilde said about Paris."

"What?" I ask.

"*When good Americans die, they go to Paris.*" He holds my hand. "And you, Oliver, are definitely a good American. And I for one am very happy that you're here, now, young enough to enjoy this moment with me."

"We'll always *not* have Paris," I say with a smile as I mangle the famous quote.

He laughs. "There he is. The Oliver I know and love is back. It was just a passing cloud."

He's right. I feel like myself again. But what happens if someday the cloud returns and never passes by me? Is that what happened to Cyril all those years ago? Was he swallowed up by a storm cloud of sadness?

We join Lily and Maud in belting the song as I heat some food on the stove. *Enough is enough is enough.* Yes, the clouds will come back. Of course they will. They can't all be sunny days. But that's another day. Not this one. Hopefully not tomorrow either. I smile, laugh, dance. I feel myself be the Oliver everyone loves. Sweet. The one who laughs at their jokes and follows their leads.

And yet . . .

Thoughts swirl inside me, little dark premonitions that I know will grow in size with time. Premonitions and unanswerable questions. If good Americans go to Paris when they die, then where do we go . . . not when we die, but when we've had enough of this turning world? When we're ready to rest in peace?

I can't go on, I can't go on no more, no.

Where do the immortal go when everything and everyone we love has deserted us? When we're ready to stop being a body and to be nothing but a soul?

BRAM. LONDON. APRIL. 1981.

I should never have promised Oliver that this year would be better than the last. A promise is a dare. To fate. To the gods. To whatever force controls the brutal dance of life. A promise is a fragile thing waiting to be broken. Mine has been broken day by day. Week by week. Month by terrible month. Oliver has finally agreed to Lily's suggestion that he talk to a professional. Finding the right therapist has been hard. His melancholy days seem to be more frequent. He goes through days where he doesn't play any music. That's how I know he's in a dark spell. When he closes the door on the one thing that always gives him hope.

"I know not whether laws be right." My thirteen-year-old student recites the poem he's studying Friday afternoon in the park. *"Or whether laws be wrong. All that we know who lie in . . ."*

"Gaol." I know the poem by heart. Of course. I know much of Wilde's work by heart.

"What is gaol?"

"It means jail. Wilde wrote this poem when he was released from prison."

"I asked Mother why Oscar Wilde was put in jail, and she said I would find out when I was old enough to understand."

"You're fourteen." I look into his adolescent eyes. So full of curiosity. Yearning. "You were old enough to ask me to teach you some of Wilde's work."

He looks at me slyly. "Truth be told, I asked about Wilde because my literature professor said I should avoid him at all costs. Said I should stick to Shakespeare and Dickens. I figured it was because his writing was obscene. Didn't expect an endless poem about prison."

I nod. "Let's dig into the poem some more."

"Why wouldn't he just say jail or prison? Why use a word like *gaol?*"

The thing I love most about tutoring is the questions. The way they remind me that I too am full of questions. Curiosity keeps me going. Persistence too. My persistence is something I cherish. A badge of honor. It's what got me here. Curiosity and persistence. And the ability to laugh at *everything.* These are the qualities that keep me alive. I'd be merely existing without them.

"Was it common back then in . . . when did he write this?"

"1898."

"Fuck me, that's a long time ago." I love when the students swear in front of me. It means I've gained their trust. That they're willing to be themselves in my presence.

"Not so long, in the grand scheme of things. Not even a century."

Wilde had been released from prison by then. A bon vivant no more. The era of green carnations had passed. The witticisms that once delighted this city gave way to cheerless verses. His words dried up as he drank himself into a stupor. Loneliness. Meningitis. An acute ear infection. He who had a talent for hearing what others were hiding could hear no more. He died too young. Too broken. Perhaps—among the many things he taught us—this is the most important one: that all beauty must fade.

"*Gaol* is a word of Irish origin. As Wilde is of Irish origin. Perhaps he chose the word to tell us something."

I wait patiently. Watch the wheels in this intelligent boy's head turn. "My father says the Irish are greedy and ungrateful."

"Mmm." I don't dare say more. I need jobs like these. I cock my head toward the book in his hand. "Keep reading. Better yet, close the book and try to recite from memory."

He closes the book. "*All that we know who lie in gaol is that the wall is strong. And that each day is like a year. A year whose days are long.*" He glances nervously at me. "I haven't memorized the rest."

"You still have time." I glance at my watch. "Let's wrap up now. The sun is shining, and it's Poet's Day. Go have some fun. Next time, we'll focus on your Latin studies again."

"Why must we learn Latin when nobody speaks it any longer?"

I shrug. "That's a question for your classics professor, but I suppose it's so you might comprehend the etymology of your language. If we don't study the source of our way of thinking and communicating, then we can never understand why we are the way we are."

"Latin is boring." He laughs. I do too. "What's Poet's Day?"

I smile. "Piss off early, tomorrow's Saturday."

"What?"

"Think about it."

He thinks. Laughs. Delight in his young eyes. The world all future for him. Nothing but revelation and possibility. "Let's piss off, then."

We walk across the park toward his parents' East London flat. Another spring. Flowers in bloom. Sunlight warms the wet grass. Cherry blossoms. Wilde's poem accompanies me as we walk.

This too I know—and wise it were if each could know the same—that every prison men build is built with bricks of shame.

I imagine my student's literature professor would become one of Thatcher's targets if he assigned Wilde. Teachers corrupting the young with the work of queers. With poems that possess the power to haunt. This one has haunted me since the revelation that Lily's Uncle Alton is in a jail cell. Possibly forever. For doing nothing but existing. Just as Wilde was imprisoned for existing. But no, they were both *living*. This was their true crime. Daring to *live* when the world needed them merely to exist.

Society grants the few life and the many mere existence.

"You're home early." The boy's mother wears an apron around her wide waist. Stained with some sort of red sauce. She has kind eyes. Overworked hands. Teeth that need fixing.

"It's Poet's Day!" My student says it gleefully.

His mother wraps her arms around her boy. "Is that a holiday I don't know about?"

I answer fast. "It just means we focused on poetry today. He's doing fantastic. He has a rich understanding of language. Next time we'll focus on Latin, which he's still struggling with."

"We're very grateful to you, Bram. You have a way with him." She pulls a fiver from her apron pocket. Hands it to me.

I hear a police dispatch from within the flat. Her husband is home. He works for the Metropolitan Police. The Black Rats. He's some sort of commander or deputy commander. I can't hear every word. Perhaps every third word. *Emergency . . . Brixton . . . now . . . riot*. Like a redacted poem.

"It's my day off." His father's voice. Husky and authoritative. The voice of a man wearing the mask of what he thinks a man must be. A voice like my own father's.

Reinforcement . . . Railton . . . Operation Swamp 81.

An association. The prime minister's words: *People are really rather afraid that this country might be swamped by people with a different culture.* The way she deployed the word *rather* to soften the revulsion in her statement. To make the fear she speaks of feel soft and rational.

A memory. Long buried. James's uppity mother, after she found me atop her precious son: *Go back to your vile country. Stop swamping ours with your savage ways.*

"I'll be going, then. Till next week." I feel dread as I walk to the Tube station to head back to Brixton. The rumbling train seems to speak the words from the dispatch to me: *Emergency. Brixton. Riot. Reinforcement. Railton. Operation Swamp 81.*

I get off at the Brixton station. Ascend the staircase into the open air. Something feels different. The smell. Not the heat of spices being cooked but the heat of fire burning. The sound. Not joyful reggae but frightened desperation. Police everywhere. Their bodies upright. Primed for battle.

I grow increasingly frightened as I near Railton Road. I clutch the bottle of poppers in my pocket. Lily recently had Archie give us each a bottle of poppers to carry with us at all times. To throw in someone's eyes if they ever try to mess with us. She got the idea when some guy accidentally spilled poppers in Archie's eyes while Archie was on his knees. Azalea was called in to care for Archie. To convince him he wouldn't go blind. Archie worried that the amyl nitrate entering his mucous membranes meant he had broken his sobriety. We all laughed about it at the time. Teased Archie until he laughed too. But the incident led to Lily's revelation: "Cheaper than pepper spray, and more inventive. Anybody fucks with you, you throw this at their eyes and run."

I walk past a burning police car. A tornado of fire. Across the street: young Black boys stand next to a group of white queers. They cheer and clap. One of the queers wears red heels and long silk gloves. He holds what looks like a box of chocolates. I recognize him. He was in one of the Brixton Faeries shows we saw. He offers me a chocolate. I realize they're not sweets. My God, he's handing out petrol bombs!

"I-I'm headed home."

At first I feel disgusted by this violence. Petrol bombs? Is this what it's come to?

But then I wonder why we didn't do this in London in 1895 when Wilde was on trial?

And why we didn't do this in Boston in 1920 when Harvard destroyed our community?

Why do we always shrug off the establishment's violence toward us?

I rush away. Gripped by fear. On the street is an old copy of *Gay Noise*. I step on its front page. The word *RAID* in big block letters. Raids. Arrests. Just like London in 1895. Just like Boston in 1920. Same as it ever was. People taken to prison for no reason but their difference. Increasing day by day. Week by week. The state is fighting back. Just as Oliver warned they would. A little over a month ago: fifteen thousand marched in the Black People's Day of Action. We were among them. All but Oliver. He was still too afraid. He was also right. Maybe he knew this would happen because he stayed in Boston longer than I did. Watched them crack down on us. Police presence in London has multiplied since the

Black People's Day of Action. Arrests have increased. The whole neighborhood has felt like it could ignite. And now it has.

"Let us through. Please let us through." A mother holds her toddler in her arms. Pleads with the police to let her across a barricade. My eyes land on the fear in the toddler's eyes. Too young to make sense of the flames. Of the cries. Of the police wielding their weapons against the neighborhood faces the toddler has grown up with. The same people she sees dancing on the street. Browsing the market for fresh produce. Her community is now a war zone.

Wilde's poem swirls around in my brain: *For they starve the little frightened child. Till it weeps both night and day. And they scourge the weak, and flog the fool. And gibe the old and gray. And some grow mad, and all grow bad. And none a word may say.* Wilde. Our imperfect icon. He warned us all the way back then. We can't let them scourge and flog us this time. We must not let them win again.

Lily is waiting for me by the front door as I turn onto Chaucer Street. She pulls me in. Locks the door. "They diverted the number two. That's when I knew."

In the living area: Maud with fire in her eyes. Oliver with sadness in his.

"They don't divert a bus for no reason. They're preparing for war. Against us." Lily pulls a machete out of the front closet.

I hear myself gasp. "Lily, what is that? Is that a . . . a *machete?*"

She laughs. "Who do you take me for? It's from the prop shop. Anyone breaks in, it might scare them off."

Maud leaps up. Approaches Lily. "There's history happening out there. The community is finally rising up. And you want us to stay locked in here with a fake machete to protect us. What happened to *living true?*"

Lily's eyes flicker with heartbreak. "This is different. The gloves are off. I have to protect you."

Maud raises her voice loud. Like she wants her voice to travel through the neighborhood. A call to arms. "The people rising up aren't afraid and neither am I."

Lily shakes her head. "Let's see how things look when the sun comes up tomorrow. Today, we're not leaving this house. My home. My rules."

We spend the day hiding. Lily seats us in front of the television. We rewatch *Mahogany*. We don't speak the quotes aloud this time. Don't laugh at the most over-the-top moments. We simply sit in silence. We watch *Valley of the Dolls*. The sound of fighting can be heard over Diana Ross and Susan Hayward. We all fall asleep in the living area. Lily with the prop machete by her side. I get the sense no one wants to sleep alone.

Saturday morning. Crust in my eyes and near my mouth. My head on Oliver's lap. Changeling paws at me. Fights me for the limited real estate of Oliver's body. The sound of the radio stirs me awake: *Good morning, you're listening to BBC Radio London. Riots erupted in Brixton yesterday after the stabbing of Michael Bailey. The neighborhood was—*

Lily turns the radio off when she sees me enter the kitchen. She's making the same breakfast she made for me on the day she saved me from the same police attacking us now. I can hear her voice from that day traveling to me: *Eat your breakfast. Porridge and—*

"Banana fritters." Lily smiles as she stirs the porridge. Next to her: a piece of paper with scribbled notes on it.

"Rich in fiber and potassium. It'll give you energy for the day ahead." I stand by her side. "That's what you said when you made this for me the day we met."

"Amazing how you remember such trivial things."

"Meeting you is the least trivial thing that's ever happened to me." I smile. "You saved me."

She smiles too. "Still trying."

I pick up the paper. "What's this?"

She tries to snatch it away. I resist. I decode her messy handwriting. There's a list of places: the Blitz. Pearl's. Chaucer. Lily Pond. Queen's Walk. National Theatre. A list of people: Archie. Azalea. Poppy. Blossom. Bram. Maud. Oliver. I feel my heart beat. "Is this . . . are these instructions for . . ."

"My memorial. Yes."

I want to tear the paper up. To burn it. Make her immortal. "How can you— What I mean is— Well . . ."

Her jaw tenses. "I won't live forever, you know. And with everything going on . . . Well, it's hard not to think of our mortality at times like this, isn't it?"

I don't answer. Of course I don't. I can't bring myself to lie. Not to Lily. "This is morbid. You've listed friends who are older than you who won't be around for your memorial. You— You'll live a long time. I know you will." I wave the paper in the air anxiously. I want—I *need* her to never die.

She snatches it back successfully. "I plan on going first. I have no interest in watching my chosen family die. Just promise me one thing."

"What?"

"I want to be cremated and have my ashes scattered in the Thames. I need to rest in water. And I don't care if it's illegal to throw ashes in the river when I go. You find a way."

I manage to cough out an "okay." Then I change the subject. Anything is better than talking about her death. "Sounds quiet out there." I peek out the window. I can see Railton Road in the distance. Some debris from yesterday. But no battle.

"For now." She releases heartbreak with each breath. Places a hand on my cheek. Her eyes land on Oliver and Maud. "If anything were to happen to any of you, I would never forgive myself."

Her eyes are misty. Her mouth tight with frustration. She seems to be aging in front of my very eyes. Her anxiety creates new lines on her faces. Or accentuates the ones faintly beginning to appear. I feel an urge to tell her everything. To confess. My father. My immortality. The truth of my history with Oliver. She deserves to know.

"Lily . . ." I wait for her to look at me. I feel weak in the knees when she does.

"Speak your mind, child." The porridge is ready. She lets the fritters fry a little longer. Then prepares our bowls.

I ask: "Do you think all secrets must be shared?"

She puts the bowls down on the counter. "Not if we keep secrets to protect the people we love. Or to protect ourselves. Why do you think I didn't tell you about Alton? Because I loved you too much to burden you with something so horrible."

"Right."

"Secrets are your personal property. You may invite others into your home, but no one may trespass." She glances out the window now. Awaiting more violence. Pondering her mortality.

Right on cue, the sound of a firebomb. It scares Lily. Jolts Oliver and Maud awake. The moment for revelations has passed.

Lily keeps us locked in all day. She does everything she can to drown out the sound of the uprising outside. Blasts vinyl from the record player. Invites us to play dress-up in her closet. Demands Oliver distract us with live music. But she can't force joy. That's one thing that must arise naturally. She suggests more movies at night. Maud says she's too tired to stay up. Says she can't sleep on the couch again. "Crick in my neck. I'll see you tomorrow."

"Go to your rooms. Tomorrow will be here soon enough. All this will end." Lily says those last words like she wants to believe them. Not like she actually does.

Oliver and I lie side by side. I can tell he's in one of his dark moods.

"It was nice to hear you play music again." I turn my head toward his. "You play so infrequently these days."

He shrugs. "I guess."

"I love you." I move my hand closer to his. My fingers brush against his.

"You don't need to make me feel better." He turns toward me. "Everyone doesn't have to be happy and in love all the time."

"I know that."

"Our whole neighborhood is burning. Listen." From Railton Road, the sound of petrol bombs. Police warnings. Powerful chants of liberation. Desperate cries for help. "I knew it. I sensed it. You didn't listen when I warned you."

"What do you want me to say? That you were right?"

"It would be a start."

"This isn't happening because of us or some feeling you had." I sit up. I can't sleep. "It's happening because people have had enough of being treated like they're subhuman."

"Are *we* subhuman?"

"What?" I search his face for some sign of what he's thinking. "Because we're gay?"

"No!" He twirls his gorgeous locks of hair in his finger. Making little spirals. Then letting them fall. "Because we're . . . immortal. It seems like a blessing on the face of it. But it's not. It's a prison of time."

"This will pass. Things will get better. And then you'll be happy you're young again. That you get to experience each new era with the energy of youth."

"What if things don't get better? I don't want to be here for the apocalypse!" His eyes are full of dread. "I tried to reverse it when we were apart. I bought as many copies of *The Picture of Dorian Gray* as I could find and burned them. Inhaled the fire. I sought out healers and psychics and witches. Anyone who might know some secret way to end this."

"I wish I could make this wish come true for you. I know it's all my fault."

"Yes it is." He thinks for a moment. Turns to his side. "People long to be obscenely rich, famous, immortal. They think it will give their lives meaning. Make them special. But all it does is isolate you. The majority of things people wish for are terrible. The happiest lives are the simplest lives. Our lives are too complicated."

"I'm sorry." I spoon him. Clutch his body. Pull him as close as I can. "Maybe we can simplify our lives. Ignore the chaos and just focus on each other."

"Stop. Just stop." He doesn't say any more. He sweats in his sleep. There's a restlessness to him that scares me.

He bolts up close to midnight. "What's that?" He looks around our dark room.

"It's just the fighting outside. Go back to bed." I try to hold him.

He pushes me away. "No, it's something else. It's Maud." He bolts out of bed. Drenched. Eyes ablaze. "It was her window."

"I— You can't hear her window—"

He throws pants and a shirt on frantically. "Not everyone experiences the world exactly as you do, Bram. My God, you have no idea how narcissistic you can be. I *hear* things. I have a musician's ear. I know the difference between the squeak of her window and a fucking firebomb."

Oliver never swears. Never swore. He's changing.

"Okay, I'm sorry, let's—"

He's already out the door. I follow him to Maud's room. An open window. A cold night breeze blowing through it. The sound of carnage is louder without glass to shield it. She's stuffed her bed with pillows. Snuck out to live life on her terms.

Oliver leaps out the window. Lands athletically. "Oliver!" He doesn't answer. Starts running toward Railton Road. "Oliver!" Lily would have barged in by now if she were up. I could wake her. But that's not what I do. I jump out the window too. Land hard on the pavement. Fall to my side. We may be immortal but we do feel pain. The impact hurts. The fear makes me forget the pain. I chase him. He searches for her.

What I see stuns me.

Our neighborhood is burning.

Police hide behind their vehicles.

Young men and women smash bricks into police cars. Drag cops out of their cars. Fight back. Make the police answer for their crimes. For their *suspicions*.

The George burns. The buildings around it still stand. Maud stands outside the old pub. Oliver finds her. I catch up to them. We stand side by side. Watch the place burn down.

"Old racist pub." There's a smile on Maud's face as she watches it disappear.

"It's not the pub that was racist. It's the assholes who worked there." Oliver takes Maud's hand in his. They laugh uproariously.

"What's so funny?" I turn to them. I feel excluded. "Let's go home."

"This is our home." Maud's eyes can't glow like ours. But they can light up with fury. "And it's about time they understood that you don't come to a person's home and lock them up for living."

Maud runs into the road. Raises her fist up in the air. High-fives every brother and sister she sees. Joins the chants. Unleashes her power.

"We have to get her home now." Oliver turns to me. "She can't be out here all night."

I follow Oliver as he chases after Maud. Police wield their weapons against the protesters. Beat them with batons. Point their guns. Young protesters throw petrol bombs at police cars. I watch one burn. Oliver must be looking in a different direction because he suddenly screams—

"MAUD."

Oliver bolts toward Maud. A petrol bomb flies in the sky. Toward a police car. Maud directly in its path.

"MAUD, MOVE."

Oliver leaps. Pushes her down to the ground. The petrol bomb misses her. Misses the car too. Hits Oliver. His hair catches fire.

A blaze.

"OLIVER." Panic on Maud's face. Her eyes full of regret. Fear. "Bram, help, what do we do?"

I see a woman sleeping on the street. Thick blanket on her feet. Watching the destruction with a resigned lack of surprise on her face. I don't have time to ask for permission. I snatch the blanket. Leap into the blaze. Wrap Oliver in the blanket. The blaze engulfs me too. We're both aflame. Maud screams. The agony of her voice. No one else seems to notice us. Too many other burning things to look at. I wrap the blanket around us tight.

Oliver's voice in my ear. Hopeful. "Bram, maybe this is it? Maybe this fire will burn away our immortality. Do you have the last page with you?"

I always keep it with me. Just in case. I push us down to the ground. Roll around on the pavement until the flames have gone out.

"Bram, tell me if you have it!"

"I do." Fire made us this way. Will these flames reverse our immortality just as flames once made us immortal?

But nothing happens. We emerge unsinged. Unharmed. Alive. I pull the page out of my pocket. I put out the fire before it could burn. I put it safely back.

Maud stands above us. Shocked. "Are you all right? I'm sorry, I'm sorry, I'm sorry. This would never have happened if I hadn't snuck out."

"We're okay." I touch Oliver's skin. Still as smooth as ever. Mine too. Our eyes still glow orange.

Maud leans forward and touches us too. A hand on Oliver's cheek. A hand on mine. "I don't understand. You're not hurt."

"It's a miracle." I look at Maud.

She doesn't look like she believes in miracles. "It don't make sense." She runs a hand through Oliver's hair. "It's not burned. You're fine. You're both . . . fine."

I try to end her suspicions with a joke. "The power of Lily's anti-aging creams."

Oliver leaps up. "Let's go home."

"Not until you tell me why you're not hurt." Maud helps me up. Looks at me with desperate eyes. "I know there's something different about you. I've always felt it. Tell me."

"Tell you what?" I brush her off. "We got lucky."

"Lucky?" Maud touches my skin. Then Oliver's. "You're not even slightly burned."

Oliver takes Maud's hand. Looks into her eyes. I'm afraid he's going to tell her everything. A part of me hopes he does. "Maud, listen." A deep breath. "You have to trust us."

Maud's lips quiver. She has questions. She's afraid of the answers.

Oliver continues. "Don't tell Lily. If you do, she'll know you snuck out."

"But that's— Well, it's nothing compared to . . . what you did . . . what you are." She breathes out forcefully. "What are you?"

I put a hand on Maud's shoulder. "He saved your life, Maud. If Oliver hadn't been here, it would've been you who burned."

"I know, but—"

"Maud, please. He saved your life. This is how he wants you to thank him."

She stares at us for an interminable minute. Another petrol bomb. The sound of violence. We have no choice but to go home. Nobody says another word. We climb in through Maud's open window. Maud agrees not to say anything. Her suspicions will be all her own. A horrible distrust that I can already feel driving a wedge between us.

OLIVER. LONDON. NEW YEAR'S EVE. 1981.

How do you describe the decline of life? Of Love? Of happiness? I can only explain through music, which allows a means of communication beyond words. Music is our only tool for capturing the intangible, the unseen, the true mysteries of life. In my darkest moods, I stopped playing entirely. Now I've started up again with the help of my gay therapist. I've even tried medicines but always stopped because of the side effects. It's a process. I'm changing. So are my tastes. I've lost my interest in the romantic melodies I used to favor. Gone are Schubert and Chopin. Gone are the optimistic synth sounds that welcomed me to London.

Bram walks into our bedroom on the last day of this wretched year. A year of loss and fear. I sit in bed, synth on my lap, Changeling curled up by my side. My hair is longer than it's ever been, due to laziness, not stylistic choice. I've grown a beard. Bram hates it. Says it itches when we kiss. But we don't kiss like we used to, so it makes no never mind. Perhaps I grew the beard as a wall between us. We all build walls, don't we? As individuals. As groups. As countries. Walls to keep the enemy out.

"*Vertigo?*" Bram asks, recognizing the melody I'm playing on my synth from the Hitchcock film we both love.

I nod. I play the evocative melody that accompanies Kim Novak as she sits in a museum, staring at a portrait of a woman named Carlotta who we think is possessing Kim. The story of the film is a web of deceit and mirrors. Jimmy Stewart plays a detective with a debilitating fear of heights, who is investigating Kim's strange behavior. When her character jumps from a bell tower and dies, his fear of heights stops him from saving her. He blames himself. Wanders the world sadly. His friend plays him Bach and Mozart to soothe him, but it doesn't work. There's only so much even the most beautiful music can do to soothe a plagued psyche. Eventually, Jimmy sees a woman who looks just like Kim. Different hair. Different voice. Same face. Same soul. He transforms her into the Kim that preoccupies him. Dyes her hair the same shade of icy blond. Dresses her in identical clothes to the ones the dead version of her once wore. Tries desperately to re-create the past as he knew it. He hasn't lived long enough to know you can never recapture the magic of the past. That's what gives nostalgia its strange power over us.

"It's New Year's Eve. Play something brighter." Bram leaps into bed. Kisses my neck. "'Don't You Want Me'?"

I raise my shoulder to gently push him away. "Not right now. Maybe next year."

He smiles. "I meant the song. Play it for me?" He leaps onto our bed and dances. Tries to make me smile by making a fool of himself. Sings off-key. *"Don't you want me, baby? Don't you want me, oh-oh-oh-oh?"*

I could pull out the most hurtful lyrics of that song and fling them at Bram like an arrow to his heart. The lyrics about moving on from someone you've loved after the good times. But I don't want to hurt him. I only want him to hear the song that's playing in my head.

"It's incredible, isn't it?" he asks. "All the superstars that have already come from the Blitz. 'Don't You Want Me' is the bestselling song of the year."

"The Blitz used to belong to us," I say. "Now it belongs to the world." I look at his eyes, fascinated by their unshakable optimism. His seemingly unkillable defiance. "Do you remember what you told me when I arrived in London?"

"What part of it?" he asks. "The part where I told you how I love you, and will never stop loving you?"

I manage a small smile. "No, that was the only true part. The rest, though, was a lie." He doesn't say a word. Waits for me to go on. "You said . . . there are spaces for us." I keep playing the *Vertigo* theme as I speak. Scoring the movie of my dizzying life. "You said we didn't need a whole city. Just a block here, a bar there."

He sits next to me. Runs a hand through my unwashed locks of hair. "Oliver . . ."

"The Blitz is gone."

Closed three months ago. It went out with a bash. A few hours of hedonism and connection. And then blackness.

"Pearl's shebeen is gone."

Closed after the Brixton Uprising changed our neighborhood. At first with an eruption. And then more slowly. Bit by bit, street life disappeared. Trust between people eroded. Something was achieved, no doubt. Even a government as vile as Thatcher's had to listen to a crescendo like the one that was heard that weekend. A report was commissioned. Lord Scarman, the ancient white man put in charge, unsurprisingly claimed not to find any evidence of *institutional* racism. To admit to such a thing would be to put the *institutions* at risk. But Scarman did find evidence of racial disadvantage and police bias. A fire had been lit that could not be ignored.

"Pearl is going to open a café," Bram argues. "She's not giving up and neither should you." He curls my hair around his fingers. "Let me cut your hair. Tomorrow is a new year. A new beginning."

"Do you promise it will be better than this year?" I ask snidely.

"How about I promise that next year will be the worst year of our lives?" He smiles. "Since my promises seem to have a way of not coming true." He leaps out of bed. Fishes our secret journal from beneath the floorboard. Writes on the next blank line, *Next year will be abysmal and atrocious and simply harrowing. I promise.*

I run my hand on the smooth, thick paper of the journal. Paper. The very thing that transformed me into whatever I am now. I read his last few notes in the journal. They're full of love and hope. Still. I don't know how he doesn't see what's happening as I do. It's a skill few have, perhaps. To *feel* the direction of history before it's become clear to others. Then again, I don't feel it exactly. It's more like I *hear* it. Like a film score playing in my head. The composer is Fate herself.

I place my fingers back on the synth. Play *Vertigo* again. Changeling meows. "Do you know how the score to the movie captures the lead character's decline so brilliantly?" I ask.

He shrugs. "You know I don't understand music like you do."

I take his fingers and lead them to the keys. I guide him in playing the score. "The easy answer to capturing a decline would be to descend in pitch. Down, down, down, right?"

"I suppose," he says quietly. There's an eeriness to his voice. He doesn't like where I'm taking him.

"But that's not how decline happens, is it?"

"I—" He tries to pull away from the keyboard, but I won't let him. I move his finger up now. Ascending.

"This is how declines happen." I close my eyes. I don't need sight to play music. It's all instinct. I hear better with my eyes closed. "You fall, yes. But then you get back up, a little weaker. Like us, wouldn't you say?"

"No," he says. "No, we're stronger. With each challenge we survive—"

"Then you fall again. And you're weaker still."

"Stronger," he insists.

"Listen to the melody. This is the genius of Bernard Herrmann's score." I make his finger play again. "You see what he's doing, don't you? He descends four pitches, then ascends two. Again and again. It gives you the sensation that you're free-falling, and then getting back up. But when you get back up, you don't rise as high as you were before. And so each time, you find yourself plunging lower and lower into the depths of—"

"It's *just* a score."

"It's madness itself. Melancholy itself. Music is never *just* music. Just as poetry is never just poetry. You should know that by now. The music is telling us something."

"Maybe we're not meant to be listening," he asserts. I turn to him, intrigued. "Maybe the whole point of life is to live free of these kind of premonitions of the future."

"It's not a premonition," I insist. "It's happening. The Blitz is gone. Pearl's is gone. Thatcher is in power here. Reagan is in power back home. Gay boys are still disappearing from the streets of London and no one cares. There's a war on our people. Our time is *not* now."

"You're being too dramatic."

"Gay men are dropping dead."

"In New York!" he blurts out. "In San Francisco! That's across the pond. It could be something about the environment there. The air."

"Do straight people in New York not breathe the air?" I ask. "It's about *us*." In the back of our journal, I've collected clippings.

I pull one out from July. The *New York Times*. July 3, 1981. One day before Independence Day. *Rare Cancer Seen in 41 Homosexuals*. Next to the thin and alarming article, sheet music for "The Star-Spangled Banner." Above the music, the words *SING OUT ON THE 4TH!* Exclamation point and all. The most poetic juxtaposition I can think of.

On one side . . . *"Doctors in new York and California have diagnosed among homosexual men . . ."*

On the other . . . *"And the rocket's red glare, the bombs bursting in air."*

On one side . . . *"No apparent danger to nonhomosexuals from contagion."*

On the other . . . *"the land of the free and the home of the brave."*

I pull out another article. From just a few weeks ago. December 13, 1981. *First UK death from mysterious gay illness*. "There you go," I say. "You can ignore the warnings all you want. Perhaps it's just a prelude now. An overture."

"The man who died in Brompton had just returned from the United States," Bram says with the kind of authority that might convince anyone but me. "All we need to do is avoid the United States. There's a whole world where gay men are *not* dying. Besides, *we* won't die."

I shake my head incredulously. "You're insufferable," I say. "It's not my own death I'm concerned with. It's that I can't—I already lost a generation of loved ones. I can't lose another so soon."

"Right." He contemplates this. He hasn't lost anyone he's loved yet. "Please. Let me cut your hair."

"Why? Do you think the hair is the source of my melancholy?" I laugh. "Like Samson's hair was the source of his strength?"

He pulls my hair back. "I think it's a symptom of your melancholy. Perhaps treating the symptoms one by one will help. First, we'll cut the hair. Then the beard gets shaved. Next, we'll get you to play the music that makes you happy again. Over time, the fog will lift. You'll see."

I take a deep breath in. "I'll let Lily cut it. Not you."

He leaps up. Opens the door. Changeling hops off the bed. "LILY! LILY, COME QUICK BEFORE HE CHANGES HIS MIND!"

I realize our secret journal is still in my hand. I stuff the articles back into the journal. Something in that *New York Times* article catches my eye. The sheet music for the national anthem is an advertisement for a bank. *"Happy Independence Day from Independence Savings Bank Member FDIC."* I hear an ominous new melody in my head. The sound of freedom itself being bought by banks and corporations. A new era of greed is upon us.

Why can't everyone else hear its ominous overture underscoring our lives?

Lily sets me up for a haircut in the kitchen. Towel around my shoulders, Bram and Maud by my side, thrilled to observe this moment. I realize I haven't had a haircut since coming to London. It seems symbolic. Frightening almost. Like I'm tempting fate by making such a drastic change. Donna Summer sings in the background. *Running for cover. I'm just so scared that he's out tonight.* Even Donna's music has changed. She used to sing of ecstatic love. Of spring affairs and hot stuff and being queen for a night. Now she's running for cover. Cautioning of devils hiding in city parks in D minor. It's still a song you can dance to, but within the song is a warning that it could be, well, your last dance. We're running for cover. From the virus killing our brothers in New York and San Francisco. From the serial killer we all know is targeting young gays in London. From the police who still gleefully stop Black youth on the streets, desperate for revenge since the uprising.

"I've made us all new outfits just for tonight," Lily announces as she wets my hair and brushes its knots away. "Poppy has been cooking all day. It will be a fantastic party."

"Are we all going to match?" Maud asks. "Like ABBA?"

Lily cackles. "Knowing me, knowing you, I decided against matching outfits." She takes a long chunk of my hair in her hands. Indicates a potential length. "Up to here, Oliver?"

"Shorter," I say.

"Here?" She moves a little closer to my scalp.

"Maybe shorter?" I can't see myself. No mirror to reflect my youthful face.

"I won't be buzzing your hair off," Lily insists. "I despise this new gay uniform of buzz-cut hair. Why do queens want to look like the skinheads who want them dead?"

"Maybe to confuse the skinheads," Bram ponders.

"Maybe because they hate themselves, yeah?" Maud offers, and Lily gives her a nod of agreement. Maud has kept her promise since the fire. She asks us no questions. Has told Lily nothing about what happened.

Lily cuts a long chunk of my hair. Still leaves enough to run a hand through. "Self-hate. That's what they're counting on. If they can't destroy us, they'll make sure we destroy ourselves. Promise me you'll never do that."

Maud nods. "Yeah, never," she says quietly.

Bram and I eye each other. Afraid of making any promises. Then again, never self-destructing is the one thing we *can* promise. We are indestructible, after all. We both make the promise. Maud's eyes seem to catch every moment of hesitation in our glances. Her eyes have been like that since the fire that left us unharmed, full of suspicion.

"I'll take the helpline shift today," I say. "Unless someone else wants it."

Lily chops faster now. Lets long heaps of hair fall onto the stained linoleum floors. "It's a holiday."

"I know, but it's still a weekday," I explain. "The sign says *weekdays*. Besides, I want to end the year doing something . . . meaningful. Something that feels . . . intentional."

I know what Bram is thinking. He's already accused me of taking excessive helpline shifts because I enjoy hearing from the maudlin callers. He said I'm looking for evidence to prove that my blue vision of the world is the right one. He's not wrong.

Once Lily has shorn off my long locks, she grabs a razor. Cleans my neck up. Sizes up my sideburns to make sure they're symmetrical. "Very handsome," she says. Changeling paws at the locks of hair on the floor like they're a toy.

Bram kisses the top of my head. "Beautiful," he says.

I long for Maud to say we make her sick. To tease me for looking stupid in my new haircut. To mock us with the playful ease that was once our trademark as siblings. But she just nods and says, "You look just like you did when you arrived." She turns to Bram. "You do too, come to think of it." She squints, piecing something together. "I've grown at least two inches since I got here. My tits got bigger. I wear a different size."

"I had my growth spurt early," Bram quickly says.

Thankfully, Lily says that she too grew early. "They say people who have a growth spurt when they're very young stop growing after that. It's the ones who grow late who grow the tallest. Maud, you'll tower over us all when you're done."

"Yeah" is all Maud says. Her eyes swirl with questions. She's getting closer to the answer. I can hear it in her labored breathing. But each time she thinks she understands us, she descends back into the unknown.

BRAM. LONDON. NEW YEAR'S EVE. 1981.
JANUARY 1. 1982.

This is what Lily made us for the last day of the year: A sharp black blazer with dramatic shoulder pads for Maud. Like the one Grace Jones wears on the cover of her last album. The blazer almost reaches Maud's knees. She wears no trousers. Just combat boots. An asymmetric vinyl jacket with matching pants for me. Buttons that come down diagonally. Starting at the left shoulder and ending at the right hip. A simple black suit adorned with a cape that flows down to his shoes for Oliver. A constellation of musical notes on the cape. A gold lamé dress with wings for herself. Lily is a disco angel tonight. Every guest seems to be wearing something Lily made for them. Archie in his top hat. Azalea in the sky-blue Grecian dress. Poppy in the crushed velvet jumpsuit. Blossom in the custom sari. We count down to the new year together. Ten on down to a boisterous chant of . . .

"HAPPY NEW YEAR."

1982. A year that once felt like a distant future. Now here.

We all give each other hugs and kisses. I whisper in Oliver's ear after I kiss him. "Don't forget my promise. This will be the worst year of all time." He laughs. He's more high-spirited than he was earlier. Maybe it's the haircut. Or the community. Oliver's always been at his best when he's surrounded by the camaraderie of a group. In the dorms at Harvard. In our living area in London. I wish I were enough for him. That he was enough for himself.

Everyone leaves our house after midnight. Archie is the last to say goodbye. He looks over at me and Oliver before leaving. "I'm going to Heaven, if you boys care to join."

Lily kisses Archie's cheek. "Archiekins, you most certainly are going to hell. Heaven would be far too dull for you."

Archie laughs. "I'm referring to the nightclub. I would invite the ladies too, but the club prefers its clientele male."

Maud shakes her head. "Pearl let *everyone* in. Black, white, gay, lesbian. The Blitz, though not my scene, was the same, yeah? Is this where our community is headed? Clubs for cute white boys only. No one else allowed."

"I certainly hope not." Archie glances at Maud apologetically.

Maud shrugs. "Go. Have fun. I don't love a dance floor full of sweaty men huffing poppers anyway."

I turn to Oliver. "Should we go? I've never been to Heaven."

"And you never will." He raises an eyebrow. Only I understand what he's really saying. That I'll never die. And heaven would be an unlikely destination for me even if I did die. "You two go. I'm tired."

I don't want to go without him. I think of the one thing that might convince him to come. "I hear the sound system is something extraordinary."

Archie steps forward. "It's true. It's not like the Blitz where you can talk over the music. At Heaven, the music feels like it's *inside you.*"

Lily laughs. "Why do you have to make it sound so dirty, Archie?"

Now we all laugh. Then I turn to Oliver again. "Come on. First day of the worst year of our lives. Let's begin by finding out what it feels like to have music inside us."

Oliver shrugs. "Sure, let's see." A brief pause. "But I always have music inside me. Maybe that's the problem."

We stand in line. Inch our way toward the arches beneath Charing Cross station. Toward the entrance of the club. The boys in line seem to vibrate. Excited for the night ahead. Perhaps a little nervous too. Standing in line does that to people. Fills them with the anticipatory thrill and dread of what's to come. Could be the best night of your life. Could be the worst.

A large limousine pulls up down the street.

The leather queen in front of us turns his attention to the opulent vehicle. "Looks like Freddie Mercury is here."

His friend turns to see the limo. "We wish. It's probably Jeremy Thorpe. Come to prey on some poor young lads."

"Derek Jarman?" the leather queen wonders aloud.

"Jarman wouldn't arrive in such a narcissistic and ostentatious way." That's Archie, inserting himself into the conversation. Archie and the two men discuss Jarman's film *Jubilee*. We all saw it together not long ago. The film is a nightmare vision of the London we've called home. Punk violence. Police revenge. Petrol bombs.

Oliver and I move a little closer to the front of the line. Archie continues to chat with his new friends. They've moved on to another topic of discussion now. The *Mommie Dearest* movie starring Faye Dunaway. They reenact scenes as they wait their turn to get in.

Oliver pulls me close. His eyes are on the limo. "Look." I turn to see the windows of the limousine are dark. Whoever is inside can see out. We can't see in. The back window slowly descends. About halfway. Revealing a man's hat and a wrinkled pair of eyes. "He's looking right at us."

The window ascends again. Not fully closed. Still enough of a sliver for me to see the old eyes. "I'm sure he's looking at everyone. Wondering if he wants to come in."

Oliver suddenly loses his balance. He sways like he might fall.

I catch him. "Are you all right?"

"I—I think so." He looks into my eyes for balance. Takes a deep breath of New Year's air. "The strangest thing just happened. I felt . . . I suppose it's what they call déjà vu. The feeling that I've seen him before."

"Who?" I gaze over at the limousine. The eyes are still on us. "The person in the limo? Well, you probably have. It must be some celebrity. I hear Rock Hudson gets around. Could you imagine? What if it's Rock Hudson? I'd love to meet him!"

"Bram, can we go home?"

I feel too electrified by the possibility of who this mysterious figure is not to go in. Archie calls us forward. The doorman pats us down. Waves us in. Archie pays the entrance fee for all three of us.

"Bram, please. I don't want to be here. I have a terrible feeling."

"Let's just see if it's Rock Hudson and then we'll go. One hour. If you're not having fun in one hour, we'll go home. I promise."

Those are the last words I speak before the music makes it impossible for us to hear a word. One more promise.

OLIVER. LONDON. JANUARY 1. 1982.

Heaven is hell. The music does feel like it's inside me, in the worst possible way. Like an alien invader entering my body. It clangs at my temples. Pierces my heart. Each beat feels like a blade. Sharp and constructed. Created not by humans but by machines. The bass is too loud, too deep. It makes the whole place shake. The vibration it creates feels like a premonition of a terrifying future. Mother always said music was our way of communicating with God. This feels more like a conversation with the devil.

Archie disappears on the dance floor. Rips his shirt off. Kisses a stranger. Then another. A possessed-looking man leans against one of the speakers, his pupils dilated. He sways his head from side to side so his left ear is against the speaker, then his right. Left again, then right. I can imagine the way the sound travels from one side of his consciousness to another, through his analytical left brain, then through his creative right brain.

"We're overdressed," Bram says, his eyes on the dance floor, where shirtless men rub up against each other. Bare chests, some hairy, some smooth, all toned. The smell of sweat and wild abandon. Bram unbuttons the asymmetrical jacket Lily made for him. Takes it off and tucks it into the waist of his pants. "Come on, join me."

I'm in a trance. Everyone around me seems so happy to be here. Smiles on their faces and exhilaration in their eyes. Arms raised high in the air, like they're reaching for heaven itself. I don't hear what they hear. What I hear is the sound of liberation as industry. I don't see a dance floor. I see a factory of uniformity. I see people celebrating the death of the individuality they fought for.

I tear my jacket off. Not because I want to be one more shirtless object in this mechanized stew of lust. But because I feel trapped. Claustrophobic. I can't breathe.

"I need a bathroom," I say.

"I can't hear you!" Bram screams into my ear.

I put my lips on his ear and yell. "BATHROOM!"

Bram catches Archie's eye. He points toward the bathrooms to indicate where we're headed. Archie heads toward us. Seems to know instinctively that I'm unwell. He puts an arm around me. Speaks some words I can't hear.

Bram and Archie each take one of my hands and lead me toward a bathroom. Around us, solitary dancers punch the air with their fists. A release of aggression. As if they're fighting an invisible enemy. Archie uses his free arm to push past men sucking on each other's lips like they're trying to inhale each other. Fear, that's what I hear in the sound of this place. Fear of what's to come.

People living like they're not sure there will be a tomorrow.

Destroying themselves before someone or something else can do it for them.

The music, miraculously, becomes softer as we get close to the bathrooms. We enter one bathroom and find a group of men in a circle, throwing their heads back wildly as they snort something. God no, not this.

I feel my stomach turn.

Dissonant chords play in my mind.

"I think I'm going to be sick," I croak.

Bram holds me tighter. Archie pushes his way into another bathroom where a handsome man with bulging muscles, wearing nothing but tight white underwear, washes his hands. "Well, hello, handsome," the man says to Archie.

"Not right now," Archie snaps.

Bram leads me to the toilet. Tenderly helps me crouch. I open my mouth and vomit.

"I'm so sorry," I say. "I'm ruining the fun."

The muscle clone makes a face of disgust as he looks at me. "Well, that's unpleasant," he says coldly.

"You're unpleasant," Archie barks.

"Leave us alone," Bram begs. "He doesn't feel well."

Archie pushes the guy back out into the club. He tries to lock the door so we can be alone. But someone pushes it open.

"Occupied!" Archie yells.

The person on the other side doesn't seem to care. He keeps pushing as Archie keeps pushing back, trying to get the door closed.

"I said it's occupied," Archie reiterates.

Bram yells out, "There's a sick person in here, give us a minute!"

Archie loses the battle. The person on the other side gets the door open. Archie falls to the floor with a thud, his skin now lying atop the drips of piss that all men seem to leave behind on bathroom floors the world over. Bram strokes my newly cut hair tenderly. I puke some more, then look over to see an old man lock the door behind him.

He wears leather shoes.

A luxurious overcoat with a fur collar.

A sharp hat on his head that I suddenly realize I've seen before . . .

It's the man from the limo.

The one who was staring at us.

I knew I sensed something sinister in him.

Something *familiar*.

Once he's secured the door, he turns to face me and Bram. Takes off his hat to reveal a balding head, sprigs of limp gray hair atop it like leftover sprouts in a withered salad. A gaunt face, all skin and bones with eyes haunted by time. He must be close to ninety years old. He balances himself with a long black cane, his hand on its ornate gold handle.

"If we are to speak accurately, there are three sick people in here." The old man looks at Archie on the floor. "Unless you're sick too. I can't be sure."

The old man's voice sounds like a long-dormant memory. Like a dream I once had, long forgotten.

"I know what my sickness is," the old man says. "Yours is the one I'm more interested in."

It's his smile that brings it all back. Bodies shrink. Skin sags. Hair falls. But the unique shape a smile makes has no age.

"Jack?" I wonder aloud.

"The Jackal," he corrects me. "It's been a long time. For me at least."

I look to Bram. Or perhaps Bram looks to me first. Neither of us can believe it. After all these years, we've been found by someone from our past.

Archie stands up. Confused. Wipes the wetness from his skin with some toilet paper.

"Nice to see you both again." There's a diabolical smirk on Jack's face.

"Bram. Oliver. What's going on?" Archie asks. "Who is this?"

Jack ignores Archie. Keeps his eyes fixed on us. "Bram?" He thinks. "Like Bram Stoker? Interesting."

"Archie, go!" Bram yells. "Please, go."

Archie moves closer to us. "I'm not leaving you alone. Lily would murder me if I didn't get you home safe."

Jack looks at Archie now. "Are you like them?" he asks.

"Like what?" Archie asks. Then he wonders aloud, "You mean gay? Is this a . . . are you the . . ." Archie's eyes widen in horror. "It's you . . . You're the reason gay men are disappearing, aren't you? You're the serial killer?"

Jack cackles. "What in the world are you talking about?"

"Gay boys are vanishing in London. Where are they?" Archie asks. "What have you done with them?"

"I may be a jackal, but I'm no serial killer." Jack narrows his gaze at Archie. "They haven't told you a thing, have they?"

"Told me what?" Archie glances at me and Bram.

"Do you think they're your friends?" Jack asks.

"They're more than friends," Archie snaps. "They're my family."

"Jack, enough," I beg. "This isn't you."

Jack looks at me with eyes full of regret. "You're right. It's not. I'm not this decrepit person. Inside, I'm still the young man you once knew and hated—"

"I never hated you," I lie. Of course I did. Still, I know he's no serial killer. He does his killing the socially acceptable way. In boardrooms.

"Of course, I don't look as lovely as you both still do. Your dewy skin. Your full heads of hair. How magnificent you both are."

Bram's eyes glow with fear. He gives me a nod that tells me to make a run for it. I can hear him without him saying a word.

Covertly, he straightens one finger. Then two. I know we'll run at . . .

Three.

Bram bolts up from the floor.

I lift myself up from the toilet.

We make a run for the door.

Jack blocks our passage out. Raises his walking cane up. Pushes the tip of its golden handle. A blade pops out from the end of it. Sharp and threatening. He points it at Archie's neck. A threat that stops us in our tracks.

"It's a scary world out there. So much crime. A man can never be too careful. These days." Jack moves the blade from one side of Archie's neck to another. "I wouldn't move if I were you. One step in the wrong direction and it's the end for you."

"I thought you weren't a killer," Archie says.

"I'm not whatever serial killer you were referring to," Jack corrects him. "But to have what these boys have . . . For that, I would gladly take your life."

"Please don't do this." Archie's voice sounds guttural. Desperate. Confused.

"I have no desire to hurt you." Jack smiles. "In fact, your fate is not in my hands. It's in *theirs*. Your *family*."

"I'll scream!" Bram yells.

Jack shrugs. "In this place? Go ahead. No one will hear you."

"Just put the weapon down," I beg. "Let Archie go and we'll tell you anything you want to know."

Jack mulls the offer over. "A fine plan, but in the wrong order. First, you talk, then I put the weapon away and free your friend."

"Did you . . . Did you know we would be here?" Bram asks. "How long have you known?"

Jack's eyes light up. "You give me more credit than I deserve. I was merely here to look at the eye candy before returning to New York. The cane was a gift from a friend in MI5. One can't be too careful in London these days, he said. Thieves everywhere." Jack's lips tighten. The lines on his face look hollow in the harsh light of the bathroom. "You're thieves too, aren't you?"

With his free hand, Jack touches Bram's chest. Runs his hand up and down the goose bumps on his skin.

"Don't touch him," I say, pushing Jack's hand off Bram.

"Thieves of time," Jack murmurs, almost to himself.

Archie's frightened eyes find my gaze. "What is he talking—"

Jack cuts Archie off. "I have access to every medicine science has discovered. The best estheticians money can buy. And look at me." Jack turns to the mirror. We all find our gaze traveling to his reflection. In the background of the mirror, our faces. All four of us. Jack, ancient. Archie, approaching middle age. Me and Bram, eternally seventeen. "Look at my forehead. The wrinkles. The lines of cruelty seared into my lips." With a sharp fingernail, he traces a line above the curl of his top lip. "This appeared after I betrayed your cousin Brendan," he says with his eyes on me. "I saw it appear with each passing night of guilt."

"You?" I dare to say. "*Guilt?* I don't believe it."

He turns rapidly toward us, the mirror now reflecting the spotted skin of his bald scalp and neck. The hunch of his shoulders. "Believe it. Why do you think Brendan was readmitted to Harvard? Who do you think gave the *generous* donation that convinced the school to take him back?"

"I—I didn't know," I stammer.

"Brendan didn't know either," Jack says curtly. "I certainly never told him. I didn't do it for his gratitude. I did it to wipe the guilt from my face. But it never left. When I was young, I looked impish, mischievous. The boys found me attractive. I looked like trouble in the best way. Now I just look old."

Bram steps forward. "What do you want, Jack?"

Jack smiles. "Isn't it obvious? I want what you have. The only thing worth having. Eternal youth."

"Eternal youth?" Archie gasps.

Jack cackles. "For that, I would give anything. My soul, even."

"Do you still have a soul?" I ask.

Jack shrugs. "Don't ask unanswerable questions. What I'm asking has an answer. How?"

Bram and I look to each other again. What do we do?

Jack raises his voice. "TELL ME HOW."

"Jack, please." Bram speaks softly. Carefully. "I'll tell you everything, but let Oliver and Archie go. They have nothing to do with it."

Jack's face hardens. A merciless mask. "If Oliver has nothing to do with it, then why does he look just as he did when I last saw him over sixty years ago?"

Archie's breathing quickens. He blinks too rapidly. Rubs his eyes. Like he's hoping it's all a hallucination. "Sixty— That was . . . Long before I was . . ."

Bram raises his arms up in supplication. "It was all me, Jack. Let them go and we can talk. I made Oliver this way. He knows nothing. Let him and Archie go and I'll tell you everything."

Jack's lips curl. "I don't think so." He shifts the blade a little closer to Archie's throat. "Archie here is the only one I can use to make you talk. I'm not sure my weapon has any power over you. Does it?"

"Jack, please," I beg.

"Can you still die?" Jack asks. "Shall I slash one of you and find out?"

"NO!" Archie screeches.

Jack laughs. He's enjoying this. "Life has been so boring for so long. My wife is ill. My children are waiting for me to die so they can take over the company. This is already making me feel like the young man I truly am again. And when you tell me your secret—"

Bram interrupts. "Even if I did tell you the secret, it's too late to help you. The pages, they don't make you young, I don't think."

"What pages?" Jack asks. "Is there some scientific formula written on them?"

"No, it's not like that," Bram explains.

"Then what is it like?" Jack bellows in frustration. "Do you realize how much humanity is suffering? How many people could benefit from whatever gave you this power?"

"It's not power," I say. "It's a curse." Jack looks at me curiously. His eyes tell me to go on. "I wouldn't wish this upon my biggest enemy. I wouldn't wish it upon you."

"Am I your enemy, *baby boy*?" he asks, using my old nickname. Two words that send me reeling back in time.

"I always liked you, Jack." I try to sound convincing by remembering the pieces of him I did enjoy in moderation. "You were fabulous. Bold. Wickedly funny."

"All I was, it turns out, was young." He bows his head down. "I tried to remain bold. I've tried to help people. To make medicines that will alleviate their pain."

Years of headlines about the company flow through my head.

New medicines. Questionable practices. Audacious experiments. Unmitigated greed. The rise and rise of Whitman & Whitman.

"Help people?" I ask. "Don't you price your medicines so only the wealthy have access to them?"

"How else would we fund research into the next miracle cures?"

"You mean the next gift to the rich and powerful." I remember something else. Something horrific. "You . . . You tested medicine on prisoners without their consent, didn't you?"

He doesn't seem bothered by the accusation. "They were criminals. This was a way for them to pay their debt to society."

"Not every prisoner is a criminal," Bram says sadly. I know he's thinking of Lily's Uncle Alton. Of the countless people thrown in prison all over the world for having the wrong skin color, loving the wrong gender.

"We were criminals when we met," I add. "According to the unjust laws of the time. But you already knew that. Not that you paid a price like the rest of them."

"Look at my face to see the price I paid. I'm hideous." I want to despise him, but a part of me also feels sorry for him. Unhappiness is indeed etched onto his face. "At least I know it. I'm aware I don't have a face aged with warmth. The face of a beloved grandparent. Wise and sweet and sexless. No, my cheeks are hollow. My life is hollow. Cold blue veins line my skin. Every bit of me is twisted out of shape."

"That's just your physical appearance," Bram says. "All that could change if you just . . . opened yourself up to love. It's never too late for love."

Jack laughs like the devil himself. "You're such a fool. Of course it's too late for love. Unless you tell me your secret. I promise not to experiment on prisoners. No, this time, I'll experiment on myself.

And once I've perfected the science and returned to my youthful form, I'll bring it to market."

"So you're doing this to be young again *and* to profit?" I ask. "My God, is there no end to your greed? Whitman and Whitman is already one of the biggest companies in the—"

Archie's body suddenly shivers. A little earthquake inside him. He freezes up as he repeats the words, "Whitman and Whitman?" Archie doesn't seem afraid of the blade grazing his neck anymore. "You— You experimented with ways to cure homosexuality, didn't you?"

Jack shrugs. "We experiment with ways to cure *everything*."

"Lobotomies," Archie says. I turn to Bram, confused. "Shock therapy." When Archie says those words, his body vibrates again. A small seizure. A memory relived.

"Ah, so it didn't work for you?" Jack says. "Well, we can't all be cured."

"Look at you," I snap. "You're a lecherous old man stalking gay clubs in foreign cities. You're not cured."

"My wife would beg to differ," Jack says coolly.

"You—" Archie releases a deep exhale. "You experimented with implanting the testicles of corpses into gay men."

Jack waves a limp wrist in the air. "It was worth a try. We made sure the corpses were heterosexual. Besides, if a person doesn't want to be gay, shouldn't they have the option? Just as one wants to rid themselves of a headache? Or diarrhea?"

Archie's face goes beet red. "Being gay is not a headache. And the people who were subjected to your evil experiments didn't choose it. They were forced into it by their hateful parents who think like you." Archie sighs sadly. "Some of them didn't get out in time like I did. Some of them were lobotomized. Operated on.

For what? Perhaps you're not the serial killer preying on London boys, but you did prey on gay boys. You did so much harm. To us. To me."

I see tears in Bram's eyes. "Archie, I didn't know. I'm . . . I'm so sorry."

"No boo-hoo backstories, right?" Archie says sardonically.

I feel my own eyes well up too. For Archie. For me and Bram. For all of us. The ones who are nothing but pawns to the Jackals of the world. "Archie, what you suffered—"

Archie raises a hand up. "Not another word." Then, "We all had our secrets, as it turns out. Now they're out in the open. So what do we do?"

"That's up to these two," Jack says, cocking his head toward me and Bram. "All they need to do is tell me the secret that matters."

"So you can gain more power and make more money!" I shout.

Jack looks at me like I'm a toddler. "*Baby boy,*" he says. "Greed is the reason humanity has dominated the planet for so long. It is our desires that have led us to make new discoveries. Yes, I'm greedy. Unapologetically so and proud of it. But this time, my greed may help others. You must know what's happening to men like us all over New York and San Francisco. They're dying. Maybe together we can help them."

"Don't!" Archie blurts out. "Don't you dare pretend you care about our community when you subjected us to torture—to unimaginable things."

"The men dying now are just like the boys we knew in Boston," I say. "You sold them out back then, and you'll sell them out today. You don't care about helping anyone but yourself." I feel my heart pound. I want to escape this horrible bathroom so badly. The smell of my own vomit is making me sick again.

"I'm not the one who turned those poor boys in at Harvard," he says. "I'm not some serial killer. Nor am I responsible for whatever is killing the queens of New York and San Francisco. I don't make the rules. I simply play the game."

"Men like you and your father made all the rules," I say.

He pulls out a black leather wallet from the inside of his trench coat. "Here's a little pocket money to gain your trust."

"We don't want your money," I snap.

Bram takes it. Counts the bills. More money than we're used to seeing at once.

"Bram!" I yell.

Bram looks at me and shrugs. "We have no choice. It's checkmate. We may as well get on with it." Bram turns to Jack. "You'll need to give me your hands."

"My hands?" Jack asks. "Why?"

"So I can cut them, of course," Bram says.

"Cut my hands?" Jack asks. "Are you insane?"

A strange, raspy laugh comes from Bram. He's up to something. "Of course I'm insane. I've been seventeen years old for almost a century now. That would make anyone insane. Now if you want me to gift you eternal youth, I'll need your hands."

Jack holds the cane tighter in his grip. His arm trembles. The blade does too. Archie holds his breath. "Pages," Jack says. "You said something about mysterious pages. What do my hands—"

"It's just your lifeline I need," Bram explains. I look at him curiously. Impressed and also a little revolted by him. By how quickly the duplicitous part of his mind works. "The magic paper works by cutting the lifeline of each palm."

"What makes it magic?" Jack asks. "Can it be duplicated? Mass produced?"

"Do you want immortality or endless conversation?" Bram responds calmly.

"Show me this magic paper!" Jack commands.

"It's in my pocket," Bram shoots back. "Now show me your palms."

"At three!" I blurt out.

Everyone looks at me. "All right then, at three," Jack agrees.

I count down. One. Two.

At three, Jack puts the cane down and raises his palms up. Bram reaches into his pocket and pulls out the bottle of poppers Lily makes us carry for safety. He throws it at Jack's eyes.

"WHAT IS THAT?" Jack rubs his burning eyes.

"RUN!" Bram yells.

I grab the cane and unlock the door. I let Archie out first. Then Bram. Before leaving, I turn to Jack with fire in my eyes. "I lied," I say. "I did hate you. I still do."

"I'll find you!" Jack shouts.

"Oliver, hurry!" Bram yells from the corridor.

I can't leave yet. My eyes glued to Jack, I speak my thoughts with breathless clarity. "All this time, Bram and I never even considered using our eternal youth for power or profit. All we wanted was to be alive in a time where we could love freely. An age without hate and greed and injustice. But now I know such a time will never come. Do you know why?"

"OH SHUT UP," Jack yells, still in pain.

"Because of people like you. As long as there are humans, there will be—"

Jack yelps in agony. Then screams, "I'll hunt you down until I die. I'll tell my children to hunt you down after that. You will NEVER be safe."

"Oliver! Now!" Archie hollers.

We rush past revelers dancing away the first day of a new year. Past pubs full of beer drinkers. Chants of *Happy New Year.* Across the bridge. Past a group of adolescents blasting Spandau Ballet from a boom box. Music born out of the blitz of our lives. *Oh, look at the strange boy. He finds it hard existing. To cut a long story short. I lost my mind.*

Past piles of trash. Past last year's last newspapers blowing in the wind. My eyes land on headlines that will either shape futures or be forgotten. Martial law in Poland. Redistricting in New York. Sanctions against the Soviet Union. Water pollution. Record high unemployment in the Netherlands. The first test-tube baby born in Virginia. More gay men dying mysteriously.

"Is anyone behind us?" Bram asks.

Archie looks back. "I don't think so," he says.

"Keep running!" I yell.

We go forward. There's no going back anymore. If we had any innocence left, it's gone now. We run past the river that flows into the North Sea, south toward what I know is our home no longer. Life will be escape again. Happiness is past tense.

BRAM. LONDON. 2025.

I try to stop Oliver from telling Tobi our secrets. But Oliver is resolute. "You've made decisions for us in the past without my consultation. Now it's my turn. Do you want to know our story, Tobi?"

Tobi nods. "I do. I really do."

Oliver takes Tobi's hand in his. "Good. Because I'm tired of living in the shadows. Always hiding my true self. Bram, you can join us. Or you can leave. It's up to you. But I think Tobi here deserves the whole truth. Was Lily your mother, Tobi?"

Tobi's eyes well up at the mention of Lily. "She took me in during my transition. Helped me find the right doctors."

Oliver smiles. "I'm happy to hear that. You realize that makes us brothers."

Tobi lets out a sad, raspy laugh. "Brothers. Sure." He sharpens his words. He needs answers. "Why did you both disappear? Why are you still so young? What is all this?"

Oliver speaks quickly. Breathlessly. "*This* begins a long time ago. Come to think of it, this begins before even I was born. In the nineteenth century."

"The nineteenth century?" Tobi throws his hands up into the air. "The fuck!"

"The fuck is right." I can't help but laugh. I can feel Lily's spirit in Tobi. "I suppose I should begin, since it starts with me. Why don't we walk toward where it all happened? Claridge's."

"The posh hotel in Mayfair?" Tobi seems confused by this.

"That's the one. Shall we walk?"

And so we stroll. Three brothers. Secrets revealed. Lives relived. I tell Tobi about my mother who died when I was born. My father, who hated me for it. James at the St. James. My desperate wish to be alive in a time and place where I could love freely. Oliver tells Tobi of his mother's love. His cousin Brendan. Harvard. The Golden Rooster. A whole lost world that did more than exist. A world that was *alive*.

And then: London.

Our golden years.

That time when we were happy.

For a time.

We tell him everything as we near Mayfair. Lily. Maud. Tuesdays at the Blitz. Brixton. Pearl's shebeen. The uprising. Heaven. Hell. Jack. Our escape.

We enter Claridge's. We ride up the elevator next to an old man holding a cane. The lines on his face tell a story. I don't know its details yet. But I see the pain. The love. The regrets. He holds the elevator door open for us with his cane.

I'm reminded of Jack's cane. The blade he threatened Archie with. Jack died not long after we escaped him in Heaven. Heart attack. Full-page obituary in the *New York Times*. Gushing praise for his leadership of the pharmaceutical company his father started. Quotes from global leaders about the lives saved by Whitman & Whitman's medicines. No mention of his experiments to cure homosexuality. His children took over after his death. Under their leadership, Whitman & Whitman has only grown more powerful. Curing hair loss. Erectile dysfunction. Injections to stop wrinkles and to fill sagging skin. Collagen and silicone. Opioids. Lawsuits. The eternal dance of industry. In interviews, the Whitman heirs have promised to find the code to eternal youth "any day now." But that day hasn't come. Yet. Despite their best efforts. Jack kept his promise in death. His children *have* tried to find us. I've been followed by unmarked cars in Lagos and in Bangkok. Narrowly escaped both times. We've been running away from them for over forty years now.

Jack wasn't the serial killer preying on London boys. The killer, Dennis Nilsen, was arrested in 1983. And Jack didn't have anything to do with AIDS, though his children do distribute HIV medicines. Perhaps if the police had cared about queers, Dennis Nilsen wouldn't have killed so many boys before he was caught. Perhaps if governments cared about queers, HIV could have been contained before it spread. But we don't live in that world. We live in a world where history seems to crash into itself at every moment. A world where viruses and violence and love and community all coexist and always will.

"This is where it all started." I stare at the fireplace. There are logs inside. I light it. The flames seem to bring me back. Over a hundred years erased by the blaze.

My father's voice. *That's where filth belongs. That's where you belong.*

My voice. *You belong in hell!*

My father's voice. *I already am in hell.*

Tobi seems just as riveted by the flames as I am. He seems to see something in them. A new future. Eternal youth. The chance to live in a time where he can do more than exist. Where he can live free.

"I want everything you once wanted. I know there's better times ahead. I'm so exhausted by the . . . the hate. The lack of understanding. If it wasn't for Lily . . ."

I speak gently. "It was worse for her. Lily and Poppy had to travel to Casablanca for their surgeries. Couldn't find a doctor in the NHS to help them. They were put through hell at the one gender identity clinic they found on Charing Cross."

Tobi nods. "I know. Lily didn't like boo-hoo backstories, but as she got older, the stories couldn't help but come out. There were nights she would ask me to stay in her bedroom with her. She was in pain by the end. The medicine she had to take seemed to transport her to the past. I know what she went through to live her life. I know what Archie was subjected to. The conversion clinic. The shock therapy. They almost lobotomized him before he escaped. She told me everything."

"But she didn't tell you about us?"

Tobi's eyes blink in surprise. "Lily *knew* about you?"

Oliver nods. "Lily. Archie. Maud. And an old friend of ours from Boston. Those are the only people who knew our secret."

The fire dies down. I grab the stoker and shift the wood. I use the iron rod to stoke the flames into wildness once more.

Oliver pulls out the single remaining page we have from the original Wilde manuscript of *The Picture of Dorian Gray*. Hands it to Tobi. "It's yours."

Tobi's hands tremble as he grips the deteriorated paper. "This is—"

"The last page we have left." Oliver puts a hand on Tobi's shoulder.

"Before you burn it, you should know that Lily, Archie, and Maud all had the chance."

"Lily could— She could still be alive?"

"If that's what she wanted."

Tobi holds the paper to his chest. Breathes in the particular scent of aged paper. I can feel Lily's presence. She's with us. She's telling me to stop Tobi before it's too late. She's telling me she's in a better place. That she wants Tobi to join her someday. Wants me and Oliver to join her too.

NEW YORK TIMES CLASSIFIED ADS

OCTOBER 31, 1983

MY WANDERING STRAVINSKY,

Did you see they arrested the serial killer at last? His name is Dennis. What a mundane name for someone who destroyed so many lives. Guess The Jackal had nothing to do with it after all. Boys like us won't be disappearing from the streets of London anymore. Perhaps it's a good sign. Maybe tomorrow the virus will be cured. Maybe the day after tomorrow you'll summon me. Please summon me. We can hide from The Jackal's family together. I'm cut in half without you. An incomplete child of the sun whose heart is freezing in Iceland.

YOUR LONELY NERUDA

BRAM. LONDON. JANUARY 1. 1982.

Oliver is angry with me. Again. He blames me. He has every reason to. "I told you we should go home. I knew there was something sinister in that limousine. I could see he was staring at us." I begin to pack a small bag. Throw some of my clothes inside. Some of Oliver's too. Oliver takes his clothes out. Puts them in a different bag. "Wherever we're going, we're not going together. It's over. Our little experiment failed. We can't be happy in our prime."

"Maybe this isn't our prime." I open up the floorboard. Pull our journal out. "Maybe our best is yet to come."

"JUST STOP." He unleashes decades of resentment at me. "Look around. You've been waiting since the nineteenth century for some fictional perfect time when we can live free of hate. Where is it? When is it coming?"

I open the journal. Read one of his notes aloud. *"I didn't think it was possible, but the world has gone from minor to major."*

"Those were the words of a fool." He takes the journal from me. "It's all getting worse. Open your eyes. It's never getting better. Our people are dying, and nobody cares. They'll exterminate us when they get the chance."

I snatch the journal back. Read more of his words back to him. *"I'm watching you sleep as I write this. You look so peaceful and beautiful. Lily is frying up fritters downstairs. Maud is in the shower. It's the simple things, isn't it?"*

"You're only proving my point." Oliver grabs the journal again. Throws it into his bag this time. "We'll be fooled into thinking things are better. That we can be happy. And just when we think the worst is behind us, they'll strike. They'll attack us. Burn our books. Ban our music. Shame our youth. Make us hate ourselves so deeply that we'd rather be dead than alive. They'll turn us against each other."

"Don't let them!" My voice cracks. My throat feels raw. "Don't let them turn us against each other."

He places his hot palm on my moist cheek. I'm sweating. Delirious with fear. Anxiety. Panic. "I'm not against you. I'm not." He places a gentle kiss on my lips. "A part of me will always love you."

"And a part of you will always hate me?"

He nods. "Let's say goodbye now. Before the hate grows any bigger. Before we destroy more than we've already destroyed. Before we put Lily and Maud and Archie in danger."

Lily's voice. "What danger?" Oliver and I turn to see Archie, Lily, and Maud standing in our doorway.

Archie steps forward. "I told Lily and Maud everything. They deserve to know. Lily doesn't believe me."

"If what they say is true—"

Maud interrupts Lily. "It's true. Ever since they saved my life from the fire and emerged unscathed—"

Lily stops her. "What fire?"

"I-I'll explain all that later." Maud stares at us with moist eyes.

"I knew something was different about them. But this . . . Immortality and eternal youth? Being chased by the biggest pharmaceutical company in the world? It's madness."

I pull out the single remaining page from the manuscript I've kept on me all these years. "Listen to me. I'm not Jack Whitman. I don't have research teams at my disposal. But I know that if this page burns, at least one person who sincerely wishes for it will be granted immortality. Maybe all three of you could be. I'm not certain. But imagine . . . All of us. Traveling into the future together. A family. The best mother any family could ask for." I see a tear travel down Lily's cheek. "A father figure like no other. The daddy to end all daddies." Archie can't help but giggle sadly. I turn to Maud. "And a sister I never want to say goodbye to."

Lily approaches me carefully. She's just found out I'm immortal. Unbreakable. And yet she treats me like I'm suddenly fragile. "My sweet boy, you were never properly loved as a child. You don't understand a thing about life."

"I've been alive longer than anyone here. I've seen the cycle of time." I hear the desperation in my voice.

"Look at you, playing the *really* big brother card." Maud is joking. No one laughs.

Lily takes my hands in hers. Clutches them. "You may have been here longer than me. But you're still a child. An unloved child who thinks he can remake the world in his image."

"No, listen to me. We can all be in this together. If you come with us, maybe Oliver won't leave me." I turn to Oliver. "Tell them, Oliver. Tell them to come with us. You'll stay if they do, won't you?" Oliver won't even look at me. "Oliver, say something!"

What he says is: "I wouldn't wish this on anyone."

Lily takes my chin in her hand. Shifts my face so I'm facing her again. "What have you learned about life, about love, about family, in all these years?"

"I—I don't know— That love is the only thing worth living for. Not just romantic love. All of it. The love of family. Of community. The love we feel for a poem or a song or a moment in time. The love I feel for you, Lily. I'm not ready to say goodbye. I'm not ready to let go. I want what we had to last forever."

Lily's lips tighten. "What we had is already gone."

"No!" I bury my face in her chest. She holds me close. Comforts me for the last time. "No, it's not. It can last forever."

"My sweet child." Lily takes a deep breath. I can feel her chest rise and fall. Her glorious heartbeat. Her power. Her will to create a life no one laid out for her. To pave a new path. To create love from the rubble of pain. "Nobody ever taught you the most important lesson before it was too late."

"What lesson?"

"That life only has meaning because of death. That love can only truly be appreciated because we know hate all too well. That beauty must fade. That's what beauty is."

"But you—you fill your bathroom with antiaging creams and shampoos!"

Lily laughs. "True. But that doesn't mean I want to be alive forever. It only means I want to look as good as possible while I'm here."

I turn to Archie. "Tell her, Archie. You must know what's happening. We're dying. This is a way to survive."

Archie shakes his head. "Lily is right, Bram."

Maud nods. "Lily is always right." Maud approaches Oliver. She pulls him into a wretched embrace. Wretched because it's so full of longing. Because she's saying goodbye. "You two need to leave now.

Before Jack starts looking. Don't write or call. They'll track you down. The less we know, the better."

I fall to the floor. I want to become one with this house. This stained carpet. This chipped paint. I don't want eternal youth anymore. What I want is to stop time. Here. Now. An eternal present on this very day.

Lily joins me on the floor. Sits with me. "I don't know what comes next, but I know this. We must love the life we're given. It's our most important job. And when our time is up, we must hand the world over to a new generation. We must give them our passions, our lessons, our art, our loves, our losses. We must give them our *souls* and hope they can find the same happiness we once did. Hope they're as lucky as we once were."

Oliver sits down too. "Lucky?" His face is ashen.

Archie sits cross-legged. "Of course we were lucky. Look at what we've had."

Maud sits too. "More than most."

Changeling paws at Oliver's calves. He picks his beloved cat up into his arms. Looks deep in Lily's eyes. "Take good care of Changeling."

Lily nods. We hold hands. I close my eyes. Imagine we're around a campfire. But there will be no fire today. No burning page.

Our family won't exist after today. But we lived. We truly lived.

OLIVER. LONDON. 2025.

Tobi stares into the fire, mulling what to do next. To be immortal or not to be immortal? That is his question. "Lily is always right," he whispers to himself. Then he turns to us. "Have you ever thought about how to reverse the curse?"

Bram nods. "I figured that burning the page might reverse it, but then . . . if that were the case, my immortality would've been reversed when I burned the page that turned Oliver."

"Water," Tobi says. "Water is the opposite of fire, isn't it?"

"In a way," Bram says.

"It puts a fire out," Tobi says. "It heals. Lily baptized me in water."

"Me too," Bram says.

I find myself traveling back in time. Mother is by my side. By the Charles. The river she loved so much. We're in Provincetown again. Staring out at the Atlantic. The endless possibilities it offered us in that moment. "Land's end," I say to Mother as much as to Bram and Tobi. "A new beginning."

Tobi walks to the suite's teakettle. Fills it. We wait for it to boil. When it does, he pours us each a cup of piping-hot water.

"What do we do?" Bram asks.

"Put the last page in the water," Tobi suggests. "It's worth a shot."

I tear the page in two. Hand one half to Bram. Keep the other in my grip. Wilde's words are like a challenge.

In my hand, *You poisoned me with a book once. I should not forgive that.*

In Bram's hand, *The books that the world calls immoral are books that show the world its own shame.*

I crumple the paper. Bram rips his piece into shreds. We place the paper in our teacups. Bram raises his cup high. "High tea at Claridge's again. Remember?"

I shake my head. "Of course I remember. I remember everything."

"The good and the bad."

"Mostly the good," I say.

"Cheers to that." Bram raises his cup.

We clink our glasses.

"Drink it," Tobi suggests.

"Wait!" Bram yells.

"What?" I ask.

"We need to speak the wish. And mean it." With longing in his voice, he utters, "I wish for one mortal life. To be alive, truly alive, in this time and only this time. Please."

I feel my throat go dry. Imagine him making the opposite wish one hundred and thirty years ago in this very room. My beautiful Bram, Shams, Shahriar. How he's changed. I swallow hard before repeating, "I wish for one mortal life. To be alive, truly alive, in this time and only this time. Please."

And so we drink.

At first, nothing happens.

"I don't think it worked," Bram says. "I'm sorry, Oliver. I wanted you to be free of this at last. All I want is—"

"Bram!" It happens suddenly. His eyes. They don't glow any longer. They're just brown. Not feline. "Your eyes" is all I manage to say.

Bram blinks rapidly. "I feel different," he says. He gazes into my eyes and gasps. "Your beautiful eyes!"

Something in us has changed. I feel it in my bones. In the beating of my heart. We're still seventeen, but not for long. We're not immortal anymore.

"It's over, isn't it?" I ask.

I smile as mortality floods my body. All this time. These years and years and more years. This century of loneliness, with brief bursts of love and happiness and music, like sunlight in a perpetually cloudy sky.

This feels like clouds parting.

Like a big bang.

Like being born anew.

Tears flood my eyes. Water flows down my face. Heals me.

"It's a new beginning," I say.

He says, "It's our chance to finally get it right."

He takes me in his arms and kisses me. I let myself get lost in time. We're by the Charles River. We're in Provincetown. We're dancing at the Blitz. At Pearl's. We're here and there and everywhere. We're then and now. We both feel it, our past and our future spinning in this very moment. We're us, but we're also all the young lovers. All the ones who came before and all the ones who will come after. We're princes who got their fairy-tale ending. Except it's not an ending. It's just a moment, like all the other moments, and in the moment is joy and pain, connection and loneliness, and the acceptance that someday there will be an end to our story, and the beginning of another story. How beautiful that is. How beautiful we are, we flawed humans who have the privilege of choosing each other, of bestowing our love on each other.

As we leave, Bram takes one last look at the suite where his life now changed twice. I see a small red light in the corner of the ceiling. *Strange*, I think. But then I tell myself it's some sort of fire alarm. Security mechanism. Modern technology.

We run to the Thames. We make it in time to see Maud, Archie, Azalea, Poppy, and Blossom throw Lily's ashes into the river. We watch as Lily becomes one with the water. Tobi leaves us to rejoin them. They're his family now. Not ours any longer. Our life will begin again. Somewhere new. Until it ends and life leaves us in peace.

"Should we try to see Maud and Archie before we leave?" Bram asks.

"I don't think so," I say. "I think we should let them grieve Lily in peace. Without making it all about us."

"Right." Bram nods. "I miss them."

"Me too."

"I've missed you."

I smile. "Me too."

"Oliver," he says quietly. I sense a troubled heart beating in his chest. "I love you," he declares. Before I can tell him I love him too, he continues. "But I understand if you want to live this mortal life without me. You deserve happiness. Uncomplicated love. Peace. If you want to part ways, I'll understand. I'll cheer you on. I'll—"

"Bram, stop." I put a hand on his cheek. A single tear from his right eye falls onto my fingers. "I can't imagine my life with anyone but you."

"But—" Another tear. And another. "I ruined your life. I cursed you."

"I made the wish, didn't I?" I suddenly realize that all these years, these decades, this century, I've blamed Bram. But I *wanted* this. I wished for it with all my heart. Perhaps the magic of the burning page would have been useless had I not craved its promises. "You're brave. You're unafraid to dream. You led me toward love and honesty and new horizons. I need you, Bram. I always have. I think in some ways . . . when I made that wish . . . what I was truly wishing for was the opportunity to grow old with you without fear."

"We have that opportunity now, don't we?" he asks.

"I think we do," I say. "No one will be chasing us once they notice we've been stripped of our magic."

Bram kisses me gently. He lays his head on my shoulder and whispers. "You haven't been stripped of any magic, Oliver. You were magic when I first met you. Your open heart. Your curiosity. Your innocence in a hard world. That's your magic. I love you."

"I love you too."

We hold each other for seconds that feel like centuries. Accepting a new kind of love. A different fate than the one we had made unstable peace with.

Finally, he asks, "Oliver, where do we go next? What do we do?"

"Let's decide in the morning," I say. "With clear heads. Enough has happened for one day."

"Enough has happened for a hundred lifetimes." His eyes are moist. I like his eyes this way. No fire blazing within them. Just a lust for life and all it has to offer. We linger by the river until the memorial crew leaves.

We approach the Thames when the coast is clear. Quietly pay our respects to Lily before heading to his suite. We sleep in the king-sized bed.

The next morning, we pack our bags. We don't know where we're heading yet. But we've decided to leave together.

As Bram checks out at reception, I see a man reading the newspaper in the lobby. In a small box at the very bottom of the front page is a headline.

WHITMAN & WHITMAN HAS PURCHASED OSCAR WILDE'S ORIGINAL MANUSCRIPT FOR *THE PICTURE OF DORIAN GRAY* FROM THE MORGAN LIBRARY & MUSEUM IN NEW YORK. IS THE WHITMAN FAMILY MAKING MOVES TO OPEN ITS OWN MUSEUM? MORE ON PAGE SEVENTEEN.

So Jack's children finally found out what the magic pages are. Jack must have told them paper was involved. They must have been waiting for us to return to London for Lily's memorial. Must have managed to spy on us in the hotel room. That red light in the corner of the ceiling. That was them. Jack's greedy heirs. Finally understanding they needed to get their hands on Wilde's manuscript. Perhaps they will be granted eternal youth. Perhaps they will find a way to mass produce it.

Or perhaps they won't. My heart tells me that Wilde's power can only be transferred to those who truly wish, with all their hearts, for the same thing Wilde must have wished for himself. A time and place where the wisher's love is not a crime. I don't tell Bram about the newspaper headline. He'll find out soon enough.

When Bram is finished checking out, he finds me and gives me a kiss on the cheek. "So, where to?"

"Paris?" I suggest. "We were meant to go there together once. It never did happen."

"Everything in its time," Bram says.

We step out of the hotel. The sun is shining. Blazing. Spring will always be spring. A season for new beginnings, when nature exhales and stretches. When the buds bloom and the colors radiate. When the clouds part and allow the sun to illuminate life for those stuck in the darkness. This beautiful season that feels orchestral each time it arrives.

"It's beautiful, isn't it?" Bram asks.

"What?"

"Life," he says. "To live is the rarest thing in the world. Most people just exist." Of course he quotes Wilde in this moment.

I take his hand in mine. "But we haven't lived yet. Part of living is aging."

He clutches me tight. "Let's grow old. Together."

All around us, people enjoy the day. They know the summers are getting hotter. They know a brutal winter is always around the corner. They're wise enough to appreciate the blooms when they come to them.

Everything in its time.

AUTHOR'S NOTE

When I was very young, my favorite book was Oscar Wilde's *The Picture of Dorian Gray*. My love for the book was likely grounded in the gay sensibility being transmitted to me through its pages, and in the way it transported me to another time and place. Throughout my youth, I was haunted by the feeling that I was alive in the wrong time. I longed for a sepia-toned past or a utopian future. I've written extensively in other books on the reasons why I felt this way. I moved to the United States at the age of ten in 1986. It was a time of terrible racism against Iranians, grounded in ongoing postrevolutionary politics, and a time of frightening homophobia, grounded in the stigma of the ongoing HIV/AIDS crisis. *Of course* I longed to lose myself in the past or future. I felt the present had no place for me.

But the present surprised me. I found love, community, and purpose in our unjust, imperfect, and maddening world. I am now an adult with the life I once thought was an impossibility: a loving husband, two incredible children, and the opportunity to alchemize my pains and joys into art. Writing books for young readers has been the greatest privilege of my creative life. My novels are often about teenagers who, like teen me, wish they could live in a different time, a better world. I know many marginalized young people feel this way today. It breaks my heart. I wish I could change the world for them. But all I know how to do is keep writing. What I hope to communicate through this book is that there will likely never be a perfect time for us to be alive. And so, the present is all we have. Every day of life is a privilege, and also a responsibility.

This novel travels through different moments in history that I myself have been consumed by. The first is late nineteenth-century London, when Wilde was put on trial for gross indecency. The second is the year 1920 in Boston, a city with a vibrant queer subculture that largely disappeared after Harvard subjected its students to a secret court that was not discovered until 2002. The third is early 1980s London, a time of freedom and experimentation, when a club called the Blitz changed culture and when the Brixton neighborhood was home to a vibrant Black and queer community.

In immersing myself in these historical moments, one thing stood out to me: the power and danger of the written word. Wilde's personal letters were key pieces of evidence that contributed to his conviction. Harvard's secret court began when a letter to a student was intercepted. Today, the written word remains powerful and dangerous. Like too many authors, I have been banned and threatened for simply writing stories grounded in my life experience.

I could have written a straightforward response to book banning. But there's nothing straight about me, so I wrote this book instead. A book where a teenage boy is made immortal through the burning of my own favorite childhood novel. A book about how trying to destroy our stories will only make us stronger. A book about how love and community will always outlast hate and division. A book about the beauty of love in all its forms: romantic, familial, communal, artistic. Wilde wrote, "Behind every exquisite thing that existed, there was something tragic." With this novel I offer you an inverse truth: *Behind every tragic thing that ever existed, there is something exquisite.*

ABDI NAZEMIAN

February 2025. Los Angeles.

ACKNOWLEDGMENTS

Every piece of this novel has been spinning inside me for a long time.

One line from *Exquisite Things*—"Everything looks better from above"—was the first line of a very different novel that may or may not ever be written. That one line helped lead me to this book. For that I want to thank and acknowledge Vitor Martins, who has translated my books for Brazilian publication, and the Brazilian readers for their love, support, and, most importantly, for sharing the magic of Brazilian music with me.

It has always been my deepest desire to write a version of *The Picture of Dorian Gray*, my favorite childhood novel. My former writing partner, Micah Schraft, and I tried doing just that decades ago. It was a very different spin on the novel, a feature film written for Gwen Stefani. I'll never forget pitching it to Jimmy Iovine, who stopped us and told us he didn't need to hear the rest because they always change the title and the ending. I'll never forget the brilliant and kind Jonas Åkerlund, the director of some of my favorite Madonna music videos ever, coming on board the project. And I'll always be grateful to Micah, without whom I likely wouldn't be a writer.

I also want to acknowledge the brilliant Toni Andres, who escorted me around Berlin during an impactful trip to a literature festival. As we shuttled around the city, we discussed art and life. Toni is a scholar who is researching intersections of queer theory and classics. When I mentioned I was writing a book that deals with Wilde, we had a robust, moving, intellectually stimulating conversation that helped me unlock both the final draft of this novel and my complicated feelings toward Wilde and toward hero worship in general. For that I'm forever grateful.

The story of Harvard University's secret court is similarly something that has haunted and consumed me for decades. I first attempted to produce a script written about these true events, written by the lovely Eric Anderson and David Hildebrand. We didn't get it made. Many years later, my great friend Susanna Fogel recommended that I write a podcast about the events. With Eric and David's blessing, I pitched myself for the job and got it. I immersed myself in research with the invaluable help of Nikita Shepard, a historian who explores LGBTQ communities and beyond. Nikita's research, and the guidance and leadership of producers Alia Tavakolian, Brigham Mosley, and Zachary Quinto, helped immerse me in the voices and textures of 1920s Boston. That project didn't get made, but the voices of those students wouldn't let me go. I'm grateful to everyone mentioned above for leading me to this fictional story set against the backdrop of real events.

The liberation and danger of early 1980s London is also something I tried to explore in a previous project, a television pilot that—surprise, surprise—didn't get made. That project dealt more specifically with what became a small part of this novel: the serial killer Dennis Nilsen, and the role homophobia played in his ability to go so long without getting caught.

I share all this because people often ask me how long it takes to write a novel. The answer is that this book took me two years to write. The answer is also that this book took me four decades to write because pieces of it have been percolating inside me since childhood and have been heavily researched for previous projects.

I want to thank the city of London and the team at Little Tiger who have given my books a UK home. I try to go to London once a year to walk, explore, see theater, and find answers to what I should be writing next. The first drafts of almost all my novels have been written in London. This novel is, I hope, a love letter to a city I love deeply. A big thank you to the Gay's The Word team for running my favorite bookshop, and also for sending me to the Bishopsgate Institute Archives. I'd like to live in their LGBTQIA+ archives. Many websites and books helped me with research, including the Revolting Gays website, Black Cultural Archives, the documentary *Blitzed!*, *Queer Footprints* by Dan Glass, and the BBC podcast *Brixton: Flames on the Frontline*. Great inspiration came from Steve McQueen's anthology series *Small Axe*, especially *Lovers Rock*, which is perfect. I also want to thank Dublin and the beautiful Irish people for inspiring me in the writing of this novel. I wrote part of these pages in Dublin, chasing Wilde's spirit in his childhood home, in the building where he worked, on the grounds of his alma mater, the pharmacy he frequented. I love the Irish, and especially Irish writers and musicians, with all my heart.

I'm so lucky to have a team at HarperCollins that believes in me so much that they've now published six of my queer Iranian books. Megan Ilnitzki and Alessandra Balzer are editorial magicians who both helped me unlock this novel with their essential guidance. I'm also deeply grateful to the Harper team that helped this book come to life and will help it find a life in the hands of readers: Shannon Cox, Erin DeSalvatore, Alison Donalty, Julia Feingold, Matt Maguda, Shona McCarthy, Mimi Rankin, Patty Rosati, John Sellers, and Jenna Stempel-Lobell. Big thanks to the authors who did an early read of this novel and gave it their valuable blessing: Gayle Forman, Rasheed Newson, Steven Rowley, Amy Spalding, Julian Winters, Rachael Lippincott, Jonny Garza Villa, and Daniel Aleman. All superstars whose books you should read. And to Carla Bruce, for joining this book's dream team and believing in this story.

I'm also blessed with an agent who encourages all the Wildest stories I want to tell. Thank you, John Cusick, for understanding me and for guiding me so expertly. I'm grateful to the whole Folio team, especially the foreign rights team. A big thank you to every foreign publisher that's helped my books travel the world.

I have too many friends to thank by name. What a blessing that is. I'm so grateful for every single one of them.

My family is the best. We're scattered across the world, we disagree often, and yet we all love each other fiercely and loyally. That is what family should be. I'm grateful to every single member of my huge extended family from both the Nazemian and Aubry side, especially my parents, Lili and Jahangir, for instilling this love of family in me, and for keeping us together forever and ever.

My mom's cousin Mandy Vahabzadeh took my author photo. Her work as a photographer and her presence as a human was and is still a model of artistry and decency to me. Thank you Mandy joon.

And finally—Disco, Evie, Jonathon, Rumi—I am nothing without you.

Jonathon, my Pally, my husband. I never imagined I would find someone who sees all of me and still loves me, someone who inspires me by living life with so much passion and kindness. Our wedding day is the happiest day of my life, the day when everything and everyone I cherish most was in one room, watching us vow to love each other and then belting out *True Blue* together. You made this last decade of our lives so big with love and life. Toujours L'amour.

Rumi, last night I drove you home from a birthday party. You were so full of life and energy, buzzing from the music and the friendship. We were listening to the early 2000s hits you love on the drive home, and you asked me about those amazing times. You said you wished you could have been young then. I promise you that now is better, because you're here, and the world is better with you in it. You're so funny, so smart, so protective of those you love. Keep growing without losing those qualities, that youthful spark of magic that makes this the best era of all time because of your presence.

Evie, Rory to my Lorelai, a few days ago, your brother admitted that I was right when I said the vile food he was eating would give him a stomachache. You hugged me and said, "Daddy's right about everything." I didn't correct you in the moment because what parent (or human) doesn't want to hear those words? Like all humans, I'm learning as I go along, and so much of what I've learned is from you. Your vulnerability, kindness, and empathy have made me a better person. The poems and lyrics you write are honest in a way I couldn't be until not too long ago. No one can be right about everything, but I know this: everything is right when I'm with you.